FORBIDDEN YESTERDAY

Aaron Goldman

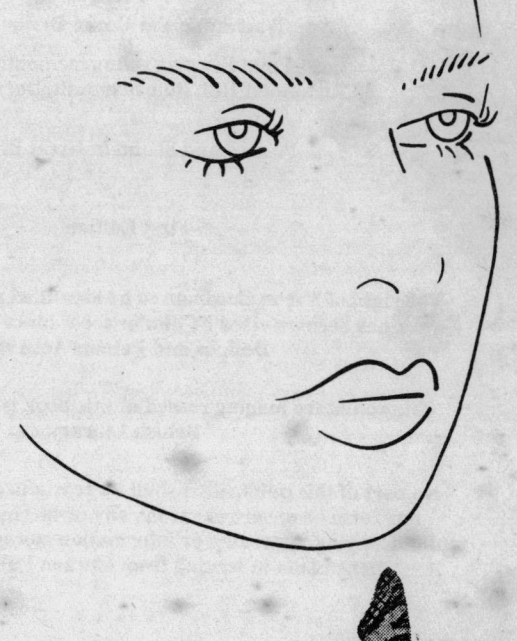

Curzon Publications Limited

First published in Great Britain by Curzon Publications in 1995

Copyright © 1995 Aaron Goldman

ISBN 0 9524926 1 X

Published by
Curzon Publications Ltd.
72 New Bond Street, London W1Y 9DD

Typesetting and Cover Design by
LaserPoint Services – Bournemouth Limited
38 Richmond Hill, Bournemouth, Dorset BH2 6EJ

Printed and bound in Great Britain

First Edition

The right of Aaron Goldman to be identified as the author of this work has been asserted by him in accordance with the Copyright, Designs and Patents Act 1988

The voluntary lodging record of this book is available from the British Library

No part of this publication shall be reproduced or transmitted in any form or means, electronically or mechanically, including photocopying, recording or information storage, without the prior permission in writing from Curzon Publications Ltd.

* * *

Future publications by Aaron Goldman

Forbidden Agenda
Forbidden Revenge

Forbidden Yesterday

DEUTERONOMY 23:24

'That which is gone out of thy lips thou shalt keep and perform; accordingly as thou has vowed of thy freewill to the Lord thy God, which thou has promised with thy mouth.'

The Jerusalem Bible

Forbidden Yesterday

Dedicated to Henry. He will understand.

Forbidden Yesterday

Summary

A Startling Exposé
Based on a true story

Forbidden Yesterday is a real-life story with all the twists and turns and improbable coincidence of a finely-crafted novel, born of a chance encounter with the enigmatic Italian temptress, Clarissa, an international, mega currency transaction and a binding Hebrew promise.

Set mainly in the decadent eighties, *Forbidden Yesterday* depicts astoundingly-enlightening chronologized flashbacks of the transforming decades — intermingled with the tribulations of business life, the lucrative fringe commodity market and the compulsive, traumatic love affair between Clarissa and Zak.

Forbidden Yesterday further reveals the remarkable chain of events that lead the adventure-seeking Zackary Levin, a London fashion-exporter turned entrepreneur, to arouse the interest of Israel's renowned secret service, Mossad.

Destiny and the elements must have collaborated to arrange the fortuitous meeting on England's South Coast, during the hot summer of 1983, between the trans-coloured eyed Clarissa and Zak. Subsequently the daring paramours rendezvous in London, Paris, Malta and then Munich where coincidence bizarrely manifests itself again when Clarissa meets her old flame, Franz, a hard-drinking West German communications expert!

Ironically, when the obsessed Clarissa flees the Bavarian capital, Zak is confronted by Franz with an adventurous five-million Dollar deal involving a *nouveau riche*, West African ex-cabinet minister and a worldwide embassy communication network. However the deal gets unexpectedly aborted when the ex-minister is kidnapped off the streets of London by 'Mossad boys' and Nigerian *provocateurs* during Spring 1984.

Phenomenally, in May 1985, Mossad 'get lucky' as the result of an unguarded remark by Zak to a close Israeli friend concerning the abandoned five-million Dollar deal. Under a commercial guise Zak is consequently propositioned by Mossad to re-engage Franz.

Unknown to Zak, Mossad start to extend a hold over the alcoholic Franz. With duplicity Mossad then plunge the Londoner into an ever-increasing maelstrom of incidents engineered to infiltrate Germany's most secret conglomerate.

The tension of life builds up for the naïve Zak when Mossad solicit him to chaperon the West German over the Austrian border on the last night of January 1986 to the picturesque city of Salzburg. Zak is unaware that Mossad intend to procure TOP SECRET Libyan defence files from Franz...

During March 1986 Zak is astonished to perceive the extent of Mossad's deception upon seeing the dramatic headlines in the National Press:-

'U.S. WAR JETS HIT LIBYA '
'TRIPOLI ENVELOPED IN SMOKE'
(See 'Daily Telegraph' inserts — pages 265 & 271)

Zak then realises what he had begun to suspect in Salzburg: Mossad had indeed been treacherous and were not merely bent on gathering West African commercial information.

Historically, *Forbidden Yesterday* divulges why the U.S. Sixth Fleet crossed Gaddafi's 'Line of Death' into the Gulf of Sidra without fear of impending danger and indeed without loss to their aircraft carriers and warplanes — which at will destroyed lethal, action-ready Libyan missile emplacements defending Tripoli and Benghazi — the first major encounter of smart weapons.

As an ethical businessman, Zak requests the Israelis to honour their *Mazel un Brocheh* (a binding Hebrew promise) and pursues his unpaid West African commission in the Holy Land, where in the buzzing 'Tel Aviv Hilton' Mossad act out their motto:

'BY WAY OF DECEPTION, THOU SHALT DO WAR'.

New Year's Day 1987, on Zak's return from the Promised Land he continues to pursue his claim despite Mossad's threat on his life. With courage and tenacity the Londoner 'takes on' the fraught Israelis, and the sexsational Clarissa, when she mysteriously appears one sizzling summer's day at London Airport!

Forbidden Yesterday

A REAL-LIFE STORY

FOREWORD

We journeyed forth to the forbidden past.
To find the truth and that which remained untold.

Forbidden Yesterday is a unique book which the author could never have envisaged writing before he became involved in the extraordinary chain of events which led Zak Levin half way round the world in the 1970's - 1980's.

Forbidden Yesterday and its nostalgic parallelisms often read like a whodunnit novel. The large number of quite remarkable coincidences and interlocking events make it appear as if an experienced fiction writer had formulated the plot. *Forbidden Yesterday* is based on a true story which stemmed from a fortuitous meeting with the enigmatic Italian temptress and a broken binding Hebrew promise. Subsequently, the author recounts the incidents as and where they actually happened for Zak. The author has himself questioned on occasion whether what transpired in fact did so, and has retraced the central character's steps and looked at old hotel receipts and flight tickets for confirmation. If the author has erred at all, it has been in good faith.

The author has allowed himself 'poetic licence' in respect of the dialogue since clearly Zak could not remember and indeed reflect each conversation verbatim, particularly in view of the circumstances in which some of them took place! Also, because of the somewhat sensitive nature of the material, the names of the main characters and that of the German conglomerate have been changed. On the other hand, the names of the fringe characters and the given names of Mossad agents are real.

Naturally, time does not stand still, so the author cannot vouch for any changes 'on the ground' which may have taken place in the meantime to the original street or hotel names or even where they may have been changed or demolished.

The narrative is written in the third person and subjectively **strays** from the past perfect tense whilst in flashback.

To keep the air of overseas ambience and conversation that took place, foreign words have been used and appear in *italics*. Their explanations are to be found in the specially-compiled seven page Glossary of foreign words, Americanisms, Commercial Terms, Curious English words and Acronyms — **see pages xvii to xxiii** towards the end of the book...

The author felt that Zak's reflections would be enhanced by the liberal use of flashbacks, since this technique has the particular advantage of introducing the reader to the origins of the main events as they occur. To ease the reader from the main story to a flashback sequence, a different type-face, and symbols (see foot of page xxiii) have been used throughout the manuscript to depict all the events prior to **9th August 1985**. Additional attention has been paid to carefully dovetail the nestling flashbacks as they slide in and out of the main storyline, since they do not necessarily follow in chronological order.

The actual writing of *Forbidden Yesterday* is indeed a story in itself, which is to be told in a forthcoming sequel:
Forbidden Agenda.

Why call this book *Forbidden Yesterday*? The author has always felt that many of the happenings should have been 'forbidden' — they just should not have occurred. But since they had, they should be recorded, as some have now become a segment of modern history!

Forbidden Yesterday

Part of the fascination of this vivid story is the almost unbelievable number of coincidences that took place around the world during the course of two decades, which continually appear in the news media and gossip columns — **see Epilogue page 351**

As did Carl Jung, the author has asked himself increasingly whether such really astounding occurrences are actually the result of pure chance or whether they represent part of some cosmic destiny slowly unfolding for each of us. As we pass down a country lane or cobbled street, who knows what awaits us and whom we may meet? Perhaps another life lesson is the only sure outcome.

Forbidden Yesterday

Forbidden Yesterday

ONTENTS

ANNOUNCEMENT	iii
DEDICATION	iv
SUMMARY	v
FOREWORD	ix
GLOSSARY	xvii
LOCATION PHOTOGRAPHS	xxiv

CHAPTER ONE 1
  London: August 1985 — Part I
  The Smiling Imposter

CHAPTER TWO 6
  Flashback: 1967 — 1981
  Time Marches On

CHAPTER THREE 15
  London: August 1985 — Part II
  Zealous Imposter

CHAPTER FOUR 25
  Recall: June 1950 — 1952
  'You're In The Army Now'

CHAPTER FIVE 32
  June 1952 — 1978
  Success in Civvy Street

CHAPTER SIX 43
  Bournemouth: September 1985
  Surprise Visit

CHAPTER SEVEN 52
  Bournemouth: The Summer of 1983
  Buongiorno Clarissa

CHAPTER EIGHT 69
  Autumn 1983 — Spring 1984
  Continental Interludes

CHAPTER NINE 80
  Estoril: July 1969
  'Pucci Nut'

CHAPTER TEN 90
  Munich October 19th 1985 — Part I
  Triple Rendezvous

Forbidden Yesterday

CHAPTER ELEVEN 99
    Munich — Part II
    The Die is Cast

CHAPTER TWELVE 109
    Munich: — Part III
    Arrivederci Clarissa

CHAPTER THIRTEEN 116
    Munich: April 29th 1985 — Part IV
    A Deal in a Million

CHAPTER FOURTEEN 122
    Bournemouth: 30th April 1985
    False Hopes

CHAPTER FIFTEEN 126
    Brussels: 17th October 1985
    Slim Pickings

CHAPTER SIXTEEN 128
    Cairo: August 1976 — Part I
    A View of the Nile

CHAPTER SEVENTEEN 142
    London: May 1976
    New Business and New Friends

CHAPTER EIGHTEEN 151
    Dallas: July 1976
    A Second-hand Remark

CHAPTER NINETEEN 156
    Cairo: Part II
    Prolonged Stay at the Nile Hilton

CHAPTER TWENTY 164
    Düsseldorf: 18th October 1985
    At Behest of Mossad

CHAPTER TWENTY-ONE 179
    Tel Aviv: May 1975
    Shalom, Lovely Tracy

CHAPTER TWENTY-TWO 185
    London: 20th October 1985
    Late Night Progress

CHAPTER TWENTY-THREE 192
    London: Summer of 1977
    The Odd Couple

CHAPTER TWENTY-FOUR 198
    Christmas 1985
    The Deal Firms Up

CHAPTER TWENTY-FIVE 204
    London: May 1985
    Mossad Butterfly

Forbidden Yesterday

CHAPTER TWENTY-SIX 210
    Munich: January 1986
    Disquieting Prelude

CHAPTER TWENTY-SEVEN 225
    Salzburg: 1st February 1986
    Disquieting Waltz

CHAPTER TWENTY-EIGHT 243
    Salzburg: 2nd February 1986
    Disquieting Reality

CHAPTER TWENTY-NINE 255
    Zurich, Kloten
    Startling Reality

CHAPTER THIRTY 260
    London: February 1986
    Suspicions Confirmed

CHAPTER THIRTY-ONE 264
    London: March — April 1986
    Startling Headlines

CHAPTER THIRTY-TWO 273
    Trieste: November 1986
    High Hopes and Shams

CHAPTER THIRTY-THREE 287
    Tel Aviv: December 1986
    On the Way to the Promisedland

CHAPTER THIRTY-FOUR 292
    Tel Aviv — Part I
    Fun and Scares

CHAPTER THIRTY-FIVE 304
    Eilat
    An enlightening 'Red Sea' Break

CHAPTER THIRTY-SIX 309
    Tel Aviv —Part II
    Broken Promise

CHAPTER THIRTY-SEVEN 329
    2nd January 1987
    Flight Back to Heathrow
    Flashback 1932 — 1949

CHAPTER THIRTY-EIGHT 338
    2nd January 1987
    Statements to Jerusalem

EPILOGUE 351

GLOSSARY xvii

DAILY TELEGRAPH INSERTS — pages 265 & 271

Forbidden Yesterday

CHAPTER ONE

London: August 1985 — Part I

The Smiling Imposter

THE 9th of this noble month found London-born Zak about to become a victim of destiny. The ex-fashion exporter was making his way to keep a midday rendezvous with Alon, a most secret agent of Israel's renowned *Mossad*. Zak knew the short journey from Kensington High Street underground station would take him past the deluxe, five star Royal Garden Hotel which dwarfed the secluded Israeli Embassy.

The very sight of the towering hotel's marble façade, flaunting an array of international flags including the Italian tricolour, brought to mind a past summer-love with an Adriatic temptress, Clarissa, lovelier and more provocative than Botticelli's Venus. Zak's vivid reminiscences with the signora from Ancona were suddenly thrust back to his memory as his presence was abruptly challenged by a uniformed Crown commissionaire . . .

Content with the rapport, the bemedalled sentinel allowed Zak to enter the restricted area of Palace Green, which led to the Embassy of the State of Israel.

Forbidden Yesterday

In the autumn of his life, Zak had been flattered by Alon's invitation to visit the Embassy, but was not sure of the engaging Mossad agent's intent, which had been extended during the Israeli's visit to the Londoner's South Coast home. Hesitating momentarily before pressing the entry device on the outside of the Embassy's palisade, Zak wondered at Alon's motive. Was he about to keep the appointment with Alon out of curiosity, or was he still seeking adventure? Zak felt the adrenalin surge in his veins as he ventured to press the buzzer to gain access to the austere-looking Diplomatic Mansion.

While waiting for a reply from Embassy security, Zak turned to view the adjoining splendour of the broad tree-lined boulevard of Kensington Palace Gardens, known to some as 'Millionaires' Row' or 'Embassy Row', whose grandiose mansions housed many of London's foreign embassies. Further on towards Notting Hill Gate, practically opposite the Russian and Iraqi Embassies, the Londoner knew the Sultan of Brunei kept a palatial *pied-à-terre* larger than the whole Israeli diplomatic mansion... As Zak gazed in awe at the grandeur of Kensington Palace, the official residence of The Prince and Princess of Wales, he became aware of the patrolling horse-mounted policemen.

Suddenly, Zak was startled by the blaring response from the hidden sentry within the Embassy.

"Yo. Who are you and what do you want?"

"Zak Levin, for Alon," he replied... Surprised at having to wait, the Londoner observed the mundane architecture and balustrade of the two-storey mansion crowned by its centre apex slate roof. The flaking flagpole over the canopied entrance to the Israeli Embassy was devoid of its waving Star of David that day.

The electronic buzz of the lock release signalled the approval of Zak's entry through the spear-tipped iron railings surrounding the Embassy. The wall-mounted security cameras instantly panned onto Zak, following his progress along the short tarmac path leading to a reinforced oak-panelled door with heavy dull brass fittings. Before being admitted into the Embassy, Zak was asked to identify himself again by yet another security device. Once inside the small fortified checkpoint, with its thick bullet-proof glass barrier, it became more than apparent to Zak that very tight security was in operation.

"Show us some I.D.," rasped one of the 'hard-eyed' guards through an intercom from behind the vantage point. Zak, trying to look composed, fumbled in his back trouser pocket. Eventually, he located his American Express card from his wallet and placed it on the ledge of the barrier.

"Hold it up so we can see it."

Zak complied by simply holding up his Amex Gold card against the protective fascia.

"Have you a current driving licence, or something with your address on?" shouted the other guard. Zak pulled his driving licence out from the other side of his open wallet. The first guard watched him closely, while the other checked out his address against a short list. The list was written in *Ivrit*, the language of modern Israel.

"O.K. Wait a minute. I'll come through and give you a body search."

Zak was given an expert frisking before being allowed to pass into the shabby inner sanctuary of the Embassy.

"*Shalom*, Zak," Alon's voice greeted his guest in the true Hebrew way as the *Sabra* appeared from the other side of the steel-lined door.

"*Shalom, shalom*, Alon. Boy, am I glad to see you."

Alon's conventional suit and tie contrasted with the casual weekend attire he had worn when they had first met in sunny Bournemouth. The *Sabra's* unpolished brown shoes jarred the picture though and made the Londoner remember his mother's advice: 'Never trust a man wearing brown shoes with a grey suit'. Of course, this could not apply to a Mossad agent impersonating an Israeli Embassy Agricultural Attaché. Modern Israel, after all, was founded on a '*Mazel un Brocheh*'.[1]

Alon's demeanour seemed to have hardened somewhat, Zak thought, as they walked together up a wide, carpeted flight of stairs that had high parget walls and decorative plaster friezes. He caught

---

[1] GOOD FORTUNE AND A PRAYER

a fleeting killer glint in the Mossad agent's steel-blue eyes, which hitherto had not been present at their encounter back in July.

Once in the busy, first-floor administration office, which had a high ceiling with ornate cornices, Alon, in a blasé manner, requested from a good-looking brunette a quiet place where they would not be disturbed. Zak's peripheral vision registered the brunette putting a couple of American passports into what looked like a diplomatic pouch, before stringing and sealing it closed 'bordero' style. The significance of her action would only strike him much later. Zak recalled having seen the big-breasted, hazel-eyed brunette before, when she'd collected Alon after their July meeting at his central Bournemouth flat. She softly answered Alon back in English, her mellifluous voice sounding similar to that of the alluring Abbie:

"What about the chart room in the attic, Alon? I have the key."

Alon thanked her in *Ivrit* as he took the ready-to-hand key. In step, the *Sabra* and the Londoner walked up a steep flight of stairs to enter a sparsely-furnished, beamed attic room.

Zak felt uncomfortable, even claustrophobic once inside the gabled attic. While chatting with Alon, a prickling sensation ran up the back of Zak's neck, intuitively alerting him to the possibility that they were being video-taped. Espying a mirror on the wall, Zak sensed he was being observed or photographed. While Alon was making small talk, Zak regarded his image in the mirror. He reckoned he looked ten years younger than his fifty-three years, due largely, he fancied, to his boyish blue eyes. His slate-blue 'Harrod's' suit and glimmering aquamarine silk shirt set off his deep tan and medium blonde hair. Zak stretched and flexed his fingers to ease his tension, catching the reflection of his precious two-tone Rolex ring, which complemented his 'Oyster' wrist-watch. The gold bezelled ring that he cherished still, had been a love gift from Clarissa last summer. She had lovingly slipped the adorable ring onto his right index finger in the 'Hilton's' bar that overlooked the picturesque St Julian's Bay on the 'George Cross Island.' He had 'touched' the enchantress's heart by reciprocating with an amethyst and pearl encrusted, gold butterfly brooch.

* * *

It had been early morning on his first day in Malta. Zak remembered the couplet he had written at the time:

'The paramours fortuitously met on the streets of Sliema
  To find they were still possessed with love fever'

Fate had allowed them miraculously to spot one another as he had stepped out of the Preluna Hotel in Sliema, just down the road from the Libyan People's Bureau, to search for the Italian butterfly. The surprised, sexsational-looking Clarissa had astonished him as she immediately desired to make love in his hotel bedroom.

After a couple of intoxicating days and nights locked away in the 'Preluna', they'd toured the romantic island in a hired car like 'honeymooners'. In perfect harmony, they experienced the 'magic of Malta' in many other hotels and in Clarissa's rented 'lair'.

Zak's reunion with the intriguing Italian beauty in Malta surpassed by far his exciting romantic interlude with Roxanne in Portugal many summers before.

* * * * *

CHAPTER TWO

Flashback: 1967 — 1981

Time Marches On

UNFOCUSSED, Zak gazed at the mirror, seeing through it as if it were to another time, another place, as images of some of Israel's great achievements and events of another yesterday crowded into his mind.

* * *

Egypt's President Nasser and the PLO threatened to block Israel's Red Sea port of Eilat that June of 1967, when the UN withdrew from Sinai. To the surprise of the Arab nations and the rest of the world, Israel triumphed in a six day shoot-out. Ironically, to this day, Egypt still celebrates the 1967 war that they had started, but lost, as a victory.

1969 saw the centenary of the Suez Canal. Built as the result of a handshake and promise *(Mazel un Brocheh)* between Benjamin Disraeli and Ferdinand Lesseps. The UAR claimed to have shot down ninteen Israeli war-planes that controversial year of '69, but Gaddifi did claim all the foriegn banks in Libya as the newly-installed Israeli Prime Minister, Golda Meir denied Nasser's claims.

The UK became decimalized in 1971 as the English pound reached parity with the almighty US Dollar and the world's athletes prepared for the coming Olympic Games in Germany.

Time Marches On

The sixth bissextile of the founding of the State of Israel in 1972 had been a year of tragedy. During the Munich Olympic Games in September, 'Black September' Arab guerrillas with sub-machine guns broke into the Olympic Village and kidnapped nine members of Israel's competing team and held them hostage.

The Palestinians' action, undertaken to enable them to trade their captives for two hundred Palestinians held in Israel's jails, had resulted in a bloody gun battle which ended with all the kidnapped athletes being shot on the tarmac at Munich Airport as German Police attempted to free them.

For America, the great Mark Spitz won seven Olympic Golds in the swimming pool, about the time two aides to President Nixon, Howard Hunt, a CIA Officer, and Gordon Liddy, a presidential assistant, were being indicted for conspiracy to break into the Democratic Headquarters in the Watergate building.

Back in London, 'Black September' claimed the death of an Israeli diplomat with a letter bomb and Edward Heath attempted to curb the UK inflation before losing his Premiership. In fact Zak had shaken the much-troubled politician's hand as he left the ITN building with his bodyguard from the Yard, before the far-seeing PM went over to the nearby BBC to go on the air again.

One year on, Syria and Egypt under their respective Presidents, Hafez al-Assad and Anwar Sadat, surprised Israel on their Day of Atonement (*Yom Kippur*), 6th October 1973, as combined Arab armies swarmed over Israel's borders. The warlike action quickly ended with the proud Arab troops' retreat and the initial loss of face for Israel, who had been caught in prayer!

Zak had been aware of the new opportunities in the clothing industry in the 1970's and had, in fact, quickly started to design and manufacture high fashion jeans in Northern and Southern Ireland (Wrangler Island) under his own brand name. The brand became very well known and sought after, so much so that oil-rich Arabs crowded into Zak's enlarged and lavish White House showroom, situated on the corner of Mortimer Street and Wells Street, practically opposite where Jeff Banks, Sandie Shaw's husband to be, operated his lively fashion company, 'Clobber'.

The newly-built ITV News Headquarters building was a stone's throw away from Zak's offices: several of the Royals had visited the sound-proof building, including Her Majesty the Queen. Why, Zak had even shaken hands with the young, bonny Prince Charles in Wells Street during one of his Royal walkabouts.

From time to time the young, dashing Terry Wogan would appear in Wells Street on his way to ITV, wearing a trendy bomber jacket and flaunting a 'Burberry' scarf, worn Italian style, wound once round his neck then thrown over a shoulder.

There was also a new newscaster in town, Trevor MacDonald, the conservative-looking Trinidadian, already renowned for his coverage of Grenada's election, in the sunny Caribbean. They'd drunk together, opposite Trevor's place of work in 'Julie's Bar', when the rooky newscaster had first visited the trendy wine bar with a couple of chaperoning TV girls.

The successful Londoner used the new, black-glass fronted ITV buildings as a landmark for his visitors and overseas buyers. When visiting Arabs phoned for appointments, to jump on Zak's 'fashion waggon', he would shout loudly down the telephone:

"We are near the ITV building. Where they make the news, in Wells Street with Anna Ford."

At first the astute Arabs gave Zak token export orders for his branded jeans, and other unisex denimwear garments before placing bulk purchases for their respective country's re-export trade — all destined to be smuggled by Iranians into Iran (considered forbidden by the Shah's regime) via Kuwait, Bahrain, Dubai and Abu Dhabi.

Having gained confidence in Zak's company's high-quality jeans and early delivery dates, the Arabs readily issued Revolving Prime Bank Letters of Credit (known as L/C's) which were payable 'sight London'. Zak became an expert in negotiating Documentary Credits, although he'd 'boobed' when putting the very first L/C into the negotiating bank for payment. Not being familiar with the exacting paperwork, Zak had three discrepancies — consequently he did not get paid 'at sight', but since the goods had been clean and competitive the buyer from Dubai gladly settled with the visiting Zak and issued further L/C's for his branded denimwear.

From then on the Londoner made no mistakes, having been told by an experienced Documentary Credits Manager from the 'British Bank of the Middle East', during luncheon in 'Wheeler's' fish restaurant within viewing distance of Tower Bridge:

"If the L/C calls for the goods or cartons to be wrapped in sky-blue-pink ribbon, then the supplier's declaration must state so, regardless."

Zak's company was further required to negotiate the difficult Arab banks' conditions, as well as to complete a Blacklist Declaration, which had to be endorsed by an Arab Chamber of Commerce, Kuwaiti Embassy or the like, before the documents could be lodged with the corresponding bank, declaring:

'The producing or supplying Company is not blacklisted by the Israel Boycott Office and is not a parent or subsidiary or sister company of blacklisted companies.'

In July 1974, Zak was obliged to fly to Hong Kong to obtain production quotes to meet the 90-day validity date of his Arab customers' Letters of Credit.

Hong Kong for Zak had been exciting from the first moment. Amazingly, the British Airways long-haul jet practically flew through the open windows and homes of the Chinese indifferently eating their bowls of rice, before landing in the Crown Colony. He'd been met and chauffeured in a Rolls Royce, to capture the past aura of grandeur and service of the Peninsular Hotel.

Wisely, Zak appointed a 'Textile Agent', Bill Chan, who had a suite of offices in Star House, situated next door to the Hong Kong Hotel. The illustrious Chinaman had asked for a five percent commission to oversee the production and shipment of Arab orders from the sweat-shops and factories of Hong Kong, but settled on two and a half percent. Zak had been fortunate in stumbling over such a well-connected H.K. agent — Bill quickly introduced him to several vertical manufacturing organisations and their RWA yellow, showroom-dolls, whom Zak did not even attempt to get into the horizontal position with. The Chinese factory owners eagerly showed the visting exporter great hospitality, inviting Zak for lunches, dinners and taking him night-clubbing, as they competed for his L/C's. After all, a Letter of Credit was as good as giving a manufacturer a free loan.

Possibly, Zak erred in his judgement by not looking deeper into the availability of suitable fabric and the viability of manufacturing track suits in H.K. His gut feeling had told him that track suits would be the mode of dress for the future. Perhaps he had known instinctively that track suits were too early for the mass market at that time and he thus embarked on supplying military clothing, improving the eighteen-second safety factor of 'Nomax', fireproof, tank-crewmens' suits with his re-design for the active Arab world.

That decade saw Zak at his best, creatively producing and exporting fashionwear from Ireland, Turkey, Portugal (where he had met Roxanne) and H.K. with profitable re-export to the Middle East, a formula which had ensured his success...

Time Marches On

In the 'Rolls Royce' class, the Londoner lunched occasionally at 'Mortons' with Nicholas 'Bunter' Soames[2] and Zak's friend Josephine in Berkeley Square, opposite where she and 'Bunter' worked for an international firm of lawyers, whose principal idolised Napoleon Bonaparte and stunning Josephine. Even in those days, 'Bunter' had a rather large stomach and big eyes on Zak's 'Roller'!

Most satisfying of all were the first-class perks of extensive travel and deluxe hotels associated with the export business which naturally included the opportunity to enjoy the local wine — and local women. Zak always treated ladies with respect, he always made a point of telling a likely 'indulging' lady his true marital status. He'd never gotten a woman 'into trouble', experienced a social disease, nor had a run-in with the law. Life and the elements during those years had been kind and had favoured the Londoner.

During the mid-seventies, when Concorde first roared into the sky, Zak started looking into other possibilities outside the jeans business. He was introduced to Paul Novey, a Vice-President of the famous 'Regency Hyatt' chain, through a close business friend, Rurik, who been introduced by Colonel Healey-Jones. Paul then operated out of Hyatt headquarters in Chicago where the password through the switchboard to the executive suite for those in the know was 'Strangers in the Night'. When Rurik introduced Zak to Paul, Rurik was a Hotel Promoter, an appointed agent for 'Hyatt'. Zak liaised closely with both Paul and Rurik in trying to convert the abandoned 'Debenhams' building in Wigmore Street into a 110-roomed deluxe hotel, as were the agents of 'Brent Walker PLC'. Alas, due to the Preservation Order on the grand architecture, 'Hyatt's' planners were unable to plan for a viable number of rooms. When Paul had given up on the idea of the 'Debenhams' building conversion into an hotel, shortly after the let-down, Rurik, in a

---

[2] CLOSE FRIEND OF PRINCE CHARLES. AGRICULTURE MINISTER IN THE MAJOR GOVERNMENT OF 1992

drunken stupor, let on to Zak that they had both been screwed by 'Hyatt' on an earlier commission for another hotel project in Morocco's running sand, which in a round-about way involved the kind-hearted Dominique.

For four days in 1977 Libya surprisingly beat off bitter Egyptian air attacks. The lesson Sadat war-planes sought to teach Gadaffi back-fired because of the lethal Libyan defence system installed by a German company. Consequently, Sadat gladly succumbed to Arab peacemakers and the war ended. Little did Zak know at the time that he would encounter the German overseer of the secret Libyan installation and the traumatic effect the bizarre meeting would have on his life.

In 1979, prior to the Iran–Iraq War, Zak was spotted by an Iranian banker in Cavendish Square, when leaving the 'Simon Massey's' fashion showroom opposite the back entrance of 'John Lewis'. Zak had just visited Leslie, one of the 'smart' Massey brothers who had sold their 'Peggy Page' shares and Edmonton factory to Benny Raven and Alf Simmons (of 'Raybeck' and 'Lord John' fame) wanting to be in the public eye. After the sale, Leslie stayed in the 'rag trade' to produce and internationally market high-class dresses from number six in the Square. Leslie's brother Gerald planned to go into the entertainment business with his share of the profits. If Zak's memory was serving him correctly, Gerald's wife had the fabulous 'Lulu' under contract. Zak then intended visiting the Zelker's of 'Polly Peck' acclaim, who later also sold their fashion public company, but to a Turkish dressmaker called Nadir. The sharp-eyed banker had by chance seen Zak leaving the 'Massey' showroom and had been bold enough to ask:

"Excuse me, Sir. Haven't I seen you in downtown Teheran?"

The fortuitous meeting with the enterprising banker nearly blossomed into an intricate legal Iranian mega-currency coup. Alas, the anticipated transaction in Zurich via Teheran was foiled at the eleventh hour when the Iranian 10,000 Rial note was withdrawn and made obsolete by the High Ayatollah's diligent Treasurymen.

In June 1980 an Italian DC-9 passenger plane was shot down by an unidentified missile near the small island of Ustica in the 'Med' when eighty-one passengers and crew sadly lost their lives. Journalists Claudo Gatti and Gali Hasmmer later alleged Israeli F-4 Phantom jets mistook the Italian plane for a French cargo plane transporting enriched uranium from France to Iraq and simply blasted it out of the sky.

Later that year simmering border incidents between Iraq and Iran flared up into the first Gulf War. That very first day of the war a cargo ship bound for Iran was attacked by Iraqi gunboats... The torpedoed ship and 2·75 million Dollars and fifty cents worth of Zak's FOB branded jeans stowed in its hull. Sunk! Zak later thought that the Persian Gulf must have turned indigo blue as he'd gone into the red. At the time, Zak could not believe that he had no claim against the insurers, even though he and his shipping agents had complied with all the conditions of the Prime Bank Letter of Credit for the delivery of his company's denimwear directly to Iran. The freight had been pre-paid, the insurance certificate was in hand, but the specially-called for certificate of docking was not. The Londoner was shocked, staggered and bewildered to find that the final letter from the insurer's solicitor opting out on the *force majeure* clause was absolutely absolute.

'There is no liability by our client, nor indeed any insurer, to pay out or make any settlement relating to: An Act of War.'

If only Zak had kept quiet and concocted a rare docking certificate, he could have lodged the invoice and other documents with the bank and negotiated payment against the L/C... but subterfuge was not the Londoner's style.

Fate had unmistakably turned against Zak. He had been obliged to sell his special LWB indigo (Rolls-Royce commodore blue)

'Corniche' to his Arab friend, Jalil — his luxurious penthouse apartment in Lancaster Gate to a wealthy Iranian dissident and to think about leaving London.

After the disaster it was 'pumpkin time', and 'inspirational moments' with wife Daphna, started getting fewer. Towards the end of 1980, when Bob Hope was looking for Persian jokes to ease the deadlock for the President, Zak took advantage of the differential in UK residential property prices…

The Londoners left London and moved to sunny Dorset, much to Daphna's chagrin. Bournemouth was where Zak intended to start a wholesale cash and carry fashion business and, in between, endeavour to pull off a mega-fringe commodity transaction with the Belgium-based Rurik. That was about the time John Lennon was assassinated in New York City by a psychotic fan.

Bournemouth, at the time of Zak and Daphna unloading their hand-made Chesterfields, was swarming with dissident Iranians and Khomeini sympathizers. Some of the Iranians had been frequent (undercover) trippers to Paris where their beloved High Ayatollah had been active in exile —dethroning the Shah of Iran.

The Londoners daughter Tracy by then was well married to an accountant. Son Henry had married a Persian beauty — or so Henry thought — who worked in the Embassy of the Socialist Peoples' Libyan Arab Jamahiriyá in Ennismore Gardens, London.

The following year, 1981, was unprecedented. It saw Sadat assassinated, along with the attempted assassinations of both Pope John Paul and Ronald Reagan. That same transforming year it was whispered that Israel could make a nuclear bomb.

* * * * *

CHAPTER THREE

London: August 1985 — Part II

Zealous Imposter

ALON'S harsh tone of voice brought Zak back to the present, suggesting they go and take a glass of black tea downstairs. Zak would have thought no more about the quick move, except Alon led him straight back down to the adjoining office where the *Sabra* had previously acquired the key from the sleight-of-hand brunette. Zak thought maybe he'd had his profile taken. Certainly, nothing seemed to have openly transpired in the attic room!

Once settled in the untidy downstairs office, Zak's particular glass and fingerprints were carefully cleared away by the dabbing brunette. Alon immediately asked for the 'Nigerian Documents' that the West German, Franz, had willingly copied from his Steilmanns Project File. Zak withdrew half-a-dozen sample pages from his inside pocket and offered them to Alon. The *Sabra* seemed to relax mentally when the presumably-important papers that Franz had photocopied in Munich were imparted into his Mossad hands.

Pretentiously Alon uttered:

"Zak, these are photostats!"

"As I told you, they list Nigerian frequencies and missions from Abidjan to Washington."

"Yea, all right, but there are only five, no, sorry, six pages."

"Surely, enough to start the ball rolling."

"You have others, Zak?"

"Some two dozen or so more that Franz's photocopied from his private file."

"I understand. Look after them, Zak. I'll call for them later, if we go ahead. By the way, have you visited the States?" asked Alon, switching the talking point.

"Several times."

"Where did you go?"

"Mainly New York."

"Anywhere else?"

"Miami, L.A. and San Francisco a couple of times to buy consignments of Levi 501 jeans and I took the wife down to New Orleans, Mexico City and Acapulco."

"On holiday?"

"What else?"

"Have you been anywhere else in the States?" Alon asked, as if he knew there was a travelogue missing.

"Oh, yes, I visited the 'Windy-City' in 1976."

"Chicago or Dallas?"

"Dallas."

"Which hotel did you stay at?"

"Loews Anatole."

After spending a couple of minutes browsing through the copy Nigerian papers, Alon embarked on probing Zak as to Franz's known capabilities and how they had met in Munich.

Oozing with charm, Alon then asked Zak to affirm how long he had known Udi from Tel Aviv and his English wife, Lena...

Seemingly satisfied, Alon went on to pry into Zak's fatherly trip to see his daughter, Tracy, in Tel Aviv during June of 1975.

Zealous Imposter

Obviously, Alon became concerned when Zak told him he had entered Israel via Teheran and Kuwait on a newly-issued British passport, void of Arab entry stamps. Zak explained to Alon that prior to visiting his daughter in Israel he had requested a one-year British passport, solely for that trip, so as not to disqualify him from entering Arab countries at a later date, since an Israeli entry stamp would have had this effect. Alon further delved into why Zak had stayed at the Tel Aviv Hilton and then requested a 'step-by-step' account of his visit and whether Zak had acquired any new friends while in Israel. Alon then brought up a past visit to Cairo and wanted to know why Zak had stayed at the 'Nile Hilton'. The Londoner's dealings with his wheeler-dealer friend Rurik were then carefully scrutinised by the smiling *Sabra*. Additional confirmation was sought about Franz's previous overseas positions with 'Steilmanns'. Zak was then closely questioned about why the now suspended West German was in possession of such an important and possibly classified file.

Alon then became even more curious, when Franz's past tour of duty in Libya came up. Further aggressive interest was shown in Franz's ex-Boss (with hindsight, Zak figured, another possible conduit for the Israelis into the multinational German Headquarters of Steilmanns in Munich).

"You know, Zak, you live very near to Bovington?" Alon said with a half smile.

"Yes I do, down in sunny Dorset."

"Do you know anyone who works there?"

"On the tanks?"

"How do you know about tanks?"

"Oh, I've had some silly enquiries from the fringe-commodity boys in the past for gun barrels. Not my cup of tea though, Alon."

"For the Chieftain?"

"What else?"

"It could have been for armour plating, Zak."

"I understand that's classified. Taboo as far as I'm concerned."

"So, do you now know anybody who works for the MOD down in Bovington?"

"So happens an acquaintance of mine worked there as a fitter with his uncle."

"Are either of them still there?"

"No, they both moved on."

To get himself off the hook and prevent Alon from 'fishing in UK waters', Zak further added:

"Did you know, Alon, Lawrence of Arabia lived near Affpuddle, just up the road from Bovington Camp?"

"I didn't!"

"Yes, he was either mysteriously killed or just fell off his souped-up motorbike on a quiet road in the spring of '35."

"That's amazing, Zak."

"Sure was, and Lawrence had a false name on his I.D. papers when his dying body was searched in the nearby Bovington Military Hospital."

"Bovington was a military zone back in 1935?"

"Must have been."

"Over fifty years ago?"

"Yes, like me, Alon. Anyway, they didn't know who the dying rider was, until the wife of the author Thomas Hardy put Winston Churchill on to it."

"Why Churchill?"

"He was a very active MP at the time."

"Very interesting, Zak."

"Well, later there were reports of a mysterious black limousine at the scene of the inexplicable accident and of wire having been stretched across the road."

"Very neat," Alon said with a sinister expression on his face.

"There were lots of rumours flying about at the time. About Lawrence's intention to meet up with Hitler to discuss reuniting the Arabs for Nazi Germany."

"You're blowing my mind, Zak. Did the British bump him off?"

"No one knows, but there weren't many 'limos' around in those slow days."

"Suppose not. Who was Lawrence of Arabia really?"

Zealous Imposter

"You must go and see Sam Spiegel and David Lean's great movie. Lawrence was an ex-Officer in the active British Army of the Middle East and the well-loved illegitimate son of Thomas Chapman, an Irish Baronet. Anyway, Lawerance was proclaimed by the Arab world: Liberator of Damascus — Hero of Aquaba — Uncrowned King of King-makers."

"You seem to be well informed, Zak."

"Not really, I've seen the film and video about a dozen times."

Alon then resumed his examination into Zak's past business trips to Iran and Arab countries, exporting jeans during the last part of the Shah's decadent rule.

The *Sabra* cut short his questioning on the Middle East when it became obvious Zak's travelogue had no military value to the Israelis. Alon did, however, make a special note about Zak knowing a Captain of Security at Cairo Airport and Fossetta, a daughter of a high-ranking Moroccan Cabinet Minister. Alon finally added to the concise notes he had made that Zak had stayed at both the 'Hilton' and 'Sheraton' hotels and also knew several VIP's in Kuwait City, underlining the names of Zak's good friend Jalil Behbehani and his partner in 'Kuwaiti Fisheries', Sheik Nasser.

Alon's main interest and preoccupation finally centred upon Franz's ex-boss of whom Zak knew little. Curiously, Alon asked if Franz had personally met either Umara Dikko or Gaddafi! To this, Zak could not answer, as he really did not know. The *Sabra* was also eager to know whether Zak would be prepared to visit Franz in Munich again…

"Alon, are you saying you're interested in purchasing the Nigerian communication installation along with their secret frequencies and codes, for commercial reasons?"

"Possibly, we could get to know more about what's going on in Nigeria via their diplomatic wireless."

It is now history that after the *Yom Kippur* War of 1973, twenty-five African states severed diplomatic ties with Israel, although strong economic relations with Nigeria later flourished.

"Sterling, but for why, Alon?"

"Many reasons."

"Such as?"

"To be able to monitor Nigerian oil outlets would be very useful to our intelligence boys, and of course, on the other hand, we could also assess Nigeria's procurement and other imports and exports."

"Clever stuff."

"For why?"

"Well, as I understand it, Nigeria's Bonny Light oil is the special ingredient for mixing heavy and light crudes."

"You're on the ball, Zak."

"Hopefully. For many years I've travelled the world seeking a residue oil contract and a would-be buyer."

"So I understand."

"So, your reasoning certainly makes commercial sense, Alon, as Nigeria has a world monopoly with their favoured mixing oil."

"Yes, we also have some two thousand technicians working in Nigeria. Israel even builds schools and hotels and we are forever looking for export opportunities in West Africa."

"Perhaps you can put me on to a deal with a good Nigerian confirming-house?" Zak asked.

"For what?"

"Like 'Peak' tinned milk, textiles, currency or perhaps you can find me a residue oil contract?"

"Could be."

"Will you keep an eye out for me?"

"Sure, why not."

Zak tried to disregard his gut feeling that the *Sabra* was stringing him along.

"I would appreciate your help, Alon. Tell me, have you full autonomy to deal on this one?" Zak characteristically asked, before the last question had been answered.

"You mean gathering Nigerian information via Franz?"

"Yes."

"No, not really, I must report back to H.Q. first."

"When can you let me know if your superiors are interested?"

"Very soon."

"Fine, but how long exactly?"

"Well, maybe Headquarters will want to check a few things out first. Bear with me, Zak. It will only be two or three days before I receive a signal back."

"So, what do I tell my partners, Rurik and Franz, in Munich about the money part of the transaction?"

"Maybe I'll also know about that side of it in a couple of days."

"Can my partners and I expect the same remuneration as we envisaged from Dikko?"

"The ex-Nigerian Government Minister?"

"Yes, you know the original idea and deal was conceived and developed with him in mind."

"That's right, but you must wait until I've heard back from Israel about the *gelt*."

"The commission only works out a mil' or so each, if one considers Sterling was nearly par against the Dollar last February."

"Yes, I know it was $1.0765."

"If you can also bear in mind I have been trying to make a deal since 1979 it's not a ridiculous amount of money we're asking for."

"If you say so, Zak."

"What does that mean?"

"I'll level with you. The 'Hercules' offer you acquired for Libya will 'rub' a little back home."

"Alon, you came to me about this one. I'm no *Sayan*[3]."

"True on both counts, but you re-designed the tank-crewman's uniform for the Arabs in the seventies," Alon answered tongue-in-cheek.

"Yes, but without gain."

"Maybe."

"Looks like you've been checking me out, Alon."

"Only by Udi."

"Whatever I have said to my good friend, Udi, over the past years has just been small talk."

"That is why we got in touch with you."

---

3 OVERSEAS JEWISH VOLUNTEERS LOYAL TO ISRAEL — IT IS WHISPERED THERE ARE SOME 1500 ACTIVE SAYANIMS IN LONDON ALONE, WITH AT LEAST ANOTHER 4000 ON CALL

"Like I said, just because I mentioned a possible deal with the *nouveau riche* Dikko?"

"That's how we operate."

"Then there's our smart little Abbie," Zak put in.

"What about her?"

"Well, she put Mata Hari to shame."

"How interesting!"

"Certainly was," Zak replied sarcastically. He continued:

"Alon, I told you when you visited me in Bournemouth — I'm a British Jew involved in trying to make a living in the fringe commodity market."

"Yes, Zak, but offering ten NATO spec' C130's to Libya is hard for us to swallow."

"Come on, Alon, I levelled with you. The offer came from a French Jew, via a prime English bank in Monte Carlo. I still have the telex offer."

"Really! Tell me Zak, what would have been your commission from your principal on such a deal?"

"As a businessman, just one per cent."

"A lot of money!"

"Not really," Zak answered, remembering how he'd nearly gone broke from all the communications, travelling and hotel bills he had paid over the past years.

"So, why didn't the deal go through?"

"Several reasons. The Greek's purchasing mandate from Libya expired, and since Kissinger withheld the EU the six C130's that the negotiating Greek had paid for on Libya's behalf, stayed in the USA. Consequently the Libyans would only release new funds once the planes were over their airspace."

"And no-one would agree to such conditions, I'll wager?"

"Right-on, but in retrospect, one can't blame the Libyan Government for not wanting to be screwed again."

"If you say so, Zak. Tell me how did you get involved in such a business?"

"Through meeting Ian Smalley and that Greek guy, Spiro."

"You know Smalley?" Alon asked in surprise.

"I did in the seventies."

"How come?"

"Ian put a tempting aviation contract on the table that sparked me off like crazy."

"And Spiro or Spiros?"

"As you must know, he acted for the Libyans as a middleman for the procurement of the C130's."

"What else do you know about Spiro?"

"Nothing really. I heard after the event, that the Greek's business holdings in Libya were confiscated because of Spiro failing to acquire the End User's certificate for the C130's release. After the E.U. episode, it was rumoured Spiro was a CIA agent."

"Well, at least it sounds like you're telling me the truth."

"Of course. Anyway, if you consider both Rurik's and my exorbitant travel and communication bills over the past decade plus lack of earnings whilst trying to close a commodity deal, then the asking price for supplying and installing the Nigerian Embassy radio network is not unreasonable at all."

"I never thought of it that way, Zak, but it makes some sense now. By the way, did you ever come across Gerald Ronson or Robert Maxwell?"

"Not guilty," Zak quickly rapped out, although G.R. was a distant cousin by marriage. But he only ever read about the property tycoon and Maxwell in the financial and social columns.

"Do you know a Manny Levy?"

Zak was stunned to hear a name from his past.

"From North London? Liked the young girls. Used to be in the 'rag trade'?"

"That's the guy."

"Sure, we were close buddies in the sixties. Last time I saw Manny he was in the lobby of the 'Hilton' in Tel Aviv, flogging uncut West African diamonds and emeralds."

The zealous Mossad agent abruptly stopped taking notes and cut the meeting!

Taking hold of Zak's flexed arm the *Sabra* manoeuvred his guest out of the office and down to the ground floor...

Forbidden Yesterday

Clearing security, then passing the Londoner out through the morbid exodus point of the Israeli Embassy, Alon, with a watermelon smile on his face, exclaimed:

"*Shalom*, Zak. I will be in touch with you shortly."

"*Shalom, shalom*, Alon. See you when you're ready," Zak said, feeling as though he was expected to jump over his own skin for the State of Israel.

CHAPTER FOUR

Recall: June 1950 — 1952

'You're In The Army Now'

ON leaving the Embassy grounds, Zak made his way past the scarred elms towards the Royal Garden Hotel to meet up with his wife, Daphna, who was hopefully waiting for him.

The military presence in the Embassy brought to mind Zak's army square-bashing days.

* * *

Zak's 'D.A.' haircut had gone with his youth in June 1950 when he had been called-up for National Service with the British Army, at the age of eighteen. God! He'd been earning £10 per week clear, a commanding man's wage at the time. It was as much as his stepfather was earning as a long distance lorry driver and certainly more than his five year older half-brother was receiving as a steward in the Merchant Navy on the 'P&O' and 'Castle Line', mainly sailing from Tilbury Docks to Australian ports via South Africa.

It took six weeks of gruelling square-bashing at the Home County's Brigade training-barracks at Shornecliffe in Kent to be moulded into soldierly shape. During the baking summer of 1950 Zak became a Royal Fusilier, nicknamed the 'Elegant Extracts', as did the actor Michael Caine a year later, (another Piscean like Zak).

Rookie Zak was billeted in a corrugated hut overlooking the English Channel, with twenty or so other recruits. Those were uncertain times and training had become even more gruelling when the Korean War became imminent. It came as quite a shock to all the rookies, during basic training, when the conscript period of eighteen months was increased to two years due to North Korean and Chinese Troops crossing the 39th Parallel, perhaps leading to an all-out mighty war!

Nevertheless, Zak faced up to the challenge and the extra training, and had been considered by a couple of dishy ATS girls to be the most athletic squaddie of the June intake. The Fusilier was also able to score the most bulls-eyes on the rifle range, and strip and put a bren gun together within the required fast time.

Having completed the 'intense' basic training, Zak turned down an opportunity to train as a PTI at Aldershot, because he could not wait to soldier abroad.

Square-bashing behind him Zak intended enjoying a much-needed home leave, spending most of the week with his loving schoolgirl Scorpion sweetheart, Daphna, 'swinging on a star' in London, before going overseas for the first time in his life...

The trained soldiers had no choice except to embark at Harwich and cross the North Sea, swinging seasick on hammocks down in the bowels of a ship, as it sailed across to the Hook of Holland...

With the rest of the troops Zak disembarked with a sigh of relief, only to be immediately directed by extra sharp-looking MP's on to a waiting troop train. They had then crossed the Lowlands at express speed travelling through deserted tulip fields, to be followed by the horrifying sight of Germany's wartime devastation, caused by Allied bombs and shell-fire.

Zak's army service was from then on served abroad with BAOR — the smart British Army of the Rhine — stationed in Iserlöhn on the top of 'kit-bag hill', wearing the cross-key flashes of the British

'You're In The Army Now'

Army's 2nd Division. At first, Zak mainly played football for the 1st Battalion, the Queen's Royal Regiment (England's senior infantry Regiment of the line), to which he'd illogically been transferred, since the Royal Fusiliers were in barracks on the other side of the German town, near to where Field Marshal Erwin Rommel lay buried, after a forced suicide and a warrior's burial! Fusilier Caine also soldiered in Iserlöhn, before being shipped off to fight in muddy Korea some months later...

As the football season finished, Zak was posted into the Motor Transport section where he was personally taught to drive by the MT Sergeant who was a look-alike for John Wayne; even performed his duties like the infamous 'Sergeant Striker'.

The MT Sergeant had taken a shine to Zak and he'd felt favoured by the 'three-striper'. When removing the L-plates, 'Striker' had immediately thrown Private Levin a set of car keys belonging to a khaki-coloured 'Volkswagen'... Later, corporal Levin became the Commanding Officer's ('Opel Kapitän') driver, having driven the young Lord Turnock, Lt. Haig (Field Marshal's Haig's grandson) and other officers around the military town.

Although he was comfortably entrenched with the 'Queen's' Zak sought further adventure, so he hastened to volunteer for combat service with the Gloucestershire Regiment, in Korea. Alas, only those who did not volunteer were drafted to the front-line and had got to wear the 'Glorious Glosters' unique double cap-badge of the recumbent Sphinx — one to the front and a smaller version to the back of their head-dress.

Zak's duties, driving the Colonel, took him all over the British Zone of Germany to many major cities. He felt he knew the route to Düsseldorf Airport and the Königsallee blindfolded. The opulent Königsallee was where Zak favoured a stop-off and a welcome coffee, schedule permitting, to watch the Germans bombastically promenading through the centre of up-and-coming Düsseldorf.

The beautiful spa town of Bad Oeynhausen was also a frequent port of call, which was then British Army Of The Rhine Headquarters and where Zak had been fortunate to watch Ike's farewell parade. Remarkably, Zak remembered actual quotes from Ike's (one of only six American Five Star Officers[4]) impressive speech, before General Eisenhower's return to America to campaign for President under his banner 'I LIKE IKE'.

"As always when I am on a British parade I get that soldierly feeling." — "If any soldier who is on this parade finds himself in the United States, and is man enough to make himself known to me, I will welcome him and show him great hospitality."

Eureka! Corporal Levin had shaken hands with the much-decorated Monty in the cook-house during one of the Field Marshal's lightening visits to Iserlöhn barracks! Under the knowing eye of the victorious soldier, the past dress-cutter cum soldier became dazzled at the sight of rows and rows of medal ribbons above Monty's dropped breast pocket.

Inspired, and for a complete change of scenery, Zak indulged in the Army's Jewish religious moral leadership courses and the 'non-kosher' intercourse, performed in the decadent city of Hamburg. Later, Zak visualized the image of the tall, angelic-looking blonde, an impoverished Lithuanian refugee girl, who had worked as a tea-maker in the Victory Club, run by the NAAFI in Hamburg. He could not remember her name… On dating, they'd taken long walks around the beautiful Aussenalster Lake of Hamburg and along the Blankenese waterway, upon whose grassy banks the Londoner had listened to her heated confessions of how plundering platoons of Soviet and German troops had treated her during her plight and flight across Eastern Europe.

---

4 EISENHOWER (IKE), MARSHALL, MACARTHUR, NIMITZ, ARNOLD AND BRADLEY

'You're In The Army Now'

Being a non-smoker and always needing local currency to wine and dine, Zak sold his weekly rations of 'Player's' cigarettes for Deutschmarks to German camp-workers. In fact, Zak managed to have plenty of German money in his pocket whilst soldiering in BAOR, even though he allowed half of his army pay to be sent back home to help his needy mother. His donation enabled her to obtain an extra Army allowance of twenty-five shillings per week, which probably paid the rent in those yesteryears.

Unbelievably, the rate of exchange from the trading camp-workers was 12 DM to the Pound sterling at the time when a certain limping Major returned to the 'Queen's'. During the war the brave Major miraculously escaped from the 'Japs' by making an impossible walk across the Gobi desert.

After five months in Germany, Zak began to look forward to a fortnight's home leave, away from *Fräuleins* with marrying eyes...

As Zak travelled back to England for the first time, he thought he'd become wiser and a more worldly person for being in the Army and having travelled abroad. He'd learnt to drive a car 'on the wrong side of the road', motored all over Germany and Holland, and managed to start speaking German and 'sow some wild oats'. The Londoner felt he'd become more aware of life and different lifestyles, having been invited into German homes and watched Regimental Officers play 'silly buggers' on mess nights.

Daphna had taken the day off from her job selling high-class leather handbags in Shaftesbury Avenue to meet her 'virgin soldier' off the troop train at Liverpool Street station. As he jumped off the train, Zak knew he looked 'BAOR soldier-sharp' in his specially tailored khaki uniform, displaying gleaming bright brass, badge and freshly-whitened flashes.

The waiting Daphna, with a kiss in her eyes, looked great to Zak, even more cuddly than Betty Grable. Daphna was wrapped up in a fashionable, belted, blonde teddy bear coat, that highlighted her 22" waist. She clutched a skin handbag that matched her handmade, high heel shoes. His pin-up girl's shapely legs were clad in fully-fashioned, American, zebra-patterned, striped, heeled nylon stockings, the likes of which Zak had never seen before. He felt he could not wait for her to unclip them from her dainty suspender belt and roll her sheer delights down for him. Daphna was also wearing the biggest smile he had ever seen...

On that home leave from Germany it was the first time Zak experienced the effect of inflation, although the Germans seemed to talk about past inflation all the time. While he had been soldiering in Germany, untimed local telephone calls in England had gone up a penny to three pence, and since he had last bought 'The Star' or an 'Evening Standard', London evening newspapers had risen by a half penny to tuppence.

Zak enjoyed a good, active home leave, when mother and sweetheart both throughly spoiled him. Although he still feared God, he had seen life and London in a different way. Having learnt to trade in the Army, he'd expected life to show a profit from then on and decided to steer clear of politics.

During the Cold War, the conscripted soldier spent two mainly 'fun years' in a 'two-up' German barrack room before he'd returned to 'Blighty' to be technically demobbed at the 'Queen's' barracks in Guildford. Zak's demob only became valid, however, after he'd slept in awe within the shadow of The Bloody Tower, the Crown Jewels and Tower Bridge. In the morning, Zak had been automatically transferred on paper, back to his parent regiment, the Royal Fusiliers. It was just about the time Elizabeth found herself Queen of England and Len Hutton's cricketers won the Ashes for England for the first time since the war. In fact, Len did a three-in-a-row job for Queen and country.

* * * * *

'You're In The Army Now'

Zak quickly marched past the Crown commissionaire who tipped his hat to the Israeli Embassy visitor as he left the confines of Palace Green. The ex-Fusilier made a sharp right, back into Kensington High Street and briskly walked up the grand slope of the Royal Garden Hotel, past privileged limousines watched over by high-hatted, uniformed doormen. Zak noticed his 'Jag' parked on the incline, which indicated Daphna had sweet-talked the link-man and was already in the hotel.

The palatial lobby was unusually quiet as Zak walked past the long reception counter and dormant lifts towards the 'Garden Café' and Bar. He immediately spotted the solitary Daphna by the window in the 'Garden Bar' and hurried over the few marble steps that led up to the tranquil dining area and adjacent cocktail bar. Daphna was perched on the edge of a winged armchair nursing an orange juice in one hand and twiddling her Rolex with the other hand, looking out towards the 'Round Pond' in Ken' Garden, with the distant British Telecom Tower phallically dominating the afternoon skyline...

After a light lunch, the Londoners went on via 'Harrods' (sadly for Tiny Rowland and lucky for the Fayhad Brothers to be later known as *'Arabbs')* to Hollywood Road, Chelsea, to visit Daphna's American cousin, Mary Schepisi and her famous Australian film director husband and their new baby son. The happy Trans-Pacific couple had rented a short-let deluxe abode whilst Fred was filming in London. To congratulate the proud father, Daphna and Zak had taken a rather expensive cuddly Kangaroo that they'd purchased from the renowned super-store. Fred cheerfully reflected several times the soft 'Harrod's' monster was 'A real bute'...

Driving on the M3 back home to Bournemouth Zak began to wonder about Alon and Mossad until the disc jockey of the hour played a Doris Day hit record of the fifties — 'What Ever Will Be Will Be'.

* * *

CHAPTER FIVE

June 1952 — 1978

Success in Civvy Street

ZAK had considered himself very fortunate to have been recommended for a good job by his old manager from Juno Fashionwear after his demob in the fifties. The manager had become a consultant designer for the Rodney Dress Company in Stewart Street, London E.1. which at the time produced exclusively for Marks & Spencer. Consequently, Zak had been employed as a marker-maker, laying out the dress patterns so as to use the least possible amount of material before cutting took place in the sewing factory in Chester-Le-Street (now a supermarket), County Durham.

Within a year, when Zak was still only twenty-one, he'd had the guts to leave his steady job with Rodney to double his salary by cutting expensive tartan dresses for a firm that made-up for the 'Scotch House', ladies' fashion retailers.

Nineteen fifty-three was the year that was, daring Daphna wanted to get married, and Mossad went public. However, Mossad's most successful achievements are never made public.

On 17th June, Zak placed an engraved, gold wedding band on his sweetheart's come-hither finger.

Somehow they'd managed to afford a white wedding under the enchanting floral-decorated matrimonial canopy, the *Chuppah*...

Success in Civvy Street

Daphna and Zak were joined together at Shacklewell Lane Synagogue, a stone's throw from where they had first met at school.

Stamping on the glass goblet to complete the beautiful Hebrew marriage ceremony, Zak heard the Rabbi and all the family joyously shout *Mazeltov*.

The look of love had been in his June bride's eyes as she watched him sip the holy wine. He knew her loving gaze would stay happily embedded in his heart and mind forever.

A small reception was held after the wedding at Zak's new in-laws' flat to which the newlyweds travelled in a smart limousine. Parents and the rest of the family, including cousin Ruth and Daphna's attractive girlfriend Lena, had been obliged to walk the short distance from the synagogue to Daphna's parents rented home.

They had collected seventy-seven Pounds in small, white envelopes by way of wedding presents, before all the family started 'to get their money's worth' by devouring the splendidly-displayed feast. The delicious, freshly-boiled, whole salmon which Ruth's father, Zak's new uncle Dave, (who lived downstairs) had lovingly laboured over all morning, was the centre of attraction. The garnished salmon took pride of place even over the superbly decorated, three-tier, pink-on-white, iced wedding cake.

Later, working for the well-known Mark Kay (subsequently bought out by 'Raybeck') as a production manager, the seal of appreciation had been put on Zak's career. Mark had complimented his manager after successfully selling seven of his dress designs in just one showing at Marble Arch to C&A Modes, during the time Karel Brenninkmeyer was running the retail UK operation. The renowned garment manufacturer proudly told Zak, about the time Andy Williams was enjoying royalties from his hit tune: 'Butterfly':

"You are the last of the old school, Zak. It's going to be a whole new world out there from now on, so always be productive and cut a true line."

Forbidden Yesterday

A year of marriage had gone by for the Levins when there was a happy event, a cute little girl called Tracy — unexpectedly, nine months later, a bouncing baby boy arrived — named Henry.

In the summer of 1956, the almighty Americans and Russians accused Great Britain and the French of being in collusion with the Israelis and causing the Suez crisis.

Accordingly, the 'Rebs' and the 'Reds' flexed their muscles, compelling the Anglo–French expedition to withdraw from the newly-nationalised Egyptian Canal Zone.

In the meantime, Zak managed to successfully work his way through the cut-throat world of fashion to become a well-paid production manager for a famous, medium-priced, high-fashion separates house, and helped to launch the new 'Hipster' line slacks at London's Savoy Hotel. Zak followed up with the first pleated 'Courtelle' box-pleat skirt for one of the Courtaulds family, and he'd even cut a pair of promotional 'Courtelle' gents' slacks (not hipsters) for master comedian Bob Monkhouse to wear on TV.

Due to Zak revolutionising its factories and creating a higher standard of workmanship in their garments, the fast-moving fashion company went public, just as China claimed to have scaled Everest.

The happily married Londoner had been at Wembley in May 1961 and saw Tottenham Hotspur, the First Division leaders, acclaimed as the team of the century. Danny Blanchflower had led the 'Spurs' to a 2-0 victory against Leicester City to win the FA Cup and clinch English Football's coveted 'Double'.

The Jew exterminator, Adolph Eichmann, had been kidnapped from Argentina by Mossad's Chief, Isser Harel, a year earlier. Walking alone in an Israeli prison, Eichmann waited to be sentenced to death as the mighty 'Spurs' went 'marching on'. Alan Sheppard at the time was preparing to be America's first man to orbit the earth.

Success in Civvy Street

About the time the Americans were asked to 'Back Jack' and the Berlin Wall started to go up, in 1961-62, Zak declined the offer of directorship with 'Highlight Sports', from Sydney Solomans; sales director and philanderer *extraordinaire*. A year later Zak chose to leave the now famous separates and dress company just as JFK was standing up to the Russians with the blockade of Cuba.

Deciding the best years of a man's working life should be his very own, Zak intended to be well established in his own business before he was forty. However, being naïve, the Londoner thought he would go through life unscathed. At the time, American Express was about to launch its new Sterling credit card. Three years later in London, Lloyds Eastern Branch automatically issued the high-flying Zak with an American Express card.

On 17th June 1963, Zak started his first clothing factory, the day prior to the Cassius Clay -v- Henry Cooper heavyweight bout, before Clay became Mohammed Ali. The champions fought at the Tottenham Hotspur football ground (or was it at Arsenal?) that hot June night. Oh, but didn't Henry do well with that superman left hook in the fifth that really rocked Clay!

The Profumo spy affair, involving call-girls, Mandy Rice-Davies and Christine Keeler, was also being knocked about at the time in London. Alas, not in a boxing ring but at the Old Bailey, due to an act of folly by one of the lovely Christine's black lovers.

'The Beatles' had made their first album and British TV debut — Beatlemania was launched as the birth control pill became readily available in 1963 to all female screamers, young and old.

By then, the Great Train Robbery was history and the elusive Ronald Biggs was still in hiding. Harold Wilson had inherited the leadership of the British Labour Party and probably went 'Silly' for long weekends.

Zak rented factory space in Dagenham Village (a stone's throw from 'Ford' where Zephyrs and Zodiacs cars were being turned out by ready-to-strike workers) from David Land, who had the good fortune after his RACS Army demob to administer and then inherit the Dagenham Girl Pipers from a retiring local chaplain. David was quickly acclaimed internationally for making the 'Pipers' famous, and then for introducing the 'Harlem Globetrotters' to the UK and Europe. The ex-squaddie, Zak understood, went on to be the 'Angel' or co-producer of the stage show Jesus Christ Superstar, achieving even greater showbiz feats by guiding Tim Rice and Andrew Lloyd-Webber with 'Evita' and other great musical hits.

Zak also made headlines in the local Dagenham 'rag' and quickly received coverage in national daily newspapers in June 1963.

'THE FIRST FOUR & HALF DAY WEEK SET BY TRENDY GOWN MANUFACTURER'

Surprisingly, The BBC requested an interview with Zak, for his voice to be transmitted over the air! Close business friends had consequently jested with the trendy gown manufacturer that he was undermining the British economy.

The media coverage attracted many skilled workers from a nearby clothing factory in Dagenham, including a well turned-out, pretty fifteen or sixteen year-old school leaver named Sandra Shaw, whom Zak engaged as a cutting room trainee. He'd wisely sold out by the end of that year to a public company located in Morley House in Regent Street, W.1. They desperately needed more production capacity owing to the loss of staff from their nearby Dagenham factory, most of their experienced workers having been attracted to come and work for Zak, because of the newspaper and TV coverage.

Oddly enough, the public company seemed delighted to buy their old staff back from the trendy gown manufacturer!

In Egypt during '63 (with the blessing of President Nasser), the PLO was born under Yasser Arafat.

That June too, JFK bestowed on Winston Churchill America's highest award, a very rare Honorary Citizenship[5] and the much-loved President toyed with the idea of a possible war in Vietnam.

Inconceivably, the following November President Kennedy was assassinated in Dallas by Lee Harvey Oswald, who in turn was quickly assassinated by Jack Ruby.

Zak had been staying in the Bahnhof Hotel in Iserlöhn with Daphna and the kids when the news of the President's death had been flashed across the stunned world. Rumour had it that only Edgar J Hoover had worn a smile on his face at the time of the outlandish assassinations.

The Beatles had captured the world with their hit song: 'She Loves You, Yeah, Yeah, Yeah' as the President was laid to rest in Arlington.

It must have been about that time, give or take a year, that Mary Quant finished fashion college and made her mark with her tight-fitting clothes that dominated the swinging sixties. Zak had been given to understand that because Mary forgot, or did not know, to allow tolerance on one of her first cutting patterns, so the tight sixties-look was born. If that was so, how lucky can one get? The so-called trendy gown manufacturer thought he knew it all, but he was slaving away trying to increase his factory's output just to keep his head above water, while lucky Mary became rich and internationally famous for a no-no.

---

5 BESTOWED ON ONLY WINSTON CHURCHILL AND RAOUL WALLENBERG IN 1981: RAOUL WALLENBERG, A SWEDISH DIPLOMAT DURING WORLD WAR II, MANAGED TO SAVE SOME 100,000 HUNGARIAN JEWS FROM NAZI EXTERMINATION BY ISSUING SWEDISH PASSPORTS AND RUNNING 'SAFE HOUSES' — BRIBING, BLUFFING AND THREATENING GERMAN OFFICIALS UNDER THE FLAG AND GUISE OF THE SWEDISH LEGATION IN BUDAPEST

Forbidden Yesterday

New Year's Eve 1963 found Daphna and Zak as guests of David Land in David's private, plush box at the Royal Albert Hall, alongside actor Roger Moore with his new Italian girlfriend Luisa, comic Bernard Bresslaw and actress Barbara Windsor, accompanied by the notorious, Ronnie Knight.

From the profit of the sale of the Dagenham factory, the trendy gown manufacturer could afford to produce fashion in the heart of London's West End rag-trade district. Zak rented premises in Mortimer Street, just off Oxford Circus, thus achieving his ambition to manufacture ladies' suits and dresses under his own label.

Zak recalled the thrill and satisfaction of cutting and styling his own original patterns and samples for his own brand lable before taking orders from the big London fashion stores, including Karel Brenninkmeyer's C&A Modes.

Being fully aware that it was hard to earn a profit on labour, Zak had given his garments out to be made, mainly by Greek-Cypriot outdoor makers, but personally monitored the production before the finished orders were delivered to his customers.

For prestige purposes, the successful Londoner designed and made clothes for some of the international cosmetic companies; 'Revlon' and 'Estée Lauder' came to mind. It was with delight that Zak dealt with an attractive female executive. A French *'papillon'* from Grasse with whom he had to negotiate and also to satisfy. She was responsible for creating, plus maintaining, the sales consultants' seasonal image. They had been strangely attracted to each other and found one another interesting in many ways. The *'papillon'* introduced Zak to Instinct Therapy and the magical smells and pleasures of Aromatherapy. She also enlightened the 'image-producer' to the healing cures of Aromaremedy and massage and the exotic aphrodisiac power of certain Essential Oils, for which Zak is forever grateful. Furthermore, the 'image-producer' became an ardent believer of Instinctology and is fully aware butterflies are drawn to the sweet honey of success.

Success in Civvy Street

Zak befriended a young Metropolitan Police Sergeant, Donald Franklin, a fingerprint specialist who had come over from Marylebone Lane Police Station to Mortimer Street when Zak's stockroom had been broken into and robbed. From then on Don used to pop into Zak's White House showroom for the odd new dress or suit for his wife, or to cadge a few pairs of jeans or a T-shirt for his kids; not that the policeman ever found a clue to the robbers of Zak's branded fashionwear.

Over a drink one evening, Don mentioned that he'd dealt with the Krays and told Zak unbelievable stories about the Twins that made the Londoner's hair stand on end. He'd never dare repeat the happenings Don had revealed, for fear of the 'copper' losing his pension. They were still friendly and met occasionally for a drink or a light lunch. The knowing Don took the time to enlighten Zak: "Only those near and dear to you can harm or hurt you in this life".

During their friendship Donald had been present when Zak bought his personalised, commodore-blue 'Corniche' from Jack Barclay's Rolls Royce showroom in Berkeley Square. The salaried policeman had obviously been impressed and amazed as he watched his exporter-friend sign the Lloyds Eastern Branch cheque for the total amount in the prestigious car showroom, on the boot of a standard white 'Roller'.

Promoted, Don became Donald and was transferred from Marylebone Lane to New Scotland Yard. Donald, to keep their friendship alive, would invite Zak to the Yard for lunch or drinks at festive times. Thank God, Zak never ever had to ask a favour of the Inspector, since Don was a policeman 'through and through' and destined to go places in the force, regardless.

In 1966 Americans orbited the moon (possibly with a little help from the special effects experts in Hollywood) before setting foot on the dusty planet three years later. England, the father of football, definitively won the World Cup that July of '66. Zak was at Wembley with the extra comfort of his newly issued American Express card in his bulging wallet to watch Geoff Hurst score a hat-trick and help beat the West Germans 4-2 after extra time. The Londoner watched with delight as Bobby Moore, the English Captain, led Alf Ramsay's (the English manager — former Spurs and England full-back) team to collect the cherished World Cup trophy, a year before the QE II was launched by Queen Elizabeth II.

The kiss of peace had been performed between the Pope and The Archbishop of Canterbury in the Sistine Chapel earlier in March of that year of '69. Back in London, to the dismay of East Londoners, the Krays were sentenced to life for killing a rival gang leader.

Becoming an active committee member of the prestigious Sportsman's Aid Society (or SAS) had given Zak some local clout and perks. Consequently, he was able to obtain much sought after tickets at short notice to main sporting events and shows, without paying 'through the nose' for them. That was how he'd been able to obtain Cup Final tickets at the right price.

Now in 'the fast lane', Zak was able to buy Daphna diamonds and furs and they started to enjoy wonderful exotic holidays and inspiration together.

Zak became a man about town, well able to sell large amounts of charity tickets to business friends for Race Evenings, Tombola and other fund-raising do's. Some of the functions were held at the newly-built 'Hilton' in Park Lane. Traditionally, the SAS New Year's Eve Ball was, and to this day is held in the Grand Ballroom of 'The Grosvenor' in Park Lane. On all of those past occasions, Daphna was at her husband's side, lovingly holding hands. Zak made sure his wife was royally turned out and to everyone's envy, they danced cheek-to-cheek.

Daphna's uncle Jack had been a founder member of the SAS and was a good friend of the great Danny Kaye and Lew Grade.

Lew always managed to put everybody to shame whilst performing the 'Charleston', before and after he was knighted.

'Never a Quarrel' Joe Coral was the President of the Society. It had been rumoured by Zak's mother that Joe Coral used to work for her deceased husband, when Dad owned a gambling club in London's East End before World War II.

Prince Philip was the Patron of the Sportsman's Aid Society during some of Zak's active time as a committee member.

The Duke of Norfolk took over the honorary position when the Prince stood down from the SAS. Joe soldiered on for many years as an able President of the SAS, sadly, never to achieve being 'dubbed' by Her Majesty.

Bobby Moore and the great Henry Cooper had both found time and given their good support to the Sportsmen Aid functions. Both, of course, had become OBE's for their special contributions to their chosen sports and other fund-raising activities.

Even though Zak never gambled on games of chance, as his late father did, another perk as a committee member of the SAS was being able to dine in any of the Coral gambling casinos and fine restaurants, such as 'Crockfords' in St James's or 'The Curzon House' in Curzon Street, 'The International' in Berkeley Square or 'The Victoria Sportsman Club' in the Edgware Road, near Marble Arch. The Londoner could wine and dine 'on the house' regardless of the size of the party or the bill, and was privileged to talk and drink with the likes of Telly Savalas before the bald-headed mega star played 'galloping dominoes'. Joe's son Bernard was an executive manager-cum-shareholder within the Coral Empire and Zak had known Bernie since their Stamford Hill Boys' Club days.

During Zak's SAS days his favourite restaurants were 'The Pescatori', 'The White Towers' both in Charlotte Street, W1 and 'The White House' in Albany Street, which also had sporting facilities and a swimming pool in those days. Daphna and Zak would take the kids swimming most Sunday mornings — later, while the family were upstairs eating a light lunch in 'The White House' fine restaurant the fast-moving Zak would play a couple of sets of squash with a friend or two.

The Londoner had been one of the first eaters at the 'imported' 'Hard Rock Cafe', before it became famous for its perpetual queue on London's Piccadilly. However, Zak's favourite 'steak joint' during the seventies was the fashionable 'Rib Room' at the Carlton Tower Hotel in Cadogan Square, later to be renamed the 'Hyatt Carlton Tower', about the time Oxford won the Boat Race in the fast time of 16·59 in 1976 and a year before Virgina Wade won Wimbledon back for England during the Queen's Silver Jubilee in 1977.

* * * * *

CHAPTER SIX

Bournemouth: September 1985

Surprise Visit

ON a typical, wet, English Bank Holiday Saturday afternoon, Zak was surprised upon answering the front door of his central Bournemouth flat to find Alon on the doorstep. Alon's extended finger still lingered on the door bell and he appeared as though a bucket of water had been thrown over him. The weathered Mossad agent looked a sorry sight indeed, standing there soaked through, wearing a drenched, open-neck, short-sleeve shirt and blue jeans, which were clinging to his skin.

Surprisingly, the *Sabra* entered the flat without regard to the *mezuzah!* He then politely refused a change of shirt from Zak, but did accept the offer of a dry towel from Daphna.

Alon took his time in the bathroom before joining Zak and his wife for a light lunch, which by then Daphna had prepared.

The Israeli appeared nervous and would not talk about the obvious impending matter until Daphna had cleared the lunch table. Only when Daphna was firmly ensconced in the kitchen, did Mossad's agent cautiously open up.

"Zak, we need to know more about Franz."

"And Rurik?"

"We know all about your multilingual friend Rurik and his nuclear-smuggling. Franz is the key to our operation, because of the position he held at Steilmanns."

Zak at the time did not think to 'qualify' Alon on his apparent knowledge of Rurik's linguistic skills and covert dealings which he knew involved the Israelis, anyway.

"What are you really asking then, Alon?"

"Zak, we may need your support to check out Franz."

"No problem, he's my partner. However, you must realise my first loyalties are to this Realm and my partners, not Israel."

"Understood, as long as you play the game with us, Zak, if we decide to gather Nigerian information via Franz and his ex-Boss."

"Remember, Alon, I will not break the law, and by the same token, as a businessman or broker, I will not sell my friends out." Zak noticed the sinister smile break across the Israeli secret serviceman's face.

"That's what I needed to know, Zak." Alon blurted out, as if in a state of glee. Mossad's agent then tactfully asked the Londoner more leading questions about how and when he had met Franz...

"Zak, did you think Franz and Rurik had known one another before the chance meeting in the beer hall in Munich last March?"

"Impossible, Alon. No-one in our party knew where we were going until the last moment. I remember it was a freezing cold Saturday night. It was a spontaneous request by my Italian *farfalla* that led us to the Munich *bierkeller*. You must know it, the one Hitler made famous?"

"The 'Mathaserbierkeller'[6]?"

"Yes."

"So, you have an Italian girlfriend, Zak?" Alon mocked.

"Just a summer butterfly, but that's a private matter."

"You're having an affair with an Italian girl?"

---

[6] THE WORLD'S BIGGEST BEERHALL WITH SIXTEEN HALLS AND THE CAPACITY TO SERVE 5000 CUSTOMERS AT ONE TIME

"Was." Zak said, not sure if Alon was asking him or telling him, or 'just taking the piss'.

"Incredible. Did your wife know?"

"Yes, I could not lie to her."

"I see."

"No, I see Alon. I'm being far too open to your rhetoric."

"Don't be *broygez* with me, Zak, just because your overseas butterfly has fluttered away."

"I'm not *broygez* with you, Alon. I'm annoyed at myself for being too 'up front'."

Alon then turned on the charm:

"But we wouldn't deal with you if we thought you were other than completely open with us, Zak."

"Perhaps so, Alon, but I have a feeling I should have played this one much closer to my chest."

"Come on, *landsman*, you can surely trust me."

Zak declined to answer that one.

"O.K., Zak, I will be in touch with you again soon."

After thanking Daphna for the meal, Mossad's agent then left with a hearty *shalom*.

Zak felt empty and none the wiser for Alon's visit, when he noticed the tagged-key on the 'Chesterfield' that Alon had vacated. The tag depicted the nearby Bournemouth Crest Hotel, Room 117. It could only have fallen out of the *Sabra's* jeans back pocket... Zak batwittedly chased after Alon, foolishly humiliating the Israeli Secret Agent by returning his lost key in front of his big-breasted chauffeuse. Zak realised later he should have allowed Alon to save face, permitting the *Sabra* to return to the penthouse to retrieve the hotel key for his naughty holiday weekend.

Alon must have been checked into the 'Crest' with the glowing brunette under a *nom de plume*... as later, out of curiosity, Zak was unable to locate the Israeli when phoning the 'Crest'. Ironically, that particular day there was a distressed Libyan freighter off Portland Bill in the English Channel. This left Zak wondering at the time if

Alon was on a double assignment, or sitting in a pub down in Bovington spotting 'Chieftains' go by.

Autumn's coloured leaves, heralding the onset of winter, were already appearing in mid-September. Zak had not heard a whisper from Alon since his Bank Holiday visit. Rurik began to make a nuisance of himself by enquiring every day if the Israelis had made contact. The hard-up Slav obviously resented the daily cost of the expensive international telephone calls to try and keep the *zugging* Franz placated.

"Zak, Rurik, here. Have you heard back from your people in the Holy Land yet?"

"Rurik, I keep telling you, as soon as the promise is confirmed, I'll phone you immediately."

"Don't let them keep us on the 'back burner', Zak. Franz is on my back, getting more desperate and nervous by the day for news and money."

"It's rumoured there might be coup in Nigeria," Zak bantered.

"They'd need Franz all the more then, my friend."

"Could be... As I told you, I'll phone you when I hear back from them, Rurik. *Ciao.*"

"Yea, *ciao* for now."

Zak's Israeli friend Udi telephoned towards the end of September from Tel Aviv, to reflect: A team of Mossad interrogators from Jerusalem had been to see Lena and him again. The team had wanted feed-back on stuff like: how long they'd all known one another? And did Udi or his wife Lena know that their friend had actively supplied denim jeans to Arab countries and Iran?

"Zak, no way must you let me down on this one. And for God's sake, don't let the Embassy know in London that I'm to receive a kick-back when and if the operation goes through."

"I certainly won't let on, Udi."

"I know Zak. But I had to vouch for you."

Surprise Visit

Zak took umbrage at what he'd heard, but 'bit his tongue'. Udi sounded very frightened, so Zak reassured Udi he had nothing to fear, before declaring:

"Udi, if you vouched for me, then you must vouch for Mossad."
"But, of course, Zak, that's for sure."

Alon eventually phoned Zak one October evening in a shallow carefree style. However, Alon had to howl over the blaring, funky music that was being played in the lively disco from where the *Sabra* had chosen to call.

"Zak, how are you? Can we meet up?"
"Fine, but no," Zak answered the two questions in one.
"For why?"
In a tight lipped manner, Zak told Alon:
"No way, Alon. I don't like the way your 'firm' side deals. In fact, I'm not interested any more in helping you." With that, Zak calmly replaced the receiver.

Alon phoned back frantically several times that night to try and persuade Zak to change his mind and 'play ball'. Finally, Zak engaged his answering machine to protect himself from Alon's persistence.

Next morning when Daphna and Zak returned home from morning coffee in nearby 'Dingles', they were both stunned to find Alon waiting for them on the door step!

The *Sabra,* entered the Levins' flat, again without acknowledging the *mezuzah!* Once Inside, Zak would not allow Alon to get to 'first base' with him. Alon worriedly argued the point about his superiors' reaction to the situation and the flak he would take due to Zak's new-found attitude.

"Zak, if you don't help me, it will leave a very sour taste in their mouths in Jerusalem."
"For you or for me, Alon?"

"For me, of course, Zak." Alon attuned to apply the redress to himself. The Israeli shrugged his shoulders as he flashed a fearful glance towards Daphna, patriotically appealing for her support.

"It's Israel's policy to trade and earn as much foreign currency as it can, Zak. We can net a lot of Dollars from exporting to Nigeria. To do this efficiently it would help if we could monitor Nigeria's commercial needs."

"Commercially, Alon?" Alon was saved by the bell, as the phone rang.

"Hi, Zak baby, what's happening today?" It was Rurik's rich, sober voice at the other end of the telephone...

"Our friend is here from the *Promisedland!*"

"You're kidding me, Zak."

"No."

"In your flat now, like while I'm talking with you?"

"At my very side."

"Are they interested?"

"I would say we're on the 'front burner'."

"Goody, are they interested enough to pay the price for the 'Nigerian Link'?"

"I would presume so."

"Then, what's the problem, Zak? We are Ready, Willing and Able this end. Get the commitment, we need the Dollars, baby."

"Alon... Rurik is on the telephone from Munich. They're RWA He wants to know if you're interested in paying the price?"

"Like I told you, Zak... four to five million USD is O.K. now that we understand your circumstances."

"Yes, Rurik. Possibly five very long ones."

"Seven figures?"

"Yes."

"Great, but when?"

"I'll let you know soonest. Keep Franz on ice. Don't let him drink too much either."

"Zak, they're not arguing about the price?"

"Not yet."

"Unbelievable. It's so out of character for those guys. Try and get some up-front money if you can."

"Good idea, speak to you later."

"Yea... Zak, try hard to get some Dollars this week."

"I'll ask, okay?"

"O.K., keep in touch." Zak replaced the receiver, then told Alon: "Rurik wants to know if we can have some up-front money?"

"Impossible."

"Why's that?"

"Because we know from experience not to do business in such a way."

"What do you mean?"

"We have been had over many times by *gonifs*."

"Got it, unscrupulous parasites and all that, hey?"

"Right, *shysters*."

"Alon, are you suggesting we are *shysters?*"

"Not at all."

"So, can we at least shake hands on the deal and the agreed payment?"

"Sure, Zak, five million US Dollars is O.K."

"With a binding '*Mazel un Brocheh*'?"

"Yes."

"Alon, do you consider a '*Mazel un Brocheh*' absolute and irrevocable when given with a handsake?"

"Yes. Absolutely cast iron."

"Fine." They shook hands there and then, with a '*Mazel un Brocheh*' on five million American Dollars, in the age-old irrevocable biblical way of the Hebrews — on the understanding that Zak would travel to Munich and tighten up on Franz's willingness to perform. Luckily for Mossad, they could take advantage of Zak's anticipated trip to a Brussels wholesaler and 'Imotex' near Düsseldorf in Neuss where Zak hoped to sell his stagnating stock of ladies high fashion Skiwear.

Coincidentally after the delights of the gourmet-city, the trip would allow a visit to 'IGEDO', the German International Fashion Show at Düsseldorf, before flying on to Munich.

Forbidden Yesterday

On 17th October 1985, Zak eagerly kept the rendezvous with Alon, in the lounge of the Post House Hotel close to London's Heathrow Airport, to collect his extra expenses from the *Sabra* and to receive last-minute instructions. Zak was given the code name 'Lancaster' before catching the 18:00 hours SABENA flight 608Y to Brussels, travelling first to meet up with the Frenchman, Jean Paul and his likely Belgian buyer for the Skisuits, before flying on to Munich via Düsseldorf as agreed with Alon to proposition Franz. Zak had previously purchased his Club-class ticket from the British Airways ticketing shop in Bournemouth. Alon closely inspected the ticket before parting with the petty cash, surprisingly requesting a full signature for the Sterling notes. However, to Alon's dismay, Zak was only prepared to initial the *'biroed'* receipt, performed on a loose leaf from Alon's notebook.

The British Airways computerised ticket was indented:

LHR-SN/BRU-SN/DUS-LH/MUC-LH/LHR

With his passport, ticket and money in place, hand-grip neatly stowed under his upright seat, seat-belt securely fastened, Zak watched a changing evening sky from the window of the taxiing SABENA jet... Zak recalled the first time he'd ever travelled by air. It had been on that very same route: the first BA scheduled flight of the new Trident T1 which had a revolutionary, rear-mounted third jet engine. Zak further recalled he had been a little hesitant to fly... after all, it had been April Fool's Day, 1964, or was it '63?

* * *

Like a clapperboard, Zak's mind suddenly displayed a vivid image of the erotic Clarissa and her incredibly-worded Airmail Express letter from Italy. The letter had been induced by his five day disappearance, hospitalised in Basingstoke General due to a car accident — the Londoner had fallen asleep at the wheel on the M4 Motorway, the very morning of his return from the sexsational, magical Maltese holiday with the Italian love-Goddess.

Surprise Visit

Friday, 24th August '84

My dearest Zak, my love,

Only a day without you ... an endless time!

You are so far away ... yet so deep inside of me, where are you?

I have just tried again to speak with you at the Crest Hotel in Bournemouth (0044 202 23262); a cold woman's voice told me you aren't there. I wanted to leave a message for you but I couldn't speak;

"There is no guest with this name." That was all.

Will you give me a call?

I miss you so much ... I need your voice ... your breath on my lips, on my face, on my hair, on my body ... can you understand me, how much?

If I close my eyes, I think you are so near that I can touch you.

I feel on my skin the heat of our last night's kisses...

I love you, yes, yes, yes.

           Your Summerlove.

CHAPTER SEVEN

Bournemouth: The Summer of 1983

Buongiorno Clarissa

RETAINED in Zak's memory was that glorious, hot English summer's morning in July. Prince Charles and Princess Di, he remembered, were just into their third year of marriage.

Akin to a fish out of water, Zak was into his third year of living in Bournemouth — a large 'backwater' of a seaside town, struggling to be a city. A place that harboured, amongst other things and people, dissident Iranians and Khomeini sympathizers. Here, the Italian Butterfly and Zak had first chanced to meet. He'd been strolling home that bright morning with thoughts of Ian Smalley, for some unknown reason, dwelling on his mind. Perhaps it was because Ian at the time of his arrest was considered by the media to be the number one arms dealer in the world, having overtaken Khashoggi. Ian's arrest in the States the previous September had caused a cold wave to roll through the International Electronic and smart-weapon market.

When Ian had been committed for trial at the beginning of the following February, after pleading not guilty as charged, the polite, chubby, bespectacled boy (who looked like Elton John) from the Old Kent Road had been acquitted by the lenient American jury, because of entrapment by the FBI.

Realising he was day-dreaming and late for brunch, Zak started to walk briskly home as he'd left the Daimler Vanden Plas with his local Jaguar dealer for a short interim service. It had been his intention later that afternoon to take the welcome heat of the sun down on the beach with his estranged wife. Mentally as well as physically Daphna had become a different person since Mr Pinker (the Royal gynaecologist — now Sir George D. Pinker — whose famous hand Zak had shaken a couple of times) had performed her hysterectomy. As 'man and wife' they were rarely able to sit down and make plans or lay down ground rules to improve their marriage. If they did appear to reach an accord, Daphna's female understanding differed from her husband's at the end of the day and she quite often frivolously abjured on what they had agreed upon.

Daphna had become obsessed with looking after her ailing mother to the extent that she and Zak didn't laugh together or hold hands any more, and the only thing they seemed to have in common since her mother arrived was the same address. Obviously Daphna needed a break from her self-inflicted routine but had refused to take a much-needed holiday. Over the years if Daphna wasn't worrying about her mother or their grown-up kids she would dig up an obscure aunt somewhere to concern herself with. Zak had thought twice when allowing his mother-in-law to move in with them from her small London flat, even though he liked the old lady and had always been able to get on with her. He really only acquiesced to appease his ambivalent wife.

June had been out of tune for Zak. The meeting with Clarissa must have been on the glorious 17th day of the following month, since the Italian butterfly later told Zak he was the best birthday present she had ever had, and wished she hadn't had to wait until her thirty-fifth birthday for her Prince Charming to come along...

If Zak's recollection was right, Terry Wogan, disc jockey supremo, on the very morning July 17th, allowed him to jay-walk, as 'Our Tel' politely stopped his brown 'Roller', enabling Zak to safely continue crossing Bournemouth's busy Richmond Hill roundabout, a sign, perhaps, of the coming incident that was about to change the Londoner's life.

For Zak, it had been 'lust at first sight' of Clarissa. How could he forget the fever that had come over him as his eyes fell upon her loveliness and held her intriguing gaze. Destiny and the elements must have ensured the incredible happenstance on a quiet street corner outside one of those tall, fading red metal and glass-panelled telephone kiosks that display the Crown of the Realm over its door, opposite Braidley Road. Visiting Libyan students considered the kiosk as something of a shrine, since in 1964 Gaddafi, at the age of twenty-four, had taken a short course at the King's School of English in Braidley Road before going on to Beaconsfield to take a military signals course.

The radiant butterfly was obviously waiting to use the kiosk, or its occupant. She had the sophisticated-looking 'Lancôme' face and features of the beautiful Isabella Rosselini. Her shapely form, attracting the brilliance of the sun's descending rays, made her appear iridescent and angelic. She appeared alone and pensive sitting on a wooden bench, framed by a low, honey-coloured, knotted pine fence. Instantly, Zak put her on the highest of pedestals. The resplendent setting, full of colour and fragrance from the over-hanging seasonal flora behind her, would be forever etched in his memory.

Clarissa had been wearing a great looking, two-tone khaki-and-fuchsia-coloured, dolmen sleeved sweater at the time, with lightweight khaki gaberdine jeans, the pocket flaps and detail narrowly piped with slubbed raw fuchsia silk. The ensemble was complemented by a divine-looking clutch bag and low-heeled sandals, both expertly styled and trimmed in flaming fuchsia slubbed-silk like her well-tailored jeans.

The very expensive looking outfit was apparent to Zak's trained eye, an exclusive one-off designer piece.

The resting '*Speyria Aphrodite*' was of medium height, between a size 12 and 14. His experienced eye also gauged that she would need the in-between size to fit those curvaceous breasts and hips. Magnificently shaped shoulders supported a gorgeous swan-like neck, pillaring a head and face that he felt sure must put a lot of class cars' fast engines into reverse. Her lustrous, fashionably-layered chestnut-coloured hair was only slightly displaced by her designer sunglasses as she flicked them down over her eyes. Her frames matched her silver and gold ladies Rolex 'Oyster' watch which, oddly, she wore on her right wrist, along with a fine two-tone gold chain.

The other ambiguity about this never-to-be-forgotten beauteous vision, was the antique amethyst-studded gold necklace strung around her graceful neck. The necklace was not in keeping with her otherwise international image and not becoming of her somehow.

Spellbound, Zak labelled the waiting butterfly as being foreign, no more than twenty-eight years of age, probably from Italy, because of the much favoured Italian combination of wristwatch and chain. A discerning, possibly a wanting or needy female on holiday, he'd thought she could be the answer to his dream

In the early autumn of his life, conjured up in Zak's head were all sorts of thoughts of how he appeared to the interesting-looking, perched butterfly. In fact, at the sight of her, he had developed a bout of spring fever and had broken out into a sweat from merely looking at her He'd felt his chest and shoulders expand in the American Army Officer's shirt which was a 'working-sample' from that attractive, young, widowed, factory-owner in Dallas. Zak's 'love-shirt' was a similar shade to his new khaki drill 'DAKS' trousers which he had recently purchased from 'Simpson's' of Piccadilly. The hems of the new 'DAKS' took the rub of his hand-made, Jermyn Street, brown turtle shoes which matched his silver and gold buckled skin belt. Around Zak's neck was a long, 'Hermes', hand-made 22-carat gold chain that he'd bought on the fashionable Rue St Honoré, which dangled over the partially unbuttoned love-shirt, revealing his *maschile petto*, as Clarissa later nick-named his manly chest. A matching link bracelet showed distinctively below Zak's neatly turned up left cuff. On the other wrist he wore the male version of the Rolex 'Oyster' wristwatch the butterfly was wearing. It was inevitable that they should notice one another. They were like two khaki 'peas in a pod' on that deserted street corner!

Zak was surprised when his trance had been broken when he came abreast of the clear-skinned beauty, her bubbly Italian-laced voice declaring:

"*Mi scusi*, I am Italian."

"*Buongiorno*. Welcome to my dreams, can I help you?" Zak asked, with bold delight.

"*Si, grazie*, I am not sure I know how to use your English *telephono*. I must speak with *Italia* by *Il'uno*."

"Do you have a problem, *signorina*?" Zak quietly requested, to be sure of her intentions and to find out if 'lady luck' was about to knock at his door.

"Pardon me, I would like to know, do I have enough money to phone Italy this time of day?" The *signorina* then displayed a clear plastic Lloyds Bank £10 money bag, over-flowing with brand new silver 50p coins.

"And can you show me how to use the telephone?" Before answering, Zak made a guarded attempt to see the colour of her eyes, behind the dark-lensed sunglasses that seemed glued to her lovely brow, but to no avail. He'd managed a close-up glimpse at her gold, antique, amethyst earrings though, that matched her necklace. A family heirloom, no doubt, Zak thought at the time.

"It looks possible to me," he dauntingly answered.

"*Grazie*," she quickly answered with apparent relief.

"I would say you have enough change to make at least a ten minute call, this time of day."

"Wonderful."

"But the girl in the telephone booth will need to hurry!"

"*Si*, it is twelve-fifty five in Italy". Simultaneously they glanced at their perpetual time pieces again.

"*Yesa*, but how do I use the telephone exactly?"

She'd euphonized her 'yes', as Italians do, before exclaiming in a tensed, anxious voice:

"Do I put the money in the phone box before I dial my number?"

The apparent *signorina* was getting more tense with every word she spoke. Zak empathised with her predicament, having been in the same dilemma himself many times — being unsure of the local telephone system and its dialling codes to get into the international network. His reminiscences of overseas trips and holidays abroad were temporarily shelved as she went on:

"Will I get through to *Italia* in time?" she asked, in a dramatic tone of voice, that cut into his very heart. It made Zak even more acutely aware of the *signorina's* pending concern. Past memories of waiting around at international airports for an empty telephone kiosk quickly flashed through his mind again…

"Have you the time to help me?" queried the Italian Butterfly, now close at the Englishmans side. She gave Zak the perception of somehow wanting him to take her strain, and had turned on his curiosity and libido by asking him for his time. Zak knew time was paramount; with time and tenacity one could climb the highest mountain and undertake the longest journey.

"Relax, *signorina*. Of course, I will help you… I'll wait with you until the blonde girl finishes her telephone call, if you like."

The *signorina*'s immediate sigh of relief expressed the tension leaving her lovely being.

She then chose to remove her sunglasses, which allowed Zak to witness her sparkling green eyes incredibly metamorphose to lilac!

"*Molte grazie*. My name is Clarissa Teresa," she said, as she stepped out of his dreams.

"Hi, my name is Zak. I compliment you on your English and your incredible eyes." He'd been obliged to shout back, because a chugging yellow bus was just passing by.

"Well, thank you, Zak. I'm a language teacher from Ancona,"

"Like 'Verdicchio' in amphora-shaped bottles?"

"*Si*, you have tasted the wine?"

"Yes. Can you believe in Ancona's 'Happy Bar'?

"Unbelievable! Drink and smile, hey Zak," the bubbly Italian butterfly affirmed the 'Happy Bar' catch phrase as she stepped into the now-empty telephone booth... Then she stepped back into Zak's dreams.

Phenomenally, a couple of days later Zak again chanced to meet the expensively-dressed Italian schoolteacher. She was on her way into Bournemouth's town centre... Zak knew the elements were on his side when he found the courage and the right moment to ask:

"How about a light lunch and a heavy date?"

"*È'un piacere*," she said in Italian as she suggestively winked and flicked her head to one side.

"And your *sogno, Signore*?" Surprise, surprise, she appeared willing to step into his dreams, with a drink and a smile!

"I would love to whisper my dreams to you, *signorina*,"

Zak knew 'lady luck' had indeed knocked on his door as she took his questing hands in hers.

"By the way, Clarissa, do you smoke?"

"Cigarettes?"

"Is there anything else?" he asked naïvely.

"No, Zak, I do not smoke cigarettes."
"Great, couldn't be better. I'm a non smoker, too."

Along the coast from Bournemouth in the Dolphin Hotel, the captivating butterfly was sitting alone, on a full-size, plum-coloured Chesterfield, opposite the reception desk. Clarissa looked adorable and immaculate after her quick splash and comb, and their enjoyable light lunch, in a restaurant that once proudly displayed the cherished 'Egon Ronay' rosette.

As Zak approached Clarissa, she put both hands up to him and uttered his name. He'd taken her hands in his, feeling the heat of her fast flowing blood through her cool, cleansed skin. The aroused Englishman could not resist kissing her junoesque neck with his fervent lips. Zak's kiss lingered on Clarissa's warm perfumed flesh as she shuddered with pleasure… Reluctantly, he pulled away from her craving being, then looked intensively into her romantic eyes before uttering:

"Lovely butterfly, we must leave now, if you want to arrive at school on time."

"My charming Englishman, I do not want to go to school!"

He kissed Clarissa's burning lips in reply, then asked:

"Tell me what do you want to do?"

The impassioned butterfly's verdant eyes miraculously metamorphosed, to a tantalizing shade of amethyst, settling to a soft blush of lilac at being kissed:

"Zak, I want to make love with you!"

He was completely mesmerised by her trans-coloured eyes, her impulsive words and obvious immediate need. He was sent spinning into a cold sweat as his fired body went weak at the knees.

"Are you sure?"

"*Si*, Zak, I cannot resist giving myself to you. Your perfume is driving me crazy."

"My concocted cologne is bottled passion."

"*Si*, it makes my libido throb."

"Your desire is my command, my *Bella Donna*."

"Wonderful, can we take a little room here?"

"Sounds good to me," he'd whispered wistfully.

"Wonderful," Clarissa cooed again.

"Wait here, butterfly, I will see if they have a vacant room, then I will give you an unforgettable experience in quintessential oils and the art of Aromatherapy."

"*Si*, smother me in concocted cologne and passion, that would make me so happy. *Cazzo, me dia cazzo*, Zak."

"You're incredible, butterfly. I will, I will," he'd vaunted.

"Can I remain here while you see if they have a little room for us?" Clarissa asked demurely, obviously not wanting to encounter the receptionist.

"Yes, if you promise not to fly away."

"I promise not to fly away, my gallant Englishman." Zak lovingly caressed her desirous body with his hands and lips, thinking only of the sexual experience which lay ahead with this bold, wanting Latin beauty.

"*Un attimo*, Clarissa," Zak said in Italian, before ambling over to the reception desk. The expressionless receptionist who had witnessed their enrapturement, indifferently franked the American Express card.

Zak turned to Clarissa, dangling the room key at her. She was smiling with delight, and apparent admiration, at his ability to handle the moment calmly and to avoid the receptionist's request for her foreign passport. Clarissa eagerly raised her lithe body from the settee as he extended his inviting hand.

"*Magnifico*, Zak, what is the room number?" He'd displayed the large tag hanging from the big old-fashioned iron key depicting his lucky number. Taking Clarissa's ripe womanly form into his embrace, he whispered:

"We only have to take one flight to Room 17 and paradise, my lovely Continental lady."

"*Presto!*"

Gently, Zak led the willing butterfly by her ring-less hand up the nearby narrow staircase to the first floor.

As Zak closed the door to the shaded bedroom, the overt seductress immediately fell to her knees and ripped open his original and rare white '501's' to grope and gourmandise him. He had somehow managed to 'isolate' her clinging body from her white designer outfit to find her erect blood-filled nipples with his searching lips, protruding behind the front fastening of her lacy, lavender-coloured bra. At the same time, Zak experienced the unparalleled ecstasy of Clarissa's sensuous tongue on his prolific erection. In all of his life, he'd never experienced a butterfly with such a 'sexsational' technique, which she joyously accomplished with the use of her devouring suction...

Embedded in the deepest cavity of her throat and with lusting strength Zak lifted the delirious butterfly onto the soft bed, managing not to swamp her ravenous mouth with his rising sap. He gently slipped his enlarged corona from her guzzling mouth, enjoying every facet of the intriguing moment. Slowly, very slowly, Zak removed her lace briefs. He'd stared in awe at her *mons veneris*, a triangular mound of provocative, silky, black hair nestling below her exquisite naval. Clarissa invitingly spread her unblemished, sun tanned thighs, revealing the most adorable, pink-lipped, moist vagina.

Still mesmerised, as if under a spell, Zak found himself holding the Italian beauty's flimsy 'Janet Reager' lavender-panties in his grasp, her ripe spreadeagled body was his for the taking...

A few days later, after loving and swapping exotic fantasies with Clarissa in Poole, in fact while taking high tea in Bournemouth's sumptuous Royal Bath Hotel, she asked Zak, in between cucumber sandwiches and exchanging presents:

"Did you have an interesting day in London yesterday, my capable Englishman?"

"Yes, I did, but I missed your pillow-talk and passionate body, my *Bella Donna*."

"*Si*, me too. Zak, can we find a little room shortly?"

"My pleasure."

"Wonderful, I need you deep inside of me."

"No problem, my adorable lady."

"Really?"

"Yes, Clarissa, Clarissa."

"*Magnifico*. Tell me, my Englishman, what did you do in the Big City yesterday?"

Zak told Clarissa all about his full day in London and how as a result of his visit he had already received an encouraging affirmative telex from a Colonel friend to start the ball rolling on a JPI contract and a mega currency deal.

"For really big money, Zak?"

"Two billion Old Nigerian Naira."

"How much is that in Sterling?"

"Well… in US Dollars, at my selling price, it's four hundred and sixty-two million.

"*Mama mia*, Zak! That's a lot of Lira. But who would want to buy such Old Naira?"

"Someone in an Ivory Tower, an Overlord in the petroleum business. Old Naira are not completely obsolete in Nigeria." He had then gone on to explain the finer technicalities, which Clarissa surprisingly appeared to comprehend. How only an oil company would be interested in buying the Old Naira with external American Dollars at a discount price, to then be credited in Nigeria with New Nairas at an increased face value.

"What would be the point in an oil company doing that, Zak?"

"A way of buying 'Bonny Light' cheaper. To get around the fixed OPEC crude oil prices and give the Nigerians all that much-needed external currency to play around with."

"It must be hard to make such a transaction?"

"Certainly is."

"I wish you luck, Zak."

"Thank you, I need it. The real problem is the buyer having the confidence in the Nigerians to honour the subsidy, which includes all royalties and commissions, within the purchase price."

"I see, Zak. What is 'Bonny Light' and JPI?"

"Black gold and jet fuel, my fast little butterfly."

On finishing their light snack, Zak suggested to Clarissa:

"Before we find a room, how about me showing you our little museum which is just along the road from here?"

"Do you mean the Russell-Cotes Museum?"

"Yes, I do. Would you like to look-see or have you already seen Earl Russell-Cotes' treasures?"

"No, but it would interest me to make just a short visit." He'd paid the important-looking bill before leaving the 'Royal Bath'. They went arm in arm. Zak, feeling like a VIP, was puzzling how and when he could wear the locket and golden key that Clarissa had presented him with or whether he should just put them in his safe deposit box until the price of gold escalated again.

Oblivious to the steep hill, hand in hand they'd walked the forty or fifty yards up to the museum, resting on the scenic East Cliff.

Having taken in the museum and its outside Geological Terrace adorned with stone columns from the nearby Isle of Wight, and the surrounding Purbeck Hills they'd gazed at the easterly view of the 'Needles', the white cliffs of the Isle of Wight, glistening across the bay in the sunlight. Between caresses they wondered at the panoramic Purbeck Hills, 'Old Harry Rocks' and Poole Harbour over to the overcast west. Entwined, they'd strayed along the East Cliff, towards the funicular, stopping to recapture the seascape from the 'View Point'. Amused at the sight of a half-naked exhibitionist flying his red-fringed delta kite from the cliff top, they stole the time to wait and watch the wind unwind the deep-sky reel, then stole another kiss... From the cliff-top the paramours observed the despondent surf-boarders in the gentle sea's swirl before the ripples magically faded on the sea shore in front of the Victorian style beach huts below. Nature seemed to call them down the Zigzag, along the sandy beach towards the rebuilt Pier; slowly, they then walked its wooden planks together. The lovers lingered for another moment to watch the anglers casting their rods from the lower deck. Unavoidably, they picked up the curses of the fishermen, mingled with the squalls of the seagulls, too busy casting their lines to notice what looked like the trim, 240 foot long, black and white hull of the sea-going paddle-steamer, 'Waverley', disturbing their fishing area. The sight and sound of the 'old lady' manoeuvring with only one of her two brightly ringed, black, white and red stacks smoking and coming into dock with flags flying, bell ringing and siren tooting, was splendid indeed. The unique paddle steamer quickly unloaded its cargo of sightseeing day-trippers from her decks. On disembarking, some day-trippers rushed to the Pier-Head Café, to quench their thirst, or to buy an ice cream cornetto to devour. Others sought out brightly-coloured deck-chairs that provided shelter from the lively sea breeze.

When paying the toll charge on entry to the Pier, Zak joked with Clarissa that he would take her 'out to sea' and later make 'sand pies' for tea. She'd immediately laughed as she'd caught on to the double meaning of his English humour:

"Zak, it's wonderful. I can laugh with you. I'm so very happy you don't just want my body."

"Really, Clarissa?"

"I cannot lie, Zak."

Acutely aware of Clarissa's presence and realising his predicament at home, Zak told her:

"Yes, you are right, I crave the comfort and the conversation of a loving woman these days."

"It's *meraviglioso* for us, Zak. We are able to just hold hands and walk and talk."

"I know what you're saying, Clarissa — we are compatible."

"*Yesa*, we are making love another way!"

"For sure."

"I think we understand one another's needs, Zak?"

"Could be. Fancy renting a beach hut for the afternoon? Or shall we go, you and I, to a sleazy motel?"

"*Si*, I love the pleasure of being a woman and the words of the American poets, T.S. Elliot and Emily Dickenson."

"Sounds very pleasurable, my poetic one."

"Wonderful, you have perceived me quickly, my Englishman. Can I pay for the sleazy motel room?"

"You are most generous, Clarissa, but that's not my style," Zak answered, puzzled and unable to define the Italian temptress's need to pay for a cheap motel room.

Before Clarissa's return to Italy, Zak organised a long weekend, transporting the exhilarated butterfly to view Windsor Castle prior to taking up their reservation at the Royal Garden Hotel (overlooking the Israeli Embassy) in London. It became routine each morning for them to share breakfast and fantasies in the well-sprung wall-bed before loving again. Once dressed, Clarissa seemed more than happy to go hand in hand and explore the London Zak knew and loved: Soho, Covent Garden, Bond Street, Mayfair, The King's Road, Chelsea, Portobello Road, combined with lunch at 'Fortnums', dinner at 'Veeraswamy's', the joy of eating a burger at the 'Hard Rock Café', a late night table at 'Ronnie Scott's.' There was a visit to Westminster Abbey, a romantic walk along the Embankment.

A kiss and a whisper in St Paul's. The Thames, Boadicea, Cleopatra's Needle, the Sphinx and The Shell Clock. When strolling over Waterloo Bridge, Clarissa seemed surprised to learn and see from that unique position that the Shell time piece was bigger than Big Ben. Unpretentiously, she mentioned that she had seen the biggest clock in the world in Times Square, New York.

"Clock or cock, Clarissa?" Zak asked inquisitively.

"Both!" she'd teased".

"*Si*, Clarissa... The Shell Clock is the second largest time-piece in the world."

"Big Ben must then be the third biggest?"

"*Si, farfalla*. Tomorrow I will take you to The Tate."

"Sounds wonderful, Zak. I would love to see the paintings of the famous English artist, Turner."

"You also seem to know all, my butterfly."

"I love the arts and the good life, Zak."

"*La dolce vita*, Clarissa."

"*Si*, Zak."

Clarissa and Zak made an expedition to the British Museum the next morning, where in the Mummy Room he'd taken some time away from Clarissa to meditate and concluded he'd finally broken the curse of the Pharaohs from the plateau of Giza.

When visiting Cairo back in '76, Zak had climbed the never-ending stairs up to the pinnacle of the Great Pyramid and its burial chamber, only to experience nausea and muscle spasms. Not to mention the ten-ton deal with Mr. Elissar, for the unlined secondhand jackets for the up-and-coming Egyptian executives, which went sour because the naïve Elissar could not acquire the necessary external currency. However, Zak had encountered Fosseta...

Seemingly, always tight for time, the romantic pair managed to visit London Zoo and then dash over to Kensington Gardens for

Zak to introduce Clarissa to Peter Pan and put himself in 'never-never land', before taking in The Tate Gallery.

However, for Clarissa, the panda in London Zoo turned out to be the main attraction, as she had never seen a performing 'black and white' before.

It was during the last night over dinner in the beautiful 'Royal Garden' roof-top restaurant just before the salacious Clarissa's departure, that she'd seriously told Zak:

"My Englishman, apart from a few misunderstandings, it has been a Midsummer Night's Dream with you."

"And wonderful for me."

"Then, I wish to share my very special fantasy with you later."

"I'm honoured, and the theme?"

"Enchanting Arabian men!"

"Arabs, tell me more." Zak requested loudly in surprise.

"Yes, you must know I prefer circumcised men, Zak," Clarissa said, searching her Englishman's eyes for a reaction to her risqué remark."

"So, that's the attraction?" Zak uttered back in jest.

"Partly," Clarissa quipped back in retaliation.

"And?" Zak asked quizzically.

"I can climax with you. And, you are my first Jewish man."

"Lucky thee and me. Is your fantasy in double vision or 3 D?"

"I will reveal all to you later," Clarissa teased.

"*De trois, papillon?*"

"*Piú tardi.*"

"Promise?"

"*Si*, I also promise to completely give you my mind, Zak."

"Sounds like a real live Peter Sarstedt gig to me," he'd bantered naïvely.

"What do you mean, Zak?"

He'd answered the impulsive butterfly in good singing voice:

"Where do you go to, my lovely, when you're *not* alone in your bed."

"I know those lyrics."

"I'm sure you do, my lovely, but I would like to hear about Hank and Luke again."

"My Berlin nightclub fantasy, lovemaking with two American soldiers, really turns you on, doesn't it, Zak?"

"You know black sex triggers my libido."

"Yes, I do… Because of Trudy?" Clarissa asked, wide eyed.

"I guess so, Trudy was my first foreign butterfly."

"Remember, my Englishman, fantasy is just fantasy with me."

"If you say so, butterfly."

"I tell you, more men have set foot on the moon than have entered me, Zak."

"Why, Clarissa, twelve men have walked the moon!"

"*Si* my Apollo, more men have put foot on the moon than have entered me."

Clarissa's lingering farewell kiss before her departure from LHR the next afternoon, the discovery of her bearing a single red rose, yet no underclothes, made Zak's emotions go into overdrive…

As a hot August wind helped catapult the Alitalia flight AZ 1263 away into the blue, Zak waved the unforgettable Italian school teacher's 'Janet Reager' keepsake knickers in the air, shouting:

"*Arrivederci*, summer love."

* * * *

CHAPTER EIGHT

Autumn 1983 — Spring 1984

Continental Interludes

THE fringe commodities business was still a non-starter for Zak after the demanding Clarissa's departure to Italy. His constant business endeavours resulted in exactly zilch as none of his many commodity deals ever made it to 'second base'. A good 'home run' was much needed to get Zak back on track.

A survivor and still 'in there fighting' that August of '83, in order to try and stop the routine of going to the bank every week for cash, Zak decided to go both to the Düsseldorf 'IGEDO' and 'Cologne Fashion Fair'. To try and drum-up some quick business and credit, and then go to Italy in September for the 'Fashions from Florence and Tuscany', and just maybe rendezvous with wanting Clarissa in midway Rimini.

However, also wanting to keep his marriage intact, Zak safely tucked mother-in-law away in an unaffordable local rest-home, and attempted to loosen Daphna's self-imposed bonds enabling them both to meet up with friends on the Continent.

Daphna and Zak departed early one morning in mid-August on 'Sealink' car ferry from Dover's Eastern Dock to Ostend...

Within two hours of driving off the ferry at the famous Belgian channel port, the Levins were sitting with Slavic Rurik and his Belgian wife, Zsa Zsa, in their flat on the Avenue Louise, situated in the very heart of Brussels.

Brussels and the Hotel Arcade Stephanie had been a great two-day stopover for Daphna and Zak, prior to going on to Düsseldorf. In Rurik's flat overlooking the 'Arcade Stephanie', on their second day in the Belgian capital, during a fine fish lunch which had centred around Zsa Zsa's decorated poached turbot, Rurik mentioned casually:

"Zak, I know a couple of big local fashion wholesalers specialising in buying and selling high-class leather clothes." Rurik, with his cunning remark, was obviously wanting to get in on his guest's intended new import-export action.

"Alright, Rurik. If I can buy the right numbers on the right terms, I'll let you have some samples of leatherwear to see what you can do with them."

"Make sure they're our sizes, though," Rurik had said with a big sly smile.

"Of course."

It was obvious from behind his Slavic generosity, Rurik was looking for some free gear. Why, even the fake Cartier tank-watch their hostess was brandishing happened to be a 'freebie'.

Next morning, as Daphna and Zak checked-out of the Hotel Arcade Stephanie and revved-up for Düsseldorf, Rurik and Zsa Zsa watched and waved them a goodbye from their flat window...

The visit to 'IDEGO' and the ' Cologne Fair ' had been rewarded when Zak's interest was captured by an Italian leather skirt manufacturer, who had taken a fancy to Daphna, and a 'hungry' German knitwear company that was based in Munich.

The rigidness between Daphna and Zak somewhat softened on leaving the 'Colonge Fair' and they'd managed to laugh and love all the way back to waiting mother-in-law.

Nineteen eighty-three ended with Arafat being forced to leave the Lebanon for the second time in sixteen months, but still alive and operational; maybe he was useful to the Israelis. They certainly did not want the PLO leader dead! The Polish Pope forgave his Turkish would-be assassin after two years, without anyone in Italy really caring.

Coincidentally, President Reagan also survived being shot in 1981, unlike President Sadat who was assassinated by Egyptian fundamentalists that very same year!

The leap year of 1984 started with a disaster for Zak.

A *coup d'état* in Nigeria by General Mohammed Burhari over Christmas had blown Zak's chances of closing a deal for a billion of the Old Nigerian Naira, with a favoured Minister from the deposed President Sheru Shagari government. The option Zak had from NNPC (Nigerian National Petroleum Co.) via his Egyptian contact for 'Bonny Light' was obsolete the very next day! Bad luck, indeed, especially since Zak had received an affirmative telex purchase order from a Dutch Chemical Company for the Nigerian crude oil.

Once more, the Londoner had been stumped because of a Nigerian bloodless coup on New Year's Day. Months of work and countless yards of telexes had gone down the drain, not to mention the earache, heartache and the communication charges connected with trying to find success and riches again.

The happy voice of Clarissa cheered Zak up a few weeks later, even though he'd made his mind up not to see the exotic butterfly again. She'd telephoned from Ancona on the 29th February, Zak's leap year birthday.

"Happy thirteenth birthday, Zak."

"Great to hear from you, Clarissa. Do you… ?" he'd asked out of bravado.

"Yes, yes, yes." she'd replied irrelevantly.

"Tell me all, butterfly."

"I want to drink 'Krug' champagne with you this day, Zak."

"Sixty-nine, Clarissa?"

"*Si*, always."

"Thanks for remembering my birthday, my *summerlove*. How are you? Tell me."

"I miss you, missing me."

"And?"

"And, I want to look into your blue eyes as you spread my loins and enter my body."

"Wow, they are inviting words, butterfly."

"*Si*. I am in Paris on 17th March — can we rendezvous?"

Clarissa met Zak at Charles de Gaulle Airport. She'd looked incredible in the new spring season colours of jade and mauve flashing under an expensive looking, three-quarter length, baby-lamb cloak. The *femme fatale* had let her hair grow long since he had last seen her and looked even more sexsational.

The paramours took a taxi to the Café de la Paix in the heart of *gaie Paris*.

"What are you actually doing in Paris, Clarissa?" Zak asked eagerly, as the cab sped along.

"I'm acting as an interpreter for our family business at the International Paris Shoe Fair."

"Sounds industrious and fitting, Clarissa."

"*Si*. How long can you stay in Paris, Zak?"

The embarrassed Zak paused before continuing, loathing to utter his next words.

"I'm sorry, my *summerlove*, but... I'm booked on the last BA flight back to London tonight."

"You cannot be serious, Zak?"

"Afraid so."

"Can you not stay over this night with me?"

"Impossible, butterfly. I have a Nigerian delegation coming to England to meet me tomorrow."

"I wanted to visit the artist's quarter and the Upper Montmartre and walk along Les Champs Elysées with you, Zak."

"Another time, Clarissa."

"A pity. We could have also taken in the Sacré Coeur together."

"Next time, butterfly. Anyway it would be torture for you to move past all those African trading-boys on the steps leading up to the big white dome."

"*Si*, there are many beautiful dark-purple boys hanging around Paris, sleeping in the streets and cheap back rooms."

Clarissa, for reasons best known to herself, quickly changed the subject of conversation although her eyes were still in the 'far-away mode'... Strange Zak thought!

"Are you still trying to make that crazy Nigerian currency deal via Zug?" the glowing butterfly surprisingly asked.

"I guess, until it happens or I die."

"Zak, tell me. If you make this Naira deal, what will you do with all the millions of Dollars commission?"

"Probably pan for gold in Alaska."

"My Englishman, you are a crazy naïve panhandler, and I need you to handle me."

"Can't wait... Do you still love me?"

"Yes, yes, yes," Clarissa whispered in passion as her burning fingers found Zak's zip. To check her onslaught, since the cabby's dark eyes appeared glued to the rear-view mirror, Zak diverted the butterfly's readiness by keeping up the small-talk.

"By the way, which hotel are you staying at?"

Clarissa surfaced without a splash.

" 'Le Méridien Montparnasse'," she said with pouted lips.

"Over on the other side of Paris. On the Left Bank," he'd slowly answered in surprise.

"*Si*," she'd quickly replied with a view to getting back to swallow some 'hot fibre'!

"That journey will cut down our time together," Zak said to keep the conversation flowing.

"*Si*…. But would you really like to make me happy, my Englishman?" Clarissa asked wistfully.

"Very much so."

With a look of glee back on her beautiful face, Clarissa excitedly requested:

"Take me to a dirty little hotel room behind la Madeleine, and treat me like a Parisian whore."

"Isn't that a bit far flung, butterfly?"

"Not for us, my Englishman."

"Give it to you like a wild Arabian stallion or a double-wild purple-boy, hey?"

"*Yesa*, like black African stallions."

"Okay, my exciting *Bella Donna*. You've got it."

"You're marvellous, my Englishman."

"Can we get some sustenance first?" Zak asked.

"*Si*, if you let me pay."

Settled in the Café de la Paix, Zak casually mentioned to Clarissa over a mundane '*salade niçoise*' and a glass of dry champagne that he intended going to Munich in the very near future.

"Why Munich, Zak?"

"I have to see a friend about a nuclear waste deal."

"What does that involve?"

"A German chemical company has trouble dumping its industrial waste in Europe."

"So?"

"So, little one, I have a Liberian connection that can possibly handle the dumping operation."

"Is it an ethical deal, Zak?"

"For sure. I would only get involved if it was environmentally acceptable."

"Good for you, Zak. I've always wanted to visit Munich."

"Next time, my lovely." The exuberant Italian vamp seemed unaware of his slight, as she made him aware of her desires.

"Zak, I'm hot for you. Can we go and find a little room now?"

"That's why I'm here, butterfly."

"Come, I will do all for you, Zak."

"Great. Cheap hotel room behind la Madeleine, here we come."

"Wonderful. I cannot wait, Zak. I will pay."

"Only if I pay for the lunch."

"Promise you won't shoot and scoot?"

"Have I ever, Clarissa?"

"Never."

"Wonderful, we have many hours to make love before the last flight to London."

"*Si*, I will tell you another naughty fantasy."

"Wonderful, Clarissa. We understand one another's needs."

"*Si.*, Zak. You will really understand all, when you read the poem I have written for you!"

During the flight back to London from Paris that night, Zak could only think of Clarissa's incredible passion and sexual fantasies that had no boundaries and he looked forward to the possibility of being with the Italian temptress in Malta, next July.

Forbidden Yesterday

On clearing H.M. Custom's 'Green Lane', Zak made straight for the taxi rank, only to argue with a young London cabby, who was not in the mood to take a fare to the nearby Post House Hotel.

"Guv'nor', I've been sitting on the ruddy airport rank all night. I can't afford to take you just to the Airport Gate."

"Okay, take me to the Saint George's Hotel in London. Same difference, I can have the extra hour in bed in the morning."

"Now you're talking my language, guv."

* * * *

Beneath a fading pink Paris sky, it had been hard for Zak to leave the half-naked Clarissa in a taxi at Charles de Gaulle Airport... Zip and *tukas* in hand he'd been obliged to run to catch the last flight to London's Heathrow...

In flight, Zak suspiciously began to wonder if Clarissa had asked the handsome Algerian taxi driver to take his place before dropping her off near the Sacré Coeur, to relive one of her fantasies. Or, for a big tip, take her to a back room in the Arab quarter of Paris at the wrong end of the Faubourg, in the Rue du Maroc or the Rue de Tanger, to introduce or recommend her to some accommodating friends. No way he decided it was all fantasy with her.

On arriving at the Saint George's Hotel, Zak thought it only fitting to give the 'butter boy' a legal fare, before alighting from the black cab. As Zak entered the hotel to check in he had good thoughts of the fabulous Roxanne, and wondered whether he might bump into Barry Norman in the lift again, although it was probably well past the film-critic's bedtime.

The meeting with the Nigerian delegation the next morning to establish new links was a complete waste of time for Zak. They just would not bank-confirm the availability of the Naira, or the Bonny

Light Crude Oil in contract form, or commit to any other binding format or agreement.

He should have stayed in bed with the demanding Clarissa on the Rue de Séze behind la Madeleine in Paris (a stone's throw away from Dominique's flat) and killed another bottle of '69', before paying the hotel bill the next day, he thought. Zak then delightfully recalled, after the third time round in the french-bed, how Clarissa had whispered a possible 'tell' in the darkness!

"Zak, would you like to watch me experiencing dark-purple silhouettes?"

"Isn't that taboo for a well brought-up Italian girl such as you?"

"Not if she's sociable," she'd answered coyly.

"Another multi-coloured fantasy, eh, butterfly?"

"*Si*. A very 'well proportioned fantasy'."

"So, its not a myth, then?"

"Not at all. Their dimension and sustained hip-moving technique is sensational when indulging."

"Sounds moving. Tell me more."

"*Benissimo*. Pretend when you leave me in the taxi and fly back to London that I proposition a desirable pair."

"A double act?"

"You must know Italian women are inclined that way."

"*Il contrasto*, hey?"

"*Si*," Clarissa answered, with a grin and grimace.

"Tell me, where would you go in Paris to find such an accommodating pair?"

"No problem. There are plenty of 'dark torsos' hanging around the Gare de l'East station or on the steps leading to the Sacré Coeur."

"It would be much quicker to stop off on the Left Bank," he'd gently teased.

"*Si*, Zak. At night there are always groups of lovely deep-purple boys over by the Notre Dame and under the bridges of the Seine, just waiting for a chance to ravish a needy white girl."

"Collectively?"

"If she wants."

"Tell me why, butterfly."

"To try and relive the bizarre times with the beautiful Hank and Luke in Berlin."

"All those zealous, puffing soldier boys were for real?"

"*Possibilmente.*"

"Can you elaborate?"

"*Si*, once a girl's sexual curiosity has been fulfilled in such a way, she forever hungers."

"I'm bewildered!"

"What do you mean, Zak?"

"Obsessed or not, I don't know if it's Tuesday night or Thursday morning when I'm in bed with you."

"Then tell me one of your fantasies, my Englishman."

"Okay... I know a couple of North African guys who live in London who specialise in wanting white girls."

"Wonderful. Are they both big and black, Zak?"

* * * *

Unbeknown to both the American citizen and Zak, about the time he was flying back to London from Paris, Jonathan Pollard, an American Jew, was heavily engaged in passing out reams of of secret US intelligence paper to Mossad. A few years earlier, Pollard, who worked in Washington as a US naval statistician, had put himself out to meet a real-live Israeli icon, when Colonel Aviem Sella was on a fund-raising mission to the United States. Because of Pollard's love for Israel, he had easily been recruited by the ace, Israeli Air Force colonel, to spy on America... Later when the FBI were alerted to the activities of the well-placed statistician, Pollard and his wife made for the Israeli Embassy in Washington to seek asylum. Undercover FBI agents watched Pollard with his wife being refused entry into the Embassy of the State of Israel before arresting them outside the Embassy gates. Promptly Mossad put up a veil of silence to cover its covert operation in the United States and to receiving military secrets from Pollard ... the Sabras from the ace intelligence corps and the PM's office, chanting *Sauve qui peut* (every man for himself), from behind an extended olive branch.

* * * *

Prior to going back to Bournemouth the next day, Zak was trying hard to forget about his negative meeting with the empty-handed Nigerian bullshitters. Yes, he should have stayed in bed with Clarissa, or made a visit to Versaillies and recaptured his 'Pret-à-Porter' days, the wide boulevards and shop windows of Paris...

On checking out of the Saint George's Hotel, Zak took the time to visit an Italian restaurant in the Edgware Road to speak with Lionel Morris, who was also heavily involved in the fringe commodity business. Lionel was working out of the basement of a third-rate spaghetti joint, trying to make a deal on 'the back' of its Sicilian proprietor. It was reckoned by the fringe commodity dealers that Lionel and Zak between them knew everybody involved in the business of trying to close the crazy, long-winded Naira Deal.

Lionel had commented during that visit:

"Zak, what did you think about Sterling going to nearly par against the Dollar, at 1.075?"

"It's too low for my liking *landsman*."

* * * * *

CHAPTER NINE

Estoril: July 1969

'Pucci Nut'

ON board the SABENA flight to Düsseldorf ('Imotex' and 'IDIGO') from Brussels on 18th October 1985, before going on to meet with Rurik and Franz in Munich, Zak's mind was at first occupied with the motive of the tight-fisted Alon at Heathrow. Zak wondered why Alon had given him the code-name Johnny Lancaster. Trying to disregard his gut feeling and thoughts of Mossad and their final goal, Zak's mind suddenly did a three hundred and sixty degree turn to recall his first encounter with the 'Pucci-nut', Roxanne in '69.

* * *

It had been prime sardine-fishing time in Portugal that summer of '69. Zak had completed his ordering and buying of T-shirts in the Oporto area. Needing to unwind, he'd decided to take a few days off before sailing with his car to Southampton on the 11,500 ton M.V. 'Eagle' via the Bay of Biscay.

With sun-roof open and all eyes on his new spec' metallic pale-blue 4·2 Daimler Sovereign, the Londoner motored down to Estoril. The luxurious 'Estoril Sol' with views of the wide Atlantic, Cascais and the Castles of Sintra, caught Zak's eye that sunny day…

'Pucci Nut'

At eight-thirty the next morning, the Londoner settled down by a stone dais, at the far end of the Olympic-size swimming pool.

Suddenly Zak realised he'd mindlessly picked a sunless spot in the shadow of the high and mighty hotel to sunbathe, and looked around to re-locate himself in the early morning August sun.

Zak's gaze fell upon a strawberry-blonde, a dream of a butterfly, with long hair all pinned up. Even though she had fair hair she brought to mind the raven-haired Elana, an ex-Israeli girlfriend, who always seemed to be on the edge of the Londoner's mind.

The last time Zak had seen the gorgeous Elana, she was all dolled-up, dining and dancing with a couple of Arab gamblers in the early hours of the morning, down in the London's 'Hilton's Trader Vic' in Park Lane. He'd been quite surprised at the time when Elana had gone off arm-in-arm with the Semitic pair, probably to the nearby 'Playboy'.

The stunning strawberry-blonde appeared to be in her mid-twenties, wearing a unique brief 'Pucci' bikini which accentuated her striking figure. Zak knew she just had to be a compatible Cancerian.

The cool Londoner was immediately attracted to her appealing jizz and luring smile.

Aroused and interested Zak did not hesitate to acknowledge her captivating smile. Amazingly, she immediately waved and gestured back to him, presumably to park himself next to her sunny, front-row lounger, lined up with scores of other empty loungers at the pool-side. To Zak's further surprise, the strawberry-blonde butterfly then stretched out five well manicured 'antennae' with large lunula markings towards him, signalling, he assumed, that she would be back in five minutes or so.

Zak smiled to himself whilst gathering up all of his paraphernalia to move closer to her, merely on the strength of his reading her 'antennae right'... The beauty then took off, leaving all her togs including her beach bag on her lounger!

The Londoner laughed again to himself, as he thought at the time the butterfly would probably arrive back with a male 'Tiger Moth' and a small flight of screaming kids.

Anxiously Zak waited for ten long minutes. He then caught a glimpse of the beauty through the pool's glass door entrance, thankfully alone. She looked even more appealing, having changed into a multi-coloured psychedelic one-piece swimsuit, which he just knew had to be another 'Pucci' creation. She was 'flying fast', seemingly just flittering through the automatic double doors as she made a bee-line towards him, wearing an alluring smile on her lovely tanned face.

"Hi! I am Roxanne De Winter from the USA. I've just flown in from Washington DC. I'm as tired as hell, but I'm a 'water nut'. I just must spend a couple of hours at the pool-side before I crash out in bed."

'Wow'! Zak thought. A fused bombshell had landed in his lap.

"Hi to you, Roxanne De Winter, I'm Zak Winterbottom from London," he'd transmuted, with a controlled smile on his face before saying:

"How about a splash together?"

Roxanne paused in wonder at his phraseology or Americanism.

"O.K., Zak, let's go." They'd both taken a running dive into the clear, cold water together... A perfect pick up.

The Trans-Atlantic couple spent a wonderful morning together, mostly swimming, diving, laughing and making a lot of small talk which came easily to both of them.

As they chatted the morning away, the time just seemed to whizz by. They had really hit it off, and appeared to have a lot in common, obviously compatible.

Roxanne appeared impressed that her new acquaintance knew about the Florence-based fashion house, and 'Pucci' psycheledia.

'Pucci Nut'

Suddenly Zak remembered Liza, the Canadian Pan-Am hostess that he'd chatted to at the pool-side the previous afternoon and who was about to keep their second date.

"Oi, Oi! and beware," the aware importer-exporter said to himself. It was nearly one o'clock! Lookout, panic stations.

Roxanne appeared thrilled when the seemingly, cool-handed Zak took the time to admire her handmade, 22-carat, sculptured ring, depicting a gold nude male and female form entwined over one another. The American butterfly was just been about to go to her hotel room to crash out, and yet Roxanne stopped and looked intensely into Zak's eyes, as she'd asked in a coy, girlish way, as only an American girl can:

"You don't think it's 'dirty', Zak?"

"Not at all, Roxanne, honey, it's beautiful," he'd genuinely answered as she'd lovingly taken and held his hand in hers. He could still hear her pleasing tone of voice telling him:

"It's a 'Sabereni', I'll have you know, Zak."

"Wow! The off-beat American millionaire jeweller who lives in that fabulous house built in a tree?"

"You're incredible knowing that, Zak! Listen, I'm staying here for a couple of weeks before going on to the 'Marbella Beach Club' in Spain. I must go to my room now to try and sleep off my jet lag. I would be more than happy to have dinner with you in the hotel tonight... if you're free."

"Fine, sounds divine, butterfly."

"Great, Zak. If we get on well... maybe we can keep one another company for the time you are here?"

The Londoner answered by boldly taking Roxanne in his arms and kissing her on the mouth...

Breathlessly, they agreed to meet on the 14th floor of the hotel at eight o'clock. As Roxanne was about to go, she ran her fingers flirtatiously through Zak's hair, and said:

"Have a good day. See you tonight big boy."

Zak watched the departing butterfly glide away, admiring her shape and style, wondering at the colour of her underwings. He had been right. She was a Cancerian and he was going to be burnt at the passion stake. Panic stations — beware collision course ahead — Roxanne and Liza, two North American girls were about to 'brush feathers' at the pool's entrance.

God! What incredible timing Zak thought; a real close shave — no troubled water until Biscay — the newly arrived Liza hadn't seen him kissing, and Roxanne hadn't hovered or bothered to look back at Zak.

Zak greeted Liza rather coldly, and treated her indifferently during the afternoon, later declining to dine with her, knowing better than to put two talkative North America girls together over a highball cocktail.

At eight o'clock sharp, Zak formally met up with the fabulously dressed Roxanne on the 14th floor... As they made their way to the reserved window table, all the diners' heads seemed to turn in the elegant restaurant, to look at the bra-less wonder, adorned and looking absolutely 'sexsational' in a very low-cut, 'Pucci' jungle-print sarong. Roxanne's full breasts were, somehow, tantalisingly concealed by a hand-made, solid gold, triangular, Inca-style 'choker' and her cleverly-styled, loose, cascading hair.

The meal had been fine, Roxanne divine. The service had been over-attentive — in fact, a hilarious farce — as a continuous line of short Portuguese waiters dressed in monkey suits, relentlessly appeared with extra side-dishes and unwanted table implements, desperately standing on tiptoe to sneak a glimpse at Roxanne's partially concealed nipples.

The delights of dinner over, Zak and Roxanne took a stroll to the then fashionable Cascais. Suddenly the cold sea breeze started blowing up from Madeira, across the Atlantic, they began to chill. Hurriedly Zak engaged a taxi, lovingly taking the opportunity to caress Roxanne to keep her warm during the short drive back to their hotel. On entering the hotel, the sound of soft music immediately led them downstairs to a swanky disco in the hotel's nightclub.

Moulded into one another on the dimly-lit dance floor, they smooched the night away…

Later in Zak's room on the 17th floor, over a bottle of iced 'Krug', Roxanne suddenly declared:

"Zak, I am an old-fashioned girl."

"What do you mean?" he'd naïvely asked.

"I will show you," she'd uttered. Without removing her gold triangle of love, she otherwise slowly stripped herself of her silk jungle-print sarong and danced to the background music as he poured the vintage champagne.

Roxanne teased and aroused Zak with her sensual belly-dance before she made ravenous love with her mouth. Unexpectedly, the tempo changed. With a melodramatic looking smile on her face, Roxanne expertly wriggled her naval as she danced around her prey. Mesmerised by her exotic movements, Zak rapturously found her absorbing his swollen hardness into her cavity of passion as though she was a love-starved whore.

Suddenly the belly dancer frantically called:

"Zak, the ice, the ice, give me the ice!"

"What ice, Roxanne?"

"I need the contrast."

"Where?"

"Deep inside of me, Zak."

"What do you mean?"

"The ice, from the 'Krug'."

"From the ice bucket?"

"Yes, floor me and pour all the ice into my quim. You can pump me then, with the Champagne bottle!"

"Wowee and hurray for old-fashioned girls."

"Yes, yes give me the contrast and Champagne treatment now and I'll take it black for you!"

Zak had been able to ask the star-spangled butterfly one night, during pillow-talk:

"Have you really slept with a coloured man, Roxanne?"

"I used to be into a certain type of black guy a few years ago, but I've outgrown the need and I can do without them now."

"Really?"

"Yes, are you ashamed of me and my past negromania?"

"Tell me more, honeychil'."

"O.K.. When I was younger, I liked it big and black, Zak."

During their time together, between the sheets and heavy love scenes, Roxanne, the high-flying politician's daughter, discreetly let Zak know she was well connected in political circles with Senators and Congressmen back in Washington, and that she knew a lot of the big boys in international banking, mainly because of her millionaire father's activities, although she was cultivating a few herself. The knowing Raxanne also enlightened Zak as to *'Novus Ordo Seclorum'*[7], the secrative 'Bilderberg group', the 'Council on Foreign Relations,' the 'Trilateral Commission' and 'Majestic,' all of which were run by current or ex-world leaders, international financiers and never-elected industrialists!

Roxanne and Zak were amazingly open and very relaxed with one another during their time together.

Zak was wise enough not to try to impress the politician's daughter in any way. Not even in the classy Estoril Casino where Roxanne enjoyed playing a little roulette and black jack.

Somehow they'd found the inclination to drive down to the unspoilt fishing village of Sesimbra in his new Daimler, where Zak

---

[7] TRANSLATION = NEW WORLD ORDER — AS DEPICTED ON THE BACK OF AN AMERICAN ONE DOLLAR BILL

introduced Roxanne to the wonderful simple Atlantic sardine, explaining to the gullible 'Pucci' admirer:

Sardines taste far better here before they pass through the Straits of Gibraltar. They quickly lose flavour when entering the warmer Mediterranean. The sardines are best, grilled in the local Portuguese way, on fallen pine cones, sprinkled with crude salt, at the sea front, preferably outside a primitive tin beach hut with sawdust on the floor." Roxanne seemed caught up in his saga of the sardine, or was it in one of those magical moments in time, when the elements were at peace with themselves?

"Zak, one of the things I adore about you is that you have not once tried to 'shoot me a line' or try to score over me! Why, my 'beaus' in Washington or Boston would not have the balls to bring me to a joint like this. I love it… and what you do to me ." Why! Roxanne had even admitted she was a 'Pucci' snob.

When the American butterfly was in the shower one afternoon, towards the end of their stay together in the more peaceful grandeur of the Palacio Hotel, Zak jumped out of bed to sneak a closer look into the blue 'Tiffany' presentation gift-case that cushioned the fabulous gold love triangle. Roxanne had earlier told him she'd received it in Washington, just prior to her flight to Lisbon. The enclosed signature on the engraved White House card more than vouched for her, and her admiring beau.

Roxanne pleaded with Zak to delay his sailing on the 'Eagle', even told him he could 'do what animals could not do' ever since man had gotten up on his hind legs and mated head on.

"Zak, you can make love with your mind as well as your body. Animals can't do that. It's the highest form of intelligence in my book. The way you look into my eyes and talk me through a climax is like going to the other side of the moon."

"Yes. I'm fully aware of evolution, the missing link, but a Bonobo chimp does it from the front, head on."

"Really! Like us face to face?"

"Yes, the only animal that can."

"But we fuck with our minds, whilst acting like animals," she stated with satisfaction.

"Oh, I thought it was my capability to supply lots of ice." Zak quipped. Roxanne laughed and then seemed to 'pitch' him even harder, suggesting once again that they drive together to Marbella and not to let their fantastic week of sun and sex come to an end.

The Londoner felt he'd had enough sun and fun, not wanting to spoil things, declined because of business commitments. Roxanne was knowing enough to back off.

"Zak, I do understand. I'm also intrigued by the way you earn your living successfully from the fashion business."

"Thanks, Roxanne. Perhaps we could set a business up in the States together? What do you think?"

"Any time, any place, Zak, as long as you bring that raging monster you keep behind your teethed-up jeans."

"You mean behind my zip?"

"You've got it, Zak."

"I'll take another rain check on that one," he'd answered obliquely.

"Zak, will you give it to me Greek before you leave me?"

"No way, I'm British," he told her once again.

Later, having exchanged contact numbers, even addresses, they loved... then kissed goodbye.

"Zak, you certainly aren't a Winterbottom."

"Yeah, I know what you mean, Miss Ice Bucket."

The departing Londoner checked out of the 'Palacio' and then went to the pool to sneak a last look at the precious American butterfly. Observing her from behind a large swaying palm tree,

'Pucci Nut'

Zak expected to see Roxanne surrounded by waiting beach boys, or with some new guy lurking in the wings. He was surprised to see the 'Pucci nut' alone, looking so very demure, silently weeping into what looked like a 'Pucci' handkerchief. The checked-out Londoner managed to tear himself away and transported himself off in his 'Daimler-Jag' to sail away on the M.V. 'Eagle' at 23 knots.

The wonderful American 'water-nut' took the time and trouble to keep in touch over the years that followed, visiting Zak in London for a week one Autumn and one hot Summer and Spring when she'd said she needed him and his mind to help her make it through the rain.

Roxanne always found time to meet up with Zak whenever he visited the States. She had somehow taken an active interest in him during the years, always finding time to ask of him:

"Zak how's business and can I help you?"

She once said to him in Miami:

"If you ever need any help, don't be shy to ask." God, Zak had no realization at the time, sitting in 'Wolfie's', that her casual remark was going to cost him dearly, much later on in his life. He'd naïvely replied:

"I'll take a rain check on that one, butterfly."

They had ravenously devoured pastrami-on-rye sandwiches, which contained a quality of beef Zak could never seem to find in Bloom's salt beef bar in the Whitechapel Road, nor in the 'Brass Rail' in 'Selfridges', before going back, fortified and with Miami spice, to test the queen-size bed springs in the Doral Hotel.

Zak felt sure Roxanne's wild screams of "give me the Champagne treatment big boy", could be heard in the 'Fontainebleau' and all over Miami's Waterfront.

* * * * *

CHAPTER TEN

Munich: 19th October 1985 – Part I

Triple Rendezvous

AS ticketed, Zak departed Düsseldorf on Lufthansa flight 982C, Munich-bound to proposition Franz at the behest of Mossad. The conversation with Alon at the Israeli Embassy in London came to Zak's mind. Why had Alon mentioned Maxwell, Gerald Ronson and Manny Levy? Also, why had Mossad's agent harped on about Dikko and Gaddafi? And indeed why had Alon closely questioned him about how he had met Clarissa's ex-lover Franz. With Clarissa back on his mind, Zak fully recapped on the incredible happening in the Munich *bierkeller* having met the fox-clad Clarissa off Alitalia flight AZ 428 from Milan last April.

* * *

Triple Rendezvous

It was uncanny, the Alitalia plane was about to land on time at Munich Airport. Zak had never had to hang around waiting for Clarissa. She was never late for a rendezvous and always appeared radiant and RWA.

The Londoner had arrived earlier that evening on Swissair via Zurich to visit Rurik about the drawn-out nuclear waste deal that had been going on for nearly a year. Rurik had been reduced to residing in a small Munich flat with his three children and overweight Belgian wife, Zsa Zsa. The unfortunate Slav had recently absconded hastily from Brussels for not having seen 'eye-to-eye' with the Belgian authorities over a clandestine plutonium transaction, in which Rurik supposedly acted as middleman for the Israelis.

* * * *

Rurik had been introduced to Zak by Colonel Healey-Jones. To be exact, it had been prior to a hurried but fine business lunch in the roof-top restaurant at the Saint George's Hotel. God! Roxanne had been waiting for her big boy in a hot bed in a room downstairs on the 10th floor that afternoon. Consequently, Zak rushed lunch even though they enjoyed a window table overlooking Regents Park…

Rurik made a big show on picking up the bill from the Londoner's favourite roof top restaurant during their first meeting. As they left the restaurant, Zak thought he'd noticed the chatting Gloria Hunniford still at lunch.

To this day Zak has not made a profitable business deal with the Slav for all their many endeavours of trying to close international currency, oil, Au (gold) and Lockheed C-130 Hercules aircraft deals, not to mention the mountain of nonsensical telexed offers for branded whisky and cigarettes from non-performers. Amazingly though, Zak and Rurik's friendship grew continually richer in those transforming years.

* * * *

The flick, flick, flicker of the automatic arrivals display indicator brought Zak back to reality — Alitalia flight AZ 428 had landed — he would soon be with the voluptuous Adriatic vamp again...

The Londoner could still vividly remember Clarissa's soft exciting Italian voice, boldly telling him:

"Zak, I want to make love with you!" That was nearly two summers ago in the 'Dolphin' in Poole, a couple of days after they'd first met in sunny Bournemouth.

Clarissa could not be long clearing customs, Zak thought. He had told her during one of their long distance, lengthy telephone conversations:

"Clarissa, only bring yourself to Munich."

"But what should I wear and how shall I fly, Zak?"

"Bareback on the cockpit of a jumbo, my lovely."

"You mean in my 'Lady Godiva' outfit?"

"Yes, 'skinsational'."

While waiting for the next few minutes to pass, Zak wondered if he would be up to par with Clarissa for the anticipated 'active weekend', after the unexpected meeting and night with Roxanne in Zurich. By chance he'd spotted the American butterfly talking with banker friends in an open air café on the Bahnhofstrasse! Carl Gustav Jung theories just had to be wrong regarding coincidence.

It had been hard leaving Roxanne in bed at the Grand Dolder Hotel, up on the hill overlooking Zurich, especially as Zak's gut had signalled there was a hiccup ahead.

* * * *

Clarissa Teresa appeared... She looked rapturous, having flown wearing a glamorous full length, silver-blue fox coat, long leather boots, lurex top, with a clinging short skirt over brightly coloured tights, complete with matching 'Gucci' handbag and luggage.

She seemed to be struggling though, with an additional see-through bag, full of duty free merchandise!

Clarissa's exhilarating green eyes metamorphosed to sparkling lavender as they found Zak's... She'd run forward, calling:

"*Ciao*, my Englishman, I am with you."

They kissed passionately, further greeting each other by uttering words of love and devotion. Zak happily realised he would have no worries about satisfying this *bellissima* creature of loveliness, as he pressed his rising hardness into Clarissa's fur-clad yearning body.

"Hey, great to see you butterfly, you've cut your hair?"

"*Si*, I've had it re-styled just for you."

"You look wonderful, its the same as I first saw you."

"*Grazie, mille*. You remember all, Zak?"

The paramours arrived at the München Arabella Park Sheraton Hotel after a frenzied fifteen-minute love-biting taxi-ride. They'd hastened to check into the deluxe suite, a reservation that Rurik had made for them. Zak could not but help notice during checking in a couple of dark-skinned airline crewmen hanging around the lobby who openly gave Clarissa the eye...

Behind closed doors, and having fortuitously met on the streets of sunny Bournemouth and Sliema, they found they still had 'love fever' and lovingly lingered and embraced. Suddenly, while taking in the view of the glittering city of Munich by night from their bedroom window, they were startled by the ringing telephone. With Clarissa 'glued to her Englishman's chest', he'd reluctantly surrendered to the calling telephone. It was Rurik...

"Zak, when do you have to see your special wheeler-dealer friend?" Clarissa asked inquiringly.

"Soon. That was Rurik on the phone."

"*Si...* do we have time to try out one of these fantastic big beds before we meet your friend?"

"Later, butterfly. Rurik is down in the lobby with Dominique. They are waiting to take us to dinner, downtown."

"Who is Dominique?"

"Rurik's French girlfriend."

"Do you know her, Zak?"

"Yes, I introduced them to one another."

"Zak... you've bedded this *papillon*?"

"Many years ago. Do you need to shower?"

"Bah. I have no need to 'wash me'. I will just change into a dress and stockings for dinner."

"Sounds perfect," Zak said. Obviously peeved, the sulking Clarissa asked:

"Will we go dancing this night, Zak?"

He'd been temporarily 'let off the hook' as the phone rang again. It was the delightful, cadence-sounding American voice of Roxanne who was phoning from Washington just to say:

"I miss the high mountains of Switzerland, and you, big boy!" He had tried to sound as though he was speaking to his secretary, giving out a load of verbal nonsense. The knowing Roxanne had come back at him:

"You lovable bastard, you're with another lay already! I don't know where you get the *kóch* from, but save some for me." Roxanne added before cutting off.

"I will see you in London shortly. Bye...eee, have a good night."

Clarissa's eyes became aflame with rage!

"That was a girl calling you, Zak. That is why you did not want me to come to you in Germany. And how did she know the hotel and the room you were in?"

God! Clarissa was so aware and smart, she'd 'cottoned on' that it was not his secretary on the phone. Zak's double-talk had not fooled Clarissa. He'd always marvelled at her comprehension of

English, including some of the dark sexy colloquialisms she used. She could only have picked up that pillow jargon in bed with a fast moving coloured guy, Zak deduced.

"You have it all wrong, Clarissa. It was an old girlfriend that I just happened to bump into in Zurich."

Clarissa retorted:

"Zak, remember we agreed last summer in Malta — when we are together, no intrusions."

"Yes, my *Bella Donna*, no intrusions or intruders."

"And I don't believe in such a coincidence, my Englishman."

Zak's flippant remark about intruders had not defused the mounting tension.

"Never underestimate coincidence, Clarissa."

"Zak, I tell you there are many coincidences every day if you look; they mean nothing and go nowhere."

"You've been reading Carl Jung, Clarissa, Clarissa?"

"Not since my Berlin University days. Tell me, Zak, what did you think the first time you saw me?"

"When we first met outside the telephone booth in beautiful Bournemouth?"

"*Si*, where Gaddafi went to school."

"Yes, a very demure, but somehow a provocative butterfly."

"No, really Zak?"

"Really. Angelic, intelligent and wanting, if you prefer."

"And what do you see now?"

"You are still radiant and desirable."

"Are you aware of another side to my character?"

"Proud and profane."

"Tell me all, Zak"

"I guess I see several Clarissas in your startling eyes. Bright, zestful, intriguing, romantic and most important, we are extremely compatible."

"*Si*, from the very beginning like *un fulmine*."

"Yes, like a thunderbolt, butterfly. I only see the beauty and intelligence inside your head, my lovely. I'm always with you, and your exciting bubbly voice never fails to stimulate all my senses."

"Really amazing, Zak!"

"Yes. You turn January into June."

"*Molte grazie*."

"However, I sense an uncontrollable force, an inner compulsion if you prefer, which exists within your being, as though you were a wanting whore at times... Excuse me, I guess I've always been infatuated with your good looks, your imaginative mind and pillow talk, which will never wane for me."

"*Meraviglioso*, Zak, you're a real man."

"An addicted man."

"*Si*, but, your mentality and understanding is king size."

"Thank you. I'm told though, broad-mindedness and fantasies can be drawn to too fine a line between serious lovers."

"Understand, but it is always good with you, Zak. Can we remain a while longer?"

"Sounds good to me, but let's get ready, Clarissa. If I know Rurik we are heading for a most enjoyable meal and a fun weekend." Clarissa lovingly apologised for the previous bad moment, and in aspiration remarked:

"Zak, something else is looking king size!"

"Could be queen size, Clarissa," he said in jest.

"Wonderful, for me just the right size. Can I have *antipasto rapido* now?"

"*Solo!*" he teased.

"*Si, solo cazzo*."

"Your pollinating my libido now, butterfly."

"*Favoloso*, give it to me now, Zak." Clarissa brazenly demanded.

Desirously, they embraced and kissed... In her denudation, Clarissa fell to her knees to unzip her lovers' zipper down to the bottom notch, then wrenched Zak's 'DAKS' down to his ankles.

Zak thought at the time the Italian temptress had purposely assulted all of his senses to sexually arousing him, obviously wanting and needing spontaneous passion...

In the shower together, Clarissa mischievously emitted:
"My Englishman, did you see those two beautiful coloured boys who smiled at me in the hotel lobby on the way in?"

Clarissa's suggestive remark to Zak brought back images of the lovely Trudy in Carnaby Street, that hot July night in the fifties...

* * * *

Zak had been surprised and shocked not having seen the Polish beauty for a year, to find her be-bopping and smooching down in a smoke-filled Soho club with black men. He still vividly remembered feeling the pang of horror and concern, seeing her in the early hours of a Sunday morning, going off hand-in-hand with a couple of West Indians, each of whom had 'narco glints' in their eyes. This unforgettable incident had deeply embedded itself in his mind and soul for some reason or other. Perhaps it was because Trudy could not look at him with her trans-coloured eyes when he had wished her 'happy birthday' that transforming night. Her darting eyes had remarkably metamorphosed as she'd suddenly broken away from her twin escorts, to hurriedly climb the stairway to the street exit, followed by her lusting dancing partners. The very thought of the Trinidadians ravishing Trudy's demanding white body, as she subjectively sought love or interracial sex, had perturbed Zak. Indeed the stark thought of the passionate Trudy enmeshed with black flesh in a dark room, still obsessed the Londoner.

* * * *

"Yes, I also noticed your trans-coloured eyes change to the colour of your necklace at the sight of them," Zak said, back in the now.

"Really. The lanky one looked as though he might be an Arab?"

"Yes."

"*Interessante*."

"Naughty thoughts, Clarissa, Clarissa?"

"Could be the *ultimo*... I wonder if I mesmerised them?"

Forbidden Yesterday

CHAPTER ELEVEN

Munich — Part II

The Die is Cast

FRESHLY showered and attired, Clarissa and Zak took the lift down to the lobby to glimpse Rurik sitting in the 'Rendezvous' bar of the 'Sheraton' with the blue-eyed blonde, Dominique. The fashionable Parisienne still looked like a young 'Brigitte Bardot'. Zak recalled he had met Dominique on the beach in Nice one September, on his way back from the Middle East to take in the 'COTE D' AZUR'S DE LA MODE D'ETE' a few years earlier.

* * * *

It had been the dawn-to-dusk fasting period of *Ramadan* during Zak's sales trip to Kuwait! There, he had been obliged to kick his heels in the oasis of the downtown 'Sheraton' and wait for confirmation of a worthwhile Letter of Credit for a jeans contract from a shrewd old Arab trader.

The potential client suddenly decided to go off to Mecca and meditate on the deal before committing himself to opening the L/C! 'Browned off', all Zak could really do apart from trying to make some new contacts during the tedious waiting period, was to deepen his tan by the 'Kuwait-Sheraton's' luxurious swimming pool...

The Londoner had not taken a drink or enjoyed any pleasurable female company for three weeks, so back in Europe he'd made a bee-line for the lonely looking girl wearing a match-box size bikini on the Nice beach...

Intro's neatly over, Zak did not hesitate to invite Dominique for a 'light lunch and a heavy date'. With confirmation of a profitable Arab Letter of Credit in the hand, he could afford to guzzle 'Krug' champagne and felt like ripe-red pepper sauce with Dominique at his side. Zak knew a true 'blue, white and well read' French girl could not resist *coq au vin*, a bottle of France's finest champagne and a *crème caramel*...

Crème caramel devoured — the *papillon* felt good on Zak's arm as they took the short walk to the 'Negresco', where he had a charming room, complete with four-poster bed. Dominique was certainly not a tart but had willingly given herself in the decadent Renaissance bedroom without asking for money or expecting presents. She had an incredible body, was very experienced in bed, but was not into pillow talk and could not compare with the stimulating Clarissa, Roxanne or Elana, as they were all Cancerians.

Later, Zak passed on the good-hearted Dominique's telephone number to Rurik after she'd agreed to put up the penniless Slav when becoming financially embarrassed during a business trip to Paris. Zak 'teed off the play' knowing the inevitable would happen for Rurik in the Virgo's little, third-floor flat off the fashionable Rue Saint Honoré, a stone's throw from Place Da La Concorde, le 'Ritz' and the romantic Seine. Later Dominique introduced Rurick to a Moroccan Minister, hence the 'Hayatt' project in the running sand.

* * * *

The Die is Cast

Dominique and Rurik appeared to be oblivious to the world, even though they had been kept waiting downstairs. The plump Rurik was heavily enamoured with his attractive and clinging *sirène*. Dominique was well turned out in a 'Hermès' outfit, looking more than capable of commanding the full attention of the suave Slav. Rurik had a different image, obviously he'd waxed his dashing moustache, and brandished a new quiffed hairstyle, and looked sleek and well oiled. Rurik's only give-away to his forty-five years was when the skin around his foxy eyes creased into a smile at the sight of Clarissa. His extrovert personality immediately took over, as the excited Slav jumped up from his seat, preening himself swiftly before rushing over to hug and kiss Zak, like a long-lost brother, yet never taking his greedy eyes off Clarissa. Finally, Rurik released Zak to allow enough space to be introduced to the fur-clad seductress. Rurik then unwisely greeted Clarissa in an over-familiar, pretentious manner. Clarissa pulled away, resenting Rurik's brash style. The moody butterfly openly showed her annoyance by her vexed expression and abrupt act when she'd sharply pulled away from the obnoxious Slav. As Clarissa turned away from Rurik, she was further annoyed, indeed shocked, to find her Englishman being kissed on the lips by the beautiful Dominique! Clarissa then refused Rurik's offer of an aperitif, openly snubbing Dominique when Zak endeavoured to present the two females. With zest, the spurned Dominique attempted to French kiss Zak. Spurned again, the daring *papillon* brazenly squeezed Zak's *yugger*! With embarrassment, he raised his eyebrows to Clarissa and then gestured at the amazed and shattered Rurik. To salvage Rurik's pride and gloss over the Parisienne's *faux pas*, Zak explained with a discreet nod and a wink:

"Clarissa drove all the way to Bologna Airport early this afternoon from Ancona to catch the internal flight to Milano before flying all the way here to Munich; she's tired and anxious to eat." Loud and clear, Rurik received the message to follow on with:

"I'm starved and shattered myself — let's go and eat somewhere interesting, my friends."

Rurik then called for the bill from the enraptured watching, uniformed *Fäulein*...

As the four of them left the 'Sheraton', Zak noticed the two coloured crewmen still hanging around the Lobby, both of whom openly gave Clarissa the eye again — this in turn caused Clarissa's trans-coloured eyes to metamorphose!

The two couples found themselves speeding towards Munich's town centre in Rurik's comfortable, hired Mercedes. Clarissa had clung to Zak earlier, when Rurik suggested the girls should sit in the back together. Clarissa appeared happy enough once settled in the back seat crushing her sultry Latin body into her Englishman even though he and the Slav were heavily engaged in open conversation.

Rurik had the good sense to ask as they were in motion:

"What sort of food do you guys fancy?"

"*Um ristorante specializzato im pasta*," Dominique exclaimed in Italian. Clarissa instantly cut into the *Parisienne's* preference for Italian food:

"I would like to eat *Blutwurst* and drink in the Grosser Bier Hall that Adolf Hitler made the most notorious in all the world."

"The 'Mathaserbierkeller' on Bayerstrasse?"

"*Si.*"

"Great."

"*Molte grazie*, Rurik." The ice had been broken, Zak thought, with Clarissa's words of thanks.

"*Prego*," Rurik said before downing Dominique's frivolous spaghetti joint suggestions further by reminding her:

"It's Clarissa's first visit to Munich, *chérie*. Zak and Clarissa are our very special guests."

The Die is Cast

The tension eased slightly with Clarissa's nonchalant thanks. She then stared at the passing puritanical German Gothic architecture of the city, whilst still tightly holding on to her Englishman as though she was fearful he was about to run away from her.

They'd all entered the vast Bavarian beer-hall to the expected furore of the oom-pa-pa of the trombone and the fortissimo hum of the massive rowdy crowd, singing, dancing and making merry in the vastness of the Banqueting Hall.

One could still easily imagine the Nazi gatherings during the Hitler era of the twenties and thirties and feel and capture the rowdy Nazi aura bouncing off the wooden beams. The whole place reeked with atmosphere from a forbidden yesterday that had impregnated its thick stone walls and high ceilings.

Smouldering, Clarissa became more than lively; to the astonishment of Rurik and Dominique. The turned-on Italian vamp vigorously started strutting and singing in guttural German to the tune of the crude beerhall march, which the Bavarian, *Lederhosen-*clad brass bandsmen were enthusiastically knocking out on the boxing-ring type stage.

Somehow, somewhere, from out of the vastness and gaiety they were offered a round table, covered and set with a fresh, clean, red, chequered table cloth and napkins, well away from the blaring stage. They'd all made their way towards the empty table, weaving in and out of the dancing throng and the heavy-breasted waitresses transporting huge fistfuls of frothing litre mugs full of fine Munich beer, as well as piled platters of smoked sausages and sauerkraut to the thirsty Saturday night merry-makers and sightseers.

As the multinationals were about to order from the extensive menu, they were all rather surprised when Clarissa was confronted by an overweight, casually-dressed, bespectacled man. The stranger stood directly behind Rurik and addressed Clarissa in very excitable German, before asking politely in English:

"Can it be you, Clarissa Teresa? Remember me, Clarissa? Franz… We were in University together in Berlin. Remember?"

Clarissa immediately blushed to the colour of over ripe, wild beetroots and quickly looked from Franz to her Englishman with complete amazement. Then uttering in her bewilderment to the intruder in perfect German:

"I cannot believe it is you, Franz. After all these years!"

"Yes, it is I, Clarissa."

"*Mama mia*… This is unbelievable. The very first time I set foot in Germany since I finished my studies in Berlin, and we meet here in Munich!"

"Truly incredible, indeed!"

"For sure, *capriccioso*. I don't believe how fat you have become, Franz," Clarissa vocalised with a certain amount of jocularity.

"It's the good Munich beer. But you look *wunderschön*, Clarissa Teresa."

"Thank you Franz. May I introduce you to my friends?" Clarissa then disconcertingly gestured towards her party before formally making the introductions:

"Zak, this is Franz, whom I have told you about."

"Yes! *Guten Abend*, Franz,"

"Franz, this is my boyfriend, Zak, from England."

"Good evening, Zak."

Coming out of shock with the look of fear in her trans-coloured eyes, Clarissa impeached herself. She then introduced her present love to her past lover. Maybe the Italian butterfly perceived her present lover's doubts about whether her intimate fantasies and pillow-talk were concocted or not. Zak immediately rose from the table to shake Franz's large, sweaty hand as he gave Clarissa a smile and a knowing wink. The disorientated butterfly then meekly introduced Dominique and Rurik to Franz as her new friends….

Franz, grinning from ear to ear, asked Clarissa:

"What have you been doing since Berlin?"

The Die is Cast

Clarissa answered her ex-boyfriend with evasive, garbled jabber in several languages! She quickly collected herself, knowing her guilt was showing on her flushed face and then in a cross tone, asked the confused Franz:

"What are you doing in Munich, Franz?"

"I've been working out of Steilmanns A.G. head office here in Munich. For years I've been a specialist overseas communications installation manager."

The astute Rurik's ears pricked up at this information. Here was a possible business opportunity with a multi-national German electronic company that had some half-million employees worldwide and held many nations' trading and military secrets.

With added charm, Rurik asked Franz:

"Would you care to join us, sir?"

Clarissa kicked at her Englishman's crocodile shoes under the table in a bid for him to get Rurik to reverse the slick invitation.

Zak had, however, immediately caught on to Rurik's line of thought and joined in and requested Franz to dine with them. Franz uncertainly babbled back:

"But my wife and I have already started our dinner."

Rurik, to Clarissa's annoyance, persuaded Franz that he and his wife should come over and take their dessert with them later. Clarissa reverted to an expression of utter shock, not believing that her past was catching up with her. The Italian butterfly unfroze to quickly fly round to the side of her ex-boy friend, who was still standing by the seated Rurik. In a fatuous manner, she'd taken Franz by the hand to whisper in Italian, guardedly in case she made a contradictory remark.

Rurik, who spoke perfect Italian and was also blessed with good hearing, raised a knowing eyebrow to Zak at what he had overheard Clarissa say, just as Franz tripped off back to his wife.

Whilst nibbling their Bavarian feast, Dominique commented something about Franz sitting with a Middle Eastern woman. No-one looked up to take notice of the informative *papillion's* remark, although Zak noticed Clarissa blush again at the mention of Franz's name...

The arrival of Franz with his tall, slim, dark-skinned wife was somehow a relief to them all, except to the stressed Clarissa, who Zak knew felt otherwise about the encounter.

Franz introduced his shy, unfashionable, jewelless wife, in the same manner as Clarissa had done with Rurik and Dominique, but did not mention his spouse by name! However, Zak was aware Franz had made an especially smooth and elaborate effort when he presented his wife to Clarissa. The semitic looking wife had obviously been enlightened on the connections between the four Europeans and was aware of her husband's past relationship with Clarissa, she only simpered and withheld her handshake, causing yet another discordant note to the evening.

Rurik acquired two empty chairs from an adjoining table and placed them deliberately either side of himself to make sure he had Franz's ear. Dominique became irritated at being separated from Rurik and found herself sitting close to Zak. In her hurt state of mind, Dominique felt entitled to flirt with her old flame, moving her chair closer, to touch him solicitously and whisper in Zak's ear:

"Can we make it together before you leave?" Zak gently shook his head.

"Will you 'talk naughty' to me in a quiet corner or in the car?" Again the Londoner shook his head in the same no-no manner before softly uttering:

"Strange as it may seem, I'm principled that way: I don't make it with a friend's wife or girlfriend."

"Can the four of us do it later then, in one of the big french-beds in your hotel suite?"

The Die is Cast

"You know that's just fantasy and pillow-talk for me," he whispered back.

Clarissa, Zak could see, was finding it difficult to take the strain of Dominique, coupled with the thoughts that had been building up in her mind... Suddenly, Clarissa pushed her chair backwards, stood up in a tantrum, snatched her handbag from the table, grabbed her fox-coat from the stile of her chair, and to everybody's horror, recklessly ran off!

Zak could not find it within himself to chase after the tempestuous Italian butterfly, but wondered if Clarissa would return to the hotel and pack, kick up her heels in spite or seek spontaneous sex for bravado.

On the waylaid Zak's return to the 'Sheraton' some ninety minutes later, he'd half expected to find Clarissa reclining in the lobby with the crewmen on one of the modern crescent shaped couches, just for a tease, or waiting in the 'Rendezvous'. But no, she was not to be seen in the down-stairs lobby.

Arriving at the suite, Zak'd found the door open. The main lounge lights were on. Surprised, he'd noticed, displayed on the console, a bottle of 'Krug' '69 next to an opened bottle of duty-free Napoleon Cognac draped with a couple of 'Gucci' cravats. Thinking Clarissa may have checked out, Zak rushed into the oversized bedroom. Clarissa was lying naked on one of the king-size beds!

She looked very dramatic, an adorable Amaranth to his eyes, lying on her stomach. From the dim glow of the lounge, her fuscous body contrasted against the shimmering, satin bedspread. Zak became filled with passion at the sight of the *prima donna* displaying her curvaceous haunches. Leisurely, she manoeuvred her shapely legs into the spreadeagled position to reveal her glistening sex, before surprisingly whispering in French.

"*Encore, s'il te plaît, encore une fois!*"

The perplexed Londoner did not succumb to Clarissa's request, instead he'd climbed into the other bed. The unfading flower then fell into a catatonic sleep. Zak noticed in the half light that Clarissa's clothes were not neatly folded on the bedside chair, but scattered over the thick-piled carpet. Zak's growing paranoia was further fuelled as he caught a fading whiff of hashish. He became disturbed and restless about Clarissa and the spicy lingering fetor.

Clarissa's needs and values started to come together in Zak's mind as he recalled some of the impetuous Italian butterfly's past remarks: '*La magia*, Zak. — I cannot lie. — More men have set foot on the moon than have entered me — I adore the contrast and taste of dark chocolate — Give it to me like wild black Arabian stallions — Don't shoot and scoot — *Cazzo, cazzo* — You must know, Italian women are inclined that way — Treat me like a Parisian whore — Once a girl's sexual curiosity has been aroused in such a way, she forever hungers — *Tu credi troppo alla mia fantasia* —Yes, yes, yes, if they're big and black, Zak!'

CHAPTER TWELVE

Munich: April 27th 1985 — Part III

Arrivederci Clarissa

RURIK had come over to the 'Sheraton' late Sunday afternoon to discuss the industrial waste problem with Zak. It was apparent at the time Rurik was very excited at the possibility of working with Franz due to the miraculous meeting with Clarissa.

"Where is Clarissa, Zak?"

"After the party I was completely disenchanted with her. She went back to Italy via Rome this morning."

"What party?"

"Doesn't really matter now. I've finished with her. Broken the habit of needing to hear her so-called naughty fantasies."

"You're finished with her?"

"I never thought it possible, but yes."

"Are you sure? Franz said she was hot stuff."

"You can say that again, Rurik."

"Franz scored with her, you know?"

"Tell me something I don't know."

"O.K. Franz bragged, she was just about to *gam* him in the quiet of her University room in Berlin when her *fidanzato* made a surprise visit from Bologna, and knocked on the door."

"She told me, her Italian fiancé nearly caught her necking with a German boy during the time she was studying in Berlin."

"Amazing! Franz reckons he just got out through the bloody dorm window before the love-crazy Italian kicked the door down."

"I can understand that. No-one can saliva a *yugger* like Clarissa."

"Really?" Rurik said after licking his lips.

"Yes, really. And just for the record, she married that love-sick, door-kicking Italian."

"Really. Did you know the last time Franz saw her she was with two American soldiers."

"Good old Franz. I bet he told you they were the deep-shade of black-purple."

"How did you know they were *Schwarz*?"

"I always thought Clarissa... fantasised Hank and Luke picked her up in Berlin and took her down to a jazz club when Franz didn't show for their date. Guess they did rub and dub her to the music on the darkened dance floor."

"Come on, you're kidding me, Zak! Black soldiers got inside her panties, because Franz didn't show up?"

"In retrospect, yes."

"Incredible."

"I thought it was all fantasy until yesterday, but she obviously never got over the extraordinary experience."

"*Fausse bonne femme.*"

"Not really. You could say, she had a dual personality."

"Is that why you let her go, Zak?"

"Suppose so. I can accept any reality, Rurik... but not a downright guarded lie!"

"How did you meet her?"

"When we met, things were on the wane between Daphna and myself, in not so sunny Bournemouth."

"How come?"

"Daphna had an hysterectomy a few years earlier and became estranged when I moved out of the 'fast lane'."

"When you lived in Lancaster Gate?" Rurik enquired.

"Yes, she and our marriage changed after her operation, which was performed by the Royal gynaecologist. Then there was her mother's illness and the kids to contend with."

"Sorry, I didn't know, Zak. Did you at least shake the hand that handled the Queen?"

"So happens I did a couple of times. Anyway, I kept it all to myself but Daphna never stuck to an agreed understanding."

"But you love your wife. You always treated her like a Queen. Took her with you to the Far East, Hong Kong and Bangkok. America, New York, New Orleans, Mexico City and Acapulco."

"Yes, I did. In deluxe style, we also visited every European capital and main holiday resort. Then there was the 'Orient Express'."

"You bought her diamonds, fur coats and a genuine Rolex."

"True, but Daphna never could come to terms with and understand why I bought a 'Rolls'."

"Daphna must be crazy. So what have you been searching for in a woman, Zak?"

"One I could adore as well as love."

"You seek the impossible, my friend."

"Anyway, I guess fate played a hand in Clarissa and myself meeting in Bournemouth."

"You don't say."

"Yes, it was like tripping over a match-stick and falling into the arms of a love goddess!"

"What were your first instincts about her?"

"Deep down... A radiant, needy female."

"And you sent her away, just because she lied to you?"

"Yes and some. The awe of pending disbelief is over."

"But it's second nature for women to lie."

"I don't want to malign Clarissa but I do have certain principles that are important me."

"Bearing in mind Zak, most women are whores. Your principles are too high, when it comes to a woman like Clarissa."

"Not in my book, Rurik. Anyway, I've finished with foreign butterflies."

"Hey, hey. A man must forget his dignity to bed a woman such as your Italian whore."

"No way, the addiction is over."

"What are you saying, Zak?"

"The flame of passion and lust was put out last night when she levelled with me."

"About what?"

"Responding to the glancing volley those two long-haul guys gave her in the hotel lobby the other night."

"You mean those big Air Mauritius uniformed pilots with the built-in tan, who were hanging around the lobby, Saturday night?"

"Yes."

"They 'balled' Clarissa?" asked Rurik incredulously.

"They weren't cockpit guys though."

"What then?"

"A couple of cock-happy cabin staff."

"How did they 'pull her', Zak?"

"I told you, Clarissa knew she had earlier caught their eye. I guess she purposely ran off from the beer hall to recklessly satisfy her ultimate fantasy. Revenge or something."

"What's with the ultimate fantasy, Zak?"

"An Arab and a Negro 'doing all' to her at the same time."

"She's capable of coloured doubles?"

"Who knows about the private emotions inside the mind and soul of a woman such as Clarissa."

"Yea, we guys are inclined to be one-sided and not very understanding about them."

"You can say that again," Zak assured Rurik.

"Anyway, tell me, what did she do when you came back?"

"I think now that she thought I was one of the Mauritian crewmen wanting seconds."

"What makes you think that?"

"The door was ajar, she was laying spreadeagled, face down on the ruffled bed. She mumbled *'encore, s'il te plaît'*, without looking up from the ready position."

"Like, 'give it to me again, please'?"

"Yes, something like that."

"Clarissa is fluent in French?"

"She's a linguist."

"Yea, that's right. I also understand among the Franco-Mauritius there are many French speaking Arabs and blacks."

"And of course in neighbouring Réunion."

"Right."

"And then there was the fetor of hash!"

"Amazing, is she into dope?" Rurik wanted to know.

"No, just a lascivious Cancerian, I guess, with lots of wanton memories in her soul."

"Unbelievable, Zak. A negromanic?"

"Maybe. I guess she was always seeking to satisfy her erotic ambition for new sensations and guys from dark Continents."

"Inter-racial sex!"

"You could call it that."

"Not taboo for Italian women, Zak."

"I can assure you the Italian female hasn't got the monopoly on mixing it under the sheets."

"I suppose not." Rurik agreed:

"So, how did you leave it with her, baby"

"I told you I'm finished with Clarissa. Not interested in her or the likes of her any more."

"So what were your last words to your Italian butterfly?"

"*Granmercé, farfalla.*"

"Beautiful, Zak... Thanks for nothing, butterfly!"

"Yes."

"You could have phoned your 'buddy-boy' to come over and give her one before she flew to Milano."

"She wanted the contrast, baby."

"No problem after I'd finished with her, Zak, baby."

"Really?"

"Really. I know Moroccan guys here in Munich that would give their right arm to let a broad like Clarissa have the contrast."

"I know what you mean, Rurik," Zak said, thinking of Clarissa's so-called fantasy about the goings-on under the bridges of Paris. Simultaneously, he sensed bad vibes from the Slav. Suddenly Zak felt Rurik was not to be trusted and that he was quite capable of cutting one's heart out, just to put bread on his own table. The Londoner liked Rurik. Even though he was living on his wits and had traded in plutonium and possibly Russian 'Red Mercury', Zak knew he could never hate the Slav. However, Zak had been unable to refrain from commenting sharply to Rurik:

"Would you have used your stiletto to make her acquiesce to your will?"

"How do you know I carry a stiletto, my friend?"

"I've known you carried a thin, flick-knife in your pocket from the first day we met."

"Yea... I remember now, at the Saint George's Hotel in London where we first met up, I thought you'd spotted it when I took the tab for the lunch with that silly prat of a Colonel at my back. He sold me out to Müller, you know!"

"No, I didn't know. But for me, the Colonel is a real gent. In fact; an officer and a gentleman."

"Yea, well you're naïve, Zak. The so-called Colonel sold my 'Johnny Walker' whisky source to that mother-fucker Müller."

"That *gonif*!"

"Yea, you know about Herr Müller, Zak?"

"For sure. Anyway, it so happened I've sat drinking 'Black Label' in Steven Watts' private office down in St James's."

"So what?"

"So the 'Johnny Walker' company will not knowingly serve any customer twice who has infringed their agency conditions."

"Who the hell is Steven Watts, anyway?" Rurik had wanted to know.

" 'Johnny Walker's' export manager; he's family and the source of the 'Black and Red' stuff."

"Oh!"

"Tell me, Rurik, what happened to your condo' in Boca Raton, Florida, U.S. of A?"

"Oh, I got cheated out of that one in the 'Bay of Rats'!"

"Kiss my *tukkas* Rurik."

"Why should I kiss your arse?" Rurik replied aggressively, obviously misunderstanding the colloquialism.

"Who cares," Zak exclaimed, throwing his hands in the air in despair at Rurik.

"Thought you'd have passed Clarissa on to your old buddy boy," Rurik said with a razor smile.

"Not this time round, buddy."

"Well, one day I'll spray her larynx."

"What with?"

"With a little help from Franz."

"Some chance with that 'beer-belly'."

"We'll see. On the other side of midnight Zak, Clarissa could have lied to you. And Franz could have been shooting a line."

"About what?"

"Clarissa, in Berlin. Or maybe she was also jealous because Dominique came on hot with you in the 'Mathaserbierkeller'. I was."

"Those possibilities never occurred to me."

"O.K. my friend, we have a money-making metting with Franz tomorrow morning."

"If you say so. I'll take a later flight back to Heathrow."

CHAPTER THIRTEEN

Munich: April 29th 1985 — Part IV

A Deal in a Million

ZAK would never forget the meeting on Monday 29th April in Rurik's rented, 'pre-war' flat, located near the Karlstor Gate's graceful fountain in the centre of residential Munich. The Londoner rang the bell for the impromptu meeting. Zsa Zsa had greeted him with her eyelashes on 'flutter'.

On entering the stuffy apartment, Zak was surprised to hear and see the churlish-sounding German already settled in. Franz was informally dressed in a black leather bomber jacket, an open-neck, check shirt and jeans. Franz was talking loudly with Rurik, drinking locally-brewed beer in between continuously opening and closing a well-used, large, black leather briefcase.

A Deal in a Million

Zsa Zsa appeared anxious as she prepared the *'zhlub'* a snack before lunch. Franz kept boasting about his wife and claimed she was a Moroccan Princess.

The visiting Londoner assumed at the time, because Franz did not ask after Clarissa, that Rurik had already imparted his account of the traumatic break-up to the bombastic Franz. Or the German knew he'd killed the Anglo–Italian relationship by his chance presence.

Franz's boastful claims changed over lunch to those of past installations and communications systems he'd either managed or helped install all over the world, whilst working for the giant conglomerate Steilmanns. Franz seemed resentful that the conglomerate had made nearly two billion Deutsche Marks profit the previous year. Apparently, Franz had joined the international German electronics company on leaving Berlin University, about the same time as his Administration Boss; consequently, the *zhlub* had enjoyed the run of the Munich headquarters of Steilmanns.

"So why were you dismissed from the company, Franz?" Zak asked.

"I drank too much on my last job in Lagos. Steilmanns suspended me because they considered I'm an alcoholic."

"Are you?"

"I suppose so, Zak... but I'm also a workaholic."

"What did you actually work on in Nigeria?"

"I was responsible for installing the Nigerian communication and telecoms system for their new worldwide Embassy network."

"To do what?"

"The system is programmed to transmit to their forty-six stations abroad. It has a very powerful transmitter and is very sophisticated; it operates on variable frequencies with secret codes."

"What do you mean by stations?"

"Nigerian Embassies in different capital cities, from Abidjan to Washington."

"Are you really able to cut in on the Nigerian transmission?"

"Yes, with the facility and installation, Rurik."

"Then that's that."

"What's what, Zak?" Rurik excitedly exclaimed

"Well, if our friend Franz here could cut in on the transmission, maybe we could earn a lot of money."

"I told you the other night, Franz, Zak would come up with something to get you out of trouble."

"Why do I have the feeling you two guys are reeling me in?"

"Come on, Zak, tell Franz who you know."

"What's the difference? Franz can't perform."

"Tell him otherwise, Franz."

"I can duplicate and install the whole transmitter system for eavesdropping. I also have Steilmanns' project file for the Nigerian worldwide installations."

"That's another ball game, Franz," Zak said, with renewed interest.

"See, I have the complete file with me." Franz then proudly took a thick, loose-leaf file from his briefcase, which he eagerly flicked through, stopping from time to time to show off key documents.

"Look, Zak, America, England, France, Canada, Germany, Italy, Libya."

"That's impressive, Franz, but what about the mast?"

"No problem."

"Would the mast be enormously tall?"

"No, Zak. It could be installed and operate from a back garden."

"Now you're talking."

"Tell Franz who you can get to in England, Zak."

"As I told you when you waylaid me in the Bayerstrasse, Umara Dikko."

"The ex-Nigerian Transport Minister?"

"That's the guy, Franz, the one that ran off with the Nigerian Treasury kitty."

"Fantastic, if he's O.K., he's very rich."

Unfortunately, Zak had not fully picked up on Franz's far-reaching hypothesis during the excitement of a possible mega-deal coming together!

"Tell Franz where Dikko is, Zak."

"I understand he's lying low in London, waiting to take over the Nigerian Government. Planning a *coup d'état*."

"Zak, he will be interested for sure, if he's O.K.," Franz had excitedly exclaimed.

"Yes, but what about the codes and frequencies?"

"Oh! They are changed regularly."

"Another 'bummer'."

"But I can get them, Zak."

"Wonderful, but how, Franz?"

"From my old executive Boss. His signature appears on the report in my box file."

"Why should he give them to you?"

"We are friends, since we started at Steilmanns together; and he gambles heavily, if you know what I mean, Zak."

"You means he loses."

"Most of the time."

"Say no more, Franz."

"You think we have a deal, Zak?" Rurik, wanted to know, sitting anxiously on the edge of his chair, with anticipation of being in the money again.

"Not sure, but I will need some proof."

"No problem, Zak."

"Enlighten me then, Franz."

"I can give you photocopies of past codes and frequencies which are still classified as secret. In my briefcase, I also have a current list of spare parts and copy invoices to the Director of Finance at the Ministry of Communications in Lagos. You saw some of the documents and reports in my file."

"Yes, Franz. But how much would the system cost Dikko?"

"He has lots of black money, Zak; let's ask for five million American Dollars."

"That's too high, Franz."

"That would be fully supplied and operational."

"How much would that cost us?"

"About a million."

"We would be sharing four million then… after expenses."

"Including my old Boss, Zak."

"That's a mil' each."

"Yes."

"I will have to satisfy Dikko on the Nigerian link and stick a mil' on for bargaining power."

"So, what do you need to get started, Zak?" Franz asked with keen excitement.

"As you offered, some copies of your classified Nigerian file to try and wet Dikko's appetite."

"But, of course, Zak. I will photocopy a few key papers for you to take back to England."

"Great."

"Zak, if Dikko doesn't bite, perhaps you have access to the 'Bilderberg group'?"

"No way."

"How about 'Majestic', Zak?"

"I wouldn't know if 'Majestic' was spelt with a 'jay' or a 'gee', Franz."

"Anyway, they're too busy negotiating with aliens from outer space," said the well-informed Rurik.

A Deal in a Million

The Londoner left Munich that damp Monday night emotionally bruised, but armed with two dozen photocopies, copied from Franz's Steilmanns – Nigerian file. They detailed station by station progress reports, headed invoices, packing notes, a list of radio frequencies, including link-ups from the main Lagos installation to thirty-two Nigerian embassies abroad.

The flight back to Heathrow was uneventful apart from there being no-duty free 'Lancôme' on board for Daphna. So Zak settled for the largest size bottle of Chanel Nº 5 — and an Aramis spray-cologne for himself, from the helpful British Airways hostess.

* * * *

CHAPTER FOURTEEN

Bournemouth: 30th April 1985

False Hopes

FIRST thing Tuesday morning on his return from Munich, Zak made a telephone call to Lionel Morris .
"Lionel, Zak here, how's the heart?"

"Not so good, but thanks for asking. What can I do for you my much-travelled friend?"

"Umara Dikko."

"What about him?"

"I need to speak with him, on the hush-hush."

"Yes, I can get to the bespecticled Umara."

"Can you set up a meeting for me?"

"Yes, but you will have to go through the 'boys in blue'."

"Why's that?"

"Because of Mossad's boys' kidnap attempt!"

"Of Dikko"?

"He was that man."

"Oh, yes. I remember now in June of last year." There and then Zak realised what Franz's subconscious had cruelly belied when the *zhlub* had said:

"If Dikko is O.K. now."

"God!" Zak exclaimed before thinking. He should have been more alert at that crucial moment in Rurik's stuffy flat to have been able to put two and two together and recall Mossad's part in the abduction of Dikko. All carried out in broad daylight, on an open West London street, so that Israel could re-establish their old ties with the reigning Nigerian Government.

"The SAS are guarding Dikko and Special Branch are vetting everybody in and out of his home these days," Lionel cautioned.

"Can we not by-pass them?"

"Impossible after Customs at Stansted found him all boxed up with a Mossad hallmark, ready for the West African export trade."

"That's right... where is he now?"

"I understand he still lives just off Queensway, W.2. under very close surveillance."

"Whereabouts?"

"Porchester Terrace, but, of course, that could be a blind now." The Londoner knew the street-cum-terrace well. One most certainly could not hide a twenty-foot transmitting mast in those neat, open front or back gardens.

"Hasn't Dikko another abode?"

"Who knows."

"Okay, Lionel, take care of yourself, see you next time around."

"Bye, Zak. Sorry I can't help you further."

"By the way, Lionel, do you have a connection into the 'Bilderberg Group' or 'Majestic'?"

"Zak, keep away from those guys, it's rumoured they're the New World Order, if you know what I mean. It's also rumoured, 'Majestic' could have been responsible for JFK If you know what I mean my friend?"

"Really… Thanks for the information."

"That's O.K. Be lucky, Zak."

"*Shalom*, Lionel. I wish you all you wish yourself."

Immediately on putting the phone down on Lionel, Zak telephoned his friend Donald on his direct line at the Yard.

"Chief Inspector Franklin, please."

"Speaking."

"Don, Zak here. How's the weather up there?"

"Fine here, Zak."

"Can I talk freely on this line?"

"Yes, the weather is fine."

"Good. I need some rather sensitive information about a privileged Nigerian exile."

"Nigerian, should be no problem."

"Good, can we meet for a coffee, next time I'm in London?"

"Sure, when would that be?"

"Like tomorrow!"

"Why not?"

"Usual place, at noon?"

"No problem."

"See you there."

Donald 'marked Zak's card' the next day over a double scotch or two, in the busy bar of the ageing Grosvenor Hotel, adjacent to Victoria Station:

"Don't get involved with the SAS or Special Branch, Zak. They'll go right through you and all your known associates from the date you were born, if you make any kind of overture towards Dikko," Don warned, not wanting Zak to chance getting his fingers burnt in sensitive waters.

"But I have nothing to hide, Don."

"Regardless, they will let you know otherwise!"

"Understand, Don. But have you any special contacts within Special Branch?"

"Yes, I have. But I don't get involved with politics or international protected persons, Zak."

"God! I hadn't thought about the deal as political."

"Then you're naïve. Leave it alone, Zak."

"Yes, you're right, Don… Thanks."

Zak remembered Rurik's tone of disappointment, when he'd been informed over the telephone:

"I've been advised by a friend at the Yard not to proceed with the Dikko deal."

"Like in, Scotland Yard?"

"Yes."

"Oh, bloody hell, Zak. Another leap in the dark."

"Yes. Will you tell Franz the deal is considered unworkable."

"Sure, say no more."

Saturday afternoon Zak bought a spring's red rose before walking Bournemouth's Pier. He'd pricked the flesh on his index finger as he entwined the spiked stem around Clarissa's 18-carat locket and key. Under the sun's rays, dejectedly, he'd thrown the rose and golden presents into the turbulent English Channel uttering:

"*Granmercé, farfalla.*" Then, with pouted lips, Zak drew a broken thorn and blood from his wound, then uttered:

"Drink and smile, my lovely. I shall adore you forever."

* * * * *

CHAPTER FIFTEEN

Brussels: 17th October 1985

Slim Pickings

ZAK was brought back from his reverie as the Belgian pilot cut back the powerful SABENA jet engines, decreasing speed and landing way behind schedule at Brussels National Airport, where Zak knew Mossad agents must be active due to NATO Headquarters being nearby, and possibly keeping an eye on him.

On arrival at the Hotel Metropole on the Place de Brouckere in the very heart of Brussels, Zak was relieved to find his reservation was still good. After further enquiry at the antiquated reception desk of the Grand Hotel, the visiting Londoner was informed Jean Paul from Marseilles had indeed checked in.

Later that evening the Frenchman and Zak made their way to dine at the renowned 'Chez Léon' on the gastronomic Rue des Bouchers, looking forward to consuming Belgium's national delight. They'd stopped *en route* to admire the early 17th-century 'Mannekin-Pis' located in the illuminated Gothic Grand-Place, an architectural gem witihout compare. The 'Pissin Boy' seemingly pointing to many other inviting fish restaurants, arrayed along adjoining narrow passageways.

Slim Pickings

The new season's *'moules à la marinière'* were incredibly good and exceptionally plump that evening. Jean Paul, a self-confessed student of the grape, favoured a chilled Sancerre '82, on which Zak complimented the Jewish man from the Golfe du Lion, although Zak's choice and palate at the time was really for one of the distinctive Chablis on the impressive wine list.

The next morning they kept the appointment with Jean Paul's buyer, a retailer-cum-wholesaler, on the nearby Rue de Marché. The keen Belgian client, quickly recognising a good buy when he saw one, readily committed himself to buy half the stock of colourful, proofed, cotton ski-suits at the asking price, on a twenty-eight day credit basis. The sale and business were concluded perfunctorily. Jean Paul was delighted at the result of their combined efforts, as it meant when the account was settled he would receive a full 10% commission. With the signed and sealed order in the hand, they wished the buyer *'au revoir'*. The Frenchman then tightened up on his commission and politely asked for an advance payment to cover his expenses. With a few assurances given by each of them, they automatically confirmed the verbal agreement with a handshake and a *'Mazel un Brocheh'* before Jean Paul confidently passed over the order. Jean Paul kindly offered Zak a lift in his Citroën Estate. The lift afforded Zak the time to keep his promise and visit Rurik's son Maurice over on the busy section of the Avenue Louise. Maurice, Zak knew, missed his parents and was serving a lonely apprenticeship with a firm of *Frummers*, with whom Maurice's father traded in diamonds from time to time.

As Zak waved goodbye from the wide, picturesque boulevard of the Avenue Louise, Jean Paul appeared happy with his cash advance, which would more than cover the Frenchman's hotel and travelling expenses back home to the Marseilles waterfront.

Later that afternoon, on a cramped SABENA sixteen-seater German-built Messerschmitt biplane bound for Düsseldorf, Zak reminisced about Jean Paul, Stan Blend, Mister Elissar and Cairo…

* * *

CHAPTER SIXTEEN

Cairo: August 1976 — Part I

A View of the Nile

ZAK had been introduced to Mr Elissar, a visiting Egyptian clothing manufacturer who did not look unlike Peter Ustinov, by a crippled Commercial Attaché from the Arab Chamber of Commerce in London. The money-grabbing Attaché had immediately expected a fat commission just for bringing Elissar over from the Arab Chamber's premises in nearby Berkeley Square to Zak's showroom in Mortimer Street!

"Mister Elissar cannot speak English. He is looking to purchase large quantities of second-hand, light-weight jackets for the up-and-coming young Egyptian executives," spluttered the unfortunate Attaché in excitable, broken English, directly after eloquently introducing himself.

The next evening, Daphna and Zak wined and dined Elissar Chinese-style, with a view to being favoured with a lovely prime bank Letter of Credit from the overwhelmed Egyptian.

A View of the Nile

Elissar later reciprocated hospitality in Egypt, when the Londoner pursued the L/C for the second-hand jackets. Elissar welcomed Zak on 27th August at Cairo International Airport on his stop-off from selling jeans in Kuwait.

Amazingly, Elissar had arranged for an English-speaking friend and his nephew Captain Hussein, the Police Chief of Cairo International Airport Security, to quickly usher his guest through Egyptian Passport Control and Customs as though the visiting Englishman was a VIP. Ceremoniously, when the comedy of greetings was done, Zak's beaming Egyptian host then chauffeured them towards downtown Cario and the 'Nile Hilton'.

Surprisingly, during the drive to the 'Hilton', Elissar would not allow the interpreter to respond to any business talk before or after the jolly small talk!

On reaching the outskirts of parched-coloured Cairo, Elissar suddenly stopped his souped-up 'Zil' car at a newspaper stand. Unbalancing the one-legged newspaper vendor with the car door of his Russian made car, Elissar, still unconcerned as to the fate of the poor, hopping vendor, took and paid for a copy of 'Al-Akhbar'. Desperately thumbing through the newspaper the delirious Egyptian pointed with childish delight to an advertisement displaying his company logos and visitor's company logo, both under a bold banner heading:

'Welcome to Cairo'

The congratulations from Elissar's Jeans Company to Zak's London company ran alongside dozens of other greeting adverts, mostly depicting the smiling Sadat who had been newly appointed as Egypt's First Minister. Zak's sixth sense signalled that Elissar, by associating the two companies in the important Arab newspaper, had hoped to pick up some extra Middle East business to the detriment of his visitor's UK company. Zak had obviously been used by Elissar. The visitor's gut feeling confirmed what his mind had chosen to ignore about the crafty Egyptian!

When checking into the 'Nile Hilton' and before Zak's case was 'bell-hopped' to his allotted room, he'd been obliged to sign a declaration that he would vacate the allocated room by the following mid-morning! Though Zak felt uptight over the strong-arm proceedings at the reception desk, he passed in silent awe through the well-worn 'Hilton's' lounges and verandahs, intrigued that OPEC had crystallised in one of the tranquil areas during the sixties over a Coca Cola. Alone in the lift with Elissar, Zak assumed the interpreter-friend had been assigned to watch the car. The Londoner managed to relax upon reaching the well-appointed room overlooking the picturesque Nile, whose soft, filtered water fed the pool below the balcony. Whilst taking a deep breath and devouring the incredible sight, Elissar cut into Zak's reverie and presented him with a bulky brown paper parcel. The parcel seemingly appeared from out of nowhere. It was lightweight and tied up with thick, coarse, hairy string. Elissar found the English words to inform his visitor:

"Mister Zak, a present for your wife, please."

Zak knew, no-way was he *shlepping* the contents of the crude, bulky parcel back to London. However, he'd courteously taken the time to unwrap the gift, only to be dismayed at the contents — a voluminous, long-length, black-net, gold-tinselled, trimmed Arab dress! The ethnic dress would certainly be ill-suited to his petite, fashion-conscious wife. Except, maybe, if she wanted to portray Salome dancing for Herod. Zak tactfully thanked Elissar for the unwanted gift.

"Wonderful, I trust I can re-pack it into my luggage."

The gloating, perspiring Elissar bowed low to his visitor's thanks, as though he'd been paid the biggest compliment of his Egyptian life.

A View of the Nile

Elissar then started to reveal bad manners by helping himself to a drink from the mini-fridge, which he guzzled down on his way to the balcony, then flopped on to a reclining chair in a hot sweat and with a loud sigh.

Elissar, pointing towards Mecca waited in a prostrate position, while Zak took a quick shower and changed...

Back in the car, without ado, Elissar drove his visitor away from the air-conditioned 'Hilton', amidst the pollution of scorching Cairo, to the fresher, cooler plateau of Giza and the Pyramids.

The marvellous sight of the three dominating peaks of the Pyramids vividly set against the skyline on the highland above Cairo had been wondrous indeed. Then, drawing nearer to the plateau, the smiling Sphinx suddenly panned into view. The phenomenon, Zak felt, was all too fleeting, as Elissar started to embark on various parking manoeuvres.

The two Egyptians and Zak entered the awe-inspiring, pinnacled tomb of the Pharaohs, balanced with some 2·3 million stone blocks, weighing up to two and a half tons each. They then laboriously climbed, seemingly forever up to the disappointing, musky hollow of the burial chamber at 405 feet...

On leaving the Great Pyramid, Elissar's friend asked with a funny wink and a smile:

"Do you want to ride a camel, Mister Zak?"

"Okay, I'll try anything once."

"Good for you, Mister Zak."

Elissar took over to barter for the camel ride. The long argument that ensued between the well turned out camel driver and Zak's host was certainly an education. The Englishman did not have to know the language to understand Elissar was negotiating a price with a very able horse-trader.

Eventually, the waiting, 'ten case' camel was grounded to allow

Forbidden Yesterday

Zak to climb aboard the two-humped monster before it did a triple-jerk movement for take off.

Holding the pommel of the saddle tight, Zak responded to the thrill of his first camel ride, as he seemingly rode the desert waves towards the grandeur of the recumbent lion, which depicted the head of King Khafre entwined with the royal head-cloth and crowned with a Royal Cobra. Close up, the 'pot-marked' head of the declining Sphinx had been all too sadly apparent, defaced on the orders of a simple gunnery officer in Napoleon's invading army.

The parched visitor was requested to pose for a souvenir photo on top of the swaying camel, with the Pyramids in the background, before gladly dismounting.

The departure from the symbolic grandeur of Giza in the jarring Russian car became tolerable as Zak's eye caught the panoramic view of the mosque of Mohammed Ali ahead. Elissar, for reasons best known to himself, drove back to the 'Hilton' as though he was Stirling Moss in a hurry.

Elissar promptly left his visitor at the 'Hilton' reception desk having reflected via an English speaking receptionist:

"You will be picked up at 8 o'clock for dinner and a night's entertainment."

Hot and bothered, Zak requested his room key from the attentive receptionist, who, along with the key, handed the English guest a telex marked 'urgent' from his numbered pigeonhole.

The guest eagerly opened and read the surprise communication from Stan Blend in Dallas, while waiting for the lift:

ZAK,
MUST KNOW BY RETURN TELEX IF YOUR EGYPTIAN CUSTOMER HAS CUT L/C FOR LIGHTWEIGHT JACKETS.
BEST PERSONAL REGARDS, STAN

A View of the Nile

Stan's short telex request reiterated the fact that Elissar, the whole day, had evaded the many enquiries about opening up the L/C for the second-hand jackets. Zak made a mental note to pin down Elissar during the evening. After all, his reason for being in Cairo at the time was to get the L/C, although it had been a bonus to have seen the great monuments of the Pharaohs and another wonder of the old world.

On the way up to his room Zak found himself alone in the lift with a well-groomed butterfly! She looked about twenty-six years of age and had the appearance of an exuberant starlet with pinned-up, henna-tinted hair. Sparkling light brown eyes were framed by long eyelashes. Her lovely neck held a proud semitic face with absolutely stunning features. Zak just knew she was not Egyptian, nor a known professional working the hotel. The curves under her silky-sapphire, brocade 'slit-shift' imparted tantalizing enzymes and an intoxicating fragrance that reeked of class, instantly making his libido go wild.

Senses alerted, Zak envisaged a way of ridding himself of the Arab dress...

The desert butterfly responded in good English to his offer:
"Where is this so-called wonderful Arabic dress?"
"In my room," Zak replied nonchalantly.
"I thought as much."
"But there are no strings attached to my devious generosity."
His witty remark must have appealed to her sense of humour, as she'd laughed and said...
"With a line like that, you've intrigued me."

Zak picked up on a possible North-African dialect from her delivery. They immediately introduced themselves before Fossetta's surprisingly accompanied the stranger to his hotel room to look at the dress!

The look of apprehension on her face suggested Fossetta was getting cold feet as Zak put the key in the door lock. From the opened doorway the desert butterfly beamed with delight as her gaze fell upon the ethnic dress on the bed.

"I'm pleased you have told me the truth, Mister Zak. The dress looks adorable. Now that I'm here, shall I try it on?"

"Be my guest, Fossetta."

The long-haired Moroccan beauty somehow had known how to qualify the situation further.

"There are definitely no strings attached if I try the dress on, are there, Mister Zak?"

"None, whatsoever. You can take it home or to your room, if you wish."

Apparently content with his offer, the Arabess touched and fondled the garment prior to caressing it against her gleaming, umber-form, studying herself in the wall mirror. She then flashed a delightful smile, kicked off her satin wedges and quickly moved her curvaceous body in the direction of the bathroom, calling out:

"Your surname is in the paper today, Mister Zak."

"Informed one, tell me about your name, Fossetta. Is it Arabic?"

"No, its French, meaning 'the dimpled one'."

"Sounds kind of Italian to me, *Mademoiselle*!"

"Do you have other languages, Mister Zak?" she called back, ignoring his previous remark.

"A strong smattering of German, Italian and some French," he'd answered with some reserve.

"*Très joli*," she exclaimed. Keeping the conversation going through the bathroom door, Zak continued:

"Tell me, Fossetta, why did your parents give you an Italian French sounding name?"

"It's rumoured my father in his youth had an affair of the heart with a French diplomat's wife in Casablanca."

"Lucky the husband wasn't the second Attaché."

"What does that mean?"

"Just an embassy joke."

A View of the Nile

"Like assassin?"

"Could be! Tell me Fossetta, is Casablanca where you were born?"

"Yes, have you been there, Zak?" He noticed Fossetta had stopped calling him Mister!

"Just for a short visit."

"Did you go to the *Kasbah*?"

"Yes, I found the visit really interesting."

"Everyone does."

To try and ascertain her age and outlook, Zak asked:

"Are your parents watchful of you, Fossetta?"

"Not since my twenty-first birthday party, five years ago now." Fossetta then appeared back in the bedroom, looking as if she'd stepped out of one of those glossy 1950's Hollywood Arabian Nights musicals, except no way was Fossetta a blonde. Pirouetting across the bedroom floor with bare feet and let-down hair, she sung out, in singsong English:

"It fits me like a glove, Zak. But it's impossible for me to accept such a gift from a stranger."

"Why?"

"Good Arab girls just do not take presents from strange men, let alone Europeans."

"I can understand your reticence and fine culture, but there really aren't any strings attached and you look a million dollars in the dress, Fossetta."

"Do you know Arab girls?"

"Just a little. I've travelled the Gulf and I took a short break in Tangier two or three summers ago."

"When you visited Casablanca?"

"Yes."

"Did you book through our tourist office, just past 'Liberty's' in Regent Street?"

"So happens I did, opposite El Al."

"That's right. Which hotel did you stay at in Tangier?"

"The 'Riff'. Can you believe, I contracted colitis from unwashed fruit there?"

"But the 'Riff' is a very important hotel."

"So the wine-waiter kept telling me all the way to the *Medina*."

"You're decadent, Zak, and you must know Moroccan girls. Tell me about your principles."

"As in 'personal code of ethics' and 'conduct'?"

"Yes."

"Ethics. I have compassion for my fellow man. Code of conduct, that's always the woman's prerogative."

"I cannot argue with that!"

"Good, then you'll accept the dress?"

"I'm surprised at myself for even thinking about accepting the dress from you."

"So, it's agreed, you'll keep the dress?"

"Yes, seeing your name is in 'Al-Akhbar' today."

"Wonderful."

"Thank you. I must go, Zak. I have a business dinner this evening, because of my work here in *Al Qahirah*."

"As in Cairo?"

"Yes. I'm with the Moroccan Tourist Department. A prompter-cum-interpreter."

"That sounds interesting, Fossetta."

He realised that was how she knew the Moroccan Tourist Office and El Al were in Regent Street. A real prize, and she was actually taking the monster dress!

"Are you checked in here at the 'Hilton', Fossetta?" Zak asked politely.

"Yes, and if I'm not too late back tonight, maybe I can buy you a nightcap, or even a snack, in return for the dress?" He'd been distracted from her possibly suggestive offer upon feeling the first twinges of muscle spasm hit his calves from the Pyramid climb.

"Perhaps, a drink but not supper. I also have a business dinner."
"Of course. You are obviously a successful businessman visiting *Al Qahirah*?"

"And hopefully victorious here."

Zak hastily agreed with the Fossetta to do a key-check with the concierge when he returned to the hotel that night.

Fossetta then slipped back into her high-wedges and picked up her discarded shift-dress from the bathroom. The Arabess left, with a *ma'a salaama*, and mentioned her room number again, which Zak did not pay full regard to, since the twinges in his body had turned into excruciating pain.

Once the Moroccan butterfly had flown away, Zak quickly went into the bathroom, ran the soft, cold water over his legs and thighs, following up with a hot and cold *Sitzbad*. The water therapy gradually dissipated the pain. The sightseeing Englishman then gently massaged his legs and thighs with essential oils of Rosemary, Juniper and Ylang Ylang based with virgin almond oil before resting, mentally blessing a lovely past butterfly from Grasse for her charming introduction to Aromatherapy.

Just before it was time for Zak to be picked up that evening, Mr Elissar telephoned and managed to explain in broken English:

"No come to 'Hilton', Mister Zak. Bad pains from climbing high the Pyramid."

Obviously Elissar had experienced a similar discomfort, but did not know about the art of Aromatherapy.

"Soon, my friend will call... Mister Zak."

The phone was then abruptly put down by Elissar.

The telephone rang again.

An over-cultured English speaking voice at the other end of the line eloquently introduced himself as Mister Abdul Khalid, the very esteemed friend of Mister Elissar.

"Sir, Mister Elissar's expedition to the great Pyramid this afternoon has caused him to acquire agonizing pains in the lower part of his anatomy. I have been given the pleasure of taking you by taxi to the performance of the *Son et Lumière* at Giza."

"Understand the pleasure's all mine, Abdul."

"Not at all, old chap. Mister Elissar will meet both of us later for dinner. Very well Sir, later we have a first-class reservation in a swinging night club."

The setting for the performance of the floodlit *Son et Lumière* had been breathtaking. A perfect setting under a silent midnight blue sky, the shrouded splendour and secrets of the Pyramids and the dormant Sphinx, ready to be further exposed.

Mister Khalid and Zak sat in a comfortable, part-upholstered chair on the desert sands amidst a gathering of many other tourists. The soft, cool summer breeze delivered the exotic scent of jasmine to Zak's nostrils from the white garlands worn by the glowing female in the audience.

Suddenly, everyone was startled as the bellowing acoustics system started to recite. Later, the booming voice of the narrator informed the enthralled audience of the ancient mysteries of Egyptology, built by the enslaved Israelites, whose inheritors were now the most formidable power in the Middle East.

The wonders of the *Son et Lumière* left behind, but never to be forgotten, Mr Khalid and Zak sat in the nightclub 'Auberge des Pyramides' in Shara City, Egypt's up-and-coming film centre.

Especially for the tourist trade, the nightclub waiters were resplendently turned out in decorative white and gold coloured turbans, complemented by gold-trimmed, red-coated uniforms. Whilst they waited for Elissar to arrive they'd both ordered Pernod on the rocks. The colourful waiter ceremoniously placed two odd

A View of the Nile

glasses on the well-worn, red chequered cloth and poured generous tots of Pernod, alas, without ice!

While they sat drinking their warm Pernod, Zak followed his gut feeling and asked Abdul about Elissar's intentions to honour his commitment to open the L/C for the reserved jackets. Having become drinking friends, Abdul opened up:

"Confidentially, I believe that there is a problem in acquiring the external currency, Mister Zak."

"Really?"

"However, it is for Mister Elissar to inform you, not I."

"I see, thank you, Abdul. I shall, of course, not mention your confidential remark."

"Thank you, Mister Zak. I know Elissar is very embarrassed about the whole affair, sir."

Zak remembered thinking his instincts had been correct about Abdul being in the know. He'd then prudently decided not to 'pump' the over-polite young Egyptian any more but to wait until Elissar hopefully turned up and levelled about the deal.

Mr Elissar's guest became jarred at the sight of his host when he appeared in a lemon coloured, lightweight Tonic jacket, white flares, blue-striped shirt and a ghastly, wide, 'kipper' tie.

The tardy Egyptian apologised for his lateness through Abdul and by his repentant manner. Elissar then spoke at length with Abdul in profound Arabic. Zak felt sure Abdul had told Elissar about the inquiry regarding the jackets before they ordered dinner. During dinner, a young, shapely Cleopatra-style belly dancer started to gyrate on stage, reminding Zak of the belly-pushing Roxanne's remarkable capabilities...

However, for Zak the fresh, colourful, plump, jumbo Red Sea prawns had been the highlight of the evening. Even more delicious than the swinging entertainment.

Leaving the nightclub's car park in Elissar's car, the Egyptian made his way slowly in the direction of Islamic Cairo... taking in the pungent odours, sights and sounds of the old quarter, with glimpses of Roman remains and the Ben Ezra Synagogue before cutting across towards the Ezra Bridge. Elissar then drove up the Shari' El Qasr El-Aine where he miraculously parked, to the sound of the recorded *Muezzin*, a recurring whine that seemed to drone for ever, calling the locals to prayer. During their downtown walk-about, the Londoner was accosted time and time again in the bustle of the holiday crowds by knowing shoe-shine boys calling out:

"I will clean and shine your crocodile shoes for free. They will bring great luck to me and my esteemed family."

At around midnight, the trio took Arabic coffee in a trendy, but fly-infested pavement cafe. The continuous noise of the city grated in Zak's ears as the traffic fumes mixed with the sickly smell of jasmine and Cairo's polluted air seemed to percolate in his nostrils.

As Elissar and Abdul talked, Zak watched young Egyptian executives go by. God! They could certainly do with a delivery of Stan's second-hand jackets, the Londoner thought.

Zak's thoughts induced him, through Abdul, to confront Elissar about his intentions to open the L/C for the second-hand, lightweight, American jackets. It was obvious from Elissar's sheepish glance and defensive manner that the Egyptian was put out by the open approach. Evidently, Elissar could not perform just as Abdul had indicated. Avoiding the challenge once more by rudely talking and jesting with Abdul at great length in Arabic, Elissar suddenly vaunted in English:

"We go to the 'Hilton', Mister Zak?"

The Londoner replied sarcastically:

"You bet, this evening has been a fiasco."

Zak then stood up and left the open-mouthed Elissar and Abdul and walked towards a nearby, parked taxi.

A View of the Nile

"Nile Hilton Hotel, please, driver." The taxi-driver clearly understood where he was expected to go, as they soon arrived at the 'Hilton'. Zak immediately sent a telex to Stan Blend from the hotel lobby communication room.

CAIRO NILE HILTON HOTEL DATE 27/8/1976

ATTENTION: STAN BLEND

RE YOUR TELEX OF TODAY:

SORRY, THE SPHINX CANNOT BITE, NO EXTERNAL CURRENCY AVAILABLE TO CUT LETTER OF CREDIT. WILL CONTACT YOU ON MY RETURN TO UK

BEST PERSONAL REGARDS, ZAK.

Back in his room, mentally weary but not tired, Zak ran a hot bath, swirling in a half dozen drops of essential oil of lavender to help him relax and possibly sleep...

The bad taste of Cairo and Elissar's obvious negative on Zak's mind made him wonder how Stan in Dallas would react to the telex, and whether the Texan would ever call him Kid again.

The lavender induced Zak to slumber, and to forget about checking with the concierge and Fossetta.

* * * *

CHAPTER SEVENTEEN

London: May 1976

New Business and New Friends

ZAK first set eyes on Stan Blend in a sparse Victoriana office of a well-established Confirming House in the City of London.

A slick, sex-mad, black wheeler-dealer called Basil Snow had involved the Londoner in trying to find a source of the famous 'Beck's Beer'. It had been by chance that bull-shitting 'Bas' with Zak called in to meet the principal of the Confirming House while trying to find a supply of the much-wanted beer for the thirsty Nigerian market.

Zak always felt he'd unwisely involved himself with Basil, which was later confirmed by his police friend, Donald. At the time, Bas's 'wised-up' Trinidadian cousin was also in town getting an abortion. She had recently been granted a divorce from her rich, New York Jewish husband and was renting one of Prince Faisal's (who bore a remarkable resemblance to his father, King of Saudi Arabia) apartments down in desirable Holland Park, London, W2.

The Londoner when meeting the polite, humble Prince, noticed he was infatuated with the bedridden female and that he consistently lit the black beauty's cigarettes, as she recovered from her operation. Zak doubted whether the Prince allowed his infatuation to blossom

New Business and New Friends

into true romance, although he had overheard the 'designing' negress tell cousin Bas over a vintage bottle of Chateau Margaux:

"The Prince is my next 'meal-ticket', baby."

When Zak first met Basil, he claimed he was earning his living dealing with commodities and had a Lebanese buyer in the hand for several regular monthly container-loads of 'Beck's Beer' for West Africa However, before Zak was wised up by Don, Zak and Bas met in the crowded lobby of the Sheraton Park Hotel in Knightsbridge with a joint offer for the 'Beck's'.

The wary Lebanese buyer's agent considered the matter was out of hand and withheld his signature on the purchase order for the German beer. This was due to the 'daisy chain' of brokers hanging about the lobby, all expecting to get drunk on the commission from the joint offer of 'Beck's'. Consequently, Zak went off freelancing with Bas to a Confirming House, in the City of London, to try and find a bona fide supply of German beer...

Stan, at the time of meeting Zak, was on a world export drive, selling second-hand clothing and wiping rags. Accompanying Stan was a fast-talking, smart Frenchman from Marseilles by the name of Jean Paul who looked like a dapper, thirty-year-old George C. Scott. Later, Zak found out when visiting Jean Paul at his run down, waterfront flat overlooking the Chateau d'If Island, that the Frenchman could hold a hundred telephone numbers in his Jewish *kop*. Jean Paul also spoke nine languages fluently, and was very well connected in both the textile and diamond trades.

Stan, in contrast to the Frenchman, was the quiet, portly American in his mid sixties, with thinning hair on top of an overripe complexion, and soft, grey eyes that looked out from a pair of thick-framed glasses. The unassuming American was dressed in a brown, synthetic sports jacket, faded grey-coloured cotton shirt, sporting what looked like a second-hand orange-coloured tie, beige, unpressed pants and heavy brown-brogue shoes.

Whatever the American lacked in appearance or dress sense he made up for with gentle enchantment. Stan's charm was instantly apparent as he captured one with his easy manner, and pleasingly slow Southern drawl. Zak found an immediate friend in Stan, maybe because of their common religious denomination.

Later that evening Zak picked up Stan and Jean Paul from their hotel. They were both checked in at the Royal Lancaster Hotel, conveniently placed near Zak's penthouse, located on the Bayswater Road, which overlooked the beautiful Kensington Gardens, the Serp' and Peter Pan...

As they crossed the Serp' in the comfort of Zak's 'Rolls', he took the time to point out to his guests the Israeli Embassy on the other side of Ken' Gardens... On leaving the parks, Zak drew the foreign pair's attention to the Iranian and Iraqi Embassies. The Londoner felt he'd further delighted his passengers when he parked his indigo-coloured, convertible 'Corniche' outside the 'Carlton Towers' over on Sloane Street, to dine in the deluxe hotel's fabulous 'Rib Room'.

The American, Frenchman and Englishman all ordered the iced Tiger prawns and mouth-watering prime roast beef with out-of-season vegetables, supped the robust Côte de Nuits and unanimously rounded off the meal with syllabub, coffee and *petits fours*. The Londoner generously tipped the head waiter and slipped the linkman a fiver for looking after the 'Corniche', before taking the well-fed pair on a grand tour of London's landmarks.

Silently leaving Cadogan Square, Zak drove down into Lower Sloane Street on smooth wheels, automatically changing gear at Sloane Square before turning right into the King's Road, Chelsea, a private road until 1830. Effortlessly, they cruised down the trendy 'blue denim road'...

New Business and New Friends

The Kings's Road, Chelsea
Where businesses are wealthy

The King's Road, Chelsea is narrow
No room for a fruit barrow

Fashion is booming
As sales go zooming

Fashion trends are featured
For adorable Creatures

The hemline is high
To attract a glad eye

The queers appear
In the most fabulous gear

The lesbians there
Very austere

The military pensioner looks in wonder
He will never know hunger

The aroma of the coffee shops
The quaint old pubs serving tots

The birds go there
For all to stare

Some unfortunate dolls
Are lost souls

The King's Road, Chelsea
Alas for some is unhealthy[8]

Passing the Venetian-designed Chelsea Town Hall on the nearside of the 'Corniche'... turning left at Beaufort Street for the panoramic view of the Thames and the iron-arched Battersea Bridge all the way down to Cheyne Walk. A left turn along the Chelsea Embankment, past the curious-looking, three span, hybrid Albert Bridge and the interesting, self-anchored Chelsea Bridge on the offside of the Rolls, gliding by the Festival Pleasure Gardens and the four-chimneyed Battersea Power Station located on the other side of the river, before arriving at the stone-arched Vauxhall Bridge.

Zak pushed the throttle down hard and crossed over the lights, curbside; the Tate Gallery housing some of 'Turner's finest', directly to the right, Henry Moore's bronze, proudly displayed on the Millbank.

Ahead, the latticed Lambeth Bridge, the castled Holy Palace south side, Westminster Abbey and Westminster Hall. The Houses of Parliament and Big Ben, Westminster Bridge, a glimpse of the bladed chariot of Queen Boadicea, oblique to Scotland Yard. The War Office overlooking the Cenotaph, the sight of gleaming helmets on faceless, uniformed, mounted Horse Guards in Whitehall... where Mossad had special privileges... looming ahead, 145-foot Nelson's Column watched over by four bronze lions, the one-eyed Admiral pillaring high in Trafalgar Square looking towards the Thames and away from the nearby National Gallery with its eight thousand paintings. Admiralty Arch, Green Park, St James's Palace, the red surfaced Royal Mail, Queen Victoria's Memorial. To the left, the tall gates protecting Buckingham Palace, left-wheel past its high wall, hiding the Royal Gardens. The glorious statue of Victory dominating Hyde Park Corner, 'Harvey Nicks' and 'Harrods' to the left. Number One London: the 'Intercontinental' with its wonderful 'Soufflé Room'. Green Park, Piccadilly, the elegant 'Ritz' with what looked like Omar Sharif waiting outside, dressed in a smart sand-coloured suit and tie. On the left, Bond Street and the Michelangelesque Burlington Arcade, quickly followed by the Royal Academy, opposite the per-

New Business and New Friends

forming Messrs Fortnum & Mason's articulated clock. 'Simpsons, DAKS' and all that. The moveable, lovable Eros now incorrectly pointing down Lower Regent Street, running parallel with the Haymarket!

To the left, Soho, within the cords, Piccadilly, Saint Giles, Cambridge and Oxford! Theatre-land. Charing Cross Station. Let's all go up the Strand. The Savoy, memories of its renowned Grill and mouthwatering 'Cherry Jubilee'. Covent Garden without flowers! The Waldorf. Around the Aldwych, Fleet Street, 'Reuter's' forever waiting for news from abroad. The appealing High Courts of Justice across from the Wig and Pen Club. Somerset House. Down Savoy Street to the Victoria Embankment. Southwark Bridge pictured in the rear-view mirror. To the right, Father Thames again, still rolling along. To the left, the huge phizog of the Shell Building, seemingly gazing down into the open roof. The sixty-foot tall sphinxed Cleopatra's Needle – sister to La Concorde in Paris, both quarried from pink Aswan stone, resting Thames side. Under Waterloo Bridge, moored in calm waters, HMS Discovery and HMS Wellington, framed by the Festival Hall on the far side of the slow running river.

A smooth approach to the City of London. The visual bliss of the Inner Temple Garden...

The eye-catching wrought iron arches of Blackfriars Bridge, closely followed by the 1972 built London Bridge (the fallen down one, exported and rebuilt in America). A flamed monument with 311 steep, winding steps; he had personally counted them with the kids. Billingsgate fish market and Pudding Lane, where the Great Fire of London actually started. A quick negotiation of Upper and Lower Thames Street. Glimpses of a flying Union Flag on the medieval Tower of London that still housed the Crown Jewels. The symbolic 'Tiger Tavern', originally supped in by Peter the Great and supposedly slept in by the first Queen Elizabeth. Tower Hill with a view of the famous bridge miraculously at attention. On a mound, a solemn-looking Merchant Navy Cenotaph. The Royal Mint, pennies from heaven. A winding left into the Minories, 'Tubby Isaacs' stall where one can feast on a bowl of 'lovely jellies'. Petticoat Lane, a busy Sunday street-market, nearby Spitalfield's veg market. 'The Three Nuns 'and none too far away, 'Dirty Dicks'. Houndsditch, "I can get it for you wholesale". Aldgate and Aldgate Pump ahead with its antique brass dog's head. 'Ye Olde' Leadenhall Market. Streets of banks. The struggling Old Lady down on the right 'thread a needle'. Left side, the raised portico and six Corinthian columns of the Portland-stone Mansion House. Cheapside towards Wren's Dome of Saint Paul's Cathedral. The demanding Old Bailey. Holborn Viaduct, trains in the sky! Smithfield's meat market, nothing quite like it. Look, the great dome of St Paul's! Newgate. Treasured Hatton Garden down on the right. The new Daily Mirror building to the left. A listed Victorian (Pru') terracotta-coloured monster to the right. Obliged to stop for a quick red light at Staples Inn — Ye Olde sixteenth century gabbled black and white Tudor shops. Over the green lights Gray's Inn, left behind to the right. On the left, the Patent Office and the Silver Vaults in the Lane. High Holborn.

Hold on guys, crossing the Kingsway into New Oxford Street.

Georgian buildings on the right obscuring the British Museum with its plundered treasures. The empty high-rise 'Centre Point' towering in front of them. Over St Giles Circus, leaving the entertaining Dominion behind on the corner of Tottenham Court Road. A slow purr along Oxford Street. Over on the left, the famous celluloid Wardour Street opposite 'Bourne & Hollingsworth' on the corner of Wells Street — overlooked by a tall revolving Post Office Tower restaurant.

To the left, Berwick Street with its street market. Oxford Circus. The BBC and the Saint George's Hotel, up by Langham Place. Left into Regent Street. A quick peep of the London Palladium all lit up in Argyle Street, 'Liberty's' and Carnaby Street to the left. A sharp right into Maddox Street. Well-cut Saville Row to the right. Berkeley

New Business and New Friends

Square, the land of Rolls Royce showrooms and Joe Coral's 'Sportsman's' gaming club oblique to the Arab Chamber of Commerce, Zak knew *sayanim* diligently monitored it for Mossad. Fashionable Bond Street again. Mayfair, 'Claridges', The 'Connaught' and other prestigious hotels. The Roosevelt Memorial — the eagled American Embassy. A left swing into South Audley Street, Curzon Street forward — 'Annabel's' to the left, Jean Paul sitting on the edge of his seat as they had passed the 'Playboy' — lots of bunnies with tales to tell. The busy 'Hilton' further on down Park Lane, taste-buds relishing past 'Zombies' drunk in 'Trader Vics'. Around Curzon Gate. Travelling north on Park Lane's carriageway. The Dorchester Hotel and 'Grosvenor House' over on the right. Swell digs forever viewing Hyde Park. Marble Arch and silent Speakers' Corner! The busy 'Cumberland' behind sleeping water fountains on the right. A left down the Bayswater Road, Kensington Gardens, the Serp' with its Royal swans. A doggy cemetery at Victoria Gate. Four cascading fountains set in an Italian renaissance garden nearby to Marlborough Gate. A signpost for 'Peter Pan' and the 'Serpentine Gallery'. Glimpsing the Swan Pub just down from Lancaster Gate Station. Silently coming to rest outside the 'Royal Lancaster'.

The Dallas businessman was sitting tall in the 'Grey Bridge of Weir' front saddle. The enlightened Jean Paul, enamoured at viewing little old London Town from a 'Roly Poly' and listening to a poem depicting The King's Road Chelsea, from where they had started their Central London sightseeing tour...

Finally, the trio rounded off the enjoyable evening with a 'nightcap' in the ground floor bar of the 'Royal Lancaster', Stan and Jean Paul, both well aware of what their right arms were for.

Prospective business talk had ensured a long night between shorts and travel stories. Stan chose to mention his forthcoming trip with Jean Paul to Nigeria and other West African countries. Later, Stan seemed to take great pride in explaining how the second-hand clothing game operated. It appeared that Stan paid the American charity organisations a tonnage price for collecting the otherwise free second-hand clothes from the Southern States' residents. The unsorted mass of clothes was then delivered by freight train or trucked to Stan's Dallas depository. At the depository or plant, the cast-offs were stored, sorted and graded, before being bailed for transporting to shops and bazaars all over the world. Unwanted assorted tonnage would become white or coloured wiping rags which Stan sold to ships chandlers or oil refineries. The astute Texan realised the Londoner was enamoured with the business and went to his hotel room to fetch an FOB price list for all the graded items of secondhand clothes which included unlined and lightweight men's jackets.

While they waited for Stan, Jean Paul enlightened Zak about the scare in the USA that year of a possible killer sickness, first brought to the worried medical authorities' attention by an ailing male airline steward who had spread it to his gay friends on Fire Island. The new illness had been named GRID (later in 1982 the terrifying illness was re-named AIDS)...

By the time Zak told Stan to watch out for the sweet-talking Nigerian women in Lagos, it was early morning. It was apparent to the new-found trio that a special bond had been struck as they shook hands and said goodbye.

It was with delight after receiving Elissar's intent to purchase via the Arab Chamber of Commerce in London and learning Stan was back in Dallas from his world trip, that Zak contacted Dallas to find out if Stan could indeed supply ten tons of second-hand unlined or lightweight jackets for the up-and-coming Egyptian executives!

Consequently, Zak made arrangements to visit the 'Windy City' to make sure of the supply, state and standard of the tonnage.

CHAPTER EIGHTEEN

Dallas: July 1976

A Second-hand Remark

ZAK departed London–Gatwick in the early, exceptionally hot Summer of 1976 on a Texan airline non-stop to Dallas. Seemingly travelling in style, seated in extra-large, tan, cowhide seats, aboard a wide-bodied 'Braniff' jumbo jet. Zak could never understand, later, how those oil rich Texans could allow an airline such as 'Braniff' to go 'bust'!

Stan met Zak warmly, with a 'Hi, Kid' on arrival at the well laid-out Dallas airport, minus the orange tie. Otherwise, the greeting American had been wearing the same clothes as when he'd last visited London!

They'd driven into Dallas in the Texan's new American 'Vogue' compact car. Zak both curious and excited, as the drive followed the same one-way causeway that introduced the weekly rave TV series, 'Dallas'. Somehow, Zak could hear and feel the rousing signature music of the soap-box opera as they sped towards the Loews Anatole Hotel on Stemmons Freeway, right opposite the Dallas World Trade Centre that bright afternoon.

Half expecting to see 'J.R.', Zak entered the opulent-looking, golden hotel with Stan in close pursuit. The large, rectangular, glass-covered atrium housed ultra-modern columned shops and six restaurants, ranging from a deluxe hamburger 'joint' to authentic Chinese, plus a café under a four-tier pagoda figurine. All the units were laid out diagonally in oblongs, enhanced by an array of square-shape gardens displaying prime foliage and fruit trees.

There were even three drop-globe lamp posts uniquely positioned on each corner of the mini gardens which appeared diamond-shaped against the grand bordered floor. 'Loews' boasted nine hundred rooms, from a demi-suite to the Presidential suite, as well as an executive conference centre, three lounges, a thousand-seater theatre and a health spa with indoor and outside pools.

Zak had been obliged to quickly unpack and shower, with Stan seemingly glued to his side in the reserved luxurious suite. Stan appeared almost over-anxious to whisk his potential buyer off to lunch, so much so that Zak felt embarrassed by the American's presence, until Stan explained:

"My wife has prepared a special meal for you."

Stan's wife, Rose, was a thin, dried-up, plain-Jane of a lady, about the same age as her husband. She obviously wore the 'second-hand pants'! Her cooking was also second-class, plain and without imagination.

When the over-cooked meal became a left-over, Rose waylaid Zak and showed off her spacious bungalow. She seemed to take pride in showing the Londoner a large walk-in closet, even bragging about the quality and grand assortment of her (hanging) second-hand wardrobe. Unsubtly, Rose let her guest know in unnecessarily bad taste that she understood the second-hand business just as well as her husband, having inherited the plant and trading company from her dear, deceased Father.

A Second-hand Remark

Zak had been eager to leave 'second-hand Rose' to inspect the plant and see the goods, but she buttonholed him again. Proudly slapping a framed photo of their pathologist doctor son into his hands, before Zak could kiss the *mezuzah* goodbye, Rose claimed her son had been on duty at Dallas Parkland Hospital the very day President Kennedy's Catholic incarnation service had been administered by Father Huber, on the 22nd November 1963.

The second-hand clothing plant was situated directly alongside the commercial railway sidings of the depository where Lee Harvey Oswald had worked and fired the historic shot that killed the President of the United States.

Or, had the shot been meant for Governor Connally, who became Secretary of the Navy after Marine buck-sergeant Oswald received his honourable discharged? Stan confided:

"Zak, as I understand it, Connally may well have signed and issued new trumped-up discharge papers after Lee came back 'from Russia with love'."

"Are you telling me that Lee Harvey Oswald was aiming to shoot at Governor Connally, not President Kennedy?!"

"Some folks from around here reckon so."

"That's unbelievable, Stan. Do the FBI know?"

"I guess so. Anyway, they won't know the truth about the President and whether there were two guns until Connally dies."

"How come, Stan?"

"Well, Connally still has fragments in his body either from the miracle bullet or another shot."

"Remarkable, Stan!"

"Yea Kid, I'll take you to see where it all happened later, it's like a shrine there now."

"And the guy who shot Oswald?"

"Ruby?"

"Yes, the 'assassin's assassin'."

"Well, the name of 'Majestic' is whispered, but we don't talk about such high flying things down here," Stan exclaimed with some corny reserve!

The Londoner recalled that he'd been in the Railway Hotel in Iserlöhn with Daphna and the kids, reliving his army days, when the President had been shot.

The inside of Stan's plant could only be described as the black hole of Calcutta. It contained huge piles of dirty, smelly clothing everywhere. There were hundreds of waist-high, well-used fibre bins into which the Mexican 'wetbacks' sorted the different types of clothes and rags, then re-sorted them and even re-sorted them again into the same kind of article, fabric, colour, or even size before baling the graded orders for shipment.

Stan further explained with professional humour:

"The more we grade the cast-offs the more they cost!"

Putting on some clean dungarees, Stan and his nervous Mexican foreman then guided the dungaree-clad Zak to the pile of reserved jackets for his Egyptian order. Under the dim lighting, the jackets looked very suitable for the would-be up-and-coming Egyptian executive and possibly they would open up a whole new market. It could be the 'Golden Fleece' the Londoner was looking for.

Stan's blend of hospitality had been fun during Zak's three-day visit to the 'Windy City.' He'd been wined on Californian white wine and dined in great style at Stan's favourite, yet inexpensive, speciality restaurants. Why, large, fresh, chilled oysters in the open shell, delicious like the Red Sea prawns but not considered kosher, had only cost $2.99 a dozen.

Stan appeared to take genuine delight in introducing his visitor to other businessmen, who were, in the main, dressed like cowboys, in stetsons or high-heeled boots.

Walking around downtown Dallas with Stan, Zak had been casually introduced to a young Dallas widow. She'd, recently inherited a run-down shirt factory, which had been making army shirts for 'Uncle Sam'. The attractive widow took an instant shine to Zak when she'd been made aware of his textile and worldly experiences... The Dallas butterfly personally delivered a gift to Zak's hotel room. A smart, khaki officer's walking-out shirt.

"Zak, honey," she later told him under a warm, starry sky:

"My heart is like a prairie fire over you." Then she tried to give the Londoner a sample of what he was going to miss if he did not take up her amorous offer. He'd taken a rain-check on that one and gone to open an account at 'Nieman Marcus' prior to his departure. Fortunately, at the time, Zak managed to speak to one of 'Nieman's' Directors whose expert opinion, regarding three of London's prestigious stores, had run like a punchy 'ad':

"Certainly, 'Selfridges' haven't got it. We have it, 'Harrods' and 'Liberty's' have it."

"Meaning class?"

"You've got it, sir!"

"Thank you."

"Thank you sir, have a good day."

•

Before Zak finally bid *adios* to Dallas and the 'dampened prairie fire', Stan made sure his London visitor had a farewell drink in his favourite cocktail bar, where and when the Jewish Texan reflected:

"Kid, I'll have you know, Racquel Welch used to serve me Margaritas at this very table... before she became a big movie star."

* * * *

CHAPTER NINETEEN

Cairo: Part II

Prolonged Stay at the Nile Hilton

THAT morning, between the Egyptian cotton sheets, Zak was suddenly disturbed from his slumber. He wondered where he was on hearing the room door slam, followed by a muffled commotion. Zak had been further surprised to hear an Arabic female voice, giving out sharp instructions. Bravely opening his eyes to the bright Cairo sunlight streaming in over the Nile, Zak felt elated at the sight of Fossetta. She was gesturing to, and ordering about, two young uniformed waiters, instructing the very bewildered pair, the wide-eyed Londoner supposed, on how and where to park the laden breakfast trolley. Amused, Zak did not interfere but just lay there, watching the early morning show, mentally stripping Fossetta from her flimsy, bright floral peignoir, as he played with his rather large erection which protruded over his 'Homs' under the fine Egyptian cotton bed sheets.

How the deuce could he have forgotten about Fossetta last night, Zak mused, as the waiters left without begging for a tip!

Since he had not been asked to sign the breakfast tab, Zak assumed that Fossetta must have charged the breakfast to the Moroccan Tourist Department! Fossetta looking like a bird of pleasure, approached Zak with a red flower between her flashing white teeth, dropped the sweet smelling rose onto his tanned chest, then planted a meaningful peck on his forehead! Certainly, a very unusual action by an Arabess even if she were Moroccan and liberated, thought he.

"Good morning, Zak."

"Good morning, dimpled one. Am I dreaming?"

"No. Get up, sleepy head. Come have breakfast with me on the balcony; it's my way of saying 'thank you' for the dress. The desert butterfly then 'tortured' the Londoner as she flew from the room to set out breakfast, calling back to him:

"How do you like your coffee?"

Jumping out of bed Zak coolly called back:

"No sugar, sugar... just honey, honey."

"Black?"

"But, of course."

"But, of course," she'd repeated.

Doing what a man has to do in the bathroom, Zak watched his erection stay up as he emptied his bladder. Arab women had always eluded him, maybe because he was the 'wrong cousin'. He began to wonder if they were as exciting as Persian women, who claimed to be God's gift to mankind. Vivacious Vahsti and the lusting Leila came to mind during past rendezvous at the Teheran 'Hilton' and 'Sheraton'. A quick splash over his hands and face, a dab of toothpaste, flick on the 'Braun', a shot of 'Aramis', bath towel in place, electric toothbrush stowed, Zak adopted a debonair style and manner, then confronted the umber-goddess. He'd been amazed to find Fossetta had discarded her peignoir and was stretched out on a lounger sporting a tight, two-way stretch, cerise bikini!

Zak could not resist placing his cool lips on an exquisite closed eyelid, becoming further excited at the touch of the Arabess's smooth, fragrant skin as his bold lips moved down her upturned face. Joyously, Zak felt her searching tongue find his as his fingertips gently encircled a ripe nipple. The telephone rang! Fossetta clung to the bold Englishman passionately, not wanting him to end their kiss. Zak willed himself to pull away from the Arabess's unquenched mouth to answer the phone. It was time-wasting Elissar! At the sound of the Egyptian's discordant voice the Londoner's *yugger* went into the flaccid position.

Zak only half listened to Elissar's laborious apologies in broken English, admitting he could not acquire the external currency to open the Letter of Credit.

"I will call for you at four to take you to the airport, Mister Zak."

Elissar then ended the conversation by slamming the phone down, obviously not waiting to hear a pissed-off reply.

"Don't bother yourself, Elissar," Zak shouted down a dead telephone.

On Zak's return to the balcony, the hungry butterfly was perched on her lounger, devouring her breakfast. Without comment, she poured a long fruit juice. For reasons best known to herself, Fossetta gave Zak a look 'boiling' at about the same temperature as the chilled grapefruit juice. The Arabess looked incredibly capable and topless, as she put a plate of *Cordon Bleu* scrambled eggs and mixed grill together. Zak decided there and then to defrost the sensitive beauty by toasting and *shmoozing* her with a delicious fruity cocktail. The Arabess did indeed melt with Zak's latent words and cosy glass clinking, before asking him a double question:

"What happened to you last night, Zak? Why didn't you contact me for a nightcap?"

Suddenly Fossetta's fascinated eyes became fixed on the rising bulge coming back to life beneath Zak's bath towel, which was beginning to slip from his waist... Spontaneously, with her new-found interest Zak took delight in letting the towel tantalisingly slide to the floor, nonchalantly revealing his mock-leopard 'Homs'. Fossetta's tell-tale sparkling eyes 'showed promise' before she scolded:

"You tease, Zak" then she sharply handed him the scrumptious looking breakfast that she arranged.

Sausages, scrambled egg, ripe banana and a passion fruit. Once devoured, Fossetta set about also revealing her exquisite dimples...

Prior to going down to the hotel pool for a swim and a late luncheon, Fossetta and Zak went to visit the nearby Egyptian Museum. They passed through the 'Hilton's' lobby into the streets of Africa's largest city, where merchants had traded internationally since the 13th century. It appeared to Zak at the time that all of Cairo's eight million inhabitants were bustling and hustling about outside the gardens of the Colonial-looking two-storey museum. The French, Zak learned later, had built the museum in 1920 to house the mysteries of the Dynasties.

As Zak was buying the entrance tickets they became caught up in a sudden rush. It had been as though everybody around them was about to catch the last train out of Cairo. The 'Hiltonites' were consequently jostled up to the first floor ... to find displayed the treasures and 'glit of gold' of 'Tutankhamun'. Both gazed awestruck at the glittering gold in the original glass cases and state Harold Carter had left the extraordinary 1922 archaeological finds. They managed to shuffle around hand in hand to find and view the gold and jewelled decorated coffin of Tutankhamun, the 'Dancing Pygmies' and other antiquities, all in an atmosphere of a crowded railway station...Back in the comparative calm of the ground floor, Fossetta and Zak came across a small group of blue-beret, Finnish UN soldiers who, apparently, were on leave from their peace-keeping duties. The blond soldiers seemed more interested in looking at the hennaed-haired Arabess in her dazzling 'Liberty' print-material midriff and skirt, that perfectly covered her dimpled cheeks, rather than view the remarkable, dead relics of another yesterday.

In harmony Fossetta and Zak passed the intriguing statue of the Goddess, Aphroditopolis, when the platoon stood smartly to attention for Fossetta's departure, calling out in obvious Finnish to her.

"*Näkemiin, viehättävä naine.*"

"Thank you, goodbye, soldier boys."

Clinging to Zak the knowing linguist half-turned and waved goodbye again to the gaping troops. A few cool steps and they had left the dark, musky museum behind and were back walking in the blazing, hot sunlight. A quick courtesy call to a nearby export customer's shop called 'Penguin 66', with the happy Fossetta on his arm much enhanced Zak's image with the astonished 'Penguins'.

Pool-side at the 'Hilton', Zak took it upon himself to order a *salade niçoise* and a bottle of iced Reim Cléopatre, before they dived into the enticing, soft water. The Londoner was tickled pink to find himself being capriciously splashed and molested by the luscious Fossetta. They'd played and swum together with great gusto until the waiter called them for their exotic chilled salads and intriguing Egyptian nectar. Zak felt he may have boobed when ordering wine for such a well bred Arabess, but no!

As they drank the last drop of cool Reim Cléopatre from the vineyards of Aby Hummais, Fossetta lured Zak with:

"I believe you chose a wine with aphrodisiac qualities. Must you leave *Al Qahirah* today, Zak? Stay a few nights."

"Impossible, intoxicated butterfly. I was forced to sign a declaration to leave the hotel by four this afternoon."

He had been stunned by the Arabess's uninhibited reply:

"Come on, Zak, I have a big double bed in my room. You can move in with me for as long as I'm here."

"Stay as the guest of the Moroccan Government, hey?"

"Yes," she said with a smile. It had been an offer Zak felt he couldn't refuse.

"But what about the wagging tongues in the bazaar, Fossetta?"

"No problem for me here in *Al Qahirah*, Zak."

"Okay, let's go and unwrap another Arabian Night's fantasy and really mess up my bed before I move in with you then."

"Wonderful, will you promise to teach me to make love with my mind, Zak?"

"If you promise not to tell the second Attaché."

Fossetta and Zak were involved in very heavy lovemaking when he heard someone enter the room.

God! Fossetta hadn't shut his room door. Zak craned his neck to be confronted by the envious, feasting eyes of Elissar gawking at the yielding naked body of the oblivious Arabess moving on top of her new-found Englishman.

The Londoner felt elated as he gave Elissar the 'V' sign with his glutinous fingers as Fossetta, unaware of the intruder, zithered the well-sprung bed springs.

"Get lost. Get out of here," Zak yelled, inducing Fossetta to excitingly exclaim:

"Yes, yes Zak: I understand, I willingly give you my mind and body. Do what you want with me."

Fossetta's sound of joy made Elissar retreat in realization of a modern Arab girl's capabilities. Slamming the door shut behind him in anger caused a rather draughty vacuum. Still zithering, Fossetta breathlessly mumbled in wonder:

"What was that *Khamsin*, Zak?"

"Only a bad wind from the Pharaohs taking it out on the door," he managed to utter, as Fossetta, gasping for air, climaxed again, screaming out:

"Is that another way of making it with the mind, Zak, or a *Haboob*?"

"Sure is." Zak uttered, not knowing what a *Haboob* was anyway.
"Tell me, Zak."
"You are beyond imagination, my uninhibited one. Yes, yes, yes, you put knowing Persian women to shame."

Elissar's depressed nephew, Captain Hussein, with his pulchritudinous young Egyptian wife, a blue rinsed blonde, had seen fit to visit Zak at the 'Hilton' during his extra stay-over. The good-looking Egyptian couple kept coming along to spy on Zak without mention of their uncle, when Fossetta was busy glozing. The self-important nephew made it abundantly clear that his wife was willing 'to be of service' during Zak's stay in Cairo, providing they received first-class British Airways tickets and accommodation in London! For safety reasons, Zak took a rain-check on that one, not knowing if the service was meant to be secretarial or sexual…

The delayed Londoner stayed on an extra week with Fossetta, without once setting eyes on the long-length, black-net, gold-tinselled, trimmed Arab dress, having completely possessed her mind and body during endless nights and hot days. Zak found Fossetta most interesting to listen to between love scenes and eating *couscous*, since she had a great knowledge of export procedures and International Banking. Eventually, the reality of pressing business and ticking bank clocks in the City started to beckon Zak back. Because all flights out of Cairo were over-booked, the Londoner persuaded Fossetta to get him ticketed direct to LHR on the clout of her father's ministerial position.

However, when the time came for Zak to pack his case in Fossetta's hotel room, he felt loathe to leave.

At Cairo Airport, Fossetta started to sob all over Zak's new pale-blue 'Montague' shirt, a present from 'Penguin 66', before telling him with unconventional Moroccan humour:

Prolonged Stay at the Nile Hilton

"Zak, you have reached parts of my mind and libido that have not been reached before."

"Wonderful for you, *Mademoiselle*. But tell me, what did you do with the black-net, gold-tinselled, trimmed Arab dress?"

"Oh! I gave it to one of the chamber maids in the 'Hilton'."

"*Touché.*"

On final departure, Fossetta promised to visit Zak when she sat for her final UN Interpreter examination in High Holborn, within walking distance of his London showroom! A promise that blossomed ...

Fossetta's metalinguistic London visits were enhanced with her substantial Arab import interests, and her wonderful marinated chicken and *merguez couscous royale*, with spicy *harissa,* side salads, all prepared in her compact Hampstead flat, near the Israeli Ambassador's residence in Avenue Road, North West London.

* * * * *

Forbidden Yesterday

CHAPTER TWENTY

Düsseldorf: 18th October 1985

At Behest of Mossad

ON arrival at Düsseldorf from Brussles, Zak promptly telephoned Herr Lieber, a well-known customer, who ran a high-fashion sportswear business from a sixth-floor showroom in the 'Imotex' textile complex in Neuss, not far from the Airport. Openers over, Zak conveyed:

"Herr Lieber, I'm at Düsseldorf airport with a fast-moving ski-suit. When can I see you?"

Herr Lieber seemed pleased to receive Zak's call and readily agreed to an immediate appointment.

Paying off the taxi driver, Zak made his way to the lifts and Herr Lieber's showroom. After a funny British joke about an Irishman, a Scotsman and a Jew, and a couple of *Schnapps* together, the overweight *Deutscher* was like putty in Zak's hands.... The visiting Englishman did not have to talk the amused German into buying the rest of the Spanish ski-suits for top Mark.

At Behest of Mossad

Having acquired a corporate signed order, Zak was offered a lift from 'Imotex' into town. The lucrative sale, coupled with a ride and an invitation to take a light meal was a nice one indeed... Zak found himself sitting in the 'Nachrichten Treff' café on the very opulent Königsalee in downtown Düsseldorf which was steeped with mixed memories from his days soldiering with the 'Queen's'.

Things were still going Zak's way as the trendy bar was situated less than a couple of hundred yards away from the Park Hotel, where Zak, the man with a mission for Mossad, had an overnight reservation...

Next morning in the 'Park', Zak took his time over breakfast before hiring a taxi to Düsseldorf *Messe*, where 'IGEDO', the 'International German Fashion Show' was being held.

During his walkabout that lasted well into the afternoon, Zak could not help but feast his eyes on the latest in *Deutsche* fashion in the huge exhibition halls. However, the *schöne,* German models were really the centre of attraction. Alas, the clock, Mossad and Munich were calling as the Londoner dragged himself away from the fabulous display — devouring a tasty, king-size *knackwurst* — during the taxi ride to Düsseldorf airport...

Quickly disembarking from Lufthansa internal flight 982C at München-Riem with inevitable memories of the distraught Clarissa crying in the 'München-Sheraton', Zak was not fully responsive to Rurik's warm greeting. Rurik looked well, although he'd put on a lot of weight around the midriff area since the Londoner had last visited the Bavarian Capital.

Rurik drove slowly into München in his bright red, sixties Oldsmobile car. Its big bumpers and chrome fittings were in noticeably good condition. Strangely, Rurik seemed apprehensive to start a conversation or talk business!

"By the way, how is the hotel business, Rurik?" Zak asked as an opener.

"Great. I hope to sign a contract for a new 'Hyatt' hotel with Mobutu and his crowd this year."

"In Zaïre?"

"You know Zsa Zsa spent her childhood there?" Rurik asked rather boastfully.

"That's right, you once told me your wife's uncle was a negrophile priest in the Belgian Congo."

"Right, and its stood me in good stead with Mobutu and his little black boys."

"Did you know Mobutu was born *Joseph Désiré Mobuto* back in 1930?" Zak asked rather informatively.

"Get away!" Rurik answered in surprise.

"True. Anyway, I wish you luck in Zaïre."

"Thanks, Zak, but I will need a 'sugar daddy' until the contract is signed. You know anyone?"

"Rurik, you know I'm counting the pennies."

"Yea, so you told me, but I will become a millionaire if the deal goes through in Kinshasa," Rurik stressed in anticipation of a monetary advance. Zak changed the subject, to avoid being asked for a risky loan by the Slav.

"Before I forget, Rurik, Maurice sends his love."

"Great, you made time to see him in Brussels."

"Sure did."

"Thanks, did you see any of the *Frummers*?"

"The religious owners?"

"Yea, the 'Palestinian cowboys', as we call them over here."

"No, only the workers."

"Oh!"

"Did you book me into the Penta Hotel, Rurik?"

"For sure, Zak. But why did you want to stay there?"

"Behest of Mossad."

"Very interesting. Tell me all about them."

As they drove towards the downtown 'Penta' Zak filled Rurik in on the past chain of events and 'sexpionage' with a Mossad butterfly, all of which had resulted from a casual chat during a meal with good old Udi.

Zak also told Rurik of the strong interest Mossad had shown in Franz, during the visit to the Israeli Embassy in London last August.

"By the way, I gave them some of the Nigerian installation data from Steilmanns that Franz copied from his private file for Dikko, the last time I was here."

"O.K. But I bet you they lifted our fingerprints, Zak."

"Do you think so?"

"For sure, baby."

"No problem for you and Franz, I copied the copies."

"Well done. Do you think they will pay for Franz's expertise?"

"I will have to tighten up on that when we have Franz's firm commitment," Zak replied.

"What commitment?" queried Rurik.

"Why do you think I'm here?"

"Yea, of course, they want to be sure."

"Right, they're set on getting into Nigeria proper."

"How do you intend getting Franz's commitment?"

"You tell me, Rurik."

"No problem whatsoever, baby. If they can shell out five million US Dollars, Franz will do anything."

"They gave me a handshake and *'Mazel un Brocheh'* on the deal, although my gut feeling tells me they consider themselves to be fishing in very deep waters."

"Zak, those Mossad guys don't fish or dish out that kind of bait for nothing, you know."

"What do you mean?"

"I wonder what they really want?"

"To be able to wade deeper into Nigeria, of course."

"Maybe," Rurik said, apparently without giving further consideration to the important issue.

"So, when are we seeing Franz, Rurik?"

"I'm picking him up later; we'll be over to the 'Penta' about nine-thirty. He's not too well, you know."

"What's the problem?"

"Stomach trouble; he's drinking too much."

"Oh dear!"

"He keeps on being sick," Rurik cried.

"What about dinner then?"

"We are both short of change, Zak. You go ahead, eat in the hotel or where you want. We can talk in the 'Penta' later; trust you will pay for the drinks?" Rurik queried.

"Yes, of course, but you're welcome to join me now for a meal."

"No, that's O.K. Hey, did you know Franz has been reinstated at Steilmanns?"

"You didn't tell me! Wow, that's really great news."

"For sure, the *shikker* has his old job back there."

"Unbelievable. Is he fully reinstated?"

"Unless he's 'bull-shitting' me; it sounds more like he's got the run of Steilmanns."

"That's wonderful news, Rurik."

"Ha, ha, ha. You can say that again... There we are, the 'Munich Penta' is ahead." As the Oldsmobile crossed over Rosenheimer Strasse into the Hochstrasse, Zak experienced a strange premonition as he noticed a road sign pointing to Salzburg in Austria. He sensed he would be going there soon.

"Look, Zak, that's the Deutsches Museum across the Isar river and behind you is the Gasteig — Kultur Zentrum," Rurik exclaimed and in turn pointed out.

"They're great-looking buildings, Rurik. The 'Penta' also looks a biggy."

"Not really, she only has some five-hundred rooms and a dozen suites."

"I can really tell you're in the hotel business, Rurik."

"Sure, I'm an established 'Regency Hyatt' promoter now."

"Who promoted you?"

"The Vice President."

"Of the United States?"

"No, Paul Novey from the 'Hyatt' in Chicago."

"Okay, Rurik, just pulling your leg. Anyway, thanks for meeting me and the smooth ride."

"Thanks for nothing, we're buddies, baby. Hang on, I'll get your case out of the trunk..."

"Thank you, see you later. Rurik, make sure Franz brings his passport with him tonight."

"O.K., if that's what it takes" Rurik managed to utter through an open mouth and dropped jaw, before asking:

"So, when are you going back?"

"I have the last Lufthansa flight back to London tomorrow evening. Franz's passport is a must, understand?"

"O.K., I know what you're asking, Zak. *Auf Wiedersehen.*"

"*Wiedersehen*, see you later in the lobby."

"Yea, for sure, Zak."

Zak quickly checked into Room 717 in the pleasant 'Penta', surprised to find a basket of fresh fruit and a bottle of chilled 'Henkell Trocken' Sekt on the writing bureau, displaying a greeting card! At first sight of the choice selection, Zak wondered why the special treatment. Maybe it was because he'd flashed his 'Penta' VIP card down at reception on registering. But the *'Shalom'* alongside his name on the greeting card made Zak wonder about the long-arm of Mossad and the special room service.

Zak wasn't hungry, with thoughts of Franz's sickness and Rurik's solemn face. The bagged snack from Lufthansa, the *Knackwurst*, and the meal in Brussels with Jean Paul from the night before were still with him. Zak decided to shower, nap and miss a meal before going down to the bar to meet up with Franz and Rurik.

By ten o'clock there was no sign of Rurik or Franz! The Londoner was just about to make a call to Rurik's home, when the pair appeared at the entrance of the hotel. Zak stayed put, sipping his Hock and watching them search him out. Franz looked more or less the same as when they'd first met, at the end of last April. The West German's mousey-coloured hair was cut shorter, further accentuating his big ears. However, the most noticeable feature about Franz was his extended beer-gut and droopy moustache. The same, well-worn, black leather bomber jacket that had fitted Franz perfectly last spring, now pulled at the shoulder seams across his wide back. Franz's tall stature seemed reduced by his extra girth, as he brashly wiped his steamed-up heavy-rimmed spectacles with what looked like a rather grubby handkerchief that the German took from his grey, baggy trousers. Zak's memory played back the blues lyrics of Johnny Mercer: 'My mama done tol' me when I was in knee pants', at the sight of Franz's brown shoes. At that moment he was spotted by the searching pair...

"*Hallo*, Zak how are you?" said Franz, as he gave the visiting Londoner's free hand a weak shake.

"*Danke, gut,* Franz, *und Dir?*"

"Apart from my stomach playing me up, I'm also fine, I suppose."

"Just take it easy on the booze, Franz, and lose some kilos."

"*Ja*... How's Clarissa, does she still like it *schwarz?*"

"No idea, Franz. Haven't seen the Italian *farfalla* since the last time I saw Munich."

"Have you spoken with her?"

"No. Can I buy you a glass of milk?"

"Are you joking with me, Zak?"

"About Clarissa or the milk?"

"No, not the *schwarz geliebte*, the *milch*."

Franz grunted expletively as they all walked towards the 'Kindl-Bar', without Rurik having opened his mouth or indulged in any body language!

"Well, if you have stomach problems, Franz, I suggest you drink an alkali," Zak suggested helpfully.

"I would rather die before I drank *milch*, Zak."

"Okay, Franz, it's your stomach and life. What will you have to drink then?"

"*Ein grosses 'Löwenbräu'.*"

"Rurik?"

"*Nock einmal dasselbe bitte,* baby."

"Fräulein... Zwei grosse 'Löwenbräu', bitte."

Zak ordered two beers from the attentive waitress, attired in typical Bavarian costume, and stayed with his Hock.

Franz listened intently as Zak repeated the events of Mossad's overture to him. Rurik took in every word, as though it was the first time he had heard about Mossad's interest in the Nigerian Embassy communication system.

Franz seemed delighted when Zak confirmed:

"I made direct contact with Mossad in their London Embassy," showing even greater delight when Zak further mentioned:

"I personally climbed the stairs into the attic at the Israeli Embassy in London, I reckon just to have my photograph taken secretly."

Franz, sitting on the edge of his chair, exclaimed excitedly:

"Zak, I consider the whole thing workable, especially as you are dealing direct with Mossad and I'm reinstated in my old job."

"And it's common knowledge Israel want in, in Nigeria," butted in Rurik from the edge of his seat.

"That's very encouraging, you guys."

"*Ja*, but will the *shysters* pay, Zak?"

"Rurik appears to have some strong views on that one."

"Can I have another beer, Zak?" Franz asked, bluntly.

The pig, Zak thought. *Bitte und danke* were not in the German's vocabulary.

"*Fräulein... Noch zwei 'Löwenbräu', bitte.*"

"Franz, how's the Princess?" Zak asked casually, not wanting the waitress to overhear their main chat.

"*Prima.*"

Later, Zak ordered another two beers from the watching waitress. He still nursed his Hock.

Franz was half way through his third beer, when he became deathly white, and then 'threw-up'. The conversation ended for the time being, as the waitress mopped up the booth.

Whilst Franz was engaged in the washroom, Zak took the opportunity to question Rurik about Franz's trustworthiness and excessive drinking habit.

"Do you really think we can rely on Franz to play the game with us, Rurik?"

"It all depends on what the Israelis really want, Zak."

"What do you think they want, then?"

"We won't know until the eleventh hour with those shrewdies."

"I think we can trust them, Rurik."

"Don't be naïve, Zak."

"Just thinking affirmatively."

"Good for you. But you're naïve if you think you can trust Mossad, Zak. Believe me," Rurik stated knowingly.

"What are you saying?"

"One thing is for sure, we must never let them break us up. You know I had a run-in once with them?"

"You mean with the Plutonium?"

"Yea, the 'RM 20/20'."

"You told me Mossad were involved, when you fled Brussels with the wife and kids."

"Right. And Mossad don't play around, my friend."

"Rurik, I have a good memory."

"For sure."

"Anyway, I've also made payment abundantly clear, along with the conditions of our ground rules."

"Any chance of a contract, Zak?" asked Rurik, expectantly.

"You must know the 'institute' policy is not to dish out contracts or give advances."

"For sure. And the agreed amount?"

"Five mil' as we wanted, but nothing in writing."

"Yea, that's their way, Zak. Did you know the British and American Government still do not recognize Israel's sovereignty over Jerusalem?"

"Yes, that's why their Embassies are located in Tel Aviv."

"Right, right opposite the 'Hilton'. But not many people realise that, Zak."

"Well, at least the Vatican acknowledges Israel's right to existence at the moment."

"I didn't know that!"

"By the way, when we get paid, where will you bank your share?" questioned Zak.

"Vienna. And you?"

"Zurich."

Franz appeared from the men's room, looking puny and smelling like a bar of insipid washroom soap. The self-confessed alcoholic was obviously weak and giddy as they supported the reeking

At Behest of Mossad

Deutscher back to Zak's hotel room for a rest... Once Franz's head touched the pillow, he immediately went into a state of suspended unconsciousness.

With promptitude and without reason, Rurik decided that he wanted to leave before Franz came back to life. The Slav then requested Zak to put Franz in a taxi back to his precious Princess when fully revived!

"It's all very well for you to run off, Rurik, but can we trust this card, or maybe he's a joker?"

"Don't worry, Zak, he'll turn up trumps in the end."

"As long as it's not the knave of spades."

Since Franz was out cold, Rurik and Zak agreed that they should all meet up at nine-thirty the next morning.

As soon as Rurik left the room, Zak got a warning signal from his gut, which had proved only too accurate in the past, that Rurik was not 'dealing from an unknown deck'.

Later, while he was wet-nursing Franz, the telephone rang!

"*Shalom*, Zak, are you well?"

"I'm okay, Alon. It's our cold friend here."

"What's the matter with him, he's not dead, is he?"

"Not yet, he's just passed out."

"Did Rurik have anything to do with it?"

"No way. Franz has been sick, that's all. Too much beer."

"Otherwise?"

"Apart from occupying my bed and looking like an undercooked dumpling, I guess he'll be okay."

"O.K. now listen to me, Zak. Did Franz bring his passport with him?"

"I told our other friend to make sure he came with it, but he's left the hotel already."

"Yes, I know. Search Franz now; if it's there take his passport down and have it photocopied at reception."

"It's not my style to pick a sleeping man's pockets."

"What are you talking about, Zak?"

"I'm not inclined that way. I'd much rather wake him up to get his permission."

"O.K., but you must get it. I'll phone you back in half an hour to make sure you've done it."

"I'll try," Zak said, feeling momentarily estranged.

"Zak, if you don't get it, keep him there until I telephone you back. Understand?"

"Not entirely." Zak slammed the phone down, then gently shook and spoke to Franz.

"Franz... *Was is los*?"

"*Ich bin terrible*, Zak."

"Did you bring your passport with you?"

"*Ich verstehe nicht.*"

"Did Rurik tell you to bring your passport with you?"

"*Ja.*"

"Where is it?"

"In my inside pocket."

"Can I borrow it for a little while, just to copy?"

"*Ja*, it's O.K., Zak, I understand."

Zak left Franz being sick again in the bathroom, having willingly parted with his passport. The Londoner caught the express lift down to the lobby, feeling hidden eyes trained on him.

At the front counter, Zak found an on-the-make German night receptionist, who spoke English with an effeminate American accent, willing to photostat the passport in the back office, for a quick ten Marks...

On returning to the room, Zak was surprised to see that Franz appeared to be in a fitter state of mind and disposition.

"Franz, you're looking better!"

"*Ja*, Zak."

"You realise you agreed to let me photostat your passport?"

"It's O.K., Zak. I told you, I understood."

"Well done."

"I need to go home now. Have you some Marks for the taxi, Zak?"

"Sure, I'll come down with you and put you in the taxi."

At Behest of Mossad

Zak felt somehow embarrassed when passing through the 'Penta', propping up the staggering German. The Londoner dug deeply into his trouser pocket to find Franz a fifty Mark note for the taxi fare. Franz then staggered Zak with a bold request as he handed over the note.

"It's not enough, Zak. Make it two hundred and fifty."

Zak bit his tongue.

"Okay, Franz, if that's what you need. See you here with Rurik tomorrow morning at ten."

"*Bis morgen,* Zak."

"Yes, in the morning, Franz. Don't be late; *zehn Uhr.*"

"*Ja, ja*, Zak, stop worrying."

Returning to the hotel room, Zak was appalled at its state and stench, so he decided to change rooms. Then and there he phoned the duty 'Kraut' to explain his predicament.

"No problem for a VIP like yourself. I will send you a key up right away for another room, no extra charge to your bill. Same floor still O.K., sir?"

"Fine, thank you very much." The ten Marks for the photostat had not been expensive after all.

"That's O.K." The Germans seemed to use the lazy colloquialism more than the Americans, the Londoner thought...

As Zak was about to take a shower in his re-allocated room to rid himself of the stench of Franz, the phone rang!

"*Landsman* Zak, why did you change rooms to 707?"

Zak was surprised that an active Mossad agent did not use code names on an open telephone line. Feeling annoyed at Alon, Zak gave a sarcastic answer, which fell on deaf ears.

"Zak, you should not have changed rooms."

With hindsight, the Londoner would have cut out from the deal if he'd realised at the time that he was under threat from Mossad. Zak was obviously naïve without realising it, just as Rurik had said he was — or was the smell of closing a deal the reason why he had bitten his tongue again? However and regardless, Zak firmly voiced his opinion:

"Alon, just because you paid part of my expenses to get here, doesn't give you the right to tell me which bedroom to sleep in."

Surprisingly, Alon quickly backed off.

"O.K., Zak, forget what I said."

"Forgotten. But Franz is eating up my expenses."

"Don't worry about the extra expenses, Zak. Have you got the passport copied?"

"Are you asking me or telling me?"

Alon paused...

"O.K., Zak, so you've got it. As arranged, I will see you on the way back at 'Venue 88 E' at the Bush. *Shalom*, Zak, and stop worrying."

"Yeah, see you there. But tell me, Alon, why is everyone telling me to stop worrying?"

"Search me."

Zak fell asleep wondering, was Alon really in Munich or was Mossad's agent phoning from London?

Rurik telephoned early the next morning to tell Zak he wouldn't be over until eleven, because Franz was still in bed nursing a hangover.

"So, he got home safely with my extra two hundred Marks?"

"For sure, Zak."

Rurik, with his curt remark and giggle, was obviously laughing up his sleeve at Zak for having given Franz two hundred and fifty Marks for a taxi ride.

"See you and Franz in the lobby of the hotel at eleven sharp."

"O.K., Zak, we'll see you then," Rurik said without any enthusiasm in his voice.

Upon Franz's and Rurik's arrival at the 'Penta', the scenario was much the same as the night before, except Franz seemed completely revitalised. The German drank twice as many beers but without any ill effects...

About lunch time, the Slav invited the Englishman and the German back to his flat for a 'light lunch and a heavy chat' to finalise their format and ground rules for the Nigerian Link for Mossad.

Zak checked out of the 'Penta', taking his light hand-luggage back to Rurik's rented flat, located by a graceful fountain, in the Slav's huge red American car...

Zak felt nausea creeping over him on entering the run-down apartment and kissing Zsa Zsa 'hello' on her chubby cheeks in the continental way. After her guests sat down in her stifling kitchen to 'talk turkey', Zsa Zsa then carried on cooking her cheap cuts.

During the meal they really only went over ground they had already talked about. Franz suddenly decided he was expected at Steilmanns that Sunday afternoon, giving Zak a closing summation that sounded as though it were rehearsed:

"Zak, the deal sounds good to me, stop worrying. You have what you came for, and I can perform for sure with the Nigerian Link via my Boss. I promise I will give you and the Israelis my full support. I will also travel wherever, whenever if necessary, as long as my drink and expenses are paid for."

"Sounds good to me, Franz."

"For sure, Zak. I tell you I would kill my Moroccan Princess for a million US Dollars, if you know what I mean." Yes, Zak thought, as he looked down at Franz's brown shoes. The Londoner ignored his adverse gut feeling and the alcoholic's wicked remark, as his memory pounded out again:

"My mama don' tol' me when I was in knee pants."

Rurik's last words at Munich Airport that evening on bidding Zak farewell sounded solid and normal enough:

"Zak, remember... You must never allow Mossad to break us up. And don't forget to keep me closely informed. Kiss Daphna for me. Have a good trip home. Love you, baby, *ciao* for now."

Away from it all, sitting in the airpot's departure lounge, Zak recapped on past events. Something wasn't ringing true, he felt he was missing a salient point. His partners were not showing the right spirit nor the expected enthusiasm, although Franz had handed over his passport with out ado. Zak tried to shrug off his gloominess by watching the passengers for Lufthansa flight to London Heathrow getting ready to board…

All strapped in, hand-luggage stowed under the upright seat, Zak watched the lights from the Munich Terminal quickly disappear. Suddenly the jet penetrated the languorous cloud. Past thoughts of a trip to Israel to visit his daughter, Tracy, billowed through the Londoner's mind.

* * *

CHAPTER TWENTY-ONE

Tel Aviv: May 1975

Shalom, Lovely Tracy

DURING the mid-seventies, when Zak was involved in exporting to the Middle East (possibly under the ever-watchful eyes of Mossad), he found himself flying from Kuwait to Teheran and then to Tel Aviv to visit daughter Tracy. Earlier... Zak had been enlightened in Kuwait City by his good friend, Jahlil Behbehani, that many Kuwaitis wanted to buy properties in Central London, as the Kuwaitis feared the Iraqis would one day invade their Arab homeland. This desire by Kuwaitis to have a *pied-à-terre* as a retreat had unwittingly launched the buying-boom for Central London flats, which subsequently benefited the whole UK housing market.

Fossetta had introduced Jahlil to Zak and in turn he had met Sheik Nasser. The Sheik was a Royal Kuwaiti, jointly owning 'Kuwaiti Fisheries' with Jahlil. At the time of Zak's visit, 'Kuwaiti Fisheries' was next in export volume to Kuwait's oil exports. Undoubtedly, the elite Kuwaiti pair were amongst the first citizens from the Arabian Gulf to help kick-start the UK property price rise of the seventies...

Jahlil had taken the time to explain the local situation in detail to Zak as they dined together in the exquisite Revolving Tower Restaurant in downtown Kuwait. When explained, this boiled down to the fact that the Iraqis wanted an easier additional outlet to the Gulf waterway for their oil exports. According to Jahlil, the Iraqis also had big eyes on Kuwait's oil production. The wise Kuwaiti predicted that one day Iraq would start a war in the Gulf and seize whatever they could lay their hands on.

* * * *

On Zak's first visit to the Holy Land he could hear the Israeli National Anthem *(Hatikvah)* playing loud and clear, on glimpsing the green fields and golden crops as the El Al jet approached Israel, a country under arms since its miraculous birth.

Zak landed at Tel Aviv's Ben-Gurion International Airport for a three-day stop-over to see his love-sick teenage daughter, Tracy. Daughter Tracy was 'doing her thing', living and working on a *kibbutz* where she had fallen in love with a Jewish Brazilian boy and she needed some fatherly support.

Zak entered Israel on his newly-issued second British passport which was duly stamped at Ben-Gurion passport control: 25. V. 75. He'd been obliged to have a second passport in his pocket to avoid being denied entry into Arab States on anticipated future business visits, because of forbidden Israeli entry stamps in his main passport.

Tracy's good looks and charm allowed her father to be met in VIP style inside the restricted transit area of the airport, along with the young, gallant duty-officer of the day!

On taking up the reservation that Tracy had made at the 'Tel Aviv Hilton', her father found he was sharing and paying for a deluxe suite with two bedrooms. Their well-appointed suite enjoyed a wonderful view of the antediluvian port of Jaffa, overlooking the clear blue Mediterranean sea, and was well worth the Dollar price.

Later that afternoon, Zak hired a taxi for his first trip to Jerusalem, via the Port of Jaffa, with his precious daughter at his side. The trip turned out to be a memorable highlight in his life, a dream come true. Stopping in front of the dramatic Damascus Gate, Zak thrilled at the sight of the Old City and its apparent different cultures that went back to 1350 B.C. Once within the walled City, Tracy pointed out the Moslem Quarter to the left and the Christian Quarter to the right. Ahead lay the Jewish Quarter, the symbolic grave of King David, the Wall, the Dome of the Rock, a magnificent Moslem shrine built in 691 A.D., crowning the Sacred Rock of Abraham's sacrifice on Mount Moria. Noticeably, many Arab traders diligently waited outside their shops to pounce upon a likely tourist. Zak quickly picked up on the unguarded hatred in the sad traders' dark semitic faces and resentful eyes. He could not help but notice also the way the Arab traders feasted their lustful eyes on Tracy's good looks, her long blonde hair, and ripe young body. The watchful traders probably thought Tracy was Zak's young girlfriend as she'd clung presumptuously to her father as they meandered through the crowded bazaar...

Zak felt he had captured the atmosphere of the Holy City, drenched in religious blood and intrigue from past shrouded centuries. Looking in wonderment at the marble and multi-coloured mosaic Dome of the Rock, decorated with arabesque inlaid quotations from the Koran, Zak felt he'd definitely experienced the divine presence that is said to hover over the city. Finding it hard to leave the magnificent octagonal edifice under the Dome, his senses seemed to become further aware of the rift between Jew and Palestinian and somehow more readily able to understand the mentality of the Arabs and their homeland problems. After all, the locals were being treated as second-class citizens in the land of their birth.

Forbidden Yesterday

Zak felt proud the way Tracy bartered in an up-market *souk* with a shrewd Arab merchant, for an expensive Bedouin, multicoloured, patch dress, which featured a beautiful, antique, embroidered bodice insert, as well as kaftan type sleeves. The *souk* was located on the same passageway in the religious city where Jesus of Nazareth had been compelled to carry his own cross that Friday afternoon, after Pontius Pilate had washed his hands of the local matter effectively sentencing the then considered upstart Jewish Rabbi to be crucified. It is written, Jesus then slowly carried the heavy cross along the via Dolorosa to the green hill of Calvary and to crucifixion, just before the Jewish Sabbath. In those rebellious times, the Romans would have been obliged to observe the local custom to release Jesus from his crucifix, since it was forbidden for a Jew to remain nailed or affixed to a crucifixion-stake on the Sabbath. Strange, to Zak's knowledge, there was no mention in the holy scriptures about any of the disciples ever trying to bring Judas Iscariot to task for his betrayal of Jesus! It is also written that Judas later committed suicide, as Pilate did. Perhaps it had been a Jewish plot to nail Jesus's father, Joseph, to the cross for a few hours, so his son could escape from the Romans and Priest, as the Dead Sea Scrolls may some day reveal, since Jesus never did have any nail holes in his wrists or in his knees or in his ankles.

'Oh boy'! The next morning, Zak would never forget the incredible breakfasts Tracy and he had enjoyed in the 'Milk and Honey' restaurant of the 'Hilton'. The overflowing *kosher* breakfast room was situated on the lower ground floor of the renowned hotel and led out to the swimming pool. The fresh smell and sight of the filled bread baskets and choice fruits on display were still implanted in his mind and his senses. The many different kinds of herrings, salted, marinated, smoked and pickled plus special *smoltz* dishes, all prepared in the traditional way from old Middle Eastern and Mid-European recipes. All were intended to be enjoyed with an assortment of soft cream cheeses on freshly baked, seeded bread, egg loaves, black bread or brown bread, bagels. There were also glazed egg brioches, crisp plaited rolls and pletzels garnished with onion and poppy seeds to be eaten between overflowing glasses of chilled, locally-grown orange or grapefruit juice. Hot, pure ground coffee and ice-cold milk, followed by hand-folded buns, shaped like miniature envelopes, stuffed with all manner of goodies, including honey, almonds, spiced or savoury cream cheese. Eventually, one could finish off with a choice of hot blintzes topped with lashings of Galillee honey, cinnamon; or mounds of juicy Israeli fruits. One could easily start the eating ritual all over again with a differing combination, with the mental justification and a self-promise that one would miss lunch, even dinner, that day.

That evening found Tracy and her father, about to break his breakfast promise to himself, waiting outside the King David restaurant in the 'Hilton' for Tracy's Brazilian boyfriend. Tracy looked incredible and turned all heads, dressed in her long Arab kaftan, which she chose to wear barefooted!

Dinner with the tall, good-looking South American 'beau' and purring daughter Tracy had been a delightful feast. In fact it was so calm and smooth, Zak wondered why he had been needed

Before leaving Tel Aviv and his contented daughter, Zak made time to visit Daphna's first cousin, Ruth, with whom many yesterdays ago they had all attended the same school.

Ruth had in her youth emigrated to Israel, to marry Doff, a *Sabra* whom she'd previously met in London whilst he was on some kind of Zionist exchange scheme. Ruth had borne Doff three children on a *kibbutz* before he was called up and killed by a land mine during an Arab border raid. Ruth's mother, Auntie Rosie, had proudly told Zak that Doff, a Master Chef cum part time soldier, was given a full hero's funeral by the Israeli Military.

Zak could still taste the superb, hot, fried grated potato pancake known as *lutke*, pitted with diced onion, that Auntie Rosie lovingly prepared as a pre-dinner 'nosh' from the original recipe passed down from her Polish mother. The tasty result only she could achieve, since it was only Rosie who had the secret recipe.

The sun-bronzed Lena came over during the evening to see Zak, along with her resentful-looking *Sabra* husband, Udi, and one of their attractive young daughters, Abbie. They had brought a gift along, a box of Jaffa oranges, freshly picked on their affiliated *kibbutz*. The Israeli couple and their two lovely daughters had lived on the *kibzut* prior to Udi bettering himself by getting a job with the Israeli Admiralty, in the *Sabra's* endeavours to survive the high inflation and troubled waters of the Holy Land.

Lena's lingering goodbye kiss, along with the affectionate Abbie's visit, had made the evening most memorable.

Astonishingly, a powerful bond and rapport had been cemented that night between Udi and Zak!

Another lasting highlight during the short stay in Israel had been a trip to Masada and the Dead Sea, on Zak's last afternoon. The opalescent moon had been shining high above the dramatic, natural, boat-shaped fortress as they had arrived at Masada on the private tour, arranged to coincide with the expected lunar sight. Still ringing loud and clear were their *Sabra* guide's humorous words:

"Religious Jews or the '*Frummers*', as we call them here in Israel, joke that there is a direct telephone line to God from the top of Masada."

* * * * *

CHAPTER TWENTY-TWO

London: 20th October 1985

Late Night Progress

THE vibration of the Lufthansa 727 from Munich-Riem cutting back its powerful engines on touch-down at Heathrow interrupted Zak's wonderful dreams and reminiscences of Israel. Immediately upon awakening, the reality of what still had to be accomplished with Alon and Mossad, before driving home to Bournemouth that Sunday night, became uppermost in Zak's sleepy state of mind.

Clearing Passport Control, Zak nonchalantly walked past the ever-watchful British Customs Officers in the 'Green Lane'. He then proceeded, as instructed in code by Alon, during the Mossad agent's last telephone call to the 'Munich Penta'.

Accordingly, Zak hired a black cab to take him to the 'West London Hilton'... but wanting to get his circulation pumping full blast before the rendezvous with Alon, Zak requested the cabby to stop short of the given destination. Having settled the fare and tipped the cabby, Zak then quickly walked the dark hundred yards or so from Shepherds Bush Green towards Notting Hill and the nostalgic Bayswater Road.

Forbidden Yesterday

With his adrenalin running high, Zak arrived at the 88 bus stop (going east), the so-called 'Venue 88E', situated directly in front of the 'West London Hilton', the agreed meeting place with Alon.

Zak managed to 'cut off' from the tense moment by mentally reciting a simple verse he had written, many autumns ago, after a Sunday afternoon walk along the Bayswater Road where he had lived at the time...

THE EIGHTY EIGHT
FOR LANCASTER GATE

PASSING HYDE PARK
WATCHING THE KIDS AND THEIR LARKS

A WONDERFUL RIDE
AND WHEN YOU ARRIVE

OTHER SIGHTSEERS ARE GOING
THE WIND IS BLOWING

IT IS AUTUMN
ONE LOOKS WITH CAUTION

THE ROAD IS BUSY
THE SIGHT OF FALLING LEAVES MAKES ONE DIZZY

THERE IS MUCH TO SEE
ONE SPOTS FASHION TO BE

THE ROYAL LANCASTER TOWERS
KENSINGTON GARDENS WITHOUT FLOWERS

PETER PAN WITH HIS FLUTE
CHILDREN EATING FRUIT

THE LAST OF THE TOURISTS MAY BUY
THE ARTIST MAY CRY

Late Night Progress

THE SWAN PUB IS TRADING
PASSERS-BY CHARADING

THE PROSTITUTE IS NO MORE
NOW PAINTINGS GALORE

THE LOCALS ARE NOT SEEN
THEY LIVE IN THE WONDERFUL SCENE
SEVERAL STOPS BEFORE SHEPHERDS BUSH GREEN [9]

The waiting Londoner was surprised to spot the formally-dressed Mossad agent appear from the 'Duke of Clarence' pub and quickly proceed to the 'Hilton'! Lingering somewhat before deciding to shadow Alon, Zak crossed over Holland Park Avenue, coming back to 'Zulu Time' as he negotiated the opaque automatic doors into the startling hustle and bustle of the bright 'Hilton' lobby.

Zak just managed to catch another glimpse of Alon before the *Sabra* seated himself in the lounge area, at a corner table, near to a chubby, coloured pianist who was playing a well-known melody. The black guy was struggling to sing 'That Old Black Magic' in the style of 'Hutch' (Leslie Hutchinson), an old song that Sinatra also helped make famous.

Alon was all smiles as Zak sat down and seemed more than pleased to order a couple of turkey and beef club sandwiches, with a much-needed pot of black coffee and fresh cream. Not considered to be *glatt kosher*, Zak was therefore surprised at Alon's choice, since milk and flesh were not to be consumed during the same meal by a good practising Mossad agent! Due to modern refrigeration, Zak thought, the Jewish dietary laws were out of date, anyway.

"Are you well, Zak?" Alon asked with his standard opening line.
"As well as can be expected under the circumstances."

---

[9] THE ABOVE VERSE WAS WRITTEN IN 1975 BY ZAK

Zak's remark obviously unnerved Alon, as the *Sabra* asked:
"Did something go wrong or have you lost it, Zak?"
"No, not at all."
"Do you have it?"
"Yes."
"Then pass it discreetly under the table to me."
Zak took the copy of Franz's passport from his inside pocket, then performed as instructed. The Londoner wondered at the expression on Mossad agent's face as he took the 'under-the-table' delivery. Was the Israeli treacherous? After a careful long-distance inspection of the photostated West German's passport, Alon, simply said:
"Well done, Zak."
"Enlighten me, Alon, why is it so important for you to have a copy of Franz's passport?"
"We have our reasons. So you had a good trip?"
"You tell me." Zak managed to utter as the 'double-deckers' arrived via the efficient, coffee-pouring, Asian waiter. They both remained silent until Alon prepaid the bill. Zak then gulped down his much-wanted coffee, never having mastered the art of nursing a slow cup of coffee as the Continentals do.
"Are you well, Zak?"
It sounded as though Alon was 'playing silly buggers' with him, so Zak ignored Alon's reflective question.
"Alon, did you realise that Franz was very sick during the first meeting in the 'Penta'?"
"Yes. Par for the course, given the situation."
"What do you mean?" Zak asked, as the tempo went slightly upbeat and the black singer started to croon, 'I've got you under my skin'.
"Zak, when someone is doing what Franz is doing, they are either physically or emotionally sick, until they can come to terms with themselves."
"What does that mean?"
"How are you then, Zak, well?"

Late Night Progress

That same bloody question again, only this time Alon wasn't playing silly buggers, as the Mossad-trained *Sabra* took the tired Londoner's wrist and placed his index finger on Zak's pulse!

"Alon, stop playing the medic, taking my biofeedback. I want to get back home tonight."

"What do you mean, Zak?" Alon asked blatantly, before letting go and then quickly picking up the nearest 'double-decker' portion.

"Come on, Alon, let's get on with this debriefing. I have a long drive in front of me and I have to get back to Heathrow first, thanks to you and your 'firm's' procedure."

"O.K. Tell me, will Franz play ball?"

"Of course. Why do you think he freely gave up his passport for copying?"

"He needs the money," Alon said with a snigger.

"Right, like all of us."

"What does that mean, Zak?"

"Well, you don't work for love, do you?"

"That's uncalled for, Zak."

"Not really, my man."

"O.K. then. Maybe we will ask you to travel again, shortly."

"No problem, as long as you pay the expenses."

"Zak, a businessman should pay his own expenses."

"I did, but your 'firm' spoilt it for us."

"Meaning Dikko?"

"For sure, when your 'firm' helped kidnap him and took him out of the game."

"That is not the way you should view it, Zak."

"I thought you understood my predicament?"

"I do."

"Good, so please stop undermining the situation."

"Meaning?"

"You are always asking more of me, Alon."

"What do you mean?"

Zak thought it was opportune to ask for a contract from Mossad.

"Give me the deal in writing, then I'll gladly pay all my own expenses, Alon."

"You know that's impossible, Zak," Alon immediately cut him dead with his impossible words.

"Why?" Zak asked, still pushing the 'cat and mouse' style conversation.

"Because we know from past experience, never, never to do business in such a way."

Zak was just too weary to argue the issue with the single-minded Mossad agent.

"*Nebbech,* let me know if and when you're ready to shadow me in Munich again. *Shalom* for now," Zak sarcastically uttered to Alon when rising from the table.

"Yea, *shalom, shalom*, Zak. You're tired, go home and get some rest. You must need it."

"If I don't fall asleep at the wheel on the M3 motorway. Like the time I left the magic of Malta behind and found myself in Intensive Care in Basingstoke General Hospital."

"You nearly killed yourself because of an Italian butterfly, Zak!" Alon mocked.

"That holiday in Malta was like an incredible movie for me, well worth the accident." Images of Clarissa in all her glory raced through Zak's mind.

"Sounds as though it must have been quite an affair with your Italian butterfly, Zak."

"Yes, but isn't this whole affair really due to Clarissa and the unforeseen meeting with Franz in Munich?"

"I never thought of it that way."

"Life is the way it is viewed, not how it is, Alon." Zak tiredly philosophised, trying to hit a nerve.

"You can say that again," Alon confirmed profoundly.

"Haven't got the time or *koách* Alon."

"Understand, I'll be in touch."

"Don't be too long making up your mind," Zak requested.

Mission completed, Zak left the sinister Mossad agent and hurried into the inky blackness of the night. Jumping into a waiting cab from the 'Hilton's' taxi rank, the out-of-pocket Londoner headed back to Heathrow...

Late Night Progress

Within twenty minutes, the old-time London night-cabby dropped Zak alongside his Jaguar, parked in the long-term car park. But the 'old lady's' battery would not come to life. God! Zak missed his lovely Daimler Vanden Plas that he'd wrecked on the M3 after his Malta holiday with Clarissa. Consequently, he was obliged to use the Airport's emergency telephone. The 'AA' arrived promptly and jump-started the dead engine, leaving Zak to face the weary miles back home to Bournemouth, alone with his thoughts.

During the drive home, Zak recalled how he had been introduced to Rurik in the Saint George's Hotel opposite the BBC in Langham Place, by the 'Colonel'.

* * *

CHAPTER TWENTY-THREE

London: Summer of 1977

The Odd Couple

A tall, debonair ex-army type, parading a fine silver-grey handlebar moustache, a 'Guards' neck-tie and highly-polished shoes claimed to have been a full colonel when Zak and the colonel chanced to meet at 32 Harley Street. The Colonel had popped into 32 without an appointment, to try and see a bone specialist. Zak had an appointment to see a dermatologist, who purported to treat the Royals. Colonel Healey-Jones introduced himself and struck up a conversation whilst they sat in a shared specialists' waiting-room. The perfumed Colonel confided to having served with the Indian Army and to have been Mountbatten's adjutant during World War II. They'd been casually exchanging business cards with a view to possibly trading together, when Zak was called in to be interviewed by the eminent 'skin-man'.

The Colonel later contacted Zak about a possible military clothing order (without an MOD number) on behalf of his principal, a Slav named Rurik. Zak made a quick note of the specification, price, quantity, destination and delivery date before informing the Colonel:

The Odd Couple

"It's an interesting enquiry, sir. I'll get back to you, if we can perform, factory wise. Or maybe I can find a 'made up' lot in the Far East, somewhere."

Looking for ways to acquire an order from the Colonel's principal, Zak's agent in Hong Kong, Bill Chan, telexed back, advising of the possibility of producing the uniforms locally. Bill's telex also mentioned that he was exploring a rumour that there was a 'job lot' of British MOD 'spec' combat uniforms, lying on the docks in Pusan in South Korea, due to a 'stale' Letter of Credit. On the strength of Bill's telex, Zak telephoned the Colonel with a starting price and made an appointment to firm up the enquiry with the aim of receiving a Prime Bank Letter of Credit.

It had been fortunate that the agreed appointment with the Colonel had coincided with his principle's visit to London. The 'old-stick's' expensive-looking card displayed his full rank and also depicted a dubious royal-looking crest of some kind. Underneath the crest was stated: 'Financial Adviser'. Zak later learnt from his policeman friend, Donald, that the crest and the Colonel were phony, and further let on:

"The supposed full Colonel only ever made Captain. He's a regular 'Walter Mitty' who became a civilian bankrupt after leaving the declining Indian Army!"

Zak kept the lunch appointment with the smartly turned out Colonel and Rurik in the roof-top lounge of the Saint George's Hotel. Rurik looked a young forty, dressed to kill in an off-white suit and pink silk shirt, set off with a shocking pink coloured tie. Rurik possessed a crop of thick jet-black straight hair, a flushed complexion and brandished a ridiculously bushy moustache, which appeared as though it could fall off at any moment. Rurik's brash outgoing manner was evident from the start. At the time Zak felt an instant dislike for the smiling Slav. Rurik was obviously a Jugoslav and spoke English with a strong American accent. Over drinks, Rurik 'bullshitted' about his wealthy Swiss and American principals and his condo' in Boca Raton, Florida.

Zak had been indifferent to lunch with the 'odd couple' and more eager to get back to the ever-loving Roxanne, who was conveniently installed in a room on the 10th floor below.

The Londoner felt bored listening to the waffling Colonel and Rurik 'shooting the shit', trying their hardest to impress him with commodity deals, C130 Hercules aircraft with NATO specs, jet fuel contracts, 'Peak' brand condensed milk from Holland, bound for Nigeria, premium Swiss Francs, US Dollars, restricted Italian Lira, Johnny Walker whisky, American cigarettes, all the way through to Nigerian Bonny Light crude oil and back to restricted, discounted Nigerian Niara and fatigue uniforms.

Zak knew from bitter experience about the 'sweet-talking' Nigerians and their phony enquiries, always requesting nonsensical offers or proforma invoices which were tantamount to seeking a licence to trade without funds.

Why, a Nigerian 'Ready, Willing and Able' or Letter of Credit, wasn't worth the paper it was written on, until it had been confirmed by a prime European bank. However, one had to be aware that there were still astute Nigerians out there, who could do a deal.

Zak remembered quite clearly how the three of them had sat at his favourite window table in the roof-top restaurant, overlooking Regent's Park. While waiting for their first course, Zak pointed out to Rurik what looked like Gloria Hunniford at lunch, and the high-rambling aviary in London Zoo which Lord Snowdon had so cleverly designed. The Colonel chipped in to point out other landmarks, from North West London to the Surrey Hills and whenever the conversation went flat during the remainder of the meal.

Humorously, Zak watched how, just to show off, Rurik picked up the bill for the fine but hurried lunch, maybe with a view to try and hook, or influence him. What Rurik did not know at the time was that his stiletto had been spotted!

Zak finally managed to excuse himself from the seemingly devious pair, to dash back downstairs to the RWA American strawberry blonde waiting expectantly in bed below.

Later he'd told Roxanne about the conversation upstairs and his visit to Nigeria in January 1975.

* * * *

The Federal Palace Hotel or the 'Bristol' were the only hotels to stay in Lagos in 1975, as the 'Holiday Echo' was not completed until the following year. It had been a waste of time for the visiting Londoner trying to do business with the Nigerians, since none of the Nigerian importers seemed to have external currency or a back-up Confirming House in those days, to enable them to trade. Ludicrously though, the 'penny ante' waiters in the Lagos hotels, while serving tasteless food, kept insisting they could do business, as they kept glancing at the 'prime black pussy' hanging around the lobby, RWA to devour a visiting 'Whitee' and his wallet.

* * * *

"Did you do it with a ravenous Nigerian chick, Zak?" the turned-on Roxanne wanted to know.

"Well, I certainly didn't lose my wallet, honey chil'."

* * * *

In due course, the Colonel telephoned:
"Can you talk, Zak?"
"What do you mean, sir?"
"Can we talk privately?"
"About what?"
"You know who, wants to know about you know what!"
"Colonel, stop playing the 'old soldier' with me, sir."

"What do you mean?"

"Come on, sir, spell it out."

The Colonel eventually requested a written quote to be sent to Rurik's principals in Switzerland. A Zug-registered commodity company! Zak knew to be wary of Zug-registered companies as they were usually 'flaky'.

However, playing the long-shot, Zak sent a quote for 100,000 desert camouflaged combat uniforms, British War Department specification, plus another quote for 8,000 tank crewmen's overalls, US specs, made from 'Dupont-Nomax' material, directly to Zug. Zak knew with a little help from his friends, he could produce the requested overalls, since he had quoted several Middle East embassies in London for the much sought-after fire-proof khaki drab. Zak also knew that every Arab Military Attaché was prepared to overlook the fact that patented 'Nomax' yarn was produced by a Zionist controlled company, and subject to the Black List.

Rurik's principal, Herr Doctor Müller from Zug, later responded by screwing everybody at the eleventh hour. With a little help from an Asian agent, the Herr Doctor located and bought the reserved parcel of uniforms behind Zak's back, during the period his London company had exclusivity to purchase the parcels from the Korean producer. Therefore, Zak despondently thought at the time, so much for Korean ethics, the dead 'Glousters' and all that, especially since the Korean company was sizeable, on a par with Courtaulds, maybe even with ICI.

Rurik's only comment, when questioned on the odious deal had been:

"The name of the game is not to pay commission, baby." How Rurik's words were to haunt Zak later on...

Foolishly Zak involved himself a second time with Müller and company, knowing now that he'd still not learnt his lesson. At the time he'd been entitled to a one per cent finders' fee for the ten

C130 transporter planes that Libya urgently needed. Zak personally received a valid contract with full spec' and delivery schedule for the C130's from a back room cockney clerk called Ian Smalley. Ian was fronting for his boss during that particular period from a little upstairs mews office at the back of Tottenham Court Road in W.1.

Disastrously, the seemingly workable deal led to Zug and Müller, but fell through, when Müller's group sent a dummy telex from Barclays Bank, Monte Carlo, offering ten NATO spec' Hercules C130's that Zak had already offered them! Checking the situation out, Zak telexed back to Barclays about a discrepancy regarding the spec' in their telex offer, only for the bank to send a cover-up telex on 6th April 1978 stating:-

KINDLY NOTE THAT OUR BANK IS ACTING IN THIS MATTER AS A SIMPLE POST OFFICE BOX.
BARSEA CARLO

Three times unlucky. Müller's group tried to screw Zak yet again with a shady Levi 501 jeans deal! However, the 'Jeans man' hadn't been too happy with the notarised and mandated copy to trade in Levi jeans via a Belgium lawyer. Supposedly the mandate was transferable. Or had Müller's group meant disposable?

Thanks to Bill in H.K., Zak found out before opening an L/C how an ex-employee of 'Levi Strauss' had illicitly started manufacturing his previous employer's brand denimwear, until Levi's special agents traced the manufacturing scam to Taiwan. Zak received by Express Post a newspaper clipping from Bill confirming the rip-off. Accordingly the American Government via 'Levi Strauss' were obliged to put pressure on the Taiwanese Government before the Far East sham jeans operation was eventually closed down.

* * * * *

CHAPTER TWENTY-FOUR

Bournemouth: Christmas 1985

The Deal Firms Up

DECELERATING his mind and Jag, Zak eased off the Wessex Way dual carriageway and drifted up the slip road to Bournemouth's Richmond Hill roundabout. Automatically, he opened the nearside window before engaging a lower gear on entering the round Square. The towered, sloping clock showed after midnight. Zak fellt delight as the fresh sea breeze swished over his fingers and through his hair. Relieved to be nearly home, Zak glanced up at his penthouse flat, overlooking the clock and the Pleasure Gardens. The home-comer was pleased to see the welcome light from the lounge window, signalling that Daphna was waiting to hear about his assignment in Germany for Mossad...

During the 'nail-biting' period that followed Zak's return from Munich there had only been a couple of curt courtesy calls from the elusive Alon. Strangely, during the weeks leading up to Christmas, neither Rurik nor Franz telephoned Zak regarding their anticipated 'Merry Christmas bonus.'

The Deal Firms Up

Ominously, Alon telephoned on Christmas Eve just as Daphna and Zak arrived home from their Yule Tide shopping at 'Fortnum & Masons' on Piccadilly.

"*Shalom*, Zak, it's Alon here. Are you well?"

"Hello, stranger. I'm well and you?"

"Fine. Listen, Zak, I need to see you urgently."

"Alon, it's holiday time here. The family will be down from London in less than an hour or so."

"When are they going back?"

"Sunday, the 29th."

"Can I see you before?"

"I don't see how."

"Zak, I need to see you before I go back to Jerusalem again, if you know what I mean?"

"Impossible."

"Could we meet half way, say Fleet?" Alon pressured.

"I would rather meet in London if we can't meet down here."

"Fine by me, Zak."

"Alright, I can make arrangements to call in and see friends in London, rather than sit around in a bleak Motorway café."

"Great: I will meet you on Friday where we last met. Mid-day, O.K.?"

"Okay, see you at the Bush on the 27th."

Zak, knowingly named the 'Bush' to avoid any misunderstanding of venue.

"Zak, come alone."

"What else?"

The Christmas of '85 had been fun with all Zak's family together. As always at that time of year he ate too much. Clarissa must have just drunk too much of her favourite Vecchia Romagna brandy to acquire the dutch courage needed to telephone her lost Englishman at home. In deference to Daphna, Zak refused to take the call from the daring Italian and continued cutting the succulent Norfolk turkey. Nevertheless, the call upset Daphna, and created an unnecessary under-current which made the Christmas spirit go 'cold turkey'!

Forbidden Yesterday

By the 27th, Zak was pleased to have a break from the Christmas festivities. Driving to London alone, he could methodically turn past events over in his refreshed mind...

There was an apparent lack of bustle on arrival at the 'West London Hilton', as Zak looked around the lobby area for Alon. The hands on the hotel's wall clock were showing past twelve o'clock when the waiting Londoner noticed a Kuwaiti friend arrive in a gold-coloured 'Roller'.

Zak hung around in the 'Hilton's' lobby where activity was gradually building up. His Kuwaiti friend having parked the 'Rolls,' spotted Zak, and stopped and wished him a happy New Year — then went off with a crowd of waiting merry-makers. Eventually Zak lost patience in waiting and decided to phone home to find out if there was a message from Alon.

Having received a negative to his phone call home, Zak became annoyed that Alon had dragged him all the way to London for zilch, or had the *Sabra* meant to rendezvous elsewhere? Zak decided to call in and see his accountant friend earlier than he'd arranged, as Alon was nowhere to be seen. Just as Zak was about to leave the 'Hilton' via the automatic doors, there was a very loud announcement on the hotel's address system, for Johnny Lancaster. Zak's given Mossad code name.

"Zak, I told you to come alone to the 'Hilton'."

"I am alone, Alon."

"You were spotted with an Arab, who is still in the hotel with his party group."

"It's not my fault if someone I know also chooses to meet in an hotel lobby, the same time as me, is it?"

"I see. O.K., Zak, come along to the 'Royal Lancaster' now. I will be waiting there." Regardless of the consequences, when Zak realised Alon had not set foot in the 'West London Hilton' that morning, the Londoner told the invisible agent:

"Forget it Alon. If you want to talk to me you'll have to come down to Bournemouth and meet me outside somewhere. I'm

The Deal Firms Up

certainly not playing 'musical chairs' from one London hotel to another," and then slammed the phone back into its wall fitting.

Having received bad vibes from the pretentious Mossad agent's telephone call, Zak could not be bothered to go and visit his accountant friend.

Quickly arriving home, Zak could not but notice the look of unhappiness Daphna was wearing on her lovely face.

"Zak, your Israeli friend has been on the phone about four times already. He keeps asking for you."

"That figures, honey."

"Really! Well he's been calling from his car and is on the way down here."

"Okay, hun', give me one of your special double-decker turkey sandwiches and a cup of strong coffee, so I can fortify myself."

"You mean like a double-decker 'Dagwood'?"

"Yes, please. I'll make arrangements to see Alon outside if he phones again."

"Don't worry, he'll phone again. Mustard or cranberry?"

"Both, please."

As reluctantly arranged, Zak met Alon in the bar area of the Bournemouth Crest Hotel.

The look of 'brotherly love' was not on the Mossad agent's face. In fact, the killer glint was back in the *Sabra's* eyes.

"O.K. Zak, I'll lay it on the line. My superiors want to know if you are prepared to bring Franz out of Germany for us."

"For what reason? Why?"

"We need to speak with him without having to look over our shoulder or worry about infringing German sovereignty."

"Does it mean we will be paid the five million Dollars?"

"Yes, but not then."

"When?"

"When Franz delivers."

"Delivers what?"

"Whatever we agree."

"Rurik and I have agreed you are not to speak with Franz, unless one of us is present, okay?"

"Don't worry about Rurik and the ground rules, Zak."

"Why's that?"

"We know all about Rurik having to run away from Brussels."

"So do I. But what's that got to do with Franz's deal?"

"Rurik told you about the Plutonium deal?"

"Yes, with your 'firm', I believe."

"No, it was with South Africa."

"If you say so, Alon," Zak said, tongue in cheek, and went on to reiterate:

"Seeing we're talking about Rurik, you know you're not allowed to split us up."

"O.K. Zak, will you bring Franz out of Germany for us?"

"If you adhere to our ground rules."

"Good, I will let you know when and where."

"It's not good enough."

"What are you saying, Zak?"

"Let's get one thing clear again. My loyalties do not lie with Israel. My partners and I expect to be paid for the Nigerian installation information. However, the ground rules remain, you cannot speak with Franz on his own."

"Yea, yea, Zak. But will you bring Franz out to a nearby country first?"

"I have already told you, if you promise to adhere to our ground rules, and, of course, pay all expenses."

"O.K. Zak, go back home. I'm sorry for disturbing you over the holidays. I'm going back to Jerusalem in a couple of days to tighten up on things."

"Like expenses and payment?"

"Maybe. I'll be in touch shortly."

"Fair enough, Alon. I trust your superiors in Tel Aviv will be made aware we have shaken hands with a *'Mazel un Brocheh'* on the deal."

"Sure, but why Tel Aviv?"

"Mossad headquarters... are on King Saul Boulevard."

The Deal Firms Up

"*Shalom*, Zak," Alon said with some reservation or maybe it was contempt.

"*Shalom*, Alon. Have a good trip."

That particular night Zak went to bed with a bad gut feeling, fearful about Alon and Mossad intentions. In the middle of the night Zak awoke in shock.

The Londoner dreamt he was sitting in a bath of clear water as three open-jawed, spitting serpents came at him through the forced plughole. The dreamer somehow quickly scurried the lashing serpents back down the drain-away with his trembling hands, before shutting the plughole tight with the stopper...

Wanting to get back to sleep and not feeling too grand, Zak counted sheep jumping a fence. He even did a countdown backwards from a hundred, fortunately falling into another wild dream at magical, and much more pleasant, sixty nine. Oh, Clarissa, Clarissa.

CHAPTER TWENTY-FIVE

London: May 1985

Mossad Butterfly

TOWARDS the end of May, Daphna and Zak's special Israeli friends, Udi and his lovely English-born wife, Lena, were expected to arrive in London from Tel Aviv. The married couple's annual visits usually coincided with the major UK Boat Show in Southampton, which Udi religiously attended whilst Lena shopped in and around Oxford Street. However, that particular Springtime, Udi was scheduled to visit a shipyard in the Southampton area.

On their friends' first full day in London, the Levins went to meet the Israeli couple at the Cumberland Hotel, looking forward to taking Lena and Udi for lunch. Daphna and Zak had however both been surprised on arriving at the renowned Marble Arch hotel that the *Sabra* was in the company of his well-formed daughter, Abbie, and not his wife, Lena!

"*Shalom*, Daphna. Don't be worried about it. Unfortunately, Lena couldn't make it, she fell down and damaged her hip, just a couple of days before we were due to take this trip," Udi explained, having read Daphna's look of despair correctly.

"At home, Udi?" Zak enquired.

"No, she slipped on the deck of my sailing craft."

"*Oy vey*! Where is she now?" Daphna asked in a state of utter shock.

"Don't worry yourselves, Lena's being well looked after in hospital back home."

"You must give me the address of the hospital, so I can send her a get well card."

"Sure, no problem, Daphna, later."

When all the *shaloms* were finished with and the Levins had been re-acquainted with the attractive, all grown-up Abbie, the four of them crowded into a waiting London taxi cab, parked on the rank, directly outside the 'Cumberland'.

As Udi favoured Italian cuisine — spicy salamis and wines from *Vento* — they found themselves enjoying lunch and a bottle of Valpolicella in the lively 'Vecchia Riccione' restaurant just off St. Martin's Lane, near Covent Garden...

During lunch, Zak casually mentioned to Udi the Dikko scheme and his Munich contact from Steilmanns.

Abbie's face instantly become animated underneath her long, loose hairstyle. Suddenly, the lurking butterfly became more attentive towards Zak.

As Abbie took her first mouthful of *osso buco*, her painted toes found Zak's shin and then his knee, to slide along the inside of his sensitive thigh and snuggle into his groin!

In the act of devouring the well-beaten *zabaglione*, Zak's libido began to froth on high-boil, as Abbie discreetly found the right moment while proclaimed 'auntie' Daphna was out of earshot, to whisper her hotel room number and a rendezvous time to her well-acquainted 'uncle'!

Intrigued, the very next afternoon as propositioned, Zak arrived back at the Cumberland Hotel. However, in the express lift, Zak began to wonder about Abbie's searching toes and why he was going towards her hotel room. He'd lost all interest in chasing butterflies since finding Clarissa spreadeagled on the bed in the 'Munich Sheraton'.

Stranger still, Daphna had completely turned away from him sexually on learning he'd finished with his Italian butterfly.

Hesitating before knocking on the bedroom door, Zak was confronted by a smiling Abbie, all dressed up in a brief-cut, silk 'Teddy', displaying a lot of cleavage and her 'silken undercarriage down'! Trying to sound casual, Zak vocalised his well rehearsed opening line:

"Hi, Abbie and how are you?"

"*Shalom*, fine, 'uncle', come in!" she said, whilst swelling her hips into her proclaimed uncle's pubis as Zak crossed the threshold:

"And how are you, 'uncle'?"

"Feeling great."

"I don't have to use my imagination to see that, 'uncle'. Abbie said with raised eyebrows, on witnessing Zak's rising bulge.

"Okay daring one, tell me, is your father around?" the appointed uncle asked Abbie cautiously.

"You must know he's in Southampton for a couple of days."

"That's right, another long-range reconnaissance mission, like the Boat Shows?"

"Maybe."

Zak knew an Israeli 'maybe' was effectively an affirmative, and let it go at that.

"Were you in the Israeli Air Force, Abbie?" he asked with intended humour.

"You know I was in the Army."

"So, why are your silk 'bomb doors' down?"

"Because I'm ready to explode." Abbie purred with a naughty giggle and wriggle.

"Okay, Abbie, tell me, why am I here?"

"I've had the hots for you ever since you visited 'auntie' Ruth's flat in Ramat Hasharom back home, remember?"

"How could you have, you were barely a teenager then?"

"You bounced me on your knee as everyone sang: 'Here Comes The Galloping Major', remember?"

"That's right. Strange, I always thought you'd turn out to be a blonde like your mother."

"Well, I had my first sexual thrill then."

"Incredible."

"And when I was older, my mother confided in me about you two under the stars on Hackney Downs and in the Hyde Park."

"Just across the road, in fact!"

"Amazing, that's even better."

"Ironic is the word, little one."

"Oh, I'm not so little, look, I wear a thirty-six 'D' cup bra."

Abbie seductively demonstrated by taking a new red-lace bra from a 'Selfridges' bag and holding it against her glowing form.

"Come, touch me. I won't tell 'auntie' Daphna, honestly."

"She's is not your auntie. Not that there a problem that end, we only live at the same address these days."

"For sure. But I didn't know you two had a problem at home, I'm really sorry."

"You're just like your mother, Abbie. RWA to take a risk."

"So kiss me. I promise you I won't *kvitch* to my father, either."

"Not today, Abbie."

"Just touch my hot-button once and I'll show you how good an Israeli girl can be in action."

"Sorry."

"O.K. be my teddy bear, while daddy's at the Boat Show."

"Fine by me."

"And maybe some pillow talk, 'uncle' Zak?"

"Maybe."

Amazingly, whilst playing at being a cuddly teddy bear, Zak managed to keep his new-given 'avuncular stateliness'. However, it became clear to him that Abbie's *'con amores'* were pandering 'up' to him and that she was involved in 'sexpionage'! Regardless, Zak played the verbal game *'con brio,'* allowing Abbie to totally confide her own sexual fantasies.

Suddenly, the Mossad butterfly changed the scenario from her mother's accomplishment over in the park to Franz's exploits in Nigeria. Zak thought at the time it was no skin off his nose to slowly unfold what he knew about Franz to the inquiring Abbie, as she dropped self-induced orgasms.

After Udi and his honey of a daughter returned to Israel, Zak received what he'd thought at the time to be a benign telephone call. The short, courteous call was from an Israeli called Alon, claiming to be a close family friend of Udi and Abbie. Alon reflected in an extremely polite tone of voice:

"I have to visit Bournemouth in a few days time, Mister Zak. Can we meet up for a coffee?"

"Why not, Alon, if you're a friend of Udi's."

Unknowingly, Zak had invited a Mossad agent into his home, who turned out to be a licensed-to-kill, undercover, Israeli communications expert...

Another Naira deal started early that summer, from an interested Italian group introduced to Zak by Lionel.

Roxanne, an obvious 'white-witch', upon crystal gazing at the situation about her London man and his wife Daphna, made a special stopover in London to 'comfort him' for a few days. The American butterfly then flew off to see if her capital was climbing in Switzerland, before continuing to the Marbella Beach Club via Malaga, probably to play her ruff in a rubber of bridge with Omar Sharif and his followers.

The rest of the year seemed to be taken up with meetings with Alon and the nebulous Naira deal...

Nineteen eighty-five ended as Arab terrorists, allegedly belonging to the PLO, staged a simultaneous assault on Israeli check-in desks at both Rome and Vienna Airports on 30th December, killing twelve and wounding some hundred, innocent by-standers in the terminal zones.

Iran and Iraq were still fighting a bitter regional war with one another for the Persian-cum-Arabian Gulf.

* * * * *

CHAPTER TWENTY-SIX

Munich: January 1986

Disquieting Prelude

NINETEEN eighty-six opened disastrously for the American space programme, when Challenger exploded ten miles up in the atmosphere, travelling at some 2000 mph, killing all seven astronauts.

The price of oil also started to slide disastrously in eighty-six, about the time Aquino's Treasury agents from the Philippines were chasing the fleeing ex-President Marcos and his gold deposits, rumoured to be stashed away in Kloten Airport, alongside an amassed two billion Nigerian Naira.

The last morning in January of that year saw Zak, driving to Heathrow... on his way to Munich via Düsseldorf and then on to Salzburg... all expenses paid by Mossad via Alon, as instructed and agreed during the *Sabra's* last visit to Bournemouth.

Disquieting Prelude

At Heathrow, Zak boarded BA flight 748C with a British Airways ticket in his hand that indicated a two-hour, forty-minute stop-over in Zurich on the return flight to London from Salzburg:

```
LONDON LHR BA 748C 31 JAN 0910 OK Y
DUSSELDORF DUS LH 958C 31 JAN 1650 OK Y
MUNICH MUC VOID — VOID — VOID — VOID
SALZBURG SZG OS 225Y 02FEB 1610 OK Y
ZURICH ZRH BA 617C 02FEB 1850 OK Y
LONDON LHR...
```

Once in Düsseldorf, Zak found it hard to play the waiting game for Mossad. Under the pretence of looking around the halls of the IDEGO Fashion Show at the *Messe* as briefed to do by Alon, Zak endeavoured to kill time...

After a light lunch Zak left the main *Messe* restaurant, taking a last look at the *schöne* models that had previously caught his eye, before liberating a Mercedes from the taxi-rank. The journey back to the airport and the Lufthansa internal flight to rendezvous with Rurik at Munich airport, as agreed and instructed, was uneventful.

Rurik did not meet Zak at Munich Airport as arranged, but there was a message at the terminal's meeting point! The message confirmed Zak was booked into the Hotel Drei Löwen, which translated means 'The Three Lions'. Zak knew the hotel displayed three stars and was located in the Schillerstrasse, a stone's throw from the main railway station. Later, in a vague manner, Zak was told by Rurik that at the time the flight from Düsseldorf landed on the tarmac of the Bavarian Capital, he had been *en route* home to Munich by a delayed express train having visited a banking institute in Vienna.

With hindsight, Zak wondered whether the whole event had been prearranged and staged by the Israelis. The situation and location of the 'Drei Löwen' appeared to be custom-made for Mossad, since it fell in nicely with Alon's instructions before leaving Heathrow:

"Zak, you should only travel to Salzburg by train with Franz, preferably sober."

"If I can, then sure."

"Take this emergency telephone number and let me know if anything unusual happens."

Alon was talking fast as he tore a piece of paper from his note book and wrote the hot-line number down.

"Zak, phone before we leave England on Saturday afternoon if you sense anything fishy. Or if there is any problem to prevent our meeting in Salzburg."

"I trust I don't have to contact you, Alon, although I'm surprised you're travelling on the Sabbath."

To which, the *Sabra* closed his ears.

"By the way, my code name for this Austrian operation is 'Donald.' Yours is still 'Johnny Lancaster'. Use it if you call me on the Embassy emergency number."

"Okay, so now I know another Donald!" Zak uttered sarcastically to Alon's cloak and dagger statement, remembering his own policeman friend at the Yard.

Rurik arrived at the 'Drei Löwen' at about nine that Friday night, looking jaded and jittery. Not his usually-vibrant self, he asked without any to-do:

"Well, Zak, tell me the score."

Zak filled Rurik in on the events of the past few days, including Alon's 'recce' to Bournemouth.

"Did the Israelis pay for your ticket?" Rurik wanted to know.

"Yes, they settled with me at my flat."

"Goody. What about your expenses?"

"They reckon to have allowed for them," Zak told the uptight Slav in a matter of fact manner.

"To include Franz?" Rurik asked with apparent concern.

"They think so. The return ticket via Salzburg and Zurich came to £260; they've allocated me in total six hundred to cover the flight, hotels and other expenses."

"Sterling?"

Disquieting Prelude

"Yes, Pounds not Dollars."

"Where have they instructed you to stay in Salzburg?"

"At the Hotel Bristol."

"They won't have allowed you enough for the 'Bristol', even though they paid you in Pounds. It's a five-star deluxe job, my friend."

"My contact said, if I was out of pocket, they would make it up to me when I returned home."

"O.K. So why are you going back via Zurich?"

"That's the way Mossad want it."

To Zak's amazement, Rurik did not ask about the expected five million Dollars if the deal went through, but astonishingly blurted out rather loudly:

"Believe me, they're going to screw you, my friend!"

"What are you saying, Rurik?"

"I don't know. I just don't like it. You told me they blocked me from going with you to Salzburg?"

"Yes, because you've been involved in nuclear smuggling."

"Bullshit nuclear smuggling. The Belgian Police only chased me out of the country, they never arrested me. I just acted as a go-between or a merchant for the Israelis down in SA."

Zak quickly cut in to ask Rurik:

"What do you mean a 'merchant'?"

"Come on, Zak, baby. A business man working for a fucking commission. I only received part commission, anyway."

"So you told me."

"They'll try and break you and Franz up, you'll see, my friend."
"It's only a trial run tomorrow, so they can speak with Franz without having to look over their shoulder."

"Don't believe it, Zak."

"Why not?"

"I know the way these guys operate, especially with someone like Franz, you'll see."

"Where is Franz, anyway?"

"The *shikker* should be at home."

"Shall we phone him?"

"No, it's O.K., it's arranged. We'll both meet you here at nine tomorrow morning."

"For sure?"

"For sure, Zak."

After some vague and nonsensical remarks, Zak left the hotel with Rurik for the beckoning railway station. The visiting Londoner then left Rurik and the slumbering railway station with the train departure times to Salzburg in his hand for the morrow...

Before going back to the hotel, Zak decided to stretch his legs in the prosaic part of town passing the 'Mathaser Bierstatt', Hitler's past stomping ground. Zak felt a sudden pang in his mind and soul that brought on the vision of Clarissa running out of the beerhall with her 'Silver-blue Fox' flying...

* * *

Zak considered he'd been lucky to have met and been loved by Clarissa, but the deep feelings he'd felt for her had been finally destroyed in the 'Munich Sheraton'. God! The first time he had danced with the 'pussy pressing' Clarissa on the dimly-lit dance floor in London's Soho had been an unforgettable sexual experience in itself. How naïve could one be? It had been 'count down to catastrophe' when he responded to Clarissa's lethal charm as he recalled not having heeded his premonition when last visiting his father's grave.

With the Italian goddess's irresistible force over-crowding his mind at the time, Zak hadn't realised the elements were sending him a deliverance signal when he'd visited his beloved father's *Alov Hasolom,* gravestone. It had been just before *Rosh Hashana*, the Jewish New Year, in the cemetery at Rainham in Essex. The heavens had angrily opened up suddenly above a cotton-wool sky with the roar of thunder, as he reached the utility war-time granite ledger that had mournfully been erected in September 1940, when he was seven. However, destiny and Clarissa had led him to Franz, thus favouring him with an opportunity to become a millionaire! He believed at the time that one could do whatever one wanted, providing one could handle it, and thus he had disregarded the adverse signs and his own premonitions.

At last, ironically, his chances were looking better than nothing. *Granmercé farfalla*... Thanks for everything, butterfly. He knew the adorable Clarissa would be on the edge of his mind until he crossed the River Jordan.

* * * * *

Having studied the train timetable, the next morning, at eight-thirty sharp, Zak returned to a bustling railway station to buy two tickets on the 12.20 p.m. express to Salzburg.

Later that bright morning, things began to dull. Rurik and Franz did not show up as promised. Zak could not conceive why his persistent telephone calls to his partners had resulted in no answer. The permutations of what might have happened to them were too frightening for him to contemplate.

Ten-thirty! Zak was sitting alone on the edge of a seat (with the 'Three Lions' on it), in the hotel lounge, waiting for a call and wondering. Could Franz have 'chickened out' or had there been an accident of some kind... At ten forty-five, Franz nonchalantly appeared on his lonesome in the hotel lobby.

"*Wie geht es Dir*, Zak?"
"I'm fine and you?"
"*Ja*, O.K."
"That's kind of good. Where is Rurik?"
"Should I know?" Franz asked, seemingly innocently.
"I thought he was coming here at nine with you."
"That's news to me, Zak."
"So, where is Rurik?"
"At home, I suppose."

"No, his phone is unattended, he must be on his way here."
"I don't think so, Zak. I think I need a drink."
"Let's locate Rurik first."
"Ah, it doesn't really matter about him. Come, I have some shopping to do for my Princess."

Shocked by Franz's attitude and reply, Zak exclaimed:

"What are you saying, Franz?"
"Trust me, it's O.K., Zak."

Not wanting to throw Franz into a tantrum, Zak strung along with the German.

"Okay, Franz, we'll leave a message for Rurik at the porter's desk saying we'll be back by noon."
"Why must we be back at noon?"
"We have an express train to catch."
"I'm not going anywhere by train!"
"Franz, I have been given strict instructions."
"Don't worry, Zak, we will go to Salzburg by car. I will drive. I have a new series Mercedes!"

The Englishman was once again taken aback by the German's startling statement.

"How do you know we have to go to Salzburg, Franz?"
"Rurik told me on the phone last night."
"But if we don't follow instructions, we might go to Salzburg for nothing, don't you realise?"
"Not at all, Zak. Come, pack your case while I have a beer. I must do some shopping for my Princess. Then we can drive to Salzburg."
"What about Rurik?"
"We can try and contact him later."

What could the Londoner do other than play along with Franz? Could Zak afford not to play along? Hardly.

"Okay Franz, if that's how it has to be. I'm all packed anyway. I'll just go and fetch my case and check out."

Back in his room, Zak immediately phoned the emergency UK number Alon had given him for such a situation.

Disquieting Prelude

"Johnny Lancaster here. Urgent message for Donald. Our man insists on driving to the 'Bristol' by car". He refuses to go by train, repeat, refuses to go by train. And at this moment of time my other partner has gone missing. Understood?"

"Yes, I understand. I will pass on your message." The voice sounded as though it could have been the Embassy's *shabbos* caretaker, or a *shagets*! Zak wondered about dialling Rurik's telephone number before picking up his case. Just as he was about to open the room door, Zak decided to phone Rurik one more time. There was still no answer...

Zak settled the bill with the 'Three Lions' with his American Express card, noticing his call to London had been billed at five Marks fifty, a cheap price to pay for such an important message, he thought. The cost of Franz's beer also showed five Marks fifty!

Zak was flabbergasted when Franz unlocked a new icon gold 230E, parked outside the 'Drei Löwen'. The Londoner was further bewildered when Franz drove to a suburban, multi-storey, supermarket car park on the outskirts of Munich.

"What are we doing here?" Zak asked Franz, in a state of uncertainty:

"I told you, Zak. Before I go away, I must buy my Princess some shopping for the weekend."

"Come on, Franz, we have more important things to do than the weekend shopping."

"Not for me, Zak."

It was a contradictory statement, since in Rurik's flat Franz had stated 'he would kill his Princess for a million Dollars'. Stranger still, the West German appeared calm, unlike the time in the 'Munich Penta', plus Franz now had a new series 'Merc'!

Inside the vast, well-stocked supermarket, it appeared bizarre to see Franz selecting costly delicacies for his Princess. Even stranger, not once during the 'trolley-pushing' did Franz ask why they were going to Salzburg, nor, like Rurik, did he even ask about the anticipated five million Dollars! Zak figured something was going on behind his back, but what and why?

On checking out, Franz, with a well-stuffed wallet, seemed to delight in paying for a large, pre-packed, prime duck, a huge choice, fresh pineapple and assorted fine foods.

Leaving the vast orderly supermarket compound, Franz drove to his nearby flat...

The flat was located in what looked like a new development, situated in an unmade and unmarked road!

Once inside the moderately-sized flat, its newness became apparent from the smell of the second fix, which could not have completely dried out yet.

"Princess, we are home."

There was no answer from within.

"Liebling, I'm home."

Still no response!

"My Princess must be in our bedroom, Zak. She is so shy, this is the very first time I have brought people into my new home." The epicurean dropped the bag of gourmet delights as well as his English grammar and left the room to find his wife...

The Princess eventually appeared, wearing an expensive looking, orange-coloured, hand-embroidered kaftan, which allowed her to freely *salaam:*

"Hello, Mister Zak, good to see you, and how are you?"

"Very well, thank you, and yourself?" Zak answered and asked in a respectful tone of voice.

"The same."

The Princess continued in a sing-song voice:

"My husband will not be long, he's just packing an overnight suitcase."

"I trust you do not mind me taking your husband away on a business trip?"

Disquieting Prelude

To emphasise her coming statement she made irked gesticulations with her bejewelled hand:

"They called him out a few weeks ago and 'marched' him all over Munich, before getting him drunk."

Zak did not catch her drift at the time about Franz having been 'marched' between Munich beerhalls. Franz broke the rapport suddenly as he rushed back into the living room.

"Come quickly, *liebling*, show me which trousers I should pack."

"Let me put all your shopping away first," she said in broken English.

Waiting for Franz and his Princess to return, Zak looked around the neat and tidy flat. The wall-to-wall, shag-pile carpet and full length, luxurious drapes were obviously new. Weird though, amongst Arabic curios and latest hi-fi equipment was an exquisite bronze *menorah!*

Hand in hand, Franz and his wife entered the lounge. The Princess with head held high, revealed a hitherto unknown fact:

"Mister Zak, did my husband tell you that I am Jewish." Zak could not believe his ears. To top everything, a Moroccan Jewish Princess no less! So, the mystery of the *menorah*[10] was solved.

Zak assumed Franz would be travelling light, but he left his Princess armed with a bulky suitcase, plus a briefcase which the German indicated contained some of Steilmanns' point-of-sale brochures. This only served to fuel Zak's qualms about Franz not merely travelling into the unknown with just a change of trouser.

Once the seemingly cool West German filled up his new 'Merc' with high performance 'juice' which the visiting Englishman paid for, and they were on the road and on their way, Zak asked:

"Franz, how long will it take you to drive to Austria?"

"Oh, I can make the 'Bristol' in an hour."

"But it's more that 120 kilometres to Salzburg, Franz."

---

10 A CEREMONIAL CANDELABRUM USED FOR CELEBRATING THE SEVEN DAYS JEWISH FESTIVAL OF CREATION AND LIGHT, WHICH USAULLY COINCIDES WITH CHRISTMAS

"Stop worrying, no problem for this machine to get there before they arrive." For reasons Zak did not understand, he refrained from asking Franz, who 'they' were. Obviously, only Rurik could have let on about being booked in at the Bristol Hotel...

It was a wonderfully bright, sunny afternoon, not a cloud in the sky. The fast drive through the scenic, snow-tipped Bavarian Alps in the 'Merc' along the A8 (known as the *'Salzburg Autobahn'*, the first autobahn Hilter built) was breathtaking indeed.

Upon reaching the German–Austrian border, the 'Merc' was not waved through by the West German Frontier Guard as the other fast-moving traffic.

"*Die Ausweise, bitte.*"

Franz's whole demeanour instantly changed, as they were challenged for their passports by the green uniformed German officer...

"Why are you entering Austria, Mister Levin?"

Franz took it upon himself to hurriedly answer the officer for Zak in English:

"We are going to *stipp s*ome Austrian girls before he flies back to London tomorrow."

The Border Guard was not amused by Franz's crude remark and further probed the Englishman:

"Can I see your air ticket, please sir?"

Zak noticed the 'smiling duck' expression leave Franz's face as his Adam's apple gulped in his German throat. Franz anxiously butted in again:

"Got your ticket handy, Zak?"

"Sure, no problem."

Zak stretched past Franz handing the air ticket directly to the waiting officer. Zak became aware of Franz's knee nervously trembling on the brake pedal as the sedulous Border Guard carefully scrutinised the ticket.

"You're going to Zurich on the sixteen-ten, from Salzburg tomorrow evening, is that correct, Mister Levin?"

Disquieting Prelude

"If you turn the ticket page over, officer, you'll see I have a connecting flight tomorrow at eighteen-fifty from Zurich to London."

"*Ach so*. So you have, with a short transit time in Switzerland. Then you're not coming back to Germany?"

"No."

"O.K., sir, you can pass."

The Border Guard on the Austrian side waved them on without incident, which abruptly halted Franz's nervous perspiration. Franz put his foot down hard on the 'Merc's' accelerator and sped off along the Austrian E52 *Autobahn*...

"Franz, tell me what were you sweating about back there?"

Franz, having quickly regained his 'froth and bubbly' manner, revealed surprisingly:

"I have additional Company weaponry data in the lining of my hand case."

"I thought this was a 'dry-run', so our friends could talk with you without having to look over their shoulder."

"*Ja*, for sure, Zak."

"So, who requested the hidden data?"

"I took it upon myself."

"But why?"

"Oh, just a visual aid. Steilmanns would send anyone radar catalogues and electronic data, such as I'm carrying."

"So why the sweat and trembles, Franz, if it's only simple radar and electronic data?"

"Zak, I need a drink badly, that's why."

Zak delved deeper into Franz's defensive reply.

"Franz, I think it's about time you levelled with me about the 'ace in the hole'."

"What is this 'ace in the hole', Zak?"

"The tucked-away data."

"*Ach, so*, like the Kirk Douglas movie?"

"Right."

Franz then came back with a challenge:

"You level with me about your ace, Zak. Why are you going back to London via Zurich?"

"Like the guard said, just in transit."

"So, why?"

"The only reason I can possibly give you is the Israelis don't want me to be on the same plane as themselves on the way back to London."

"That makes sense to me."

"Glad something is making sense, Franz," Zak uttered without conviction.

"So, you're not staying over in Zurich to deposit money in your bank on the Bahnhofstrasse, Monday morning?"

"No, wish I were. The Israelis haven't talked about any settlement money yet."

"No private deal?"

"For God's sake, what makes you think I have a private deal with the Israelis?"

Before Zak could further probe, Franz sublimely blurted out with a run-away tongue:

"Yesterday, with my Boss in Steilmanns' computer strongroom, using secret Libyan deactivating codes and videos we simulated air-attacks on outlying mobile radar and missile sites protecting Tripoli and missile boats in the Gulf of Sidra..."

Franz decelerated off the E52 *Autobahn*, entering the ancient city of Salzburg via the Münchner Bundesstraße on the right bank of the Salzach river. They then crossed the Lehener Bridge over the racing river into the suburbs on the left bank. Franz seemingly knew the town, pointing out the Romanesque Mirabell Palace and gardens as he sped along the Schwarzstraße before turning left into the 14th-century Makartplatz. The charming, cobble-stoned square and central gardens were further enhanced by a church dome bearing a cross, centred between geometrical, twin-domed, clock towers. As they drove around the square Franz took the time to point out the Mozart House — it was the composer's birthday-week! The well-preserved house was next door to the Austrian

Disquieting Prelude

Airlines office, opposite a taxi-rank and across from the impressive glass-fronted Hotel Bristol.

Passing the Post Office and the magnificent copper domes of the Holy Trinity Church, Franz finally parked alongside a tall, barren magnolia tree.

According to Franz, the well-appointed 'Bristol' backed onto the famous Mirabellgarten, which in Spring and Summer was alive with blossom, flowers and the sound of music.

The 'Bristol' also offered superb views of the inspiring Cathedral's dome and the commanding eleventh-century Hohensalzburg Fortress, which crowned the snow-covered Mönchsberg peak on the other side of the river in the old part of town.

They were not greeted under the 'Bristol's' glass canopy by either doorman or linkman! So they pushed through the double swing doors under their own steam. The impressive lobby was graced by a grandiose oil painting, portraying Nero and Messallina watching Rome burn as naked female courtiers entwined themselves erotically with desirous coloured slaves. Under heavy crystal chandeliers, assorted leather Chesterfields were positioned on a large Persian carpet, mirrored by antique glass columns...

Whilst waiting at the marbled reception counter, Zak started to flip through the sophisticated hotel brochure, having observed a full complement of room keys in place! He could not help noticing the line: 'The 'Salzburg Bristol' is more than a first class hotel — it is a second home for first class guests.' Very comforting words indeed in the brochure, but in practice they were not being treated as first-class guests. A nervous, 'well-worn' blonde receptionist eventually confirmed their booking. She then, to Zak's surprise, double-franked his American Express card, before handing them their heavy iron turn keys. As the uncommunicative blonde took off her spectacles, Zak asked her about the lavish oil painting.

" 'Burning Rome' was painted by the celebrated Salzburg painter Hans Makart, about a hundred years ago; it's priceless", was the brief reply, delivered in perfect English.

Without the offer or sight of an Austrian porter, the Englishman and German carried their own luggage up a few steps to the blue and gold panelled lift door. It seemed an age, hanging on the ornate lift button in the empty, echoing lobby...

Zak became apprehensive in the confined space of the lift and wondered why Mossad had chosen such an exclusive hotel for the dry run. And why an apparently uninhabited one, where, according to the brochure, guests, if any existed, could tread on Persian carpets in individually-designed rooms.

On reaching the top floor, Zak again thought it odd for such a deluxe hotel not to have a baggage-handler on duty, but since none had appeared they were both obliged to make their way to their respective rooms, unaided!

CHAPTER TWENTY-SEVEN

Salzburg: 1st February 1986

Disquieting Waltz

ZAK unpacked in Room 489 before having a quick wash and brush up. The red and gold-leaf stationery folder caught his eye on the highly-polished console, alongside the room service menu. Automatically, Zak familiarised himself with the hotel's facilities and expensive tariff. Then he went to check on Franz across the hall in 492. Purposely entering Franz's room without knocking, Zak saw in disbelief that Franz had already started spending Mossad's allowance with an 'express delivery' from room service! There he was, the gross German, acting as though he was 'Bacchus', reclining in his vest and long-johns, enjoying *Escargots au beurre à l'ail*, at 140 Austrian Schillings a throw, and supping wine from a fine crystal goblet! Also tucked away were two bottles of Pinot Gris Rulander Kabinett behind the *chaise longue* in a large ice bucket. Zak, having studied the tarrif, knew the wine showed 320 Schillings a bottle on its price list. One did not have to be a genius to figure out that Franz had already spent nearly a thousand Schillings or more and intended to wine and dine in style.

"Franz, what the blazes are you playing at, ordering all this expensive food and drink as though you are a privileged guest?"

"Don't worry, Zak, your friends have plenty of money," Franz said with new-found glee.

"How do you know that?"

"Everyone knows the Israelis are ripping off the Americans with their two-way trade agreement."

"Maybe so, but I have to pay your bills from the little allowance they gave me, at only twenty-two Schillings to the Pound!"

"I don't know from English Pounds, Zak," Franz said, forgetting his English grammar.

"Then take it easy."

"Don't worry, Zak, they need me. I will tell them to pay you extra when I see them again."

"What do you mean, 'again'?"

"Slip of the tongue, Zak."

"You're too cocksure and glib for my liking, Franz. What have you been up to and how come you received room service and gourmet-snacks and fine wines so quickly?"

"Nothing. Don't be silly, it's just normal room service, Zak."

What could Zak do with an alcoholic, who was making the most of his new found 'predicament' with ghost-like express room service and expensive delicacies?

"Come join me. Order some more wine, Zak. I will tell them, it will be O.K. No problem, Zak, you'll see."

"Not for me, Franz, I want to be sober when Donald phones."

"Ah, Israelis are always in a state of crisis, Zak."

Alon, code named 'Donald' for that particular Mossad operation, phoned about eight o'clock.

"Zak, how are you and your friend?"

"You got my message?"

"Yes, it's O.K. the way you came."

"If you say so, Alon."

"Donald, please."

"Sorry, but I'm supposed to be Johnny Lancaster."

"O.K. Johnny, in fifteen minutes I want you to leave your hotel alone and meet me in the lobby of the Hotel Stein, alone; understood?"

"You must be kidding me?"

"No, it's nearby, just in front of the Staatsbrücke, the Central Bridge. Zak, don't take a taxi, walk... it's not far. Just cross the square, pass the taxi rank, keep walking past Austrian Airlines, you will come to the Hotel Stein, it's on this side of the river."

Bizarre, but straightforward enough, thought Zak.

"Okay, see you soon in the lobby of the Hotel Stein."

"Good. And Zak, remember you're Johnny Lancaster, come alone, understand?"

"Okay, Donald."

Before leaving the 'Bristol', Zak checked to see if Franz was sober. The door was ajar! Franz, still in his underwear, was curled up on the bed surrounded by discarded chocolate wrappers and wine bottles, apparently out cold.

In the half light filtering in from the bathroom, Zak hurriedly printed a note to the alcoholic-chocoholic, with pen and paper taken from the stationery folder on the mirrored lowboy:

20:15 hrs:
FRANZ,
HAVE JUST RECEIVED A CALL FROM OUR FRIENDS: I WILL SEE YOU ON MY RETURN.
AS AGREED, PLEASE DO NOT LEAVE THE HOTEL OR SPEAK WITH ANYONE.

Z

The tip of Zak's nose told him it was a dry, freezing night as he nudged through the swing doors of the forsaken Hotel Bristol's lobby. Mindlessly, the Londoner scanned the quiet Makartplatz. He immediately caught the tell-tale signs of two hot streams of exhaling breath vaporising in the cold night air from the dark doorway of the Mozart House. The vapours tantalised Zak's curiosity... two lovers in a nest, he deduced. Otherwise, the Square appeared deserted, no one around, no other sign of life. Under a starry sky, with a little trepidation, Zak stepped out into the unacquainted town, without even looking over his shoulder. With 'his manhood dressed to the left and feeling alright', Zak crossed the square following Alon's directions along the frost covered streets towards the Hotel Stein. Oblivious to the female passers-by clad in high-class furs, Zak passed bright, elegant shops and expensive jewellers' windows situated along a narrow dropped walkway opposite the swanky-looking Hotel Österreichischer Hof in the Schwarzstraße.

The Londoner spotted a bridge ahead but could not see the Hotel Stein! Zak's heart quickened as he fleeted over a few concrete steps, which brought him up to road level.

For the first time that night Zak's heart missed a beat. He was in front of the Staatsbrücke but he could see no Hotel Stein. The scattered street gravel pushed at his soles, as he walked a few steps along the bridge towards the old part of town, feeling exposed and out on a limb, before turning to face the newer part of town from which he'd come. Sure enough over on the right was the Hotel Stein, obscured by the corner wall of the Giselakai. There was no hoarding sign on the hotel side wall, and Alon was not to be seen, either! However, it had been obvious to Zak as he did a quickstep over the entrance mat and pushed through the stone-flanked brass and glass double door of the Hotel Stein, that he had been followed. Over the years, Zak had become an expert in instinctology, being able to perceive in advance whom he was expected to meet in a hotel lobby.

Zak was totally ignored when he openly 'showed-out' to a portly Middle Eastern looking man, who had been on his tail. Zak knew then and there that because he was so completely disregarded by the semitic looking man, he'd spotted Mossad's tail...

Zak was aghast when the receptionist, telephone in hand echoed his given Mossad name across the dowdy stone lobby:

"*Herr* Lancaster!"

"I'm Mister Lancaster."

Disquieting Waltz

"Eine Minute, bitte, I'll put your caller through if you go to the telephone cabin just up the stairs."

Zak followed the direction of the receptionist's extended finger to a light-oak cabin door with a quaint porthole window, marked 'TELEFON 1' in dull brass castings...

"Zak, Donald here. I have another hotel for you to call at before we meet."

This call was the start of a tour of Salzburg, playing 'musical chairs' to the sound of *Amadeus la Chasse* and *Abendempfindung*, to-ing and fro-ing from hotel lobby to hotel lobby, café to café, telephone booth to telephone booth, always surrounded, or so it seemed, by Mozart's chocolate balls, and watching Mossad eyeballs...

After a march around Mozart's statue and a call from inside the delightful Altstadt Hotel, things started to go awry. Alon directed Zak back towards the Österreichischer Hof! Manoeuvring the Londoner down the narrow Judengasse, back to the Rathausplatz through the 'second hole in the wall' (the Bankhaus Berger arch), and then over the Salzach by way of the Makartsteg, a narrow, metal, open footbridge leading to the illuminated Österreichischer Hof a fine, palatial, old-fashioned hotel. Its foyer was adorned with a glass-panelled ceiling, a grand staircase, ornamental wrought ironwork, oriental rugs, potted palms, a decorative mosaic floor, and chocolate balls. However, Zak was starting to get 'pissed-off' until he saw a red-uniformed, brass-buttoned page boy, paging him on a hand held message board...

Tipping the page boy, 'Johnny Lancaster' quickly left the Österreichischer Hof, crossed the Schwarzstraße to the Mirabellplatz and wearily made his way down the Rainerstraße. Preoccupied with following Alon's instructions, Zak did not register the Saturday night traffic on entering the wide, residential Franz-Josef-Straße. But he did notice the busy Winkler Hotel on his left, a block before his next port of call, a café on the corner of the Hubert-Sattler-Gasse and Wolf-Dietrich-Straße, at the junction with the Franz-Josef-Straße, where a big-breasted female waited, or was she a watching Mossad butterfly? The elegant Café Tosca appeared in a pink glow, obviously part of the four-star Hotel (believed to have still been the Vier Jahreszeiten). The vibrant café was full of old-world charm, paintings, antique furniture, sophisticated ambience and interestingly provided two entrances, one from the hotel's reception area on the Hubert-Sattler-Gasse and the second, a curtained angled glass door which afforded a double exit or entrance from either the Hubert-Sattler-Gasse or Wolf-Dietrich-Straße. With hindsight, a carefully 'recced' and chosen location by Mossad.

Zak, well and truly 'conditioned' by now to wait for further directions, kicked his heels at the well-stocked bar, lined with high pink-topped leather stools near the angled entrance. Although Zak felt he was at the final venue, he moved over towards the reception area in case there was a call summoning him out yet again.

Hey Presto! As the moonlight danced over a cloud, Zak peeked through a nearby window and caught a glimpse of Alon! Alon was with another man. Both resembled a pair of lean, hunting wolves seeking their quarry, as they stalked past the low market sheds in the one-way Hubert-Sattler-Gasse. Zak anxiously watched the venatic pair through the parted drapes, both now following the little tubby man who had tracked and ignored him in the Hotel Stein. Zak waited a few protracted moments, before the three prowling Mossad agents entered the bar via the hotel's reception entrance. The 'lean pair', who were wearing similar, close-fitting, dark-grey, slippery 'Tonic' suits and slim ties, immediately split rank in order for the 'faceless one' to cover the entrance, leaving Alon and 'Tubby' free to make contact with Zak.

"Ah, there you are, Zak."

"What does that mean, Donald?"

The *Katsas* had chosen to ignore Zak's peevish question and instead introduced 'Tubby'.

"Zak, this is Robbie, my field supervisor."

Zak was nonplussed on being introduced to the tubby man who had followed him, and under the light looked like a Greek-Cypriot motor mechanic. Zak was, however, astonished at the openness of the élite secret service's introduction, and how easily he'd been

Disquieting Waltz

aware of his 'tail'! Robbie, without attempting to shake hands with Zak, butted in rather aggressively:

"Yes, Alon, he tumbled me in our first observation lobby."

"The Hotel Stein?" Alon exclaimed in amazement.

"Yea. O.K., Lancaster, until we know what your man can come up with, you're asking too much money," stated Robbie curtly. Well, at least Robbie played the game and used given Mossad codename, Zak reasoned, before glibly replying:

"Then there's nothing to talk about, Robbie."

"Wait a minute, Lancaster."

"Wait for what? It appears you lot are dealing from the bottom of the pack again."

"Hold on, what I am saying, Lancaster, is that you are not the power-broker, we can only pay according to what we get."

Annoyed at Robbie and being unnecessarily waltzed around Salzburg, Zak let rip:

"I don't consider myself a power-broker, I'm just a business man trying to earn a crust for introducing Franz on the Nigerian deal."

"O.K. then, Lancaster," Robbie immediately acquiesced, having seemingly been backed into a hole, at least for the moment.

"Well, stop 'back pedalling' and let's talk about it," Zak said defiantly, still locked into Robbie's gaping stare.

"O.K. Lancaster, you have a drink with Donald, he's the communication expert. I'll see you later," Robbie chirped as he started to move towards the angled exit, which gave the abrupt Mossad field officer and his minder the double choice to leave the café undetected from possible hidden-eyes in the street...

"What gives with your supervisor, Alon?"

"'Donald' please, Zak."

"What a turn out this is, 'Alon-cum-Donald'"

"I don't know what you mean, Zak. Robbie's probably upset that you're not on anyone's 'firm', yet you spotted him going into the Hotel Stein," Alon explained in apparent embarrassment.

"Forgive me, it was so obvious."

"Forget it, Zak."

"No problem for me, Alon."

The Mossad agent's look and manner immediately hardened, presumably because his code name had not been used.

The interruption of the *Fräulein* asking them for their order prevented the situation from heating up. They both ordered Sacher Torte and black coffees, which were quickly and elegantly served on beautiful lambrequin porcelain and matching demitasses.

"So, what's happening, Alon, and why did you dance me all over Salzburg?"

"We needed to speak with you alone, about Franz." Zak's gut responded with a sharp pain at Alon's obvious ploy.

"Are we playing charades here tonight, 'Alon-cum-Donald'?"

"Forget all that, Zak. We must talk to Franz by himself."

"Come on, Alon, you're breaking the ground rules again."

"Maybe, but we need to consult with Franz alone."

Alon placed his cupped hand over his mouth in a precluded lip-reading position, to whisper:

"I'll level with you, Zak, for your ears only. We now believe Franz has important information regarding Libya."

"What do you think he has?"

With his hand still in the precluded mode, Alon murmured in a low tone:

"He's met with Gadaffi."

"Really?"

"We think he was the field manager on the current secret Libyan radar defence system."

"So he is a 'Privileged Person' by your 'firm', hey?"

The affirmative was confirmed by 'Alon-cum-Donald' signalling silence!

"So, that's what he meant earlier when he blurted out: 'We secretly played war games over Tripoli on a module yesterday'."

In a shocked tone of voice Alon cried:

"Who are you talking about?"

"Franz and his 'Top Priority' Boss of course, down in the classified computer vaults at Steilmanns."

Disquieting Waltz

Alon reacted with a sudden start that made Zak pause, as Mossad's agent moved to the edge of his seat to capture the rest of the hot news.

"Tell me more, Zak?"

"Okay. Franz told me they went into a basement strongroom at Steilmanns H.Q. in Munich. 'We homed in and destroyed the Libyan outlying mobile radar command posts and missel boats before the computer could lock on to our video air-attack. We then destroyed missile sites protecting Tripoli and Bengzi at will. Fire... boom, boom. Without losing a single attacking aircraft. Easy because we had the Libyan radio frequencies and deactivating codes'"

"When was this said?"

"Coming here in Franz's 'Merc'. Sublimely, with lots of 'froth and bubbly', if I may add."

"He shouldn't have told you that."

"He obviously couldn't help it. Brought on by a bout of sudden nervousness, or conscience maybe," Zak dirged mockingly.

"Have another drink, Zak," 'Alon-cum-Donald' said, to obviously save face.

"Not so ridiculous, hey?" Zak jabbed.

"Don't know what you're talking about, Zak."

"No wonder you guys are willing to pay five mil! What did Robbie say before he dashed off? We'll only pay for what we get."

"Drink your coffee, Zak."

"No, thank you. I don't like what I've seen and heard so far and I'm reeling from being twisted around Salzburg."

"We're not playing around here, you know."

"It appears not."

"By the way, Zak, are you getting on O.K. with Franz?"

Alon's sidetrack worked with Zak responding to the casual question:

"I can take him in small doses, but the *shikker's* drinking up my measly allowance."

"He's a *nebbish*. Don't worry about the outgoings. Like I told you, I'll reimburse you when we get back to London."

"Via Zurich?"

"Normal procedure, we can't be seen to be travelling with you."

"I'm beginning to get the picture. Dealing with you guys is as good as putting an eye-glass to a blocked keyhole."

"I tell you what, Zak. You bring Franz along to the 'Sheraton' in the Auerspergstraße, just past the Mirabellgarten, in an hour's time. We can then sort it all out together."

"Come on, Alon, your 'firm' has blatantly duped me."

"Zak, the name is 'Donald'."

"Okay, 'Donald', but it does not alter anything. You've acted deviously and I'm probably drifting in the wind without knowing it."

"Don't be silly."

"That's what I mean. As far as I'm concerned now, this whole affair and Salzburg has been a charade."

"What gives with a charade?"

"You know, like *yiddisher* business on the Sabbath," Zak said with a shrug and up-stretched hands.

"Don't know what you're saying, Zak. But make sure you walk with Franz to the 'Sheraton'."

'Alon-cum-Donald' was getting meaner by the minute.

"Johnny, please," Zak quipped back at Alon.

"Yea, yea, see you in the 'Sheraton' in exactly one hour."

"Don't count on it, Donald."

Zak noticed the big-breasted female again as he left the Café Tosca, and wondered was she a prostitute or a Mossad butterfly.

Back at the 'Bristol'... Franz, without a change of trouser, was ready, willing and eager to 'shake a leg' in a nightclub.

"Franz, we have to see Donald at the 'Sheraton'," Zak informed the revitalised Franz.

"Good, Zak, maybe there will be some American girls there we can pick up and go dancing or bring them back here to *stipp*"

"I'm not interested. By the way, what gives with Libya?"

"Nothing."

Franz did not even try to answer Zak's inquisitive remark.

"Well, the way Alon spelt it out, it's way out of my league."

"Don't know what you mean, Zak. Come, stop worrying."

Disquieting Waltz

"Reluctantly, Zak left the 'Bristol' with Franz and they made their way along the well-lit Schwarzstaße, beside the hibernating Mirabellgarten. Zak noticed, with a mixture of disgust and humour, that Franz even waddled like a bloody duck and not only smiled like one! It was not long before they came to the 'Sheraton's' illuminated green street sign on the corner of the Auerspergstraße. Most probably their arrival was being monitored by attentive, watching Mossad eyes, Zak thought.

Having become a connoisseur on hotel décor in the last couple of hours, Zak swirled through the 'Sheraton's' revolving glass door into the ritzy lobby. He quickly observed a blaze of light gleaming down from designed lighting around the octagonal atrium highlighting a pair of welcoming, large, L-shaped, mock chesterfields.

Surprise, surprise! Alon was sitting alone, in the 'Night Capers Piano Bar' decisively positioned, deep down inside the bar with a clear view of the lobby.

"There's Donald over there in the piano bar," Franz uttered from the side of his mouth. One needed no special powers of deduction to realise Franz recognised Donald from another time and place. A possible reason for Alon to revert to his present code name. Zak bit his tongue as Franz remarked smirkingly:

"He looks just like the other one."

Regardless, Zak could not refrain from asking:

"Which other one, Franz?"

To which the sly German answered:

"Sorry, just a slip of the tongue. I meant my brother-in-law, of course." The penny began to drop a little deeper as to why Alon had adopted another name. They walked through the open doorway, brushing against the 'swagged and tied' velvet curtain before passing the well turned-out barman behind the plush bar...

"Donald, meet Franz."

The German and the Israeli shook hands whilst Zak's gut confirmed it was not the first time Franz and Alon had 'slipped skin'.

"Can I order you guys a beer?" A 'double-stop'. Both Franz and Zak simultaneously accepted Alon's offer as they sat on conveniently-placed, moquette and polished, bow-framed chairs. The beers came during the small-talk.

"Franz, I need to speak with you privately," Alon said in a demanding tone. Stunned by Mossad's agent's forbidden request, Zak asked as the dimmer went to low and the pianist started to play a soft tune:

"Where the blazes are you coming from, Alon?"

"Let Franz speak for himself."

Zak felt he should argue his objection. However, knowing it had been agreed and instilled into Franz that he must not be interviewed alone, Zak prompted:

"Fair enough, spell it out for Donald, Franz."

"Zak is the boss, Donald," said Franz, displaying his silly 'Donald Duck' smile again as he evaded the issue.

"So you're the boss, Zak?" the man from Mossad retorted excitedly.

"Franz doesn't mean I'm the boss, Donald. What he's trying to say is, we have an understanding."

"What understanding?"

"Come on, you know the ground rules."

"Enlighten me, Zak."

"You know, we agreed that your side would not speak with Franz on his own."

"Who is 'we'?"

"Come on, Donald, you know what was agreed with my partner, Rurik, and Franz here."

Big boob — Zak allowed Alon to turn on Rurik again.

"Rurik does not exist as far as we are concerned."

"Don't tell me you've burned him."

"Don't be foolish, Zak."

"Well, he went missing before we left Munich."

"He'll show up, he's probably lying drunk in a Munich beerhall somewhere."

"If you say so, Donald. Well, like it or not, he's a major partner. But somehow, you two guys seem to know one another from a forbidden yesterday."

Disquieting Waltz

Alon flashed his killer glint at Zak, simultaneously delivering in a threatening tone of voice:

"Zak, you are standing in our way."

"Not at all, Alon. You are breaking the ground rules."

During the crescendo, Franz was just calmly sitting there with a silly grin on his face.

Zak experienced a lightning 'spasm of lucidity' at that particular moment, fully realising for the first time that something wasn't *glatt kosher* about the whole trip. Almost like a smell, one could not put one's finger on it. And Franz was too quiet, wasn't even sipping his deluxe beer!

"Franz, put Donald right on the matter, will you?"

"Zak, if we do not go along with them, then it's a stalemate, which I personally can't afford."

"What are you considering then, Franz?" asked Zak, now in a state of bewilderment.

"Zak, stop worrying — you are the paymaster," Franz replied coolly.

"Just a minute. Tell me, what does it mean, Franz, 'Zak is the paymaster'?"

"We agreed in Munich, Donald, Zak would have all the money paid into his Swiss numbered account by your people. Then he would pay Rurik and me to split with my Boss."

"There you are, Zak, a solution," Alon jeered.

"That's not a solution. It's a carefully-planned formula."

"Come on, Zak. Let's help Donald to do his job." It was obvious by Franz's remark that he was prepared to talk with Mossad privately and break their Munich agreement. Under duress, yet wanting to be loyal to both parties, Zak reluctantly accepted the position.

"Okay, Franz, on your own head be it."

The dejected Englishman walked away from the table too 'choked' to make further comment. Leaving the glitzy 'Sheraton' to walk back to the Hotel Bristol alone, Zak felt his gut gnawing at him. The Israelis were slicing him up with their very well-rehearsed 'Salami Technique'.

Forbidden Yesterday

It then appeared clear to Zak, Mossad had 'involved' Franz prior to their trip to Salzburg. They must have agreed to meet Franz on his days off, which meant travelling and planning the operation on a Sabbath! Alon or another *Katsas* had probably already been in touch with the temperamental drunk in the 'Bristol', just as soon as he'd left to be 'waltzed around' Salzburg, hence the laid-on 'express' room service. Those weren't love birds either that he'd spotted in Mozart's very doorway; they were watching Mossad operatives, waiting for him to leave the 'Bristol'. What had the Princess said about Franz in their newly-furnished flat? "They'd dragged my husband out a few weeks ago — marched him all over Munich." And Alon never did ask for the rest of Steilmanns' papers in spite of the fact that they had proceeded! If he'd had the presence of mind to have rushed back to the 'Bristol' instead of 'playing musical chairs' with Alon and Robbie, he probably would have caught Franz selling out to Mossad and Alon phoning out marching instructions. Zak then realised he was out on a limb and that the chilled wine and garlic *escargots* must have already been delivered for Franz in the German's allocated, unlocked room — not express room service at all — but ready and waiting.

Zak wandered back to the 'Bristol' with a heavy heart, taking a different route. He crossed over the Rainerstraße into the Franz-Josef-Straße, passing by the 'Winkler' before coming upon the Hotel Vier Jahreszeiten again.

Looking closely at the neat hotel and the strategically-positioned Café Tosca and exits, it became plain to Zak that Mossad ran a 'tight operation' and that this was no 'dry run'. This was a real operation!

On reaching the T-junction, Zak turned right into the narrow Linzer Gasse, chock-full of patisseries, delicatessens and small hotels. Further along there was a nightclub called the 'Casanova', displaying an array of performers and hostesses' photographs either side of the entrance, which gave the apparent 'clip-joint' a vaudeville image...

Disquieting Waltz

Franz arrived back at the 'Bristol' some two hours later looking quite sheepish, but somehow pleased with himself.

"Okay, Franz, play me back the *intermezzo*!"

"*Ich verstehe nicht*, Zak."

"Tell me all about the 'blues in the night'."

"What do you mean, Zak?"

"The bloody conversation you had with Alon in the 'Sheraton', of course."

"You mean Donald?"

"Yes."

"Zak, it's better we don't talk at all in the room, nor in the hotel. Let's go for a walk."

"Walk or another dance?!"

"Come Zak, let's leave the hotel."

Once outside in the silence of the Makartplatz, Zak immediately started to 'third degree' Franz:

"Alright, Franz, what have you agreed with your friends?"

"They want to go ahead with the Nigerian situation."

"Good, tell me more."

"They are going to pay the money via your account."

"How much and for exactly what?"

"Because of their security, I promised not to tell you and Rurik."

"So, you've already done whatever you're just supposed to have agreed to, without consulting your partners?"

"Forgive my English, Zak."

"Franz, your English is A.O.K., it's your loyalties that are seemingly questionable."

"Not at all, Zak. They are paying me through you."

"Are they? For what and when?"

"I cannot tell you now, Zak."

"I insist upon you telling me here and now, Franz. Isn't that why we left the 'Bristol'?"

"Not really Zak. I want to go to a nightclub."

"You're a *shyster*, Franz."

Zak's provoking remark was like water off a duck's back to the slippery German.

"Come, Zak. There's a nightclub just round the corner."

"Yes, I saw it."

"Let's go and have a drink there."

"No, thank you very much, it's not my 'cup of tea'."

"Zak, for a hundred Marks we can both have a good time there."

"You're on your own, Franz, it's a 'clip joint'. I tell you what, Franz, I'll give you a hundred Marks, you go whoring alone."

"No, Zak. I want you to lend me ten thousand Marks, until we get paid!"

"No way, Franz. I need someone to lend me ten thousand Marks until I get paid."

"Come on, let's have some fun."

"Franz, I'm going to bed now, I'll see you in the morning."

"If you must.... By the way, Zak, Donald said that he'll phone you early tomorrow morning."

"Thanks for remembering to tell me. Do you want a hundred Marks to go night-clubbing?"

"No, Zak, I told you I want ten thousand."

"Me, too."

"Come on, Zak, only ten thousand Marks until we get paid."

"The whole episode seems to be a put-up affair to me, Franz."

"What is a put-up affair, Zak?"

"Ask Donald."

Zak fell asleep in the comfortable tranquillity of the 'Bristol', recalling once again in greater detail the conversation at the Royal Bath Hotel in Bournemouth, brought on by thinking about Nigeria, Dikko, Mossad, and his visit to Munich with Clarissa. The only thing he had in common with Franz was they had both been intimate friends with Clarissa...

* * *

"How wonderful, Clarissa... Is the present really for me?"

"*Yesa*, Zak, for you. I missed you so much yesterday, I bought you a present as a symbol of my love."

"Thank you very much, butterfly," he had said in surprise, as he unwrapped the gift.

"I could find no other, Zak. It was so difficult to choose in such a short time."

"I understand now, butterfly! I will always cherish your gift while you love me." He had given her beaming face an affectionate kiss, feeling all the while a pang of upset for the high price Clarissa must have paid for the 18-carat key and heart shaped gold trinket. Nevertheless, he had been flattered by her show of affection.

Oblivious to the waitress serving their order, he'd picked up the silver-plated coffee jug to pour, joking with Clarissa at the same time, in order to take the pressure off the moment:

"I'll be Mum."

Just as she had started to pick at one of the cucumber sandwiches, Clarissa, uncannily understanding his English sense of humour, nervously laughed before she inquired:

"Did you have a successful day in London yesterday, my Englishman?"

"Yes, but I missed your pillow talk and love, my *bella donna*."

"*Si*, me too, Zak. Tell me what did you do in the big City?" He'd told Clarissa all about his full day in London and as a result he had already received an encouraging affirmative telex from a Colonel friend, starting the ball rolling on a mega currency deal and a JPI contract.

"For really big money, Zak?"

"Two billion Old Nigerian Naira."

"How much is that in Sterling?"

"Well... in US Dollars, it's around four hundred and sixty-two million!"

"*Mama mia*, Zak, that's a lot of lira. But who would want to buy such old Naira?" she had asked intelligently.

"Someone in an Ivory Tower: an overlord in the petroleum business. Old Naira are not completely obsolete Naira." He had then gone on to explain the finer technicalities, which she had surprisingly appeared to comprehend. How only an oil company would be interested in buying Old Naira with external American Dollars at a discount price, to then be credited in Nigeria with New Nairas at the agreed increased face value.

"What would be the point in an oil company doing that, Zak?"
"A way of buying 'Bonny Light' cheaper. To get around the fixed OPEC crude oil prices and give the Nigerians all that much-needed external currency to play around with."

"It must be hard to make such a transaction?"
"Certainly is."
"I wish you luck, Zak."
"Thank you, I need it. The real problem is the buyer having the confidence in the Nigerians to honour the subsidy, which includes all royalties and the commissions, within the purchase price!"
"I see, Zak. What is 'Bonny Light' and JPI?"
"Black gold and jet fuel, my fast, wanting butterfly."

* * * * *

CHAPTER TWENTY-EIGHT

Salzburg: 2nd February 1986

Disquieting Reality

ALON phoned Zak at the 'Bristol' at eight-thirty the next morning, without a "good morning", just as Zak was about to join Franz down in the ground floor breakfast room.

"Zak, Robbie wants you to take lunch with him before you fly from Salzburg."

"That sounds cosy, Alon."

"Donald, please."

"Oh, yeah."

"Can you meet him at noon at the Hotel Winkler on the Franz-Josef-Straße?"

"What about Franz?"

"I will be interviewing him elsewhere over lunch."

"About what?"

"Zak, not on the phone."

"Johnny please, Donald."

"O.K."

"What has Franz agreed to?"

"Maybe I can tell you later."

Possibly a parryng 'maybe', thought Zak.

"Will you be at the 'Winkler', Zak?"

"Looks like you're calling the shots now, Alon."
"Do you know where the 'Winkler' is?"
"Is that a sick joke, Alon?"
"Why?"
"You had me doing a turkey trot past there last night, as you must have done with Franz last December in Munich."
"What on earth are you talking about, Zak?"
"I know you know, Alon."
"Don't be *schmendrick*, Zak."
"Not any more, 'Alon-cum-Donald'."
"Be at the 'Winkler' to meet Robbie, at twelve-thirty sharp," Alon commanded before the phone was slammed down.

Franz, still without a change of trouser, had already ordered in the ground floor breakfast room and was well into his *Frühstück* and extra *Schinken mit Ei* by the time Zak sat down opposite the vulpine German. Zak was starving; he hadn't eaten a meal since breakfasting alone in the 'Drei Löwen', which seemed an age ago.

The famished Londoner ordered four eggs 'sunny side up, to tempt the elements', toast and black coffee with honey, before laying into Franz.

"Franz, isn't Rurik going to be upset about you speaking with the Israelis alone last night?"
"Don't worry, Zak, it will all be O.K. in the end."
"But you promised not to let them split us up."
"I told you, it will be alright in the end."
"All very well, but for whom?"
Evading the question, Franz astutely begged again:
"Are you going to advance me some money, Zak?"
"Franz, I thought I made myself quite clear last night."
"But Donald said you are loaded."
"Apparently, he's winding us both up. Anyway, you forget I saw all the money in your wallet in the supermarket."
"I gave my wallet to my Princess."
"For safe keeping until you're back home, I'll wager."

Disquieting Reality

Franz just stuffed his mouth with another piece of fruit-loaf, as Zak's eggs arrived in an upside-down mess!

"Have you noticed, Franz, we're the only ones staying in this seventy-four room mausoleum?"

"*Ja*, Zak, it's deserted," Franz answered disinterestedly.

"Looks as though they opened up the 'Bristol' especially for you and me!"[11]

"Impossible, Zak."

"Maybe. By the way, where were you when I telephoned your room early this morning, Franz?"

"I could only have been sleeping."

"I also knocked on your room door a couple of times, very loudly indeed."

"Sorry, Zak, but when I sleep I'm dead to the world."

"Did you go night-clubbing last night, Franz?"

"*Kein Geld*, Zak."

Franz started *zugging* again for money, then suddenly suggested that they both check out of the 'Bristol' directly after breakfast. In fact, Franz had already lodged his case with the brittle-sounding receptionist, who was wearing the same stained blouse. Zak did not reflect on why Franz wanted to check out so early at the time, although it had always been the norm for him to keep an hotel room until the last possible moment, even asking for extra time to coincide with a pending flight.

Due to the lack of attentive service and staff, coupled with the sloppy breakfast, Zak marked his particular 'American Express' payment slip: 'I dispute this bill'. Directly after the kerfuffle over settling their accounts, Franz showed benevolence, offering to carry Zak's luggage. But before picking up the luggage, Franz, the self appointed baggage-handler, with a melodic voice, asked:

"Zak, may I have the bills, please?"

"Why do you need the bills, Franz?"

---

[11] ZAK LATER CHECKED ON THE 'BRISTOL' IN THE RAC PUBLICATION 'EUROPEAN HOTEL GUIDE' WHICH CLEARLY STATED: HOTEL BRISTOL, OPEN 6 MARCH — 2 JAN — AND THEY WERE CHECKED IN ON FEB 1ST.

"So I can claim expenses with them, from the Company." Zak naïvely gave Franz the bills to try and stop him from further begging. The bill for Room 492, bearing the West German's name and address was for 2846 Schillings, some £60 more than Zak's bill, notwithstanding the differential of the long-distance telephone calls to Daphna. Why not, Zak thought foolishly: I have the 'American Express' payment slips as proof of payment. He then bought a stamp for Daphna's postcard of the Mirabell Gardens in full bloom. Come rain or shine, Zak always sent a card home when away. In fact, Daphna had quite a collection of foreign views mingled with her cookery-books.

Too late, it struck Zak that the loan-seeking Franz had pulled a dirty trick, probably on Mossad's tutelage. The whole performance had been rigged to remove the evidence of their stay. That's why Franz, as a pretence kept begging for a hand-out and requested the hotel bills!

With the hotel bills safely tucked away in his jacket pocket, Franz stopped his begging and quickly stowed Zak's luggage in the boot of the 'Merc' intending to drive round the Makarplatz on that cold and frosty Sunday morning. Seeing the Post Office, Zak stopped Franz in his tracks to post Daphna's card...

Franz, for reasons best known to himself, parked the car in the one-way Paris Lodron Straße (only 200 metres away) opposite the holy Loreto Kloster, which Zak noticed displayed a delightful ceramic plaque over its ancient arched entrance.

Walking away from the carefully-parked 'Merc', Zak's casual interest was also drawn to the decorative wrought iron gates, bearing the inscription 'FCS 1949' which guarded the Franz Carl Seidel archway at Number 5 Paris-Lodron-Straße.

With nowhere to go until high noon, they made their way aimlessly across the river. At the Staatsbrücke, Zak did not think to ask Franz why he had moved the car from the comparative safety outside the 'Bristol' in the Makartplatz, and, secondly, where he was going to be meeting Alon...

Disquieting Reality

Once over on the old side of the city, Franz suddenly decided he wanted his first beer of the morning...

As Zak retraced his last night's steps along the opulent Judengasse, stuffed with windows full of Mozart and Amadeus chocolate *Kugeln,* they crossed the Rathausplatz and came upon Mozart's birthplace in the Getreidegasse.

"Franz, let's kill some time and see where Mozart was actually born, over there obove the chocolate shop-cum-deli."

"I'm not climbing up all those flights of stairs to see an old piano and stool. Let's go up the stairs to the Café Mozart over there on the other side of the street and have a beer."

"Okay," Zak agreed reluctantly, suspecting Franz had been in that part of town before...

It was immediately obvious the Café Mozart's décor and menu were rigged for the tourist trade. Franz had a couple of long 'Hüber Weiss' beers. Zak tried the Strudel and coffee before leaving the comfort of the patterned moquette couch, having decided not to sit on the bent-wood chairs. They walked back over the parquet floor, down the marble stairs and out through the swing doors of number 22 into the cobbled street of the Getreidegasse.

Side by side they then strolled the length of the Getreidegasse. and all of its many trendy side-alleys, inevitably stopping at Alpine type bars and hotels to satisfy Franz's never-ending thirst. Franz became increasingly niggled, showing no interest other than to drink, never wanting to linger and admire the beguiling archways, shop windows or ancient wrought-iron displays.

Just before noon, they made their way towards the Makartsteg passing the closed fish market sheds by the main bus stop. The uplifting sound of a tenor-saxophone filled the air with the tune 'If I Was A Rich Man', played by an old man wearing a threadbare duffel coat, cords and worn out boots, whom they found sitting on the cold stone steps leading to the footbridge. With a smile, Zak dropped a handful of Schillings into the shabby green-lined velvet instrument case. The saxophonist blew harder in conspicuous acknowledgement as they crossed the Salzach, a Mossad signal, perhaps?

Forbidden Yesterday

In the daylight it was apparent the Österreichischer Hof on the other side of the footbridge was built in impressive Neo-Classical style — the Austrian, American, German and Italian flags fluttered gently from its four central towers.

The river was running slow as the metal, sprung Makartsteg bridge seemingly bounced them on their way across the Salzach.

At the traffic lights on the corner of the Makartplatz, Zak noticed the 'Bristol' was in darkness, apparently all locked up!

On arriving back at the 'Merc', Zak observed the car had been moved and told Franz so.

"You're crazy, Zak. My car is in exactly the same place as we left it," Franz said with new-found annoyance.

"So it's your car again, not Steilmanns' car?"

"Excuse me, Zak, for my English. But only I have the key."

"It's been moved, I tell you. The boot was exactly level with the ceramic plaque and just past the wrought iron gate."

"Impossible, Zak."

"Well, it may be in the same parking place, but it's certainly not in the same position."

"Impossible," Franz repeated.

"Okay, Franz, let it go. Where are we meeting when you've finished with Donald?"

"At the 'Sheraton'."

"Will you drop me at the Airport on your way back?"

"Which one?"

"Salzburg, of course."

"Why not come back to Munich and fly direct to London?"

"I don't need the extra expense, nor to upset 'Alon-cum-Donald'."

"But Munich would be cheaper and give you a rebate."

"Possible."

Zak then realised Mossad were bent on Franz and himself leaving Salzburg separately, even if Franz thought otherwise.

"Come with me then, Zak?"

"No, I'll play it their way."

Disquieting Reality

With hindsight, Franz was conveniently parked in the complex one-way system to drive off and enter the elm-lined Franz-Josef-Straße before stopping at the Winkler Hotel, presumably then to go on to the nearby 'Sheraton'...

Robbie was waiting in the inviting lobby of the 'Winkler', wearing the same short, navy anorak as the night before. Underneath the unzipped anorak he wore a casual blue jumper and navy cords unlike his formal attire of the night before.

Without a handshake, Zak was ushered into the grey-and red-trimmed restaurant for lunch by the smirking Robbie. There was only one couple ordering from the menu as the Londoner was bundled deeper into the brasserie-style restaurant! Nothing was said between Robbie and Zak until they'd ordered, when Robbie opened the conversation with a sporting remark:

"Well, Zak, are you fit?"

Robbie appeared less officious, having ceased calling Zak by his given Mossad name.

"Fit for what, Robbie?"

"Don't be upset over our little run-in last night."

"I thought you were the one who was *broyges*?"

"No, Zak, I'm not annoyed about you spotting me."

"Good, but I am perturbed."

"About what?"

"About you and your team."

"Can we talk business after lunch?"

"It seems like dirty business to me, Robbie."

"After lunch, Zak," Robbie said with steel in his voice.

"Have I any option?" Zak ventured to ask.

"I don't think so," Robbie answered with a set jaw.

"Why do I feel like a stuffed *kebab* on a long skewer, Robbie?"

"No idea, Zak," Robbie uttered casually, yet curtly.

The silence during the fish lunch, Zak thought, rather 'fishy'. However, they had both licked their lips after the apple Strudel dessert when Zak venturesomely asked Robbie:

"Can we 'talk turkey' now?"

Forbidden Yesterday

"Let's finish our coffee first, Zak," the *Sabra* commanded, just as the head waiter came and informed Robbie in a half whisper that there was a telephone call for him in the lobby phone booth...

On Robbie's return to the table, he arrogantly called for the bill from the over-attentive waiter.

"Zak, I must go now. Franz will meet you outside in five minutes or so."

"What's the hurry-up all about, we've hardly talked, let alone discussed why I'm here in Salzburg?"

"I've been ordered back to base. We've got what we came for."

"Surely you can give me five minutes more?"

"Sorry, orders are orders."

"The Nigerian deal is on, then?"

"Yea, something along those lines, Zak."

"And the procedure for payment?"

"Franz will put you wise regarding the banking."

"Can I have your handshake on the deal?"

"If you want."

"With a *'Mazel un Brocheh'* that we will get paid in full, as agreed with Alon?"

Robbie answered indifferently:

"Why not, the shopping list is complete."

The two Jews shook hands, both of them chanting the binding blessing of the Hebrews — *"Mazel un Brocheh"*.

As Robbie was about to dash off, he anxiously fumbled through his pockets before tossing a bunch of keys at his uninformed luncheon-guest.

"Give Franz his car keys, will you, Zak?"

"How come you have Franz's car keys, Robbie?"

"I must dash now, Franz will tell you!"

The Londoner flopped down in resignation, and slowly drank his black coffee...

Franz was nowhere to be seen outside the 'Winkler' as Zak started to have ugly thoughts again. Waiting five minutes or so before accepting his paranoia, Zak cleared his mind and speedily took off

Disquieting Reality

down the Franz-Josef-Straße towards the ornamental Mirabellgarten and the 'Sheraton'. Wishing he had time to study the three statues in the garden, Zak hurriedly crossed the Rainerstraße.

On turning the corner at the Auerspergstraße, Zak espied Franz, reclining against his new 'Merc'...

"What happened, Franz?" Zak asked as soon as he was abreast of the apparently nonchalant German.

"Stop worrying, Zak. It's O.K."

"Then, tell me about it."

"I cannot for now."

"Why?"

"Come, I will buy you a drink, Zak, and try to explain."

"You'll buy me a drink?" exclaimed Zak in utter amazement at Franz's offer.

"Yes, I have some Austrian Schillings over from last night," Franz expressed without batting an eyelid...

It was just after ten-past one when they sat down in yet another bar, but with Franz doing the ordering for the first time!

"They've paid you your commission already, Franz?" Zak accusingly asked whilst the waiter poured their *Schnapps*.

"How can you say that, Zak?"

"Because they had your car keys and now you have spending money in your pocket!"

"Yes, my spare set fell out of my pocket last night."

"Like your big, fat wallet, or teeth, hey. But Robbie gave me your keys, not Donald."

"Why are you thinking such things, Zak?"

"Because of what's apparently done, plus you've stopped asking me for money."

"I told you, I had some Schillings left over from last night, Zak."

"You're also much calmer, probably conspiring together with our so-called friend, who resembles your brother-in-law. You've obviously done a private deal."

"No, Zak, I'm not cutting you out," Franz said with feigned concern.

"How can you say that?"
"Because you are the paymaster, Zak."
"Paymaster for what?"
"Later, Zak, on the way to the airport."
"Another put-off."
"Shortly, Zak."
"Okay, Franz, then give me your banking details."
"Sure, Zak, I will phone you tomorrow with my co-ordinates."
"I can feel it, Franz, you've already deviously performed for the Israelis."
"I will telephone you tomorrow, Zak, with my banking details."
"Yeah, if you had my telephone number."
"No problem, Rurik will give it to me."

Bloody Rurik? They had not contacted Rurik, and Rurik, to the best of Zak's knowledge, had not contacted the 'Bristol'!

Zak put two and two together fast, realising Mossad and Franz made FIVE, and that the whole operation had been carefully planned by Israel's 'Double Cross Committee', perhaps even allowing him to spot Robbie in the Hotel Stein! Zak decided there and then to be rash and try the long-shot, drawing Franz out as to whether he had made a private deal with Mossad or not. After all, the Londoner felt he had nothing to lose.

"Franz, remember on the way to Salzburg you told me about secret Libyan codes and air-attacks over Tripoli and Bengazi you and your Boss simulated on the computer?"
"Please, Zak, do not mention my Boss's name to anyone."
"Well, Robbie told me you passed over the secret Libyan computer files and radio codes."
"Robbie told you that?!"
"Yes, radar secrets, deactivating codes and all that other classified stuff." Franz's complexion went a thousand shades deeper at the stark realization that he could be impeaching himself, by acknowledging Robbie.

"I don't want to talk about it, Zak," Franz flummoxed somewhat nervously.

"You're not denying it, then?"

Disquieting Reality

"I told you, Zak, I don't want to talk about it. Come, I will drop you off at the airport when you give me my car keys."

"No more drinkies?"

"Come on, Zak, give me back my keys."

"But you have another set?"

"Come on, Zak, stop being difficult."

"Franz, I resent your attitude and what you've plainly passed on to Alon. I think Rurik should visit you in Munich tonight."

"I'd rather he chased me than Muammar."

"Who is Muammar?"

"Gaddafi."

"You're a swine, Franz. It seems life and you are playing a dirty trick on me. I'm not sure if this is the beginning or the end."

"It will be O.K. in the end, Zak. I'll tell you Rurik's opinion when I phone you tomorrow with my banking details," Franz proclaimed with his silly 'Donald Duck' grimace. Without full comprehension of the moment, Zak threw the 'Merc's' keys at the West German with a gesture of disgust...

Franz, seemingly unperturbed, drove out into the Rainerstraße, turned left past the Pitter Hotel, under the railway bridge, before turning left at the Saint-Julien-Straße, picking up the combined Flughafen and München signpost.

The sign triggered a 'reverse thought' in Zak's mind; he remembered how, as he had crossed over the road in Munich to the Penta Hotel in Rurik's red 'Oldsmobile' he'd experienced an odd but vivid premonition on seeing the road sign to Salzburg.

Listening to Franz outside the main entrance of Salzburg Airport, Zak felt as though his chilled stomach and soul had lodged in his burning throat. Franz sounded 'flaky' as he reconfirmed before parting:

"Zak, I will phone my Swiss Bank account number through tomorrow, for sure."

Franz then had the gall to ask Zak to reconsider flying back to London via Munich, to which Zak just shook his head. However, to make sure Franz didn't 'have an out', Zak gave the weird-looking West German his personalised card and then asked the five million Dollar question:

"Just between you and me Franz, did you work on secret installations in Libya?"

"Everyone at Steilmanns knows."

"And have you really met Gaddafi?"

"*Ja.*"

A fickle moment of truth in Franz's life brought home the stark reality: He, Zak Levin, was the outsider, and he was dealing with a Judas. Zak avoided shaking Franz's 'dirty hand'. The Londoner pondered on the ramifications of this revelation and what now lay ahead as he passed through the automatic doors, checked in for the OS 225Y flight to Zurich...

Sitting waiting in the departure lounge until four-fifteen, Zak figured out that Steilmanns must have unknowingly been infiltrated by Mossad agents via the well-placed Franz and the indebted, gambling, high priority 'Boss', and that they had both already collected their 'Turkey Money'.

CHAPTER TWENTY-NINE

Zurich, Kloten

Startling Reality

THE first part of Zak's journey from Salzburg seemed empty and ghost-like. He managed to acquire a pile of Swiss coins while in transit at Zurich's (Kloten) Airport and made the pressing call to see if Rurik was still alive and kicking. Amazingly, Zak was quickly able to get Rurik at the other end of the line. Zak was surprised that Rurik lacked enthusiasm and was unenquiring. It was as if Franz's bizarre behaviour, obvious sell-out and Mossad's dirty tricks in Salzburg, fell on deaf ears! Zak began to wonder why Rurik did not even ask about payment, and began to brood over Rurik's prophetic statement in the 'Drei Löwen'.

"Zak, they're going to screw you."

Rurik had said not 'us' but 'you'. Still, Rurik did say he would phone his banking details through the next day or Tuesday.

Feeling just about better than nothing, caught in the inevitable airport trap, Zak had no other choice than to wait for the last flight out of Zurich to Heathrow that evening.

The Londoner could not help but wonder about the mythical two billion Nigerian Naira that had been reportedly stacked away in two 30 foot containers somewhere within the confines of Kloten or its *Freilager*. God! The time and effort he had devoted with Rurik, Lonel, the Colonel and the rest of the fringe commodity boys to try to sell the Nigerian paper over the last seven years, from about the time gold had feverishly started to escalate at the end of '79...

* * *

Zak had met the flamboyant Nazih Nayman from Nigeria, a deported Lebanese-Nigerian Naira currency dealer, during the 'silly period' between the decades. Nazih had earlier been thrown into a rat-infested solitary Nigerian police dungeon in Lagos for illegally exchanging Naira for external currencies. When Nigerian Treasury men had chosen to 'find the lost key', Nazih was transferred to more comfortable surroundings, then 'rewarded' with house arrest for keeping his mouth shut about converting Nigerian currency into US Dollars with, and for, Nigerian Government officials!

Subsequently, Nazih considered himself fortunate to be able to boast from his swanky, rented residence overlooking Marble Arch:

"Zak, when I was arrested at home in Lagos, half the Nigerian Government decided to go for winter sports in the Swiss Alps, even though it was midsummer in Switzerland."

Nazih, the deported Lebanese and Van Darlen, the exported Dutchman had both fired Zak's obsession to close the mega Naira deal in the early 1980's. During those years he had known both the mechanics and format laid down by the Nigerians was dubious and not considered respectable by prime banks. Regardless, he intended to *kosher* the bizarre deal as it progressed, and had seen fit to spend a small fortune on communications and travel trying to find a bona fide buyer for the massed Naira. And, of course, there was the possibility of legalising the expected 'Amexbank' telex from Hamburg to the Midland Bank in Poole for US$ 462 million:

Startling Reality

Hamburg, May 23 1986. 13:45 hr

To:-
Central Head Office, Midland Bank, att. Mr P Garland
Longfleet Poole

PRO FORMA INVOICE

1 billion old Nigerian Naira price 23.10 USD per 100 O.N.N
Delivery Zurich (Kloten) Switzerland to be accompanied by documents:-
1/ Certificate of repatriation (Issued by Central Bank of Nigeria)
2/ Certificate of authenticity (Issued by prime European bank)
3/ Certificate of counting (Issued by prime European bank)
4/ Bonded warehouse receipt
5/ Packing list.

Terms:
Transferable irrevocable letter of credit, issued by prime bank for 462 million USD without deductions: valid 30 days.

Pls confirm by return tested telex that you are RWA

Best regards
Amexbank Hamburg

* * * * *

Forbidden Yesterday

During the BA flight 617C from Zurich, Zak read in one of the Sunday tabloids that the British Government had issued a 'Green Paper', with a view to replacing the then current property rating system with a new-fangled Community Charge or 'Poll Tax'. One could not guess at that moment in time what far-reaching consequences the revamped taxation was going to have on the UK and its citizens...

Neither Franz nor Rurik telephoned through their bank co-ordinates as promised. This could only mean one thing — they both knew Zak was not going to be their paymaster.

Reluctantly, Zak phoned International Enquiries to obtain Steilmanns' main telephone number in Munich, with a view to sorting Franz out. Zak obtained the number and dialled it. He was quickly put through to a rather nervous sounding Franz Jilg, who instantly recognised the Londoner's voice on the other end of the phone.

"Zak, why are you calling me at work?"

"Because you haven't phoned as agreed."

"Zak, don't call me here again, understand?"

The line suddenly went dead. No, Zak did not understand and immediately phoned Steilmanns number again, only to be told by a muffled male voice in Franz's office:

"Herr Jilg has left the office for the day!"

Zak then called Rurik...

"Hello, Rurik, have you spoken with Franz today?"

"No Zak. Can't locate him at home or at work."

"That's weird, like his voice!"

"Why?"

"He's screwed us, you know."

"How do you know?"

"I spoke with him just a few minutes ago."

"In his office?"

"Yes, he hung up on me."

"Bloody hell, Zak! Franz's and his Boss's office is at the nerve centre of Steilmanns' organisation."

"Bloody hell, nothing. I suggest you catch Franz on his way home tonight."

"What can I do?"

"Show him your *stiletto*!"

"Come on, Zak, I'm only a lodger in this country."

"I see, Rurik. Tell me why you can't locate Franz at work as I did a few minutes ago?"

"Who knows?"

"Who is 'who'?"

"Come on, my friend, give me a break."

"Okay, Mister Who. Why have you always been so certain Mossad would not pay me?"

Rurik's weak reply was no answer at all and the Slav did not even mention his bank co-ordinates!

After Zak's disturbing telephone conversation with Rurik, Zak phoned the Israeli Embassy and left a message for Alon to call back to Bournemouth.

The following Thursday afternoon, the international telephone system's high-frequency tone heralded Alon's long-distance call.

"Zak, *shalom*, Alon here. How are you?"

"Thanks for calling back, Alon. I'm bewildered and I certainly don't feel a million Dollars."

"Really?"

"Really... Are you going to settle up, as agreed?"

"Sure."

"When?"

"Next week, when I'm back in England, I'll phone you and make the meet."

"Can you elaborate on that one, Alon."

"Please, Zak, next week."

CHAPTER THIRTY

London: February 1986

Suspicions Confirmed

DUE to heavy traffic on the M3 that morning, Daphna and Zak were delayed getting to the Royal Lancaster Hotel. While Zak went to see if Alon was in the hotel, Daphna went to a payphone in the lobby to explain their lateness to daughter Tracy, before seeking a much-needed coffee...

Zak found Alon sitting with his back to the wall in the plush lounge-bar on the first floor, with coffee for two already laid out.

With the *shaloms* and small talk over, Alon carefully drew a bundle of money from his pocket.

"There you are, Zak, two hundred and fifty English Pounds for your additional expenses," Alon uttered in a splendorous manner as if the money had come from the 'Holy Ark of the Covenant'.

"Are you happy now?"

"Not at all, 'Alon-cum-Donald'."

"Why?"

"What about the Nigerian commission you owe for?"

Suspicions Confirmed

The killer look appeared on the Mossad agent's face once more.

"Come on, Zak. Franz did not give us the correct information about the Nigerian installations and transmissions."

"Shylock, I bet you squeezed two lots of blood from Franz."

"What do you mean, Zak?"

"Stop playing silly buggers, Alon."

"What on earth are you hinting at?"

"You duped me."

"What are you talking about, Zak?"

"We both know now, you deceitfully used me to chaperon Franz out of Germany into Austria, so he could pass on the Libyan defence secrets, radio frequencies and computer codes in Salzburg."

"How do you know that?"

"Alon, I'm not an utter *'schmuck'*, I was there, albeit confused at the time."

"Keep your nose out of this game, Zak."

The deadly glint appeared stronger than ever in the ruthless Israeli's eyes.

"I'm not the Aswan dam, Alon," Zak spat in contempt.

"What does that mean?"

"Israelis are callous."

"Really, Franz didn't give us anything."

"If Franz did not perform, I'm sure you would not be topping up my out of pocket expenses; in fact, there is forty Pounds too much."

"A deal is a deal!"

"Right, so stop hiding behind a few English pounds and pay up as agreed."

"Stop talking in riddles, Zak."

"Alright, Alon. You were at my side in the Café Tosca in Salzburg when Robbie said: 'We will only pay for what we get.' The next day over lunch Robbie told me in the 'Winkler': 'That he' d got what he came for', so explain that." Zak harangued.

"Robbie told you that?"

"Yes. Then he left suddenly after a phone call, probably from you or your superior. Just like you told me about Franz having secret Libyan radar defence information, remember?"

"O.K., Zak, maybe you can understand this: 'The name of the game is not to pay'!"

Gutted! Zak cursed Alon in *Ivrit*, as he noticed the Mossad agent's brown shoes again and Rurik's past words about Herr Müller..

"That's brave talk, Alon."

"Believe it, Zak, and don't ever contact Franz again."

"You *gonif*, you completely reneged on your '*Mazel un Brocheh*', 'Donald cum Alon' you can take your soiled money back."

"What are you saying?"

Zak threw the Sterling notes with all the strength he could muster at the startled Mossad agent.

"I will be pursuing your firm's disgusting conduct with Robbie's superior."

"Like who?"

"Nahum Adonni, Mossad chief."

"Why not also tell the *Knesset*, Zak."

"Don't worry, I will if I have to. I understand the Likud party is broke, maybe my commission has been used for a short-fall or misappropriated by one of your indicted ministers. Or maybe the Pollard affair is on your chief's conscience. *Sauve qui peut,* hey?"

"Maybe," Alon jeered, as he got up from the sumptuous couch, only to be further devastated on realising Daphna had been standing within earshot!

"Maybe I'll even send a Statement into your P.M.'s Office."

"Remember what the British did to Lawrence of Arabia, Zak," Alon cried as he collected and stuffed the money into his jacket pocket, before scurrying off.

"You're only assuming, Alon. Remember, I was there when you screwed me," Zak called after Alon. Daphna, still standing there, frozen in shock at what she had seen and overheard.

The meeting aborted, Zak sadly left the 'Royal Lancaster' with Daphna to meet Tracy in the 'Green Man' over at Harrods.

Suspicions Confirmed

The conflict with Alon left a bad taste in Zak's mouth and as far as he was concerned the State of Israel's halo had been well and truly tarnished. Was this now the Government of the Promised Land? Jewish officials who could not be trusted to keep their word to fellow Jews? A *'Mazel un Brocheh'* obviously meant nothing to them! Could any State that was set up to be ethical and moral expect to retain respect or even to survive if it were not just? Mossad could be bringing retribution upon the Land of Israel with its web of deception and deceit, Zak thought sadly.

CHAPTER THIRTY-ONE

London: March — April 1986

Startling Headlines

TUESDAY March 25th, not quite a hundred years since the Indian Chief Geronimo surrendered to an American cavalry General called Nelson in the Arizona desert, and the mighty US Sixth Fleet[12] was sailing off the shores of the Libyan desert!

Zak was staggered by the startling headline looming up at him from the 'Daily Telegraph', reading like a playback from the time Franz had blurted out about playing simulated war games over Libya, during the ride from Munich to Salzburg:

---

[12] THE AMERICAN SIXTH FLEET IS THE MOST DEVASTATING WAR-MACHINE THAT MAN HAS EVER KNOWN.

Startling Headlines

Daily Telegraph

No. 40,669. TUESDAY, MARCH, 25 1986 Printed in LONDON and MANCHESTER

Retaliation for missile attack

U.S. WAR JETS HIT LIBYA

Two ships blasted, says White House

By RICHARD BEESTON in Washington

WARPLANES of the U.S. Sixth Fleet attacked two Libyan missile patrol boats and a SAM-5 missile site yesterday after six Soviet-made missiles had been fired at U.S. planes and ships which defied Col. Gaddafi's "Line of Death" and entered the Gulf of Sidra.

The White House spokesman, Mr Larry Speakes, said one Libyan patrol boat, thought to have a crew of about 27, appeared to have no survivors and was "dead in the water," apparently sinking. The other Libyan boat was seriously damaged.

Mr Speakes said there were no U.S. casualties and denied a Libyan television report that three American aircraft had been shot down.

He said damage to the Libyan missile site on the shore was still being assessed.

Saying that the United States does not consider the episode closed, Mr Speakes added: "We now consider all approaching Libyan forces to have hostile intent."

In response to a question, Mr Speakes said he "couldn't characterise it as a war" between the United States and Libya.

President Reagan was kept informed throughout the day of the dramatic developments in the Gulf of Sidra and Congressional leaders were called to the White House to be briefed on the action.

'Russians have trained Libyans'

At a Pentagon briefing the Secretary of Defense, Mr Weinberger, asked if the Russians were operating or assisting at the missile sites replied: "We don't know for sure. They have been there training them."

Mr Weinberger described the seven-hour gap in the U.S. response to the firing of the first Libyan missile as "an example of our forbearance."

There were about four Soviet ships in the area, he added.

The Democratic chairman of the House Foreign Affairs committee, Congressman Dante Fascell, expressed concern that the confrontation could erupt into a significant conflict resulting in the loss of American lives.

And the Democratic vice chairman of the Senate Intelligence Committee, Senator Patrick Leahy, said he was worried that Col Gaddafi might retaliate by taking terrorist action in the United States

'Gulf open to all nations'

A United States Navy fighter being catapulted from the deck of the carrier Saratoga during yesterday's exercises off the Gulf of Sidra.

Tougher warnings for young smokers

By DAVID FLETCHER Health Services Correspondent

A BAN on cigarette advertising in cinemas and tougher, more prominently displayed, health warnings on cigarette packets and posters, were announced by the Department of Health yesterday.

The Government has drawn up a new agreement with the tobacco industry which will impose stricter controls on all forms of cigarette advertising, particularly that likely to be seen by children and young people.

There will also be tougher action, banned with £1 million a year to the industry insert, to stop sales of cigarettes to children under 16.

In place of the existing warning, Cigarettes Can Seriously Damage Your Health, six new ones will appear, used in rotation. They will appear on 30 per cent of the area of all advertisement—that will be up from a more specific warnings, which must take up at least 8%, 5% per cent of the space.

These will be printed in rotation and will say:
● Smoking can cause fatal lung and heart disease;
● Smoking can cause Heart Disease;
● Smoking When Pregnant Can Injure Your Baby and Cause Premature Birth;
● Stopping Smoking Reduces the Risk of Serious Disease;
● Smoking Can Cause Lung Cancer, Bronchitis and Other Chest Diseases;
● More than 30,000 People Die Each Year in the UK from Lung Cancer.

Advertisement cuts

New rules will prevent cigarette posters being positioned close to schools, and spending on poster advertising will be frozen at half the amount being spent in 1980.

No cigarette advertisement will be allowed in magazines with a female readership of more than 200,000 where a third or more of the readers are aged 15 to 24.

Cigarette advertising will also be banned on free gifts distributed to children at events sponsored by tobacco companies such as roadshows and airshows.

The Tobacco Advisory Council and the new plans to combat under-age smoking would

A clear message to combat under-age sales.

THE GREAT COAL TRAIN ROBBERY

By LIN JENKINS

TWO coal trains have been ambushed by a gang thought to be about 50 strong, it was revealed yesterday.

The gang placed sleepers on the track in a remote area near Fourthwcober, Tyne Valley, South Wales, forcing the trains to a halt. Then the hoppers were opened, spilling the coal near the track.

The gang shovelled the coal into waiting lorries and it was sold for around £2 a hundredweight.

THATCHER REPLIES TO 'SMEAR'

By JAMES WIGHTMAN Political Correspondent

THE PRIME MINISTER faced an intensified row over shares last night after issuing a statement giving details of a shareholding which she had started in 1971and trying to refute allegations that she had acted improperly.

Opposition MPs said that the statement raised more queries than it answered and threatened to tackle Mrs Thatcher directly during routine questions in the commons this afternoon.

The purpose of the statement was to deny allegations, first made in a Sunday newspaper last weekend, that she had bought and sold shares in the Australian company, Broken Hill Proprietary, making a profit of £2,500.

None sold

The Prime Minister said that she had shares in Broken Hill Proprietary as well as other shares, all held on her behalf, but none had been sold.

The statement, carefully drafted after consultation between the Prime Minister and advisers, said:

In 1971 Mrs Thatcher bought a small shareholding in BHP (Broken Hill Proprietary) which was registered in her own name.

Between 1971 and 1986, through a series of rights issues, dividend reuses and share splits the holding was increased to its current level.

Last year Mrs Thatcher made arrangements for her holdings of shares, including her holdings in BHP, to be transferred to a firm of investment managers.

Continued on Back Page, col 3

OIL PRICES DIVE AS OPEC DISAGREES

By Our Business Editor

Prices of North Sea oil fell sharply yesterday following a breakdown in talks among the members of the Organisation of Petroleum Exporting Countries on production-sharing arrangements.

The price of Brent oil for delivery in June dropped to £11.75 a barrel, close to the low set level since the slide started last month.

The 13 oil ministers agreed at the need to cut output by two to two and a half million barrels a day to 16 million to try to push prices back up to $28 a barrel by were divided on how the cut should be allocated. They met again on April 15.

City Report.—P.17.

POUND AND SHARES FALL

By Our Economics

Upon reading Richard Beeston's (from Washington) account of the attack on Libya, Zak immediately telephoned Rurik...

"Hi, Zsa Zsa, is Rurik there?"

"No, Zak, he's gone to find Franz."

"Because of the attack on Libya?"

"Yes, of course."

"Okay, tell him to phone me when he gets back, will you?"

"Yes, of course, Zak. Kiss Daphna for me."

"Thank you, will do."

Later that day while Zak was listening to his Barry Manilow records, Rurik telephoned back:

"Zak, Rurik here; you've heard the news?"

"About jets from the US Sixth Fleet bombing secret Libyan missile sites?"

"Yes. Franz swears he never received a penny from them."

"When did he tell you that?"

"I just came from his house."

"Any sign of affluence since you were last there?"

"It's the same, except he has some new clothes and a pair of Christian Dior sunglasses. You know about the 'Merc'?"

"Do the glasses match the car?"

"So happens they are the same colour frames."

"What about the Princess?"

"I don't know. She's gone to see her family in Morocco."

"An obvious show of affluence, I would say."

"I suppose so, Zak," Rurik answered zestlessly.

"Okay, I will speak with Udi in Israel to try and ascertain if he knows anything."

"O.K., Zak, keep me informed."

Zak cut the line to Rurik and then connected with another international line and tapped out the telephone number of Udi's flat in Tel Aviv...

"Udi, Zak here. How are you?"

"*Shalom*, fine. How is Daphna?"

"She's great... and Lena?"
"She is also good."
"And Abbie?"
"Abbie's Abbie, if you know what I mean, Zak."
"Yes, a devious Mossad butterfly."
"Zak, you know not to let on about her, understood?"
"Of course not, Udi."
"Anyway, she's in America."
"Really?"
"Come on Zak, give me a break."
"Okay, Udi. Have you heard the news about the Americans bombing Libya?"
"Yes, it's big news here, everyone's rejoicing," Udi let slip.
"Did I not tell you, your friends screwed us?"
"Are you associating your adventure in Salzburg with the American bombing of Libya?"
"With hindsight, absolutely."
"But who knew it would lead to this, Zak?
"Well, it did. You must know, Franz sold your countrymen the deactivating codes of the Libyan radar defence system as well as supplying the whole shebang and location of their lethal missile sites."
"Zak, please, not on the phone."
"And next to Italy, Germany is the largest trading partner with Libya and I bet Israeli exports have gone up with Nigeria in the past few months."
"So?"
"So, tell your side to settle up for the Nigerian info."
"Impossible, you know Mossad told me to keep my nose out of the matter."
"Did they threaten you?"
"Yes, and you know our position over here."
"*Gonifs*! I'll have to send them an invoice for payment."
"Don't do that, Zak."
"Why not?"
"It will cause Lena and me trouble this end."
"Another visit from *Shabak*?"

"Maybe."

"Oh dear."

"So what do you think happened, Zak?"

"It's quite obvious that Mossad used me as chaperon and traded off Franz's information to the Americans."

"You really think so?"

"Yes, the coincidence of events and the timing of the Americans' action plus what has been said and done by both Franz and Alon since Salzburg fits too neatly."

"Maybe."

"Udi, President Reagan's open attack on Libya, unlike Pearl Habour, coupled with the US Sixth Fleet combat jets sustaining no loss when trying to teach the Colonel a lesson, all gells now."

"What's with Pearl Harbour?."

"History."

"Oh! How do you know we traded with the Americans?"

"It's been in all the newspapers. Two-Way trade and all that stuff."

"I see."

"Reagan's taken all the bloody glory this time and your guys are playing it like *shtoomers*."

"Why *shtoomers*?"

"Because Israel is keeping quiet."

"Maybe."

"In fact as far as I'm concerned, your cowboys secretly passed on the classified Libyan information to *Va'adat*, who would be obliged to inform the Prime Minister's Office in the *Knesset* in Jerusalem. The rest is also history."

"Who the hell are *Va'adat*, Zak?"

"Udi, don't play the innocent with me."

"No, seriously, I don't know anything about *Va'adat, Rashei Hasherutim*."

"*Va'adat*, my friend, as if you didn't know, controls Mossad. The Chairman of *Va'adat, Rashei Hasherutim*, who you most elegantly mentioned, has direct access to Israel's Prime Minister's Office in Jerusalem."

"Unbelievable, Zak, how do you know such things?"

"Because I've been duped, cheated by Nahum Adnoni and his team, as sure as olives are olives."

"Who is Nahum Adnoni?"

"Come on, Udi, he's Mossad's present Chief."

"O.K., Zak, I will speak to my contact here in Tel Aviv from the 'Institute' and make the point for you."

"Udi, also ask your friends if they received those C130's lying in Burbank in the U.S. of A. that belong to the Libyans and about secret arms deals with Iran."

"How do you know about them?"

To try and loosen Udi's tongue without mentioning the informative Roxanne in Washington, Zak let rip:

"It's common knowledge in Washington; Libya paid for six 130's, but Kissinger wouldn't sign the E.U."

"What's an E.U.?"

"Ask Oliver North, as if you didn't know."

"Strange you should mention that name, Zak."

"Which name?"

"Olly North."

"Why?"

"Because there are rumours circulating that we traded some very special information with the Americans so that Washington would not prevent us selling over-priced weaponry and Hawk missiles to Iran."

"That's what I've been saying: The Israeli-American Agreement of '85, an alliance with the CIA – Two-Way trade coupled with the Pollard affair. Follow it through, hey."

"O.K., I will keep you informed," Udi promised weakly.

"By the way, Udi, it's also rumoured in Washington that Israel wants the Sixth Fleet based in Haifa!"

"You have contacts in Washington?"

"You could say that."

"Maybe. I heard the aircraft carrier 'America' or the 'John F Kennedy' is paying a visit to Haifa shortly from the American's Mediterranean naval base in Italy," Udi volunteered.

"To pay their respects to Israel or unload some secret missiles dockside?"

"I've no idea!" Udi confessed and promptly changed the subject: "Zak, would you come over to Israel, if need be?"

"If it meant getting paid as agreed, then yes."

"Good, it's a possible starting point."

As requested, the well-placed Roxanne phoned Zak back from Washington that night with her inside info' on the historical US naval strike:

The first major World Electronic Encounter of Smart Weapons took place on 24th March 1986:-

The USA mounted 'Operation Prairie Fire': An armada of 30 ships (The Daily Telegraph had differed by reporting that there were 45 ships), including Aircraft Carriers USS 'Saratoga', 'America' and 'Coral Sea', complete with 200 aircraft (The 'Daily Telegraph' had reported there had been 200 warplanes). Nuclear subs of the Sixth Fleet deliberately provoked the Libyans on 22nd March 1986, before crossing Gaddafi's 'Line of Death' in the Gulf of Sidra. The American Sixth Fleet, under a protective umbrella of some 100 planes, attacked Libya with A-6 and A-7 intruder aircraft, launching stand-off missiles which easily homed in on and destroyed the secret German-installed Libyan radar station, without any loss being incurred to the Americans from the six Soviet SAM-5 missiles which were fired at them.

According to the papers on Tuesday, 14th April, the trigger-happy President Reagan gave direct orders for F1-11 bombers stationed and waiting in Britain to attack Tripoli and Benghazi again.

By 15th April, Libya had fully repaired its command system from the US Sixth Fleet's attack of the previous month, when large headlines in the 'Daily Telegraph's' broad sheet absolutely convinced Zak that the Americans had obtained the smuggled Libyan Defence files via the Israelis and that Franz or his Boss were still at work!

Startling Headlines

Daily Telegraph

No. 40,686. TUESDAY, APRIL 15, 1986 Printed in LONDON and MANCHESTER

Tripoli enveloped in smoke

U.S. ATTACK ON LIBYA

1 a.m. bombing raid 'on terrorist targets'

By RICHARD BEESTON in Washington

THE United States early today launched air strikes against Libya in retaliation for what it called terrorist attacks on Americans. Some of the planes were from bases in Britain.

The Presidential spokesman, Mr Larry Speakes, said: "U.S. forces have executed a series of carefully-planned air strikes against terrorist targets in Libya."

He said Libya "bears direct responsibility for the bombing in West Berlin on April 5", that killed an American serviceman and a Turkish woman and wounded 230 others at a discotheque.

Speakes said the U.S. warplanes that conducted the attacks were returning to their bases. He said: "Every effort has been made" to avoid hitting civilian targets.

Some of the strikes occurred in the Tripoli and Benghazi region, Mr Speakes said.

The strikes began at 1 a.m. London time.

American television correspondents reporting from Tripoli said attacks had been launched against Libyan Navy craft in the harbour at Tripoli and other targets inland.

Some rockets whined over the capital and struck buildings in the southern part of the city.

Steve Delaney, an NBC correspondent, reported that the southern part of Tripoli was enveloped in smoke.

Most of the action in Tripoli appeared to be directed at targets in the harbour. Power went out in the capital.

It is more than two weeks since Mr Leigh Douglas 35, from Stalham, Norfolk, and Mr Philip Padfield, 40, from Bideford, Devon, were kidnapped by "gunmen" as they walked home from a West Beirut nightclub.

Mr Brian Keenan, 35, from Belfast, who travels on an Irish passport was kidnapped as Thursday morning as he walked to work.

Huge increase in radio traffic

The attacks began after monitors had reported a huge increase in coded radio traffic between United States ships and planes off the Libyan coast.

In the darkness there was no immediate indication whether the attacking planes were carrier-based or were F-111s from American bases in Britain.

President Reagan was to explain the military action in a televised address to the nation at 3am London time—8am in Washington.

Tripoli was hit by at least four air strikes, witnesses said.

Volleys of anti-aircraft fire could be heard from the direction of the port and an explosion was seen at the western part of the city.

Tripoli radio broadcast martial music interrupted only by patriotic slogans.

LIBYAN COMPLICITY ESTABLISHED

By NICHOLAS COMFORT Political Staff

THE Government is now convinced from its own intelligence sources that Libya was directly involved in recent acts of terrorism, and is playing as great a part in the planning of further attacks.

Mrs Thatcher and senior colleagues see this confirmation as strengthening President Reagan's case for military action against Libya.

STUDENTS STRIKE OVER KIDNAPS

By Our Staff Correspondents

All universities and schools in Northern Ireland were yesterday on strike in protest at the kidnapping of two English teachers and an Irish teacher.

Bombs being moved at Upper Heyford, Oxon, yesterday as an F-111 fighter took off. Meanwhile, at Lakenheath an American sentry was dressed in full anti-nuclear battle dress.

America maintains war of nerves

By JOHN BULLOCH Diplomatic Staff

AMERICA yesterday kept up the psychological pressure on Libya with ostentatious air exercises at bases in Britain, top level meetings in Washington, and continuing consultations with European allies.

Libya repeated its pledge to respond to aggression, but also offered half a chance of a compromise with statements dissociating the country from past terrorist incidents and condemning violence.

At the base at Upper Heyford in Oxfordshire, a red alert was declared, bomb loads were moved obliquely within camera range and F-111 fighters took off to rapid succession. There were also extra movements of tanker planes.

A spokesman insisted that an exercise planned months ago was in progress and the Libyan crisis was "just plain coincidence."

American officials said military action would be credible if Col Gaddafi stopped backing terrorist operations.

Libya's denial

In Tripoli, the Libyan People's Foreign Bureau—the Foreign Ministry—said Libya was against all "terroristic operations, the hijacking of airplanes or the murder of the innocent."

The statement also denied any Libyan involvement in recent terrorist incidents, particularly those in Germany.

"Libya does not desire aggression, and is interested in making the Mediterranean a lake of peace and co-operation among the countries surrounding it. Including those of Southern Europe."

ANTI-HUNT DEMO FOR QUEEN

Admirers of the Royal Family prevented anti-hunt demonstrators from displaying a banner at the Queen and other members of the Royal Family left Gloucester Cathedral yesterday after a memorial service for the Duke of Beaufort.

Police arrested four people, who were later released without charge, and two other men were being held concerning separate incidents.

Cathedral service—P14

ROYAL BRIDE'S COAT OF ARMS

Miss Sarah Ferguson has been named, said last night "hopeful of contact with the kidnappers today."

The businessman revealed for the first time that when the three men left with Mrs Guinness, 48, they set the ransom deadline at seven days before charging their minds and making it three.

The man, who cannot be named, said last night "hopeful of contact with the kidnappers today."

EURO CURBS IMPOSED

By ALAN OSBORN Common Market Correspondent

THE TWELVE Common Market countries agreed last night on new diplomatic measures to isolate the Gaddafi regime in Libya.

The chief decision was to impose undefined restrictions on the people's bureaux maintained by Libya in most of the EEC capitals. These quasi-embassies are alleged to provide cover for organised terrorist campaigns in Europe.

But it will be up to each EEC member country to decide how far to limit freedom of movement of Libyan personnel, to reduce the size of the bureaux and to toughen visa requirements.

Murdered WPc

The bureau in London was closed in 1984 following the murder of WPc Yvonne Fletcher. Britain's diplomatic relations with Libya were severed at the same time.

Sir Geoffrey Howe, Foreign Secretary, had evidently hoped that the rest of the Community would follow the British example. While careful not to show disappointment, he noted that the other countries "have not gone as far as we have gone."

However, the EEC has for the first time explicitly accused Libya by name of complicity in the support of terrorism.

In their formal statement, the Community Foreign Ministers stated "states clearly implicated in supporting terrorism should be actively to denounce such support and to respect the rules of international law." They called on Libya to "act accordingly."

Sir Geoffrey declined to say whether or not the EEC move would dissuade the Americans from taking military action against Libya.

But West Germany and other officials conceded that the response was likely to be thought feeble by Washington. The statesmen takes the community much further than before, and the Americans have to realise.

EQUITY CHAOS ON ISRAEL

By HARVEY LEE

LEFT wingers vociferously demanded a complete cultural boycott of Israel caused the annual meeting of Equity, the actors' union, to break up in chaos yesterday.

Carlo Redgrave, reading a motion proposed by his sister Vanessa and 30 other members, called for a ban on performing in Israel and an end to all sales by the television and film industries of recorded material involving Equity members.

He referred to the Jewish state as "occupied Palestine" and to its laws as "fundamentally racist" and was greeted with a barrage of shouts of "anti-semite" and "Hitler" from angry opponents.

Mr Redgrave's supporters, meanwhile, added loudly to the chaos and the meeting at the Novelty Theatre, had to be suspended by Nigel Davenport, who was in the chair.

Equity officials and council members explained to members: "It was necessary to stop because the presiding became completely out of control. I am aware that the proposals may not be to your taste, but you should listen to them and if he vote against them."

Mr Redgrave then resumed his tirade against the state of Israel and its Zionist founders.

He said: "Israel cannot be a democracy. It is not founded on democratic foundations."

Continued on Back Page, Col 3

£300m ORDERS WON BY ROLLS

Rolls-Royce, the state-owned aero engine firm, was a record £500 million worth of civil orders in the first quarter of this year.

The group now has orders totalling £2·4 billion, representing between 9 months and two years work, providing further evidence that the civil aviation market is recovering.

CONTACT ON KIDNAPPING 'TODAY'

By JOHN WEEKS Crime Staff in Dublin

A BUSINESS associate of Mr John Guinness, whose wife Jennifer was abducted in Dublin a week ago and held for a £2 million ransom, said last night that the family was "hopeful" of contact with the kidnappers today.

LATE NEWS

London Phone: 01-353 4242

Wedding dress design—P14.

LOVABLE CHARLES

Dagmar Koller, 45-year-old wife of Vienna's mayor, said after meeting Prince Charles on his visit to the city yesterday: "I was surprised at how good-looking he is. I wanted to hug him. He is the sort of man I love."

GEMS CHARGE

Jeffrey Taylor, 53-year-old

Special Article—P14
Crisis in Med.—P17

Forbidden Yesterday

In a nutshell, the American bombers flew onto their targets without the Libyan batteries, containing SAM-2s, 3s, 5s, 6s and 8s defensive missiles scoring any hits, thus allowing some thirty-two 2,000 lb laser bombs to be dropped with utter impunity, causing considerable damage. The Libyan missiles that did get fired at the attacking US planes fell on city suburbs, one very nearly causing the death of Colonel Gaddafi himself.

This second action, of course, had been prompted in part by an event on 2nd April when a scheduled TWA flight from Rome to Athens had a cavity blown in its side, instantly killing four passengers and sucking another three out of the jet. The pilot miraculously managed to land the damaged aircraft safely at Athens Airport. No group claimed responsibility for the action, but Arab Revolutionary groups whispered (see UN resolution 748 [1992]) that it was in retaliation for the first US attack on Libya, a fact which Colonel Gaddafi strenuously denied, coupled with the bombing in a West German discotheque on 5th April, which killed an American soldier and a Turkish woman and wounded some 200 military and civilian persons. Consequently the Americans rapidly planned another air strike against Libya.

Having read the full account of how US F1-11s, with Prime Minister Margaret Thatcher's blessing, had taken off from an American base in Britain to bomb Tripoli and Benghazi with at least four air strikes, apparently without loss to the Americans, Zak felt obliged to phone Rurik and Udi again...

They both meekly agreed to probe their respective contacts, which Zak somehow felt they would do with ever diminishing interest. They knew the Londoner was 'out on a limb'.

CHAPTER THIRTY-TWO

Trieste: November 1986

High Hopes and Shams

MAYTIME brought no news nor flowers for Zak, let alone results, from either Rurik or Udi. However, there was strong interest being shown in purchasing the Old Nigerian Naira from a Swiss Italian lawyer called Tramezzani.

Tramezzani's apparent interest started with a telex from his office in Como, on behalf of his Italian principal, Carrado, a likely buyer of the Naira. It transpired that Carrado had been enlightened about the mechanics of the lucrative Niara deal by the Sicilian restaurateur (Lionel Morris's partner from the Edgware Road!). Later it unfolded that Carrado was an honorary Italian Consul to an island in the Indian Ocean, and lived outside Venice, on the road to Trieste — Italy's most northern sea port.

In July, because of the 'sweet sounding' telex traffic from the Swiss lawyer, Zak took the opportunity to meet Tramezzani in St. Moritz, while on a trip to visit known commodity dealers in both Zurich and Berne...

At six thousand feet, Zak was nearing the end of the long winding train journey from the Swiss capital. He looked in awe at the scenic mountains of the Upper Engadine towering above the lake and the splendour of St. Moritz itself. The breathtaking first sight of the alpine village in summertime was worth the dizzy trip regardless...

It came as no surprise to Zak, upon arriving at the famous out-of-season ski resort, to find the steep high street immersed in tranquillity. Noticing the appointed Rolex jeweller's shop nestling in old-world charm on the bow of a mount, Zak made a mental note to have the clasp adjusted on his 'Oyster' and view the cuckoo clocks.

Tramezzani had chosen to holiday during that warm, quiet time of year at the Hotel Albana, located in the centre of the old village. The 'Albana' was cosy-looking, displaying four stars and, amongst other comforts, boasted a fine cellar, grillroom and wine bar. Zak didn't hesitate to check into the charming hotel for a couple of nights with a view to discussing the format to sell the two billion Naira, and sample the fare from the grill via the limping *Maître d'*...

Leaving the optimistic lawyer enjoying the delights and comfort of the 'Albana', Zak concluded that the chances of closing the Nigerian currency transaction had strengthened, if Tramezzani was really Tramezzani. So much so Zak had agreed in principle to visit Tramezzani's principal in Italy to close the deal. Before leaving St. Moritz by train, Zak stopped off at 'Club Med' (Victoria Hotel) for a look around...

However, not until the Sicilian restaurateur promised to pay the price of a return air ticket to Italy in November, did Zak agree to meet Tramezzani's principal, Carrado, in Venice.
On Guy Fawkes day, before boarding the Air Alitalia AZ 295 noon flight to Venice from Heathrow, Zak was obliged to sign a commission note with the Sicilian, in exchange for the £370 cheque for the air ticket and introduction...

High Hopes and Shams

Zak was met on the tarmac at Marco Polo Tessera Airport by Carrado, accompanied by the Sicilian restaurateur's old aunt and her twenty-year-old-looking grandson. The aunt was obviously there to protect her nephew's £370 investment! The old Sicilian aunt reminded Zak somewhat of an Italian looking Dame Margaret Rutherford, with a big croc' bag doubling for the famous Dame's umbrella. The attending grandson was not unlike a curly-headed Frank Sinatra in his younger days. The grandmother spoke no English, but the skinny grandson did speak pidgin English.

Carrado was a dapper man, with a jet-black 'designer' beard surrounding a roman nose, deep-set, dark eyes and looked a polished, forty-five years of age.

When the polite smiles and weak handshakes were 'put away in the Italian's top drawer', they all boarded a waiting motor launch in the nearby *Laguna*, bound for the Luna Hotel. Zak knew his chosen hotel (the sister hotel to the 'Danieli') was situated between the Piazza San Marco and the gourmet 'Louis Bar'. Due to the noise of the high-speed launch cutting through the choppy *Laguna* there was little attempt to make conversation until the launch moored at the 'Luna's' private berth...

In the lounge of the 'Luna', over frosted Camparis, Zak deduced from the strained conversation that as he was now in Venice, Consul Carrado would begin to make the necessary appointment with the buyer of the Naira who apparently lived in or operated out of Trieste. And why not? Zak sighed to himself. Carrado was not funding the hotel side of the visit and he wasn't even the buyer's partner! Zak bit his tongue on being instructed to wait in the 'Luna' until contacted. The whole deal was loose and Zak knew it was going to be costly waiting in Venice. Furthermore, Zak was not happy about the possibility of waiting in the damp, water-logged city for days and possible *sayanim* eyes — as since the seventies when a Trieste oil refinery secretly producing for Israel was blown up by 'Black September', Mossad affiliated Italians were forever watchful — and Vanunu was lured by a Mossad Butterfly in Rome. Alas, Venice in the winter time was far removed from his last, fabulous stay at the

'Luna' with Daphna, during a warm spring and a hot summer holiday at the renowned Excelsior Hotel over on the Lido, with Daphna and the kids.

The next afternoon, after enjoying lunch at 'Louis Bar', there was good news awaiting Zak in his hotel pigeon hole. A signed message from Carrado's son-in-law informed the waiting Londoner to be ready at nine the next morning to go to Trieste. Special mention was made: Not to check out of the 'Luna', which presumably meant a one-day return trip to Trieste to see the Naira buyer.

Back in the comfort of the hotel room, the message induced thoughts of a past trip to Trieste, where the 'Iron Curtain' terminated at the shoreline of the Adriatic.

* * *

Zak had visited Trieste before, in the mid-seventies, travelling there by road in a racy, hired 'Hertz' car from Venice Airport. At the time, Zak had been investigating an Italian wholesaler who was rumoured to be producing his firms branded jeans across the border in Yugoslavia. The 'rip-off' was personally causing Zak much aggravation with his Middle Eastern customers.

It was realised when nearing the outskirts of Trieste that the broad sidewalk overhanging the sea was used for sunbathing by locals and passing motorists alike. Zak had earmarked a scenic point for a sunbathe when his investigations in the back streets of Trieste were concluded. Directly behind the delightful spot he'd chosen stood a commanding villa built on a rise in a lightly-wooded area, protected by tall iron gates that displayed a large oblong brass nameplate.

Snooping around in Trieste, Zak had been offered bulk lots of false Levi and Falmer jeans via an obscure shipping agent in the freeport zone. However, trying to find his own firms brand of 'shams', he'd come up against a solid 'brick wall'. Sadly, unable to pursue the illicit manufacturing further in the Adriatic town, he'd given up for the time being. Happily though, the old part of town stayed in Zak's mind. A local restaurateur had told the snooping Londoner: Trieste was given to Italy after a secret treaty was signed in London on 26th April, 1915, by the British, French and Russians as a peace settlement. Then, for reasons best known to themselves, the Italians did not occupy the city until 4th November 1918. Italy had lost it again to the United Nations after the Second World War, to have it revert back to them in November 1954.

The visiting Londoner mentally nicknamed Trieste, 'ping pong city', as he soaked up hot sun rays and local amber nectar at the earmarked spot before departing for home to prepare for his trip to the Middle East.

* * * * *

The next morning as informed, Carrado's son-in-law collected Zak from outside the 'Luna' in a water taxi. The young Italian spoke 'good broken English' so they'd chatted freely on the calm waters of the canal before arriving at a vacant *'vaporetto'* mooring opposite the 'Tronchetto', (the ever-busy arrival and departure terminal of Venice), where Carrado was waiting in a shiny top-series Fiat car.

The seventy-mile drive to prosperous 'ping pong city' along the A4 Autostrada in Carrado's Fiat was uneventful, not at all enlightening for Zak. Although he was amused to be returning to the city that had been given to Italy by the United Nations and later found it nostalgic to pass the place where he'd sunbathed for a few hours during another yesterday.

Zak knew the name of Carrado's principal, a certain Professor Querci, as his name had been coupled with the Consul's name on the Sicilian's commission note as the buyer. The Professor was purported to be a legal advisor to the Italian Government, according to the Sicilian's side-kick at Heathrow, when Zak was indifferently passed the £370 cheque for the outlay for the air ticket to Venice.

Forbidden Yesterday

The two Italians and Zak met up with the Professor in the lobby of the 'Duchi d' Aosta', a grand hotel in the Piazza Unita d' Italia, facing the Trieste waterfront. The eccentric-looking Professor had long straight hair, thin-rimmed specs and was clad in a voluminous 'Loden' coat, just like the one the British Foreign Secretary, Douglas Hurd, sports every winter time. Zak assumed that Carrado and the Professor were meeting for the first time because of the formal manner in which they introduced themselves. The Professor did not speak English, but his demeanour oozed with class and breeding when cordially inviting them all to lunch in a nearby fish restaurant, the 'Nostro Azzurro' on the Riva Suaro. Because of the Professor's apparent love of sport he managed to communicate and joke about football by continually mentioning the learned man's idol, Bobby Charlton, until the *antipasti* arrived.

After a good munch in the much-acclaimed restaurant, whose *alimento* surpassed the mundane wine and decor, they were all invited to the generous Professor's villa to talk business.

Due to a premonition, Zak was not surprised to arrive at the villa overlooking the Adriatic, with the oblong brass plate bearing the Professor's title and name, which he had mentally noted during his last trip to look for his brand of sham jeans. Karl Jung's theory just had to be wrong, Zak hoped...

Judging by the priceless-looking paintings, furniture, stuffed lions and tigers that were dotted all over the palatial villa, it was apparent the eccentric Querci was either a very successful lawyer or possessed a rich wife. To Zak's mind, the lavishly-furnished villa, where every thing had its place, could have been the abode of Salvador Dali. Suddenly, they were greeted by the magnificent-looking *Signora* Querci with a trayful of tall Camparis. Sadly, the smiling *signora* quickly disappeared, not to be seen again.

Before settling down to business, the Professor called for his English-speaking son, Gabrielli, to act as his personal interpreter. It then transpired the Professor was not the buyer after all, but another middleman acting for a client, who turned out to be the director of Texaco-Eastern Block.

High Hopes and Shams

The meeting, nonetheless, was encouraging, inasmuch as the Professor promised to call a meeting with the actual buyer and to strongly recommend the purchase of the two billion Naira in the next few days. It was finally agreed that Zak would wait in Venice, ready to act fast on the Professor's summons. The Professor humorously bade Zak farewell exclaiming in a high pitched voice:
"B-o-b-b-y C-h-a-r-l-t-o-n"!

Carrado appeared pleased with the level of enthusiasm, yet disgruntled that the Professor was not affording him the opportunity to be in at the close with the actual buyer.

Zak's mind was in a whirl as Carrado's car whisked him down the Professor's drive through the tall, open iron gates towards waterlogged Venice...

All the years of pursuing a buyer for the crazy Naira was nearly at an end, thought Zak. A few more days and he would be worth a cool eighteen million Dollars. At last, he was going to see his share of the commission for having been willing to gamble all his time and money to sell the two billion Old Nigerian Naira. The chasing, the racing, the anticipating, the costly communication and hotel bills to keep the deal on the 'front-burner', were all now behind him.

As Carrado's car exited from the *Autostrada's* pay toll on the outskirts of Venice, they were suddenly intercepted by a lurking, black Mercedes Benz 280E. To their complete surprise, the old Sicilian aunt jumped out of the mysterious old 'Merc' waving her battered crocodile handbag, shouting and screaming at them in excitable Italian... When the commotion was over, Carrado's shaking son-in-law explained nervously:

"Mister Zak, the old lady insists on taking you back to your hotel alone."

"Why is that?"

"She thinks we are cheating her nephew in London."

"Do you think I should go with her for a chat?"

"It's O.K. by the Consul. You can then tell her exactly what happened with the Professor, if you like."

"Is it safe with them? The driver looks *Mafioso* to me."

"Yes, that's why we don't mind at all, Mister Zak."

Reluctantly, Zak turfed himself out of the 'Fiat' just as the heavens opened up with a thunderstorm.

Drenched and slumped in the back seat of the old 'Merc', Zak found himself being 'grilled' in pidgin English by the grandson, with frantic prompting by the grandmother, all the way back to Venice...

Entering the Piazzale Roma the tough-looking, scar-faced driver parked the 'Merc' near the water front.

Zak was amazed and embarrassed to find himself being closely chaperoned to the open deck of a wet, cramped *motoscafo* before it chugged down the Grand Canal. A marked change from the water-taxi ride on the calm canal earlier. Zak showed his resentment on arriving at the 'Luna', by ignoring the dripping *Signora* and her wet escort and going directly to his room.

Sodden and completely 'knackered' back in his room, Zak felt swamped, not caring any more about possible 'death in Venice'.

During the next two days Zak did not venture out, not even to 'Louis' Bar' for fear of missing the Professor's summons, or possibly being kidnapped by the old aunt or Mossad.

While idling in the 'Luna's' lobby, Zak was surprised to read in a discarded English newspaper:

ISRAELIS ADMIT TO KIDNAPPING VANANU

The idling Englishman wondered why the Israelis should choose to climb down over the Vananu affair! Maybe there was still hope for him. Zak wished for an angel to shine down on him, as he turned over a page and read on...

Precisely at 4 p.m. on the third day of waiting, the Professor telephoned, shouting a distorted greeting down the line, 'Bobby Charlton!' Then a distinctive Italian-sounding voice, which Zak thought he recognized, took over to inform him in perfect English:

"Good afternoon, I am the associate of Professor Querci. We are on our way from Milano University by car to Venice. Please be at the Piazzale Roma in one hour so we can pick you up before going on to Trieste."

Sudden thoughts of Clarissa came to mind, of her studies and sexual exploits in both Milan and Berlin Universities...

"Thank you for calling, *Signore*. But where exactly shall I meet you in the Piazzale Roma?"

"The Hotel Santa Chiara at the far end of the Piazzale. Please be there on time."

"No problem for me, *Signore*, see you at five."

Zak hurriedly packed before settling the ludicrously expensive bill with his American Express card.

The 'Luna' behind him, Zak fortuitously caught *motoscafo* number 2 up the Grand Canal to the Piazzale Roma...

Zak waited some ten minutes in the 'Santa Chiara' bar before he spotted a Volvo 964. The chauffeur-driven saloon with its two passengers in the back seat slowly entered the Piazzale Roma from the early evening darkness into the light of the square...

"B-o-b-b-y C-h-a-r-l-t-o-n!" the Professor shouted out in greeting as he entered the comfortable hotel bar.

The 'turned on' Professor warmly shook hands, as his associate struggled to introduce himself.

"Good evening, I'm acting as the interpreter for the Professor, just for the evening."

"Good evening to you, sir, have we met before?"

"I don't believe so."

Zak was given to understand in the comfort of the front seat of the Volvo (much favoured by *Frummers* worldwide) that the Professor's interpreter was a well-established Shipping Agent, with a large network of clients who moved goods mainly in and out of Austria and Yugoslavia. The 'Shipper' elaborated:

Forbidden Yesterday

"Trieste is the import–export port for all Austria's sea-going cargo. I am given to understand you were in the jeans business, Mister Levin." A giveaway, as none of Zak's immediate Italian contacts knew he was a 'Jeans Man'!

"Yes, I was, *Signore*." Zak bit his tongue quickly so as not to jeopardize the Niara sale...

Upon arrival in Trieste, the chauffeur was dismissed outside the 'Saban' on the via Comici, an historic old trattoria which offered a high class and varied mid-European menu and wine list.

Whilst the Professor slurped his *Spaghetti al turtui nero* and gulped down the young Merlot, produced and bottled in the nearby hills of Gorizian, Zak and the 'Shipper' convened. It seemed that the buyer, the Vienna-based President of Texaco – Eastern Block, was flying in from Moscow at midnight, especially to discuss purchasing the two billion Naira in the Professor's office. Zak was further given to understand over the tasty meal that the proposed buyer fully realised 'Bonny Light' could be traded from Nigeria at a discount, with a mixture of Dollars and old Niara. It was all music to Zak's ears and also a prize to his eyes to watch the ever-smiling Professor mentally counting his own finder's fee.

After the enjoyable feast and splendid wine, which the Professor paid for in cash, they made their way to the Hotel Savoia Excelsior on the Riva Mandracchio where Zak was to stay. To the Londoner's' astonishment, the price just to sleep in the deluxe hotel was 125,000 Lira, far more over the moon than even the 'Luna'.

Once installed in the hotel room, Zak did a quick rescue operation on himself in the shower... With a clean shirt on his back and feeling revived, the visiting Londoner was confronted by Gabielli. The Italian Professor's son seemed to have appeared from beneath an orange-coloured sky in the hotel lobby! They hastened to the eccentric Professor's nearby office, just off the Piazza Unita d'Italia, located in the most prestigious commercial section of Trieste.

High Hopes and Shams

The offices of the Professor's firm were an eye-opener indeed, like a fancy Victorian-type summerhouse, displaying expensive, floral, covered furniture that matched long, pretentious drapes.

From out of the darkness the exceedingly well-dressed Naira buyer arrived earlier than expected. The man from 'Texaco' was a short, squat man with white hair and a striking Albino complexion.

Handsomely early-forties, the Albino splendidly belied his somewhat mixed features. The Professor formally introduced the buyer as Rajko Milutinovic, who Zak found out later was half Mexican and half Yugoslav.

The glowing Professor happily cracked open the waiting bottle of 'Remy Martin XO' for Rajko before commencing the proceedings. Sitting at the attentive Professor's side, the 'Shipper' translated every word into the learned man's optimistic, legal ear.

It was not long before the Albino dictated in Americanised English, the pros and cons regarding the scope of the offered Naira. Zak, who had refused the deluxe cognac, was also lectured by the informative Albino about his recent attendance at an OPEC meeting in Vienna at which George Schultz, the American Secretary of State, had made clear: 'Any big profits made by oil-producing countries or oil-companies should also benefit the local economy, not arms dealers or the like'.

The virtuous buyer therefore imposed an important condition of purchase:

"I need a declaration from the Nigerian Government prior to my commitment, that profits from our transaction will benefit the Nigerian economy. To be item number seven on your offer." Zak knew item seven would pose a problem for his seller Van Darlen, who only had the option on the Naira until the end of the year. Then the offer would expire — dropped and considered obsolete forever by the Nigerian Treasury. Zak also realised the Albino's predicament and did not challenge the request.

On settling the price for the two billion old Nigerian Naira, Zak issued the appropriate pro-forma invoice. All subject to item seven, with validity until the end of the last day of 1986.

Forbidden Yesterday

Rajko quested the Professor's consent, then gave Zak his business card to confirm the undertaking as soon as possible. The expensive card bore the Texaco logo, a Vienna address, telephone and telex co-ordinates. Zak left the convivial meeting after handshakes and a wink from the 'Shipper', who never did reveal his name.

A hard night's sleep and another 125,000 Lira shelled out, Zak had his air ticket endorsed by a local travel agent for his return flight to LHR from Trieste via Milan. Before heading out to the airport, Zak kept a lunchtime appointment with the Professor's son and business partner in the hub of the city. Gabielli had 'button-holed' Zak the night before to arrange the lunch, wanting to import textiles from the UK, on DA terms with his partner, which Zak knew could leave him out on a limb. Lunch devoured under a clear-blue Trieste sky, the Londoner politely declined the risky export opportunity.

With his head really 'in the clouds', Zak took off from Trieste Airport at 15:35 for a short hop to Milan, there to await departure of flight BA 513 at 18:55 back to London.
Still 'flying high', Zak could not wait to close the deal as he pinched himself in the clouds to see if he was still in the real world!
Later during the flight, Zak's mind was in a whirl, with the anticipation of closing the currency deal with the Albino, who hopefully lived in an Ivory Tower. The mere thought of becoming a multi Dollar millionaire was mind-boggling. But first things first, he had to get the undertaking from Van Darlen before the pro-forma became operational.

As soon as Zak returned home that night he was on the phone to Van Darlan to discuss item seven. The stout Dutchman, for reasons best known to himself, had exported himself over the Dutch-German border in Emmerich in Germany, where with Daphna in tow, Zak had visited Van Darlen and his now deceased German partner earlier that year. To Zak's utter dismay Van Darlen resented being called at such a late hour and did not seem to want to talk about such an undertaking nor indeed closing the deal! However, during the ensuing, protracted, telephone conversation, the Dutchman agreed to approach his Nigerian principal for the requested undertaking.

The very next morning, Zak phoned the Sicilian in the Edgware Road 'spaghetti joint' to ethically reflect the 'Texaco' man's affirmative intention to purchase the Naira, subject to the requested declaration. Zak further informed the excited Sicilian during the call about his aunt's over-concern in Venice.

"O.K., I understand. Don't worry about that one, Zak."

"Thanks for understanding. *Signore,* is it okay to pay your cheque in this afternoon?"

"Sure, Zak."

"Thank you. Regards to Lionel."

It looked as though the wish Zak had made in the lobby of the 'Luna' in Venice for the angels to shine down on him was starting to come true. As though by a miracle, Udi had left a message with Daphna for Zak to arrange a visit to Israel before the end of the year, to speak with the *kosher* boys about settlement!

However, because of the negative vibes and feedback Zak was getting from Van Darlen, on 17th November, he took KLM 116 flight to Amsterdam Schiphol and caught a fast train from the Central Station to Emmerich to discuss the details of closing the deal with the Dutchman...

Van Darlen courteously met Zak at Emmerich station, before taking him to a nearby lady friend's flat for a private discussion and light lunch.

Later, Zak spent a sleepless night in a nearby small hotel 'Onder de Poort' situated alongside the smelly Rhine, on the Rheinpromenade in Emmerich.

The next afternoon when they met again, Van Darlen didn't appear convinced that Zak had a serious buyer, until V.D. was shown Rajko's personal business card. The overweight Dutchman then promised Zak that he would acquire the necessary declaration in order to close the deal.

It wasn't until 26th November that Zak was able to send a telex to the Albino in Vienna:

```
ATT: RAJKO MILUTINOVIC
RE: PRO-FORMA INVOICE 1332
(1) CONFIRM PRICE 18 USD PER HUNDRED O.N.N NETT: WITHOUT
    DEDUCTIONS.
(2) THAT THE REQUIRED DECLARATION IS AVAILABLE AS ITEM
    7 ON YOUR CONFIRMATION TO PROCEED. TRUST YOU CAN
    NOW COMMIT TO A MEETING AT YOUR EARLIEST WITH
    INTENTIONS TO CLOSE TRANSACTION BEFORE 17TH OF
    DECEMBER 1986.
    BEST REGARDS, ZAK LEVIN
```

Alas, on second and third presentation, the Sicilian's cheque, issued on Barclays Bank Maida Vale branch for £370, bounced, never to be honoured.

The 'willingness to proceed' telex chasers Zak sent to Rajko, the Texaco man, during December were all totally ignored. Even Zak's many telephone calls to Rajko's secretary in Vienna resulted in no response.

Still hopeful, Zak informed Rajko's office before leaving for Israel that he could be contacted at the Hilton Hotel in Tel Aviv.

As Zak listened to his Barry Manilow records, he began to wonder whether the Nigerian currency transaction had taken place behind his back. There was no way of knowing if Van Darlen had made contact with the anticipated buyer direct. After all, Van Darlen had intently perused Rajko's business card. Or just maybe the 'virtuous' Albino had made a quiet trip to the Nigerian Treasury Department in Lagos looking for the base price.

On 18th December, Daphna and Zak left Heathrow on BA's midday flight 576M, bound for Tel Aviv. He felt glum and terribly let down by the Italians and their so-called buyer in Vienna, yet optimistic and resilient, with high hopes of a settlement in the *Promisedland*.

CHAPTER THIRTY-THREE

Tel Aviv: December 1986

On the Way to the Promisedland

THE packed BA flight to the *Promisedland* consisted mostly of English orthodox Jews, making a fleeting visit to be with relatives or friends for the festive season. The *Frummers* and the few Israelis on board, verbally fought for the under-supply of 'Bloom's' *kosher* meals, which should have been specially ordered when they'd purchased their air tickets. Consequently, Zak became caught up in the humorous traumas during the flight. The liliaceous Daphna on her first trip to Israel was simply enthralled with everything that was happening around her...

Kosher and *trafy* meals devoured and coffee cups squared away by the very capable BA cabin staff, the smooth hum of the Rolls Royce jet engines and what lay ahead induced Zak's memory cogs to revolve... Back to a period of creative adventure in his life, that turned sour due to the 'big boys' connected with the fashion trade getting it all wrong. But with tenacity and right on his side, Zak had taken on the big-guns of the thriving textile industry and finally won through.

Forbidden Yesterday

During the lull in flight, Zak's thoughts focused on Rurik and Franz and why neither of them had ever enquired if he'd received the money owed by the State of Israel! Coming to rest on 'cloud nine' after his deliberations, he concluded that the Israelis had decided to pay up for the Nigerian intro after all. Zak otherwise treated the flight as a sideshow all the way to the *Promisedland*.

BA flight 576 landed at Ben-Gurion Airport precisely on schedule: 19:15 local time. Conceived in the year 1909, Tel Aviv was a mixture of neatly laid out fields and light-painted buildings plus slimline-looking skyscrapers. From 'cloud nine', a mega boost for Daphna.

The inspiring scenery aside, Daphna and Zak were both surprised that neither Udi, nor any of the city's third of a million Jewish inhabitants, were at Israel's main airport to greet them[13].

It transpired that the missing *Sabra* had left a message for the Levins at the terminal's information desk...

For Daphna, it had been a further treat to ride in a taxicab to downtown Tel Aviv, into Independence Park, where the deluxe Tel Aviv Hilton was located. The noticeably strong military presence and the short-skirted girl soldiers hitching lifts from any condescending *Sabra* was another eye-opener for Daphna during their eight-mile journey to the 'Hilton'...

With a new-found togetherness, Daphna and Zak eagerly checked into their allotted room on the eighth floor, which overlooked the dark Mediterranean. Their immediate jubilations, however, were dashed when they wondered if the room was on the sunny side of the hotel. That time of year, possibly, the winter sun would not orbit and shine on the room until late afternoon when it would be low and weak in the sky. However, they did have a bird's eye view of both the American and British Embassies in the foreground.

---

[13] THERE ARE SOME 14.5 MILLION JEWS IN THE WORLD, APPROXIMATELY HALF LIVE IN THE USA. 2.5 MILLION LIVE IN ISRAEL, 4 MILLION LIVE IN EUROPE (UK SOME 400,000). THE REMAINDER ARE SPREAD OVER THE REST OF THE WORLD INCLUDING JAPAN'S 860 AND LIBYA'S 20.

On the Way to the Promisedland

After tipping the porter for *shlepping* and parking their heavy cases in the room, Zak phoned Udi as requested in the *Sabra's* message.

"Udi... *Shalom.*"
"Zak, *shalom, shalom.* You got my message?"
"Yes, that's why I'm phoning."
"Thanks. Have you checked into the 'Hilton' already?"
"Yes, Room 817."
"O.K. I'll be right over. Meet me in the main lobby in ten minutes."
"Sure, is everything alright?"
"I'll tell you in the lobby. Zak, be careful." Udi then cut the line before he could be questioned on the meaning of his last remark!
"Honey, Udi's meeting me in the lobby, shortly."
"Will my best friend, Lena, be with him?" Daphna shouted back through the bathroom door.
"I don't think so this time round."
"If she is, send her up."
"Of course, see you shortly."
"O.K. darling, I'll start unpacking in the meantime. See you when you've finished downstairs with Udi."

The spectacular 'Hilton' lobby was alive with people coming and going, going and coming. In the much-tavelled Londoner's opinion there was not another hotel in the world that could produce the packed hum of excitement being generated through the 'Tel Aviv Hilton'. Moving around the lobby waiting for Udi, Zak absorbed the action and the energy. The waiting Londoner gazed in awe at the tax-free diamonds, wrist watches, rings and dazzling things in 'Stern's' lobby shop window. Zak's focus came to rest on the dramatic works of Frank Miesler and Ya'acov Heller's 'Judaica' sculptures of animated biblical themes in solid silver and gold, all outlandishly priced in wanted US Dollars. Undoubtedly, a perpendicular, defiant silver goat some twelve inches high with gold horns and hooves displaying virile oversized gold testicles, was the centre of attraction. The Billy Goat had an engraved card by one of its golden hooves stating:

Forbidden Yesterday

'President Reagan accepted from the State of Israel a similar piece, which sits on his desk in the White House Oval office.'

Suggesting, Zak thought, the President had balls as well as jelly beans, or was he just an unknowing, 'bugged' caprine?

While he waited to receive Udi, Zak felt he'd drawn inner strength whilst watching the lobby's activities. Ironically, Zak caught a glimpse of Manny Levy making a hasty exit as Udi simultaneously walked through the swing doors of the 'Hilton', exactly fifteen minutes after the *Sabra's* last words uttered on the telephone: 'be careful'. Obviously, Udi was being security-minded about the pending meeting, or was Many Levy somehow involved?

With an anxious expression on his face and without greeting Zak, Udi asked with an uncertain ring in his voice:

"Has anyone contacted you yet?"

"About what?"

"The meeting."

"I thought you had that all set up for tonight?"

"Not really."

"What do you think I came over here for?" Zak bellowed at the bewildered looking *Sabra* as the visiting Londoner suddenly visualised a million Dollars being sucked down a drain.

"Forgive me, Zak. That's why I wasn't at the airport to meet you and Daphna."

"What does that mean?"

"They called off the meeting for tonight, so I went over to see my contact, who is an ex-Mossad man."

"Great! Another 'bum ride'."

"No, Zak. The 'Institute' promised they would contact you direct, maybe tonight, but definitely by tomorrow afternoon."

"If that's how it is, I guess I can endure another restless night tonight."

"Thanks for understanding, Zak. Is Daphna with you?"

"Of course, she's upstairs unpacking. Udi, will you and Lena join us for an evening meal here in the hotel later?"

"Sure, Lena is dying to see you both..."

On the Way to the Promisedland

Later, the four friends enjoyed a great 'nosh-up' in the deli-style restaurant, opposite the unflowing 'Milk and Honey' breakfast room. Unfortunately, the evening was overshadowed by Udi's obvious state of nervousness...

As they were about to part at midnight, Zak decided to button-hole Udi as Lena and Daphna made small talk.

"Who can I expect to contact me tomorrow, Udi?"

"Michael Perry."

"Who is he?"

"He is a *Sabra*. I've known him for years."

"Yes, I know all you *Sabras* know one another. But what does he actually do?"

"He's Robbie's chief. I knew Michael when he was a lawyer."

"An active ranking Mossad officer?"

"Yes, on Nahum Adnonni's staff."

"Good, a top man, hey?"

"For sure."

"Great. Anything more on the Americans or Oliver North and Two-way trade, Udi?"

"No, did you hear any more from your source in Washington?"

"Apart from the magnitude of the strike, my source's closed down on that one for the time being."

"You mean the American Sixth Fleet?"

"Yes, and your lot. It's really under tight raps how the Yanks did what they did without loss or casualty."

"It's under raps here too."

"I was also given to understand Reagan doesn't want to further upset the Arab World."

"Right."

"By the way, Udi, do you know a Manny Levy?"

"From where?"

"He's English."

"Don't think so."

CHAPTER THIRTY-FOUR

Tel Aviv — Part I

Fun and Scares

DAPHNA was totally overwhelmed at the delightful ritual of eating the *Sabra's* breakfast the next morning in the 'Milk and Honey' Room…

Leaving the overflowing restaurant with full stomachs, vowing to eat no more that day, they sauntered off to window shop in the magnetic Ben Yehuda and Disengoff shopping zone.

Zak, that mettlesome Friday morning, acquired an inspiration to visit the Hadar Dafna Building and café on its second floor, but had thought better of it when buying a couple of bottles of fine local wine from a liquor shop.

Fun and Scares

Later, on the way back to the 'Hilton', Zak began to wonder about the many German Mercedes cars and taxicabs being driven around in the Jewish State. Bearing in mind that Mossad agents, led by their Chief at the time, Isser Harel, had scoured the world bent on hanging the German SS officer and Jew exterminator, Colonel Adolf Eichmann, it just did not make sense! Thinking about it, Daphna and he had arrived at the 'Hilton' in a German-made taxi. Obviously the Israelis did what suited them, regardless.

Zak put his thoughts and notions to the back of his mind, not wanting to spoil Daphna's first full day in Israel, as they made their way past street cafés and trendy boutiques and then back to the hotel to meet cousin Ruth. Zak reminded Daphna:

"Remember, honey, we promised Udi not to mention anything to Ruth about Mossad and their past behaviour."

"Sure, darling, do you think I want to upset her?"

"Of course not, but don't let on, okay?"

"O.K. already, Zak, stop worrying."

"Darling, you know my motto: be concerned, but don't worry."

"True," Daphna replied with conviction.

There was no message from Michael Perry in their pigeon hole on returning to the 'Hilton'. Maybe Mercury retrograde was in force in the atmosphere...

Ruth, however, was sitting waiting for her cousins, being early for their one o'clock lunch appointment. She was pale and drawn and wore a faded cotton dress. The much awaited reunion was emotional and tearful, as Aunt Rosie, Ruth's mother, had died recently. Zak was on edge, up and down like a yo-yo, torn between comforting Ruth and checking every ten minutes for a message from Perry at the front counter. Zak discreetly indicated to Daphna that there was no news, as they settled down in the 'Buttery' off the main lounge area of the hotel, to take a light lunch with Ruth.

Ruth had just finished work for the *Shabbut* (the Jewish sabbath) and started to smile and relax with her cousins over their 'mischievous' stuffed cream *blintzes*.

"When do you start work again, Ruth?" Daphna wanted to seriously know.

"Sunday morning, after *Shabbut* is fully out."

"Why not Monday, Ruth?" Daphna asked in surprise.

"Sunday means nothing here in Israel, just a weekday."

"Oh yes, of course. And how are the kids, Ruth?"

"Oh, just fine. And yours, Daph?"

And so the conversation went on well into the *Shabbut*.

A fat chance of Mossad contacting him before Sunday or Monday, Zak thought to himself as they kissed Ruth goodbye...

Daphna and Zak broke the long-forming ice and made love that Friday night in the peaceful Holy Land...

The next day the Levins began to unwind, soaking up some sun at the pool side, going through the motions of being sweethearts again. Enjoying short walks, holding hands in the tree-lined streets of Tel Aviv and along the nearby sandy beaches, they gazed at the seafront and sailing craft. During the evening... they stared at late-night strip clubs and funky discotheques, oblivious to other strollers and possible muggers.

Zak was right about Mossad; Michael Perry did not telephone until well into Monday morning. To Zak's amazement, the high-ranking Mossad officer was surprisingly open, fully describing his appearance to Zak over the phone, prior to their scheduled meeting in the 'Hilton'...

They sat where they met, at the far end of the quiet 'Hilton's' lounge on a soft upholstered couch, facing the main lobby. When shaking hands, the representative of Mossad politely offered Zak a glass of black tea, but the waiter brought a pot of coffee instead.

Michael Perry who was tall and slim, appeared extremely calm and sure of himself. Perry was noticeably good-looking and 'clean-cut' with short hair, in his mid-thirties. The *Sabra's* high and angular shoulders helped carry off his blue-grey, Harris tweed jacket to full advantage. Underneath his jacket Michael wore a casual, open-necked shirt with grey cords and brown shoes... Oh, dear! Those darned brown shoes again. With 'deaf ears' Zak heard his mama's voice ringing out again the lyrics from 'Blues in the Night'.

As they took it in turns to sip their coffee, Michael seemed easy to confide in, about both 'Alon-cum-Donald' and Robbie having reneged on the cherished *'Mazel un Brocheh'* until Michael asked Zak the five million Dollar question:
"So why do you think we owe you money, Zak?"
"Because Robbie told me in Salzburg, that he had what he came for and would only pay for what they got. What else do you need to know, Michael?"
"Whatever you want to get off your chest, Zak," Michael said casually without movement, obviously trained in the art of body language.
"How about this, Michael?" The *Sabra* moved to the edge of his seat to take the folded newspapers and two pages of text from Zak, listing all the venues and his dealings with Mossad — from the one-that-got-away conversation with Udi and Abbie in Covent Garden, right up until the last meeting with Alon at the Royal Lancaster Hotel in London when Alon callously delivered the *coup de grâce* by saying: 'The name of the game is not to pay.'
Perry seemed intrigued with the list and the two Daily Telegraph newspapers, depicting headlines of the bombings of Libya during the previous March and April.
"Can I take these papers away with me, Zak?"
"Sure. By the way, Michael, I don't like what you did with what you got in Salzburg."
"But you had nothing to do with Libya, Zak," Michael said as he started to pour himself another coffee.
"Yes, I know now I was not privy to your operation and you were the *provocateurs*."
"What do you mean by *provocateurs*, Zak?"
"Instigators. Come on, Michael, your guys duped me."

"Maybe." The give-away: no denial of the dupe. In fact, an affirmative Israeli 'maybe', uttered during an unguarded moment whilst pouring coffee.

"Maybe for sure, as far as I'm concerned, Michael."

Starting to look dishevelled, Michael boasted from over the top of his coffee cup:

"It was unimaginable at the time, Zak."

"I'm sure. However, I want my commission for the introduction and situation as agreed. Not because your team got lucky with Franz and his Boss at the end of the day."

"Zak, I'll get back to you in a couple of days, after I've checked these papers out," Michael said with some new-found officialdom, as he gestured at the bundle firmly held under his non-saluting arm.

"Sterling. By the way, my wife and I are going down to Eilat on the morning of the twenty-sixth for a few days."

"When will you be coming back?" Michael asked with wide, searching eyes.

"We are due back here at the 'Hilton' on the afternoon of New Year's Eve."

"Where will you be staying in Eilat?" Michael asked in a rather abrupt manner.

"In a private apartment, near the beach," Zak fabricated in guarded response to Michael's abruptness.

"And, when exactly do you intend going back to England?" Michael further inquired.

"Early morning, the second of January."

"O.K., Zak, I'll get back to you before you leave Israel."

"Michael, just for the record, my solicitors are fully aware of the situation here in Israel and have full documentation and instructions if I should have an unfortunate accident or a fatal encounter."

"Like what?"

"Like, tripping over a matchstick," Zak said, tongue in cheek.

"Understood, Zak, *shalom*," the man from Mossad H.Q. replied obsequiously, on getting up from the couch.

"*Shalom*, Michael, see you on the way back."

Fun and Scares

"Yea, enjoy Eilat and don't worry, Zak."

Openers over, the next planned high-spot was dinner Wednesday evening at Cousin Ruth's flat with Lena and Udi present...

Tuesday morning, with Michael Perry hopefully making his enquiries, Zak booked an 'Egged Tours' to show the loving Daphna the Israelisation, and the many wonders of Jerusalem: particularly the symbolic tomb of King David, the mystical venue of the Last Supper, the 691 A.D. Dome of the Rock and the 1966 Knesset, Israel's parliament building.

Wednesday evening, in their newly-acquired room on the sunny-side of the 'Hilton', Zak was about to zip up Daphna's dress as they were getting ready for dinner with Cousin Ruth, when an almighty 'hammering' startled them, Udi's voice simultaneously shouting out from the other side of the room door!

"Zak, it's me, Udi. Open up quickly."

Their chauffeur for the evening was obviously all shook-up! On entry, Udi whispered breathlessly:

"Zak, my Mossad contact wants you and Daphna to move out of the 'Hilton' tonight!"

"Like, now?"

"Yes."

"What on earth are you saying, Udi?"

"My contact has just been round to see me."

"So?"

"So, Zak, if he's to guarantee your safety, you two must move out of the 'Hilton' tonight."

"Why, is the hotel going to cave-in?" Zak said in jest, noticing Daphna practically plastered to the wall in fright.

"Zak, a certain arm of Mossad or Shabak may come and take you away. You must stay in our flat tonight," Udi said with a quick blast.

"No, thank you, Udi, I don't consider your flat a 'safe house'."

"For real, Zak, you must move out now."

"No way, Udi. They can quicker *shlepp* me out of your flat than the 'Hilton'."

"Don't underestimate these guys, Zak. They are only a stone's throw away."

"Yes, I know, in the Hadar Dafna Building."

"How do you know that?" Udi asked with shifting eyes.

"Come on, Udi, everyone knows Mossad Headquarters is run from behind the cafeteria on the second floor on King Saul Boulevard."

"You're naïve if you believe that one, Zak. Anyway, they can kidnap you easily if they choose to."

"I know the FBI under American law can legally kidnap its citizens abroad. But I'm a British Jew in Israel."

"Doesn't mean a thing if they want to take you out over here."

"Perhaps so, Udi. However, it's your *Sabra* friends who are looking for an 'out' if they are rousing me."

"You should not have given Michael Perry such a detailed list and the English newspapers."

"Why not?"

"Because you can show them up."

"Hey, hey, hey. I thought Perry was trying to square the circle with me?"

"Who knows with the 'Institute'."

"Udi, Michael Perry is fully aware a full set of papers are lodged with my solicitors, along with my instructions."

"What instructions?"

"Well, if I should as much as trip over a matchstick, they'll blow the whistle on your lot."

"I didn't know that."

"Udi, I'm certainly not going to allow your guys to 'put me on a slippery slope'."

"Zak, be careful how you talk in here."

"Why, is the room bugged?"

"Maybe."

"I bet that's why they moved us to the sunny side of the street without extra charge!"

"Could be, Zak," Udi said with new-found humility.

"Come, let's go. Ruth must be waiting to serve us dinner."

Fun and Scares

"Zak, please reconsider your position here," Udi said, obviously still in a nervous state of mind.

"Udi, you enticed me here, at my own expense. You worry about it. And make sure I get paid as you indicated."

"That's a tall order, Zak."

"Shouldn't be. Anyway, where is Lena?"

"Yes, where is Lena?" the pale-looking Daphna piped.

"She's downstairs in the car."

"Come on then, let's go. Ruth will wonder where we are."

"O.K. Zak, be it on your own head."

Udi's shifting concern brought to mind Zak's own remark to the double-crossing Franz, in the 'Sheraton' in Salzburg: 'Be it on your own head, Franz'.

"Daphna, honey, don't forget the bottle of Special Reserve Askolon and the Presidents sparkling wine in the mini-bar chilling for Cousin Ruth.'s dinner."

"O.K., darling."

Udi had conveniently parked the car right outside the front entrance of the 'Hilton', obviously expecting to stack their luggage in its boot. It had been advantageous, because as the three of them walked out of the lobby, the holy heavens chose to open up. God had decided to activate a combined whirlwind and tornado causing one hell of a storm, as they leapt into the car. Roads seemed to disappear under the gale force ten storm, as the motor car struggled on towards Ruth's home, over at Ramat Hasharon.

Ironically, a full circle was about to be completed, as Lena and Udi escorted the Londoners to the very place where Zak had first met Udi.

The four were all drenched from the short run from Udi's car to Ruth's front porch, where dear Cousin Ruth awaited with bath towels in her well-worn hands.

Ruth's hungry guests kissed the *mezuzah* on entrance into her spick and span ground-floor flat, the sensational smell of her cooking was in the air and instantly commented upon. As though it was

Shabbos, cousin Ruth had already lit the candles, placed in her dead mother's engraved silver candlesticks on the old oak sideboard. The Levins had a similar set of traditional candlesticks at home, a wedding present from Daphna's dear departed parents. The dining table was decorated with flowers and set for soup, fish and flesh. In the centre of the table was a fine looking butter-glazed *challah* which reflected in the long-stemmed cut glassware. Cousin Zak's selection of local wine that was nurtured in the hot, dry vineyards of Zichron-Jacob, had been correctly anticipated... Simultaneously they all shouted *"Lechayim, lechayim"* as Zak popped open the sparkling wine.

"To life." Zak toasted before Ruth traditionally broke the fresh *challah* to commence the joyous meal...

"Ruth, you make better *matzo* balls than your mother — *Alov Hashalom.*"

"That's the biggest compliment I have ever had, Zak. Thank you very much."

"Yea, your mother certainly could make *matzo* balls, Ruth," applauded Lena and Udi simultaneously.

"And what about her *lokshen* soup?" Daphna added.

"That's right and her *lokshen* pudding was also out of this world!" Zak eulogised in a state of comparative relaxation.

"Zak, you'll be able to make the comparison for yourselves later," Ruth said with a delightful grin on her happy face.

"Surprise, surprise, Cousin Ruth." Zak cheered.

The weather had subsided by the time they drove back to the 'Hilton'. They all felt reinforced by the wonderful *haimisher* meal of chicken soup, *gefilte* fish, strong horseradish, pickled cucumbers, boiled garlic chicken, green figs and two helpings of *lokshen* pudding. Udi mentioned that he was pleased none of the earlier dramatic events had been mentioned to the lonely Ruth.

"Udi, I certainly didn't want to disillusion Cousin Ruth or spoil her wonderful meal."

"I know, Zak. Have you reconsidered your position yet?"

"Yes, we are going to get our money's worth at the 'Hilton'."

Fun and Scares

"I second that," said Daphna, from the back of the car, with Lena at her side.

"Bravo, honey." Zak exclaimed at his wife's brave support. However, Udi dampened Daphna's courage by cutting in with:

"Zak, be careful. Mossad don't play around, you know."

"Udi, I know they don't."

"So, take my advice then."

"That's why I'm here." Zak said with sarcasm.

"I know what you're saying, Zak."

"Good, then make sure we get paid."

"Zak..."

Zak stopped Udi in his tracks with a vexing statement:

"Udi, what can they do — confiscate my passport for a few days — lock me up. Or what?"

"Why should they do anything like that, Zak?"

"I'll tell you one day about your countrymen, my naïve *Sabra*."

Udi parked the clapped-out car and they all entered the 'Hilton'. Daphna stayed down in the lobby with Lena, Udi looking after the girls, while Zak went to 'recce' the room.

Once in the hotel room, Zak carefully checked the furniture and drapes for any obvious tricks or hidden bugging by Shabak, Israel's internal 'Dirty Tricks Brigade.'

Suddenly, Zak was startled by the sharp ring of the bedside telephone as he was about to cover the large wall mirror with a spare blanket...

"Hello."

"Zak, is everything O.K. up there?" With a calm voice, so as not to frighten Daphna any further, he assured her:

"Yes, no 'buggers' to be seen up here. Hang on, honey, I'll be down shortly for you."

At sunrise the next morning the Levins were comfortably snuggled up in the 'Hilton's' lush bed. Alive and in one piece without incident, however Zak's lovely wife's nipples were no longer in the 'introverted' position.

Having taken a light breakfast served in their room, they decided to re-visit Jerusalem, to see and feel the religious aura on that Christmas Day.

The headlines in the 'Jerusalem Post' (delivered on the breakfast trolley) read:-

PARIS NEGOTIATING WITH TEHERAN

FRENCH HOSTAGE FREED IN BEIRUT XMAS GESTURE

Down in the lobby, the anxious-looking Udi and Lena caught Zak about to buy tickets for the 38 mile journey to Jerusalem. The excited pair took over and invited their friends for a drive in their new French car!

The car was a 1987 spec' Peugeot, which the proud Udi handled well as they went motoring up the Allenby, past the Central Bus Station and the Camel Market before going way out past the tall Diamond Exchange Building. Whether it was out of excitement because of the new car or not, neither Udi, nor indeed Lena, mentioned a word about their safety or Mossad's threat of the stormy night before!

The tour continued across sleepy Tel Aviv to the artists' colony and then onto a new multi-media complex 'Israel Experience'. Udi later parked the new car in old Jaffa, so they could walk its historical restored port and take in the closed Arab-run nightclubs...

Daphna and Zak were then driven back to Lena and Udi's fifties-built flat, situated off the Sokolov and the nearby Maritime Education Centre.

Upon acknowledging the *mezuzah,* the Londoners entered the mundane residence. The flat reminded Zak of a cheap, self-catering, low-level holiday condo on the Costa Brava, with its dull stone flooring and utility-look cupboards. In fact, it was just like the flat he'd once refused to occupy when holidaying in Spain with Daphna.

Fun and Scares

After a light lunch and the friendly ritual of eating fresh green dates, choice fruits and nuts, Udi and Lena invited their guests to view their new flat across the nearby Yarkon River!

The well-appointed block on opulent Zlochisty Street, along the coast from the 'Hilton' was not far from Yarkon Park and its happy-looking picnickers. Outside the brand-new block, wires were not yet fixed to the entry phone casing. But the security cameras and the mint condition *mezuzah* were guarding the splendid entrance hall and newly-laid plush carpet of Udi and Lena's new abode.

The balconied flat was in a state of second fix – with fine views, glimpses of the Mediterranean and the road to Haifa. It did not occur to Zak at the time how Udi could afford such a valuable apartment — one that had two en-suite bathrooms with expensive fittings, luxurious built-in cupboards and imported decorative ceramics adorning the walls and floors. And then there was the new car that Udi had parked in Old Jaffa!

CHAPTER THIRTY-FIVE

Eilat

An enlightening 'Red Sea' Break

DAPHNA and Zak left the 'Hilton' by taxi Friday morning, with a shared suitcase for Tel Aviv's Central Bus Station, thankful to still be in one piece.

They departed from the busy terminal, both of the Levins looking forward to the interesting southeasterly ride ahead through the Judean Desert to Eilat.

The Bus journey traversed Massada and the Dead Sea coast before crossing the Arava-Negev Desert on the way to the duty-free Red Sea resort of Eilat. With grand thoughts of the Dead Sea Scrolls and Lawrence of Arabia, they travelled on. The Londoners knew Eilat was squeezed in between the mountains of Jordan and Sinai and was within clear viewing distance of the Port of Aquaba, just across the closed Jordanian border.

Eilat was not as warm as Daphna and Zak had envisaged, after travelling the 220 miles. However, they were delighted to find the four-star Neptune Hotel better appointed than they had expected. Later, they sat together holding hands and watched the surrounding rocks turn a stunning shade of peach as the sun set.

An enlightening 'Red Sea' Break

Saturday morning's weather looked dull and cold. The 'Neptune's' weather glass gave them palpitations as it danced from 'anticyclone' to 'wedge and veering'...

Sunday morning the weather warmed up, as they were looking around the modern port of Eilat. At the first rays of sun they made their way back to the 'Neptune' to collect their beach-gear and have a quick 'elevenses'.

Leaving the 'Neptune', they noticed an Israeli transporter flying overhead. Zak watched the military plane make an extraordinary U-turn manoeuvre over the Gulf of Eilat, then sharply level up over the Lagoon, before neatly landing in the nearby mixed civil and military airport.

"What plane is that, Zak?" Daphna wanted to know.

"It's the much-favoured C130 Hercules Transport plane, honey. The Israelis used them for the Entebbe raid in the seventies when they freed some one hundred odd Jewish hostages."

"Oh yes, we saw the film in the Odeon cinema Marble Arch, way back, remember?"

"Yes, 'Raid on Entebbe'."

"That's right, all about the hijacked Air France flight from Tel Aviv to Paris via Athens."

"Right again."

"Who did the hijacking?"

"The PFLP led by a female German terrorist, I believe."

"Yes, she ordered the plane to stop at Benghazi for refuelling before flying off to Uganda."

"You know, Daph, that was about the time the Americans were celebrating their 200th anniversary."

"My, the Americans have come a long way in two hundred years, Zak, haven't they?"

"Yes. God bless America. Honey, the C130 symbolises America somehow — it's like a graceful hippopotamus in flight — its production spec' ranges from a flying ambulance to a mighty destructive weapon."

"C130's like the ten you offered out for sale once?"

"Yes, the Hercules saga, you've got it, baby. Pity that deal didn't happen."

"What would you have made if that deal had happened for us, Zak?"

"One per cent."

"How much is that in terms of real money?"

"One million US"

"We could do with that right now!"

"You can say that again. Hopefully, we're still in the ball game."

"With a chance?"

"If the Israelis haven't got the needle to me that the C130 offer was destined for Libya."

"Is that why they did what they did to you?"

Flash-point!

"Maybe you've hit the nail on the head, honey, although Udi's never really mentioned anything about Libya. Mind you, I levelled with Alon when I met him in the London Embassy."

"About trying to acquire C130's for Libya as a broker?"

"Yes."

"You were too forthright, darling."

"Guess so."

"But, didn't Udi vouch for you?"

"Yes, but your best friend's *schmuck* husband didn't get us properly covered here."

"Obviously."

"And I'm a bigger *schmuck* for being duped if I don't get my commission this time round. I think Udi's one of them, anyway."

"Meaning Mossad?"

"Yes, or affiliated."

"Why do you think he's one of them?"

"Well, he's a *Sabra*."

"*Arrière-pensée*," Daphna said with a calm matter of fact voice.

"And he never talks money or seems concerned about his agreed secret kick-back."

"Like I said, Udi had other motives," Daphna remarked sagely.

"For sure, just like Franz and Rurik. You know, it has become

An enlightening 'Red Sea' Break

common knowledge about Oliver North and 'Two-Way trade'. And Udi comes on with: 'His source is closed to him now'."

"Which means?"

"Udi and Abbie must be Mossad. She's a regular Marta Hari, in my opinion."

"Lena never told me."

"There's a lot of things your best friend hasn't told you, honey."

With their beach gear stowed away under the deck chairs, they settled on the beach by the Marina that led to the Lagoon. Within minutes an Israeli couple and their small son took over the empty deck chairs at their side. After the opening *shaloms*, the couple made some friendly small-talk. The male *Sabra* was obviously an active military man, as he was wearing khaki 'dog tags'. Later the *Sabra* let on that he was a major in the Israeli Air Force and boasted he'd piloted a C130 to Eilat from Tel Aviv and more specifically the one they had seen in the sky earlier. During the afternoon, the major took off to buy ice cream with his offspring. The high-flying wife, in a rather loud whisper, took the opportunity to proudly inform Daphna:

"My husband, David, was the Flight Leader on the Entebbe raid, in July of seventy-six!"

"He must still be an idol here in Israel?" the amazed Daphna enquired.

"Yes, a very handsome, decorated hero."

The demigod obviously had the run of the Israeli Air Force to be able to use the C130 hippo for a family charabanc ride, Zak thought to himself.

The all-conquering, briefly-clad major returned, laden with goodies. Both Daphna and Zak warmly responded to the ace-pilot's thoughtfulness of ice-cold choco-covered 'joy-sticks'. Zak later asked the major:

"Can you tell me, why did you do that sharp U turn over the sea before landing your C130?"

"Because either side of the airport is considered hostile Arab territory by us."

Forbidden Yesterday

The visiting Londoners had taken the opportunity to visit Solomon's Pillars, some 15 miles inland, and the nearby Taba beach on the Egyptian border, where the grand Aviya Sonesta Hotel stood. When Daphna was putting a penny in the big 'white-telephone', Zak was given to understand by a bitter Palestinian waiter that the Israelis had really stolen the 'Sonesta' from Egypt. And for the first time the Londoner heard the name of the spawning Hamas mentioned...

Other than perfume and liquor, there were very few duty-free goods worth buying in little ol' Eilat!

Daphna and Zak left Eilat behind them on the last day of '86, having visited most of the delightful sights, including the Coral Beach, where they'd collected a few forbidden sea shells. They had also cruised the Coral Sea in a glass bottomed boat, watching the colourful Butterfly fish swimming in pairs around a sleeping Octopus. They even saw a Manta ray spread its wings trying to catch a scrambling Sea Cucumber for an *hors d'oeuvre*.

CHAPTER THIRTY-SIX

Tel Aviv —Part II

Broken Promise

BACK at the Tel Aviv Hilton, there were no messages. However, both Daphna and Zak thought it curious to have been checked back into the very same room they had previously occupied prior to going to Eilat! Zak wondered if the allocated room had been well and truly bugged by Shabak or Mossad to pick-up any conversation or incident which could be misconstrued for a possible future blackmail.

Once inside the vacuum of the lift, Zak took the opportunity to enlighten Daphna as to the possible dangers lurking in the room...

Having unpacked, tiredness and disappointment quickly descended upon them when they fully realised there were no messages from either Texaco or Mossad. The only good news was their other case, which they had left behind at the 'Hilton' for safe-keeping, was still intact.

There were no apparent tell-tale signs of their reclaimed case being tampered with or a 'set-up'. The precious 'Krug' '76 that Zak had purchased at Heathrow to drink in the New Year was still sealed within its deluxe presentation pack.

Unfortunately, Zak developed a bad cold on the Bus journey back to Tel Aviv. Coupled with the lack of the expected communications, he felt like nothing on earth. Cuddled up with Daphna, Zak phoned Udi to see if there was any news from Mossad and what the New Year's Eve arrangements were.

As arranged, Lena and Udi called from the hotel lobby about 10 p.m. However, Zak and Daphna were both crashed out in bed. When entering the room, Lena looked disappointed, as she and Udi were expecting to take them to a *Sabras* New Year's Eve party. Zak declined to go to the party because of his 'flu taking a turn for the worse, so Daphna willingly chose to stay and look after him. Zak thought he was maybe showing too much respect towards their amused and half-smiling so-called friends, by offering them the choice champagne chilling in the minibar. Begrudgingly, Zak nevertheless popped and poured the bubbly nectar, which he felt could never be fully appreciated by their so-called 'friends'.

Zak watched Lena and Udi with distaste as they greedily gulped the expensive 'Krug'. The Israelis then wished them a Happy New Year and conveyed Abbie's best wishes, prior to kissing goodbye. Lena somehow managed to sneak her tongue into Zak's burning throat, as Udi was giving Daphna a peck on the cheek. Zak thought it was unreal that Udi had not asked if he'd been contacted by Michael Perry, before leaving with a last *"Shalom "* and a weak handshake – as Lena and Daphna hugged one another in loving friendship.

The Londoner awoke to the first light of 1987 feeling healthier, thanks to his aromatherapy treatment, and of course the good effects of the 'Krug' from the night before...

The headline in the New Year's 'Jerusalem Post', which came *post-gratis* in the "Milk and Honey" room that day, was taken up with a report about Israel's aircraft industry:

'Lavi Jet and its maiden flight'.

Broken Promise

The report stated that the jet had been doused with fizz from dozens of bottles of champagne as it taxied up the runway at Ben-Gurion Airport

Zak wondered if the American tax-payer was aware it would cost another $4·5 billion Dollars before the Israeli Air Force took delivery of the new fighter jets.... While waiting for Daphna to join him at breakfast, a sub headline caught Zak's attention on page three:

SENSITIVE PAPERS REMOVED
UK RELEASES 1956 SUEZ RECORDS

London: The British Public Records Office revealed yesterday, after 30 years, sensitive government papers regarding the Suez affair have been removed and destroyed!

Zak recalled the Americans had made the joint forces of the British, French and Israel retreat from the Canal Zone, which caused a split in the Western alliance at the time.

Zak was amused as he read:

The case of the smuggling Rabbis

A bizarre story about a group of American Rabbis using an unorthodox method, back in 1956, to raise funds for Israel by selling smuggled South African diamonds via Antwerp, all having hood-winked New York customs with their long beards and over-the-top religious officialdom.

Nothing new, Zak thought, Rabbis and Hebrew Priests had smuggled since the reign of the radical King of Judah, Manasseh, in 687-642 B.C. when the priests of the day sneaked the Sacred Ark of the Covenant from Solomon's temple, then journeyed up the Nile to the sanctuary of Elephanti, where the Ark rested in a newly-built temple for many centuries. Due to conflicting religious disputes the Ark was again sneaked out of the temple and smuggled out of Egypt to be hidden until quite recently on a secret island on Lake Tana, the source of the Blue Nile in Ethiopia.

Two items on page three weren't so amusing:

Arafat lists 4,000 casualties in refugee camps

Black man's death stirs U.S. racism anew

NEW YORK (Reuter): It started with the death of a black man hit by a car while fleeing a mob of white youths with baseball bats.

It was ten minutes past noon on that 'nail-biting' New Year's Day. Returning from some last minute shopping, Zak's heart missed a beat. There was a message from Michael Perry waiting for him at the front desk, timed 12:05 stating: 'Will call again'. Zak became unsettled at having missed Michael's call and therefore declined lunch with Daphna.

At two o'clock, the bedside phone came alive.

"Zak?"

"Yes."

"Michael here."

Surprise, surprise. But there was no *shalom* from Mossad! Zak's heart missed another beat, either in anticipation of a negative or with excitement over a possible affirmative.

"*Shalom*, Michael."

"Can I see you, Zak?" Still no *shalom* from Mossad!

"Of course, that's why I came to Israel. When and where?"

"I'm on the house phone down in the main lobby."

"I'll be right down."

"O.K. I'll be sitting in the main lounge."

Travelling down in the lift, having left a timed note for Daphna, Zak thought if Perry's bothered to come, it must mean an affirmative. However, unless the money was in the bank, it counted for nothing. Zak recalled the night-light burning words of Arthur Scargill, the English coal-miners' union boss: 'The art of negotiation is to negotiate'. Michael surely had no compulsion to come, other than to personally take particulars for setting-up a transfer to his numbered account in Zurich, or to barter a little. Zak descended along with his reasoning, confirmed by a cutting gut feeling.

Broken Promise

Zak found the Mossad supervisor settled in a quiet corner of the 'Hilton's' main lounge. Michael immediately did the 'how are you' bit before ordering a pot of coffee and portion of almond crescents.

"Did you have a good time in Eilat, Zak?"

"Yes, thank you, Michael."

"Tell me, did you enjoy your Bus ride through the Negev to the Neptune Hotel?"

"It sounds as though you have been watching me."

"Not at all, don't be silly."

"Bet you know we have some forbidden sea shells from the Coral Beach for export?"

"Come on, Zak."

Hesitatingly, Zak responded to Michael's cable-gram type statement:

"Come on yourself, Michael."

"O.K. Zak, both Robbie and Alon are on an assignment outside of Israel at the moment."

"What does that mean?" Zak asked with uncertainty.

"It means I can do nothing about following through on our first meeting here."

"Michael, are we still at square one?"

"Maybe."

"But you are their supervisor, you must be able to reach them."

"Who told you I was their supervisor?"

"You *Sabras* are the masters of the double-act, Michael."

"That Udi just won't keep his nose out of this one."

"Who said Udi told me?"

"It's obvious it's him. You haven't spoken with any other likely *Sabra* in Eilat."

"So you have been watching me?"

"Maybe."

That Israeli maybe again.

"Zak, the whole matter is under a 'cloud'."

"You mean it suits you to hide behind a 'cloud', because you duped me." Michael was not enamoured by Zak's cutting remark.

"This is not the time for puns, Zak," the *Sabra* exclaimed with an over emphasised shrug.

"Who's giving out the witticism, let's negotiate," Zak said, still hugging his emotions.

"Alon told you in the 'Royal Lancaster': 'The name of the game is not to pay'."

Zak's hopes waned with Michael's cruel reminder. Or was it another Mossad ploy to cut the commission, Zak wondered.

"Are you telling me you're not here to settle?"

"Not really."

"You're giving me a prime bank draft then, Michael?"

Zak answered back with just the right amount of sarcasm.

"Not at all," Michael retorted sharply.

"So, why have you come to see me here at the 'Hilton'?"

"Orders."

"From whom?"

"Orders are orders."

"Under the circumstances, can I see your superior?"

"What's with superior?"

"I understand you're on the staff of Nahum Adnonni."

"I'm as far up the ladder as you can go."

"So, where do we go from here, Michael?" Zak challenged.

"Search me, Zak."

"Maybe I'll find a bank draft in an envelope when I go back to my room, hey?"

"I don't think so," Michael disparaged.

Zak thought possibly Mossad were doing a psychological number on him before asking for his Swiss bank coordinates.

"So, why are you here?"

"I told you, Zak, orders. Anyway, you had nothing to do with the Libyan affair."

"True. But I performed as agreed."

"Maybe."

Again, that Israeli 'maybe'.

"Maybe, one of your chiefs or ministers have misappropriated my commission or paid Franz, Rurik and your team via some external account?"

"It's against the law in Israel to have an external bank account."

"Is that why you lot blew the whistle on Rabin or was it to get Begin elected in seventy-seven?"

"Could be. But I don't know from politics, Zak."

Perry was starting to play the devil's advocate.

"Eloquently put," Zak uttered in order to gain some breathing space and get Perry to open up.

"Maybe we used it to help pay a debt or two, Zak."

"Not just idle speculation then. From what I hear, you Israelis don't even pay your internal debts," Zak stated attackingly.

"What does that mean?"

"I understand there are some half a million writs out for bad debts here in little old Israel."

"Issue another writ then," Perry uttered without using too much of the heated oxygen.

"Hope it doesn't come to that."

"It's your problem, Zak." Perry said with a weak shrug of his broad shoulders.

"Tell me, Michael. Why are you here and why did you invite me to Israel?"

"Another *Sabra's* idea."

"Like wanting to curb the Egyptian water supply above Aswan?" Zak said in rebuke. Keep the *Sabra* wondering and talking, Zak figured, perhaps Perry will let something useful slip.

"In the Sudan?"

"No, not the Roseires or Sennär dams."

"Where then?"

"Higher, on the Blue Nile, possibly where twenty-eight construction workers were killed and two hostages taken on the wrong side of the Sudanese border earlier this month."

"Lake Tana in Ethiopia?" Perry did let slip!

"Could be. I'm informed Israel anticipates negotiating a technical and financial package with Ethiopia, when diplomatic relations fully resume again."

"Keep your assumptions to yourself, Zak," Perry said with venom in his tongue.

"A water-war is a loud and clear whisper in the Arab bazaars, not assumption, Michael."

"A water-war?"

"Yes, Egypt and the Sudan under threat."

"What are you talking about, Zak?"

"One day Israel, with a little help from a friend, will hold Sudan and Egypt to ransom."

"When is 'one day', Zak?"

"When Ethiopia eventually constructs a high dam across the Blue Nile."

"Well, tell your Arab friends to keep their snide whispers and remarks to themselves."

"And what about the black Jews in Ethiopia?"

"The *Falashas*?"

"Yes, another Jewish saga."

"Zak, we paid to take the *Falashas* out of Ethiopia to conform with the holy scripture," Perry exclaimed with great emotion.

"Not such proud words, Michael."

"What do you mean, Zak?"

"Israel wompstered at the eleventh hour just before the *Falashas* were about to perish back in eighty-five."

"Really?"

"Yes, really. Israel offered only thirty-five mil' against the original hundred and twenty million Dollars, and topped up the deal with some rumoured weaponry."

"In eighty-five?"

"Yes, last year about the time I was sitting with Udi and Abbie in an Italian restaurant in St Martin's Lane in London."

"Where do you get such information, Zak?"

"It's now a well-known fact, Israel in May 1985 herded and smuggled some eighteen thousand Ethiopian black Jews in military C130 transporters and commercial Boeings across Sudan's sandy border."

"You know about 'Operation Moses', then?"

Broken Promise

"Yes, I believe Libya called a special meeting of the Arab League over your illegal action." A sudden thought was sparked-off in Zak's mind by his mention of Libya! Had Franz's Princess been used by the Israelis to influence her husband? After all, Colonel Gadaffi overtly stated, when King Hussein of Morocco met Israel's Prime Minister, Shimon Peres, in July 1986 that Morocco had 'violated the Treaty of Union, signed in August 1984, between Morocco and Libya'.

"Anyway, what will Israel do with the *Falashas*, Michael?"

"Probably put them in the front line, if there's another war with the Arabs!"

"As the Yankees did with the American negroes during their 'bloody' Civil War?"

"Exactly, Zak."

"Why, you Israelis are worse than Nazis."

Perry went deadly white as he recited the Israeli 'Riot Act' back at Zak for daring to compare a *Sabra* to a Nazi.

"Perry, you really are a 'twicer', and in the dirty tricks business. You can't frighten me with your Nazi-type riot act. Your 'firm' and the State of Israel have reneged on a *'Mazel un Brocheh'."*

"So?"

"So, it's sacrilegious and against the *Torah*."

"How can you expect the State of Israel to pay out that kind of money, Zak?"

"Because it was agreed."

"How?"

"You must know?"

"Tell me."

"Come on, the deal was agreed twice with Alon in London and confirmed with a triple *'Mazel un Brocheh'* by Robbie, in the Winkler Hotel in Salzburg."

"Neither Robbie nor Alon had authority to agree such a figure."

"Just leading me on all the time, hey? You are worse than a Nazi, Perry!"

"Don't you ever say that again in Israel, Zak."

"By the same token, how can you expect a British Jew to have respect for the State of Israel?"

"What do you mean?"

"Perry, your 'firm' has acted with deceit from the very beginning as far as I'm concerned."

"What are you saying?"

"Seeing you've asked: with the benefit of hindsight, Mossad via Alon had it all worked out to dupe and double-cross me right from the start."

"In what way?"

"Take Salzburg, for instance. By then your 'firm' had already infiltrated Steilmanns."

"You have conclusive proof about the 'Institute's' infiltration?"

"Verbal, with 'very strong indicators'."

"What do you mean 'very strong indicators'?"

"Franz's Jewish-Moroccan wife unknowingly let on. Your agents marched Franz around Munich and pumped him dry after getting him drunk."

"The Princess told you that?"

"Yes."

"You're inventing this, Zak!"

"Not at all. In a similar way your team used me to unknowingly chaperon Franz across the German border with stolen Libyan computer files. And waltzed me around Salzburg whilst another *Katsas* deviously dealt with Franz back at the Hotel Bristol."

"How can you begin to prove that?"

"With twenty-twenty vision you ran a tight operation in Salzburg; you even opened the Hotel Bristol up, especially to accommodate us."

"What on earth are you talking about, Zak?"

"Come on; the particular locations of the hotels you picked out and the call-outs from hotel lobbies. The open walk across the footbridge over the Salzach River. The quick close meetings in the Café Tosca bar with its three exits. The goings on in the 'Sheraton' and Winkler Hotel. Maybe the sax player blew out a signal or two to your team."

"Maybe."

"And what Franz blurted out and divulged to me on the way to the 'Bristol' in Salzburg?"

"Tell me, what did Franz divulge?"

"That he and his Boss simulated computerized air-attacks over Libya on the computer using the secret codes and radio frequencies, down in Steilmanns strongroom in Munich."

"I can't believe you know this!"

"I didn't put it together until I saw the headlines in 'The Telegraph'. But, it's now crystal clear your 'firm' or 'institute' had already infiltrated Steilmanns via the privileged Franz and his well-placed Boss, prior to your deceitful rendezvous in Salzburg."

"But for why?"

"Why else, than to pick up the goodies and pay Franz on the other side of the German border?"

"How can you begin to think that, Zak?"

"Well, Alon never did ask for the rest of Franz's Nigerian file, yet you proceeded."

"You're *meshuggeneh*, Zak," Perry ranted as he threw his hands in the air in self-defence.

"I was naïve, but I'm certainly not crazy, Perry. Franz passed your team the Libyan deactivating codes and radio frequencies in good old Salzburg."

"You're still assuming."

"Thank you. But Franz gave the game away many times and certainly didn't play for a handshake."

"For instance?"

"Franz never did attempt to pass on his Swiss bank co-ordinates to me, the designated and so called paymaster."

"I wouldn't know about that, Zak."

"Then there was his attitude and strange behaviour in the 'Bristol' — especially the way he checked out. And what about the over-sized suitcase?"

"What do you mean, 'the way he 'checked out'?"

"Mister, what do you mean?"

"You tell me?"

"Okay seeing you asked, Franz was obviously under instructions to get the bill with his name on from me, when I settled the account at the 'Bristol'."

"Can you prove it?"

"Well, I have the separate Amex slip for Franz's part of the bill."

"Which proves?"

"There are too many inconclusive incidents."

"So?"

"So, if the whole matter, including Salzburg is closely looked at, it would prove conclusively that Franz was with me at the 'Bristol' at Israel's behest. Doing a COD deal, I'll wager."

"Not in our book. Is there anything else you want to get off your chest or not?"

"You must know, Franz and Rurik both 'let the cat out of the bag' several times."

"Really, how?"

"Well, neither of them phoned to find out if I'd received payment. Let alone phoning me their banking details, did they?"

"What does that show?"

"Hey! The disgruntled Franz wasn't the *nebbech* your 'firm' thought he was."

"What exactly are you saying, Zak?"

"Franz was not the *schmuck* you lot took him for."

"What are you saying, Zak?"

"You sound like a recurring record, Perry. You're exasperating."

"Really?"

"Really. Obviously, Franz didn't trust your 'firm' when you cut me out and made a side deal with him. That's why he took the large suitcase, to carry the Dollars back over the Austrian border."

"You're crazy, Zak."

"Can you believe Franz had the gall to try and *shlepp* me back to Munich in his new 'Merc' as his cover. And what about Robbie and the car keys?"

"What car keys?" Perry asked, as his adam's apple jerked in his Mossad throat.

"Well, Robbie, in the 'Winkler', gave me Franz's car keys to return to him. He also told me face to face: 'We've got what we came for'."

"I don't know anything about the incident with the car keys."

"Which means Robbie did not submit a full report to you or you're 'stone-walling' me."

"What is 'stone-walling', Zak?"

"Nice one," Zak blurted in disregard to Perry's quibble.

"And what about Alon's error of judgement?"

"Error of judgement, Zak."

"Yes, Alon told me in Salzburg that Franz had classified Libyan radar information and that Franz personally knew Gadaffi."

"We don't know anything about that."

"Which means Alon didn't submit a full report about Franz and his Boss, playing war-games over Tripoli and Benghazi in Speilmanns' basement vaults; or you're lying?"

"I don't know what the hell you're saying, Zak."

"Why are you treating me as though I'm an imbecile?"

"If you say so, Zak."

"Thank you. Why must I suffer this indignation before you start cutting my Nigerian commission?"

"What commission?"

"Michael, you certainly haven't the ethics of Isser Harel," Zak exclaimed in hope.

"Meaning?"

"Meaning, when Isser kidnapped Eichmann from Argentina, compassion was extended to the 'out-and-out Nazi'."

"Do you know Isser, Zak?"

"Yes."

"How come?"

"I went to a lecture given by the author of *'The House on Garibaldi Street'* at a synagogue hall in North London."

"Did you speak with him?"

"You must know I did, but that's history now Michael, I'll ask you again, are you going to settle my account?"

"I've told you, Zak. Be very careful from now on in Israel. It would not be difficult for us to declare 'open season' on you."

"A foreign Jew is just a tourist or an alien to you *Sabras*."

"Consider yourself 'on notice', Lancaster."

"Brave talk, Michael, using my given Mossad code name. What will you do? Confiscate my passport, put me in prison or shoot a helpful Jew?"

"Maybe."

"It's contrary to the *Torah* to act in such a way against a Jew."

The *Sabra* closed his ears to Zak's remark concerning the ancient Hebrew Law.

"What are you saying about passports, Zak?"

"Oh! I remember seeing American passports being put into a pouch when I visited your Embassy in London. They were all wrapped and strung with a wax seal."

"Why should we put other nationals' passports in a diplomatic pouch 'bordero' style.?"

"Because the way you guys tie them, they're not tamper-proof."

"For why?" Perry goaded.

"To gain obscurity for your combat assassin, operating out of Israel on undercover targeting, maybe."

"For why?" Perry goaded again.

"So Mossad can do what it wants, without tarnishing its world image. Anyway, as far as I'm concerned, Israel has lost its ethics since Begin got in."

"Be careful I don't fix you, you're not 'in the game' you know, Zak Levin cum Lancaster."

"Blowflies... If I had insisted on a receipt from Alon for those Steilmanns' papers in your London Embassy, I could have avoided this odorous situation."

"You're stepping over the line, Lancaster."

"Why? I was led to believe I came to the *Promisedland* for settlement, not insults."

The Mossad supervisor became lost for words at Zak's pent up outbursts.

"The truth cuts doesn't it, Michael Perry? I thought you'd cover up with a ridicule or two. I can see, I'll have to start sending invoices to the Paymaster's office in Jerusalem via your Prime Minister's Office: Nazi."

The insulted *Sabra* picked himself up from the edge of the settee, upon being called a Nazi again.

Zak could not contain himself from shouting at the departing

Mossad supervisor, as the Londoner's obsession for payment started to set in:

"No insult intended, a fact. One day you will pay... I will somehow make you *Sabras* pay."

"Yea, yea, Zak. Try sending in your invoice to our Paymaster for settlement and we'll let on to your wife about you and Abbie in the 'Cumberland'!"

"Have you proof?"

"Sure, Abbie taped the session."

"Bet you dubbed it, before putting it in a bandoleer."

"Maybe."

"*Gonif!* Thought I came to the *'Promisedland'* to be paid for the Nigerian intro' not to get blackmailed."

Zak returned to the hotel room, to telephone Udi about the negative outcome of the meeting, wondering why Michael had bothered to come to the 'Hilton', and why he had been requested to come to Israel by Udi...

Zak was so overwrought by the way the meeting had gone that he disregarded Daphna's concern to know what happened with Perry. Zak became further strung out when Udi's telephone number was engaged.

When Zak eventually obtained the ringing tone, he managed to calm down and quickly told Daphna:

"Honey, you can listen in while I talk with Udi, if you want."

"Thank you very much, you were only down in the lobby for an hour and a half."

Spelling out the long conversation with Michael Perry to Udi, the listening Daphna eagerly hung on to every one of Zak's words, in the hope of hearing a settlement figure mentioned. Zak was stunned by Udi's first affirmative comment:

"Zak, you should not have called Michael a Nazi."

"Udi, he wouldn't talk settlement. And that's why I came to Israel. Isn't it, Udi?!"

"That's what I understood."

"Then, tell me why did I come to Isreal?"

"Who knows now, they obviously changed their minds."
"Because I had nothing to do with Libyia?"
"Probably and you have never asked for blood money, Zak."
"No way. But I performed as agreed."
"That's for sure."
"No one could have imagined what the double-crossing Franz did would lead to the bombing of Libya."
"We got lucky for sure," said Udi.
"Yeah, if you can view it that way. I thought Israel would just store Franz's information in a data-bank for retaliation purposes."
"It was too important for us to store, Zak," said Udi, confirming unwittingly, for the first time, a fact of dramatic significance which Zak suspected all along: namely that the Libyan deactivating codes and radio frequencies had been acquired and passed to the Americans.
"Obviously. We all know now that it became a devastating operation," Zak uttered in remorse.
"Sorry about the heavy bills though, Zak."
"I'm sure. Money down the drain. Can you believe it, Udi, I forgot to mention to Perry about the rousing last week here in the 'Hilton'."
"You did the right thing. But you should not have called him a Nazi, you know."
"*Mavin*, you must have been listening in. Or you're already informed. Anyway, it's a fact as far as I am concerned. Regardless, when I get back to good old England I shall send an invoice in as Perry told me to."
"Be careful what you say, Zak, they may stop you leaving the country tomorrow."
"They can also blow up the Aswan dam if they want to."
"What does that mean?"
Vexed, Zak let it all out on Udi:
"Israel has been secretly holding Egypt to ransom ever since they realised the high dam over the Nile at Aswan was vulnerable."
"But the construction of the dam was complete in seventy-two."
"Right, but it took a real long time for your 'Dirty Tricks Brigade' to realise that."

"So, what could that achieve?"

"Blackmail, water-wars. With one little guided missile, Israel could flood the Nile Delta and obliterate Cairo and Alexandria, the two most populated areas in Africa."

"You're kidding me, Zak!"

"Think about it, Udi. The ever-flowing Nile has been Egypt's strength over the centuries, it's now it's Achilles heel, as I'm sure the late President Sadat well knew before signing the miraculous Peace Treaty for Egypt with Israel.

"Where do you get such information from, Zak?"

"You forget Udi, I've walked, talked and listened in the market places of Dubai, Bahrain, Kuwait and Cairo, not to mention Teheran and Istanbul. I know what many Arabs and other Moslems 'whisper' in their crowded bazaars and cafés."

"Yes, you've certainly been around, Zak."

"For sure, and I've been through the loop and know Israel thrives on blackmail. Egypt is quite prepared to play Israel at its own game in the future, you'll see."

"For instance?"

"Blow the top off a newly-constructed dam sitting high up on the Blue Nile in Ethiopia, if need be."

"But that would flood Egypt."

"Only the Sudan. The Aswan Dam and the desert would help protect Egypt."

With this ghastly spectre to ponder over, they bade each other their farewell *shaloms*...

The next morning at 6:30, cloaked under the dark vaults of heaven, Daphna and Zak nervously tip-toed out of the sleepy 'Hilton'. Seething about the let-down and the expenses, they took the waiting car to Ben-Gurion Airport, pleased that there appeared to be no 'wrongdoing at dawn'... Finding themselves in yet another Mercedes on the way to check in for the 08:35 BA flight back to Heathrow, Daphna became unnerved and questioned Zak as to what might lie ahead.

"Anything can happen at the airport, honey. You know they drugged and kidnapped Vanunu in Rome, not to mention what happened to the boxed-up Dikko at Stansted Airport."

"*Oy, veh*, Zak! Remind me, who was Vanunu, now?"

"Mordechai Vanunu was the Moroccan-Israeli atomic engineer who blew the whistle on Israel's secret Atomic Plant after nine years of working for them. He then deserted to Melbourne; Mossad learnt Vanunu had been a PLO sympathiser when it was too late. Just goes to show, even the Israeli internal security can get it wrong."

"Blew the whistle about what, Zak?"

"That Israel had a secret atomic bomb programme."

"Ah! I remember now. But you said Vanunu was kidnapped in Rome?"

"That's right, it was a messy business. 'The Times' tried to lure Vanunu to London for his story, but the Israelis stole him back. In fact, an attractive Mossad butterfly enticed him onto a yacht in Italy, to stop him getting to London and spilling the beans."

"Are you saying 'The Times' helped the Israelis?"

"Not at all. They just took a long time to verify Vanunu's story. Most of the world's press at the time reported the incident completely wrong."

"Amazing."

"Yes. However, there was a 'Chinese whisper' in Fleet Street that a reporter, or the like, was a Mossad agent and tipped off the Israelis where Vanunu was really located."

"Maxwell?"

"Only the Israelis know, darling. By the way, I caught a glimpse of Manny Levy in the 'Hilton's' lobby when I was waiting for Udi to make his first show."

"If my memory serves me right, you haven't seen Manny since the last time you were here."

"That's right, although Alon asked me in their Embassy in London if I knew a Manny Levy."

"How very strange!"

"Those are my sentiments exactly, honey."

"So, why have they been treating you in such an underhanded way, my darling?"

"They knew my loyalties lay at home and with my so-called partners. Consequently, Mossad just used and screwed me."

"I understand now," Daphna whispered in the darkness and protection of the 'Merc'.

"I never did like the hand Mossad dealt me and what the Yanks did over Libya."

"But you were not part of Israel's hidden agenda or the hostilities, darling."

"I know, I know. Unlike Jonathan Pollard, I was deceived. Never even knew or had any control over the double game Mossad was playing."

"In their eyes, I suppose the Israelis really scored?"

"For sure, honey, a prize catch."

"Rough for the Arabs, but you are no way to blame for what happened, darling."

"Perhaps I was born to be duped!"

"Who knows. But we must be careful at the airport," Daphna cautioned quietly.

"The worst that can happen to me is to have my collar felt before experiencing an embarrassing body search."

"They could set us up for drugs."

"No, it would only back-fire on them during a trial."

"My, you're a cool one, darling."

"I wish. Daphna, I think we were saved when the heavens opened up, the night we went over to see Ruth."

"You mean the hurricane?"

"One could call it that. I bet Rurik doesn't even phone up to see if we received any commission over here."

"That would really give the game away."

"Right. Tell me, honey, how can Udi and Lena afford such a luxurious apartment," Zak asked searchingly:

"I wondered about that. Maybe they had a little help from a friend!" Daphna suggested knowingly.

"Maybe."

"So why did we come to Israel, Zak?"

"Good question. Just for a ruddy expensive holiday, I guess. Or I'm paying for my past sins!"

"Only you know, darling."

"I know what you're implying, Daph."

"Anyway, Eilat was great fun."

"Yes, we have some forbidden shells."

Zak's mind churned over Michael Perry's 'black' statement concerning Abbie! The Londoner knew Perry was bluffing, as it had only ever been one big verbal cuddle in the Cumberland Hotel with Abbie. Unless dark-haired 'Abbie' wasn't Abbie, but a special 'under-the-cover' agent.

At Ben-Gurion, Zak expected to feel the heavy hand of Mossad! But their luggage, unbelievably, sailed through the stringent search procedure! They thought it strange that they were dealt with so quickly, since on departure at Heathrow, Israel security had practically taken the linings out of their suitcases.

The nervous Londoners' tension went with their cases and somehow, as if by a miracle, the awe for the land of Israel returned to their hearts and conversation...

Holding hands, Daphna and Zak boarded British Airways Flight 577, understandably lacking the euphoria with which they had originally boarded for Israel. However, they were thankful the 08:35 departure was on time and uneventful.

With the plane heading towards Heathrow, Zak started to review his dilemma. Suddenly, the 'low-flying' Londoner realised he had not heard from Rajko while in Israel. And if the Naira deal had been completed, it had been without him. Zak wondered if his luck could get much worse. All the time, energy, money and high hopes that the Naira deal had involved! All for nothing. The Londoner's reflections unexpectedly took him back to his early yesteryears.

* * *

CHAPTER THIRTY-SEVEN

2nd January 1987

Flight Back to Heathrow

Flashback 1932 — 1949

ZAK Levin had been born within the sound of 'Bow Bells' the very same day Britain abandoned Free Trade, as Royal Assent had been granted to the Import Duties Bill, on that 29th February, 1932 — born and supposedly circumcised on a lucky bed of five Pound notes — earned from his father's card winnings...

Noel Coward had recorded 'Mad Dogs and Englishmen' that same leap year, as the British Empire itself was on the brink of declining.

Later he'd gone to Christian Street School during the mid-thirties at the time Mosley and his pro-Nazi Blackshirts had tried to march through London's barricaded East End.

Within eight weeks of armed German troops crossing over the Austrian border and sixteen weeks before Prime Minister Chamberlain signed the Munich (policy of appeasement) Agreement with Adolf Hitler, an England football team made Hitler's regime respectable by giving the dreaded Nazi salute at Berlin's Olympic Stadium, on 14th May 1938, just before England's cricketers respectably allowed Australia to retain the Ashes with a well-fought draw.

He recalled as a young boy seeing the German 'Graf Zeppelin'[14] flying over London one Saturday afternoon on an apparent 'goodwill visit' using the opportunity, it emerged later, to secretly film the South Coast and its airfields.

Great Britian had been obliged to declare war on Germany 3rd September 1939 and the ensuing *'Sitzkrieg'* had been followed by the very different *'Blitzkrieg'* on England's 'green and pleasant' airfields after the brave retreat from Dunkirk. Later, the sound of screaming bombs being dropped from German dive-bombers on London and 'Anderson' shelters, still remain engraved on his mind.

From then on the destructive Nazi aircraft tried in vain to demoralize the brave cockneys with their nightly bombing raids. While incendiaries bombs lit up the London sky-line, base rate was averaging 3·88 per cent. Gold was fetching something like $142 to $146 per troy oz. A five Pound note was large and white and was being counterfeited and circulated via 'Hitler's back room boys', as London was being blown to smithereens during the Battle of Britain.

---

14 THE GRAF ZEPPELIN, 'LZ-127' — 3·3 MILLION CUBIC FOOT (HELIUM) AIRSHIP — COMPLETED IN 1928 AND SAFELY CARRIED SOME 1300 PASSENGERS — FLEW OVER A MILLION MILES IN ITS NINE YEARS OF SERVICE

Flight Back to Heathrow

Because of the extensive bombing of the British capital, he had been labelled and evacuated along with his gas mask, four times. First to Swindon in 1940 when his father had seen fit to take him back to the continuous bombing of London rather than leave him with the anti-semitic family. Then to Hertford to whom he'd been allocated lodgings by the kind but unaware ladies of the Women's Voluntary Service[15] as the fearless Home Guard drilled with broomsticks and the all-seeing A.R.P. kept the blackout.

Shortly after his return to the blacked-out, battered London from Hertford, his home was bombed and blasted. With his Ration Book and Identity Card tucked away in his cardboard gas mask case, he'd then been re-evacuated to Cornwall.

His mother, the granddaughter of a Rabbi, with her new husband, had seen fit to visit him after a year down on the Cornish farm near Bodmin in the Summer of 1942. His beloved, Russian-born, father's body could hardly have been cold before mother re-married, he'd sorrowfully thought as a boy.

He never could quite understand why, at the age of ten and a half, when the war was still at its height, he'd been taken away from the Cornish farm, where he was safe and happy. How he had enjoyed milking the grazing animals, picking the apples, running free in the fields, playing and jumping with the knowing farmer's twin teenage daughters on the hay-stacks at weekends. God! They'd had such tantalizing, cuddly breasts and ripe, identical nipples...

Only a month after returning to black-out London, he'd been re-evacuated yet again from the debris of his London home to Stocksmoor, not far from Huddersfield. He had liked the nice family that he'd been allocated to by the W.V.S., but missed life down on

---

[15] W.V.S. DID NOT OBTAIN 'ROYAL' STATUS UNTIL 1966

the farm and the twins' soft voices and fingers, secretly 'showing him how'.

At the small Yorkshire village school he quickly became teacher's pet. He'd certainly got on well with the unfamiliar, broad-speaking, Yorkshire children. The fragrance of Spring was in the air when the seed of promiscuity was planted in his hot young blood by the big-breasted, blonde, sweet-smelling teacher as she enlightened the class as to the wonders of the 'birds and the bees'.

The government war-time evacuee allowance of ten shillings and six pence was paid weekly to the fairly comfortable Stocksmoor family where he was to lodge.

He'd written some verse before he was twelve, to 'Auntie', the lady with whom he was billeted. It had been about the W.V.S. women who had delivered him to the semi-detached house... The short poem, he thought, said it all for him.

THE EVACUEE

I arrived a little boy,
But too old for most toys.

The time was war,
I wondered at what I saw.

I arrived with the W.V.S.,
Having left London's bombed mess.

He had been obliged to attend Methodist chapel every Sunday morning and had become a choirboy to please 'Auntie and Uncle'.

His voice had been so sweet that he'd sung solo as well as in the chapel choir. He also travelled around the West Riding on Saturday nights with 'Uncle', who sang tenor with the celebrated 'Holme Valley Male Voice Choir'. He'd delighted adult audiences, who applauded his clear cockney boy's treble voice. 'Bless This House, O Lord We Pray' and 'I'll Walk Beside You' were his repertoire in those days.

His mother and his elder brother had visited him in Stocksmoor, about a year after his leaving London. They'd arrived in time for a cooked rabbit lunch on his twelfth birthday.

Without rhyme or reason (maybe the rabbit had done the trick) to his young mind, his mother chose to take him back to war-torn London again, which was by now swarming with American and allied soldiers. If there was ever any justification for his L.M.S. train journey back to Bow, it had never been explained to him...

Education was 'thin' in a London school in those days due to the constant wailing of the air raid sirens and the overhead dog fights, the sound and sight of which always produced a fever in him. As did the death of his favourite uncle at the time, killed in Italy in 1942, whilst serving and fighting with the Royal Fusiliers. Another uncle had been Army heavyweight boxing champion while patrolling with the Military Polic in B.O.A.R. before being promoted R.S.M. of the 1st Battalion Irish Guards...

Uncle Harry, the big, ginger, R.S.M. was featured on the cover of 'Picture Post' during the war, his immaculate appearance seemingly putting all other N.C.O.'s and Officers to shame. (The ex-R.S.M. was now an old-time London taxi driver — he'd seen ginger-Harry just the other day with a fare, driving down Old Bond Street before doing a left into Piccadilly.)

Why, the windows of his little bedroom where he'd lived in Antill Road, just off Grove Road, had been blasted out by the very first killer 'V-1' that had fallen on London, which also destroyed other terraced houses and a nearby railway bridge. (The 'Doodle-bugs', of course, were far more numerous than the 'Scud' missiles that fell on Tel-Aviv nearly fifty years later during the second Gulf war in 1991, which caused the Israelis so much alarm, unlike the British who had kept their cool in far worse conditions.)

Towards the end of the Second World War, the accurate German rockets fell without warning, causing great damage in 'Buzz Bomb Alley', as visiting American Forces nick-named little ol' London Town. Bless them all, without America's big guns, bands and Ike, the British battleship would surely have sunk, although Great Britian did have Churchill and good old Monty.

Moving from Bow to the border of North London (a stone's throw away from Ridley Road street market), he'd been enrolled in Shacklewell Lane Secondary School, situated behind 'Simpson's' clothing factory where, later, the famous 'DAKS' trousers were produced to be sold in fashionable Piccadilly.

He became Head Boy at Shacklewell Lane during the period when the noisy 'V-1' 'Doodle-bugs' were followed by the silent 'V-2' Rockets of both 10,000 were launched, many causing devastation as they exploded on their launching ramps in occupied Europe. Remarkably, several thousand flying bombs were destroyed in flight (not V-2') by the R.A.F., 'Gunners' and Barrage-Balloons over Britain. Alas, some 3,000 fell and exploded in and around London killing some 8,000 civilians before the last 'All Clear' sounded.

He remembered the Headmaster's timeless words of advice to the school:

'Always say 'I'll do it' and you'll get on in life.' To the delight of the Headmaster, he had been selected to captain Hackney Boys' football team...

Sadly, because of the War, his *Bar Mitzvah* at the age of thirteen (when according to Hebrew tradition, a boy enters manhood) had been a mere formality. His father was dead, elder brother and uncles were all in uniform fighting the Nazis overseas, aunts and cousins were evacuated and scattered all over England. Only his poor mother *Alov Hasholom* had been present in *shul* (synagogue) to witness her son in his *capel* and *tallis* , before the rabbi, read his designated portion from the sacred *Torah*.

He still had the wondrous image of the first time he had set eyes on his future wife, Daphna, all 'pink and starched' at the age of thirteen. She'd brightened the morning when she walked into the school hall with her mother, to register for classes with her cousin Ruth, both of them having just returned from evacuation...

To his later delight, he'd found out the cousins had been evacuated together, along with a pretty, friendly girl called Lena, to Marlow in Buckinghamshire.

Engraved in his memory was Daphna's lustrous, long, fair, wavy hair, which bounced on her perfectly contoured shoulders. With sparkling eyes she'd beamed him a big smile that increased the height of her lovely cheek bones. Her soft, saxe-blue eyes, as they looked into his, told him she would become a woman who could only love but once. Her lovely eyes enhanced the blueness of her pretty, spotted cotton dress, that her full young breasts strained against. She'd also worn a delightful navy blue coat which had a matching velvet collar and cuffs — her comfortable looking navy shoes had square toes and cuban heels. Surprisingly, her shapely legs were clad in real, fully-fashioned, American nylon stockings. The stockings, he knew, were a rare luxury in those war-rationed days, not liquid stockings with eyebrow pencilled seams. He'd realised later that the stockings were a present from her Canadian uncle, who was considered the Stocking King of London, and not a gift from a Yank as he'd first jealously thought. Indeed, Daphna's uncle in those yesterdays served most of the spivs in Petticoat Lane and further enjoyed the patronage of many West End lingerie shops and departmental stores.

Forbidden Yesterday

Then it was the 6th of June (Frau Rommel's birthday) 1944, and 'D' Day, when the Y.M.C.A. had double cause to celebrate their centenary... Four million battle-ready Allied troops, harboured in the South of England and nearly six years of war brought the final All Clear, 'VE' Day, Bonfires and Street Parties. 'VJ Day' shortly followed when America dropped an atom bomb or two on Japan. Then there were more Bonfires and Street Parties!

The newly-formed dress company of 'Levy & Green' in Stoke Newington High Street, London N.15 seemed pleased to engage him as a cutting room trainee-cum-errand boy. They'd paid him the princely weekly sum of seven shillings and six pence (the equivalent of 37p! Not even the price of a glass of water today in the Royal Garden Hotel). His dear, job-finding mother kept five shillings of his hard-earned cash to help with the house-keeping. A large loaf of freshly-baked bread in those lean days of 1945 (when GATT had its first open discussion in Zurich prior to being concluded in Geneva a couple of years later to keep grain prices down) had cost eleven old pence. For an extra penny, namely a total of an old shilling (5p), the loaf could be sliced at the counter! Wrapped, sliced bread was not to be had then. Bottled water was rare and only drunk in deluxe hotels. Unbelievably, a shilling in those days had been the lowest price to pay to see a movie in a cinema, although he had always managed to find the money for the 'one and nine's', the posher seats.

About six months elapsed when he'd left Levy & Green to better himself. He went to work for the Juno Fashion Wear Company in the Commercial Road in the East End of London, travelling five days a week on a number 647 Trolley Bus for a fourpenny fare, earning the grand wage of two Pounds, ten Shillings (£2·50) at the end of the week. That was serious money, for a fourteen-year-old, when Cambridge won the Boat Race in 1948, and Don Bradman landed in England with the most formidable force since William the Conqueror.

He remembered changing jobs every few months or so, whenever he felt he could not progress, learn or earn any more from his present employers.

His well-paid jobs cutting dresses before going into the Army, enabled him to travel around the country at weekends to watch his victorious football team, 'Spurs', winning their matches, whenever he was not captaining Wingate F.C. Under Eighteen's football team. Wingate had been founded by an ex-major called Sado, in memory of the British General, Ord Wingate, who was, incidentally, very pro Israel and a talmudic scholar. The Major had been the General's adjutant, serving in the Holy Land in the days when Mossad was just another rebel cell and a thorn in Rationed[16] Great Britain's side.

* * * * *

---

[16] WARTIME RATIONING ENDED IN OCTOBER 1951. HOWEVER, RATIONING OF MEAT LASTED UNTIL JUNE 1954. THE BASIC WEEKLY WARTIME RATION ENTITLEMENT PER PERSON FROM JANUARY 1940: BACON OR HAM 4 OZ, SUGAR 8 OZ, TEA 2 OZ, BUTTER 4 OZ, COOKING FAT OR MARGARINE 2 OZ, MEAT TO THE VALUE OF ONE SHILLING AND TEN PENCE (8p). JEWISH PERSONS WERE ALLOWED TO SWAP PORK COUPONS FOR DAIRY PRODUCE.

CHAPTER THIRTY-EIGHT

2nd January 1987

Statements to Jerusalem

ON Zak's return home that afternoon from the *Promisedland*, he searched for a message or a greeting from Rurik. But, there were no Noëls from the Slav on the flashing answering machine! Zak finally got the message. There and then he decided Rurik's silence was an admission of the double-cross with Franz and Mossad. With no other sensible option open to him, Zak prepared a Statement on his own behalf for his share of the agreed commission for the Nigerian deal.

The invoice-cum-statement was addressed to the Israeli Paymaster and sent via Udi to the Prime Minister's Office in Jerusalem. The demand was sent under Zak's ZL reference and named Alon, Robbie and Michael Perry. After all, Zak had the original dated and timed Tel Aviv 'Hilton's' front desk message-slip with Perry's name and message on it:-

Statements to Jerusalem

INVOICE / STATEMENT

THE ACCOUNTS/PAYMASTER
THE PRIME MINISTER'S OFFICE
THE STATE OF ISRAEL
THE KNESSET
JERUSALEM
ISRAEL

2nd January 1987

Our Ref ZL 2187

<u>Your assumed Ref: ALON/ROBBIE/MICHAEL PERRY</u>
TO MONEYS OUTSTANDING: 1.3 MILLION US DOLLARS
NETT, WITHOUT DEDUCTIONS.

THE ABOVE AMOUNT IS OVERDUE. THEREFORE YOU LEAVE
ME NO ALTERNATIVE BUT TO REQUEST FULL PAYMENT
WITHIN 14 DAYS, OR TO TAKE THE APPROPRIATE ACTION
NECESSARY TO RECOVER MONIES OWING.

For & Behalf of,

Zachary Levin

Forbidden Yesterday

Surprise, surprise, on 19th January, Zak received a letter and a postal receipt from Udi confirming that he'd posted on the Invoice of 2nd January to Israel's Prime Minister's Office as requested.

There was, however, no response to Udi's registered demand, so Zak, in a new state of agitation, sent further demands for the outstanding 1·3 million US Dollars, plus compound interest, directly to Jerusalem and the Israeli Embassy in London.

On the 21st January it was feared that the Archbishop of Canterbury's Special Envoy, Terry Waite, had been kidnapped by the *Shi'ites* in Lebanon, possibly because of a rumour that Terry had a CIA label! Gerald Ronson, a prominent 'city-gent' (and a very distant relative, twice removed, on Daphna's side), whom Alon had asked about in the Israeli Embassy, also made headlines on the very same day as the Waite snatch. The startling news about Gerald was not good either, in spite of the *intrapreneur* paying back the £5.8 million advance from Guinness to purchase Distillers' shares as part of a take-over bid strategy. Zak wondered what the outcome of the trial would be in the real-life 'Monopoly' game — would Gerald pass go and collect... or go to jail? (In September 1990, 'G.R.' without giving testimony was fined £5 million, the biggest individual's fine in British legal history, and sentenced to one year's imprisonment — down on the 'open farm' at HMP Ford in East Sussex, along with convicted Ernest Saunders, the former Guinness chairman and stockbroker, Anthony Parnes).

It was then July 1987 and Zak, together with all the monthly invoices he'd sent to Jerusalem and London had been totally ignored. Zak felt the silence told a story — it confirmed Mossad's guilt and the double game they had played. Clearly, if someone kept sending him unexplained invoices he would surely inquire as to what they were for.

Statements to Jerusalem

On the July invoice, Zak added a rider:-

I TRUST I WILL RECEIVE ADVICE THAT THIS ACCOUNT WILL BE PAID WITHIN THE NEXT 28 DAYS, OTHERWISE YOU WILL LEAVE ME NO ALTERNATIVE OTHER THAN TO PUT THE MATTER IN THE HANDS OF MY SOLICITORS FOR THEM TO DEMAND PAYMENT ACCORDINGLY AS PREVIOUSLY ADVISED TO MICHAEL PERRY DURING OUR MEETING IN THE TEL AVIV HILTON.

Summer went by and Zak's invoices to Jerusalem still kept going South...

During October, Zak issued an invoice with a detailed covering letter to Israel's Prime Minister's office in Jerusalem, which the P.M. chose to ignore.

However, on the last Sunday in October, 'lightning struck. Zak received an anonymous telephone threat!

"Lancaster, stop sending in statements to Jerusalem or risk your name being whispered in the wrong ear." warned a sinister Israeli sounding voice ominously.

Zak was so perturbed by Israel's threat that he reported the matter to the London Board of Jewish Deputies (established 1760 in England) which theoretically monitors and safeguards the well-being of English Jews worldwide.

In a large, austere upper room at LBJD Headquarters in Woburn House (opposite Euston Station, where the UK Chief Rabbi's office is also located) Zak told his story to the special committee of three gaping men.

Bewilderingly, the Committee wanted to know where Zak had been married and his wife's maiden name! During the interview, Zak had cause to mention Daphna's cousin David, 'Big Dave', a past tough, front man for AJEX (Association of Jewish Ex-servicemen). Zak recalled that David had been obliged to emigrate to Australia with his second wife and her young son after a London Crown Court Judge warned David that he would receive a stiff penal sentence if he cracked any more heads whilst attempting to break up anti-semitic meetings in Britain.

The Committee members appeared to lose their composure when Zak stated his complaint across the dark, polished table.

However, Zak felt at the time that he'd been taken seriously, because he'd mentioned their hero, 'Big Dave'!

There weren't any handshakes offered or given when Zak was about to leave the unprecedented meeting in Woburn House. With a rather sour taste in his mouth, Zak said goodbye to the three young men and made his way home.

Zak was somewhat surprised at the Committee's speed at informing him: "Mister Levin, your complaint has been lodged with the appropriate body in Jerusalem. There is need for you to worry or concern yourself any more".

Zak, not allowing himself to be fobbed off by the LBD. call, telephoned Woburn House again. Later, there was a return telephone call from another member of the Committee, informing Zak ostentatiously: "You have nothing to fear from the Israelis, as they have been put on notice." Whatever that meant.

Because of the unconvincing explanation by the LBD, Zak made an appointment with an important local firm of solicitors, with a view to them sending a stiff letter to the Israeli Embassy in London. After all, it had been at the Embassy alongside 'Millionaires' Row' that he had been propositioned by Alon, and it was where the verbal contract had been instigated.

It took no brainpower for Zak to realise that he had been ostracized by Mossad and in turn the Board of Deputies of British Jews. However, by a strange twist in fate Zak was favoured by 'the elements', following the result of an Israeli Supreme Court ruling concerning the general behaviour and the perjury and torture by Israel's secret services, primarily Shin Beth and Mossad. In 1987 a special inquiry, headed by Justice Moshe Landau, a former president of Israel's Supreme Court, had been appointed to look into the countless, sordid allegations made concerning Mossad and Shin Beth's past activities.

Statements to Jerusalem

The Landau Committee laid down new guidelines for Israel's security service; simply put, they should use only trickery and deception in the future, but not physical brutality.

In Zak's opinion, these guidelines curbed Mossad's threat to his life, but not their practice to dishonour promises and agreements.

One bright morning, Zak had the inclination to phone the Nigerian High Commission in London's Northumberland Avenue. On dialling 01 839 1244, Zak was greeted by a friendly West African female voice:

"Good morning, Nigerian High Commission."

"Hi, good morning to you from sunny Bournemouth sunshine."

Having sweet-talked the telephonist and a couple of her informative secretary friends, Zak was enlightened: 'After the *Yom Kippur* War, some twenty-five African countries had severed diplomatic relations with Israel'. Accordingly, there were no official trade figures kept between Nigeria and Israel! However, unofficially, imports from Israel had recently greatly increased. Which, to Zak's mind, more than suggested that Mossad had also acquired the Nigerian Embassy radio links from Franz and that Israel had the 'inside track' on Nigeria by being able to monitor their intended National procurements.

Zak's chosen solicitors on Richmond Hill, whose London office he understood acted for the Thatchers, sent an 'or else' letter to the Israeli Ambassador in London, dated February 1988.

The letter fully explained Zak's position and requested payment of the outstanding 1·3 million US Dollars. The Ambassador completely ignored the 'or else' letter, in spite of the hard line stating: 'Otherwise our client will take further action — through the courts, if necessary'.

On 23rd March, the prestigious firm of solicitors took it upon themselves to send a reminder and to request an answer to their previous letter. This did result in a reply, albeit a negative one, in March 1988 from Consul Karni at Israeli's London Embassy.

After conferring with Zak, his solicitors replied back to Consul Karni on 5th May.

The letter of 5th May did produce a further reply from the Israeli Embassy, dated 25th May but, it was so negative, Zak, contrary to his solicitor's advice, took it upon himself to make an appointment with Consul Karni...

Having walked past the Royal Garden Hotel and the challenging sentry before pressing the buzzer at the Israeli Embassy in Palace Green, Zak was given a tough time, down to a double body search by the security boys (not just because Peres was expected to visit the Embassy that particular day) on the door, before being allowed entry...

The meeting with Consul Karni was a farce, insomuch as the Consul played dumb to Zak's commission claims and about Israel always seeking back-up information for their reprisal raids. Karni had nothing to say either about Mossad peddling the Libyan radar secrets and deactivating codes to the peace seeking Americans, which the Israelis traded for 'Hawk' missiles and other much wanted equipment in order to keep the resale price of USA arms 'sky-high', or maybe to compensate for the Pollard affair. However, Zak's strong statement about the Yanks and the *Sabras*, under 'Two-Way' trade, covertly supplying Iran in 1986, did succeed in unnerving the Consul. Karni's only significant utterance to Zak's fiery rhetoric being:

"I've been ordered to drop the matter."

"Sauve qui peut, hey Mr Karni... Just like the Pollard Affair."

In Zak's opinion the Consul's unguarded remark had more than suggested that the Israeli Government, more so than many other governments, are a law unto themselves, as are Mossad with their Motto: 'By way of deception thou shalt do war'.

If need be, Zak knew he had the required courage and tenacity to take legal action against the State of Israel, just as he had done against the mighty 'Courtaulds'.

* * *

In the late sixties, the British conglomerate 'Courtaulds', produced a new jersey fabric called 'Duospun', which it had developed by blending two different synthetic yarns. 'Duospun' could be produced very quickly on 'Courtaulds' fast, modern, automatic knitting machines, for a new market which the company believed existed for young men's unlined jersey suits and for the lucrative trouser trade. Accordingly, 'Courtaulds' calculated the demand for 'Duospun' would break all records in the traditional menswear trade. The production of 'Duospun' was also expected to shorten the lengthy forward ordering period needed by the mills to produce conventional woven suiting materials.

Zak involved himself in designing a range of trendy, slim-fitting men's suits from 'Duospun', with some help from Sidney Brent, one of the founders of the retail chain 'Take Six'. Sidney apparently started from a market-stall and had then rapidly opened teenage boutiques in every major London shopping area, including Carnaby Street, as well as in most UK provincial cities.

Zak had been so caught up with the trend that was born from the spirit of the old 'Club Eleven' in Carnaby Street, that he'd felt compelled to write a poem called 'Carnaby Street'[18]...

> *Carnaby Street West One*
> *The street of fun*
> *There's a karzy*
> *More shops than Bengazi*

'Courtaulds'' subsidiary, 'Exquisite Knitwear', from whom he actually bought the fabric, had raved that there was a quick, needy market for 'Duospun'. Exquisite's super-salesmen further claimed that there would be even more business by way of repeat orders in

---

[18] SEE 'FORBIDDEN AGENDA' — FOR FULL VERSE

the men's' trade, as similarly enjoyed in the ladies' fashion trade, when there was a 'bren on'. Another super-salesman ironically coined a phrase: 'You'll use mileage not yardage once 'Duospun' takes off'.

The 'Duospun' sample suits were ready for the 'IMBEX' (International Mens & Boy's Exhibition) held at London's Olympia, or was it Earls Court? Bright and early the very first morning of the exhibition, Sidney Brent signed bulk orders for immediate delivery of 'Duospun' suits, thereby confirming the beliefs and inspirations of 'Courtaulds' market researchers.

'Duospun' took off alright — but in the wrong way! This was because of the adverse effect of the unequal strengths and performance of the two blended yarns from which it was knitted. Consequently, 'Duospun' lacked stability and stretched out and out like a cheap dish cloth during cutting and mass production. Regardless of his knowledge of cutting and handling jersey fabric and the long working hours spent with the operatives in the factory trying to put some shape into 'Take Six's' urgent first order for six hundred 'Duospun' suits, he was not entirely surprised when Sidney ruthlessly rejected a token delivery of the ever-expanding 'bumfreezer' suits. But he was stunned when Sidney washed his gentlemanly hands of the 'Duospun' commitment.

However, getting mighty 'Courtaulds' to admit their original error was a costly and time-consuming ordeal for Zak. Still, five years later, with the help of a Professor of Knitting at Leeds University (due to a kind whisper from M&S Testing Department), a substantial settlement was reached in Zak's company's favour by an unassuming barrister on the steps of the High Court.

Maybe at the end of the day the Israelis would react similarly.

* * * * *

Statements to Jerusalem

In July, Zak received a surprise call from Clarissa. Unbelievably, he had not spoken to her since they had parted emotionally in Munich. Clarissa's appealing voice, words and attitude as reflected over the phone convinced Zak she was not a *'Sciccolina'*, and had only intended to make him a little jealous in the 'Munich Sheraton', just as Rurik had indicated. Apparently, the passage of time had not dampened the Italian vamp's ardour for her Englishman.

Amazingly, Clarissa avowed she had overheard Dominique's sexual advances and her suggestion to make love in the back seat of the 'Merc'! Clarissa, further avowed she was unable to handle the moment, so she ran out of the beerhall and took a taxi back to the 'Sheraton', and cried herself to sleep that night. The supposedly covetous butterfly also claimed she'd invented the whole story about the airline crewmen 'doing all' with her. Maybe, Zak had just been unduly paranoid at the time about Clarissa and her fantasy.

The Londoner was not too enthusiastic about meeting up with the trying Italian persuader, even though the new found closeness which had blossomed between Daphna and himself during their trip to the *Promisedland*, and seemed likely to continue once they were back home, was in fact, 'frayed around the edges'. Zak did not know why this was but hoped time would be the healer. To pacify Clarissa, Zak took a rain-check to meet the Italian butterfly if she came to London.

Zak's solicitor on Richmond Hill, prior to going on summer vacation, agreed to send a final letter to the Embassy of Israel.

The statement in Karni's reply: 'We shall advise you accordingly' kept coming to mind. Zak knew the word 'shall' is acknowledged by the legal profession to be the most affirmative word in the English language, but did Consul Karni know that? Or was 'shall' just a 'never-ending piece of string' before being confronted with diplomatic immunity.

It then dawned on Zak that Mossad were hiding behind bureaucracy and had a *carte blanche* licence to cheat. He then felt compelled to commission a book about the whole amazing affair, from beginning to end.

Zak wondered what else he could try. Unfortunately, 'Dun & Bradstreet' were not willing to collect the 1·3 million debt on the instructions of another local firm of solicitors. The accommodating solicitors did, however, inform Zak precisely of the complicated procedure involved under Order 11 to issue legal proceedings against the State of Israel, a so-called immune state in the eyes of the English High Court. If the costly writ was ever sealed, leave to continue would then have to be granted by the Court before it could be served on the State of Israel, along with written *Ivert* translation via the Senior Master of UK Secretary of State for Foreign and Commonwealth Affairs... Such a procedure could leave Zak in a very vulnerable position and not necessarily feeling 'too' Grand but at the same time relieving him of maybe Five.

By this time the old Niara had all disappeared, either as a credit on some oil company's balance sheet, or perhaps through an incinerator. A new and not so stringent two-tier currency exchange system was successfully being operated in Nigeria.

Subsequently for adventure and a slice of the two-tier cake, Zak endeavoured to put a new Nigerian Niara deal together with a cockney-Italian, called Luciano. Luciano lived in Maidenhead, working with a close friend, Thomas (well known at Lambeth Palace) who was trying to arrange an agenda with the Lebanese Shi'ites for the release of Terry Waite... partly for humanitarian reasons and partly for a promised long-term oil contract.

Unfortunately for Zak, Daphna's estrangement fully resurfaced. She became shrew-like and rigid towards him, but she would not tell her husband why. Zak wondered if it was due to his obsession about getting paid the commission owed to him by the double-dealing Mossad or his intentions to commission a book about the whole drawn-out affair.

Unbelievably just as life on the home front was becoming intolerable for Zak, Clarissa called, seeking to rendezvous in London when she told him:

"You are my island. I need to look into your eyes."

Reluctantly, Zak responded to the persistent butterfly, and the very next day drove to Heathrow's Terminal 2...

Surprisingly, Clarissa's direct flight from Milan touched down late. But Clarissa looked 'out of this world' as she entered the UK magnificently, pushing a laden trolley. Zak was struck by the fact that the 'high flying' *farfalla* was wearing his butterfly brooch. She was dressed superbly in a coffee and cream safari outfit, sporting beige-skin, high-heeled shoes and long, flowing hair! The knowing vamp was showing off a lot of deep tanned skin from a rather long, open vent in her wrap-over skirt as well as cleavage from a low cut silk blouse. With his expert eye, Zak knew the Italian vamp just had to be naked under her revealing, tiger-print, silk blouse and cleverly designed linen skirt, since there was no bra nor panty-line showing.

Clarissa's sparkling eyes metamorphosed as she paused to look into Zak's fixed 'forget-me-not' eyes — she then engaged overdrive and steered the trolley straight at him.

"*Ciao*, my Englishman, I'm with you at last", she uttered lustfully on parking the trolley, then embraced and passionately kissed him. Clarissa's deep-kiss miraculously rekindled the infatuation and emotion, long dormant within Zak.

On the way down to the romantic 'Ye Old Bell' at Hurley, an exquisite rendezvous, situated by the slow moving waters of the Thames, winding its way to Maidenhead from Henley, that Zak had intuitively chosen on the spur of the moment at the airport, the oblivious Clarissa's amorous amours nearly caused the car to swerve into a ditch before they reached their destination. Zak, *yugger* still at attention, attempted to describe the quaint hotel to a delirious Clarissa, as she decadently douched him in duty-free

'Armani' before wrapping another stunning 'Gucci' tie around his neck.

"Sounds great for our reunion, Zak!" she gasped, with a naughty chuckle and smile.

"For sure, butterfly, the vintage hotel is steeped in history, enchantment, good English fare and fine wine."

"*Bellissimo la dolce vita!*"

"Drink and smile, hey Clarissa?"

"*Si,* like the 'Happy Bar' in Ancona.".

Zak was also sure the fragrant lavender patch within the rambling gardens of the charming hotel would still be alive with droning bees and adorning butterflies gathering and gavaging the lingering nectar. Indeed, later the salacious Clarissa gave up her tanned body and tantalising mind upstairs in 'Ye Old Bell's' sumptuous four-poster bed, imploring to be stretched and bound with a bunch of colourful 'deep-purple', gossamer 'Gucci' cravats.

EPILOGUE

THE letter from Consul Karni was not the last between the State of Israel and Zackary Levin. In fact, the unsatisfactory correspondence dragged on for years.

Zak was nothing if not tenacious and believed in playing the long shot, but he knew that the oft-repeated words of Mossad 'the name of the game is not to pay' meant that it would be unlikely for the Israelis to have a change of heart in the normal course of events.

What perturbed Zak particularly was that his two 'partners', Franz and Rurik, had been paid for their services. It took him a while to find out that this was the case and that the payment from Mossad had been split three ways, the third share going to Franz's Boss. Some partners!

The pay off, the exact amount of which Zak was uncertain, which apparently ran into six figures in Dollars, had seemingly benefited its recipients little. Franz and Rurik, Zak learned, had both left West Germany and were leading lives almost in exile, one in Eastern Europe, the other apparently in North Africa. Maybe some kind of poetic justice...

But Zak was no longer interested in Israel's Shekels. The *'Mazel un Brocheh'* had been with Mossad and they had reneged. They had three times broken the sacred pledge and in turn put Zak's life in jeopardy.

So, early 1988, against all the odds, some preliminary work started on the book (titled *Breach of Sovereignty,* then *Mossad Butterfly*) Zak had resolved to commission which became, eventually, *Forbidden Yesterday*. Maybe the book would be some kind of recompense. Anyhow, it would make Zak feel better about things he was sure, and he was right.

Forbidden Yesterday was delayed as Zak found himself becoming immersed in another exciting saga, involving Terry Waite and the Middle East, which forms an astonishing sequel:
Forbidden Agenda.

Zak actually issued a writ and received judgement against the State of Israel. That in itself was no mean accomplishment. Zak learnt rapidly that governments quickly close ranks when one of their country's average citizens tries to 'take on' another country's officials through the High Courts. Irrespective of the merits of the case, the Londoner reckoned he went about as far as he could 'down the writ road'. Zak wasn't sure but maybe, just maybe, with the sealed writ of the realm in the hand he could try once more to push things along but he held off.

Zak had never considered himself much of a philosopher or such; still, he could not help but look back on the extraordinary events which had taken place and try to make some sense of them.

And what had happened had been really extraordinary. Zak could hardly comprehend the way things had unfolded. Everything had fitted together like a jigsaw and had seemed to lead easily from one situation to the next. Chance or coincidence had played an amazing role. It was Abbie, the supposed daughter of Udi, the husband of Zak's wife's best friend, Lena, who had led Zak, by chance, to Alon, the Mossad agent. A chance meeting with Colonel Healey-Jones had led Zak to Rurik. Through another chance encounter Zak had met Clarissa and through yet another one-in-a-million chance meeting in Munich, the Italian temptress had been reunited with her old University flame, Franz. Zak's two main partners in the soured deal, Franz and Rurik, had thus emerged, ready for their part 'on stage' at just the right moment in time. Presumably

Epilogue

Alon or Michael Perry had already known Rurik anyway. So many connecting coincidences.

It further occurred to Zak and the author that many events of '*Forbidden Yesterday*' had taken place in Munich. That was the place where the main elements of the story had come together or coalesced, preparing the way for the 'main event' in Salzburg.

What was special about Munich, the author wondered? The city had been as significant for Zak as indeed for Chamberlain and it had brought no 'peace in our time' to either of them. Maybe Munich was a 'city of destiny', a 'karma thing'?

Salzburg, on the other hand, 'played' like a surrealistic film. The especially-opened Hotel Bristol, the absurd dance around Mozart's statue, the 'forced' waltz around the musical town, the bizarre meetings in deluxe hotels with *Katsas*[19]. The plethora of partly-told stories with Zak having to guess why he was considered a 'sugar daddy' by the begging, without a change of trouser Franz. Then there was the West German's parked Mercedes, which was mysteriously moved a couple of feet... boy, this was heady stuff. At any rate, Zak had learnt never to put himself 'out on a limb' again... or so he thought.

Unfortunately, Zak never did quite 'get the measure' of Salzburg, that picturesque Austrian town, the focal point of the story, where the Israelis out-manoeuvred and then double-crossed the Londoner. Zak could see now he'd been naïve to play along as he had, but nevertheless felt he needed to know more. So, in 1994, exactly eight years to the day after Zak had visited Salzburg at the behest of Mossad, for the supposed 'dry run', the author and Zak went to Salzburg and re-traced his steps. The trip was most illuminating and the Hotel Bristol was all locked up. It confirmed beyond almost any reasonable doubt that what Zak had previously experienced in Salzburg had been part of a well-rehearsed, precision Mossad

---

[19] THREE KATSAS (ACTIVE OVERSEAS MOSSAD OFFICERS) WOULD REPRESENT ABOUT TEN PER CENT OF MOSSAD'S FORCE.

secret operation. The author had to 'hand it' to Mossad — it had been very well planned and executed. Certainly, no 'dry run'! The type of hotels, for example, where the various meetings took place, had obviously been expertly selected for their strategic location within the game-plan. This was even more evident with the passage of time.

On a broader scale, the coincidences had been nonetheless remarkable. Against the back-cloth of a deal which, although never intended by Zak, ended up including Libya as well as Nigeria, it seemed uncanny that Zak had first met Clarissa in Bournemouth only a few yards away from where Colonel Gadaffi, the Libyan leader, as a young man, attended language school. Clarissa was a Cancerian, like Zak's mother and Trudy, the Polish girl, who had left such an indelible print on Zak's memory. In addition, at about the time Clarissa slipped the rare Rolex ring onto Zak's right index finger in Malta, Libya had started to dig another eighth wonder of the world: the largest civil engineering project undertaken, creating a man-made river network (some four thousand kilometres long), from an ice age reservoir under Libya's Sahara Desert, from Kufrah to Sitre. The underground reservoir is located on practically the same latitude as the Aswan Dam just below the Tropic of Cancer.

Well, one could take the analogies too far, but so many things had been like interlocking pieces, connected to one another. It surely didn't happen like that in real life. But it had!

Libya hadn't been in Zak's head when he had first been buttonholed by Mossad. In fact, Zak had only ever sought a commission for helping Israel get a better shot at lucrative Nigerian Government tenders. The sale of Libyan air defence layout, deactivating codes and radio frequencies which were probably fed into an orbiting American satellite or a 'Hercules' fitted with AWAC represented completely unexpected escalation, as did its aftermath. However, for some and indeed the media, the attack on Libya by the American Sixth Fleet was considered a strike for the Free World. Or just maybe,

Epilogue

Israel wanted its Mediteranean 'oxygen-pipe' to America and Europe secured for their import-exports by the American peace keepers

Alas the Israelis had been prepared to threaten a Jew's life — just because Zak asked for an agreed payment for doing a job (Zak was no *Sayan*) they had asked him to. Also, the Israelis had traded the Libyan deactivating codes to the Americans without a second thought, it seemed. Or had it been to compensate for the Jonathan Pollard affair? Now, Zak wasn't defending Libya's past actions, but at least that country never preached morality. For reasons best known to themselves, the British took no action against Israel for three of its citizens' (who all pleaded guilty at the Old Bailey in February 1985, in order not to give testimony) part in the kidnapping of the exiled Nigerian, Dikko, from the streets of London in broad daylight during Spring 1984. However, according to Justice McCowan: "The finger of involvement almost certainly pointed at Mossad."

Zak realised that Mossad's deal was in some respects like the Old Naira deal: both had dragged him off on many expensive trips all over the place and he certainly was not financially richer for the experience. Quite the contrary, although of course the airlines and hotels were happy to 'see the Londoner coming' again.

Was the Londoner richer in any way for his experiences? Zak, by nature was definitely tenacious as his past experience seemed to prove, as in the case of the faulty Courtaulds' fabric, that tenacity paid off. Still, Zak also knew from experience that some deals were, by their very nature, harder to put together than others, but the baffling thing was that his commodity deals took off and indeed continued with great ease and flow, up until payment time. Deals were always magnetising to an adventurous businessman when all the signs were that the deal would be closed and everyone would walk away from the table happy. But what happened to Zak was that in the closing stages of his commodity transaction unlike most of his textile deals, the deals would suddenly unravel. The Londoner had heard the phrase 'don't worry, Zak' far too often. That was the danger signal. And even though Zak did concern himself and tried to take sensible precautions, it hadn't helped when dealing with Mossad.

As Zak played it through the rain, it struck him — you can get paid from another source, an unexpected one. Zak reasoned, God doesn't forget. The Londoner could be assured that he'd tried his best and his efforts would be noted. Zak also concluded that he would not, in the end, have felt comfortable about taking money from the Israelis in view of what happened...

In May 1994, a House of Commons motion was signed by an all-party group of British MP's who were snubbed by the State of Israel when it accused their UK Ambassador of discourtesy when not replying (as the Israelis had done with Zak) to their written request to discuss why Mordechai Vananu had been held in solitary confinement and that after eight years in prison Vananu could be no possible threat to the State of Israel.

A bitter paradox, Zak eventually figured it out — Mossad kept its most successful achievements secret. The sudden awareness of a simple fact. Now Zak was a better man for telling his story and attempting to put modern history right, regarding how the Yanks openly bombed Libya without loss (not a lucky strike) to their Sixth Fleet and its marauding warplanes. Yet, at Pearl Harbour on 7th December 1941, the Imperial Japanese Navy made a surprise attack on the American Pacific Fleet and sleepy garrison. The Japanese lost 41 planes, 3 subs and 100 men before their Fleet sneaked away, not without loss and casualty as the 'finger-wagging' American Sixth Fleet did some 50 years later, even though the battle-ready Libyan garrison fired smart-weapons at the Yanks.

Finally, bearing in mind Mossad's motto, the State of Israel's miraculous Peace Treaty with Egypt and the new relaxed attitude towards all Arab States, Zak feels fortunate for Israel's belated change of heart which enabled him to recall his forbidden yesterdays.

GLOSSARY OF FOREIGN WORDS PHRASES AND THEIR MEANINGS

ARABIC

Al Qahirah (= Victorious)	Cairo
Couscous	North African dish of crushed wheat (semolina) steamed and served with various meats and vegetables
Harissa	Chilli paste
Hamas	Moslem fundamentalist
Haboob	Violent sand storm
Kasba — Casablanca	Native Quarter — tourist shopping area
Khamsin	Hot Sahara wind of 50-day duration
Ma'a salaama	Goodbye
Medina — Tangier	Native Quarter — tourist shopping area
Muezzin	A crier who calls Muslims to prayer
Merguez	Beef or lamb chipolata-size spicy sausage
Ramadan	High Moslem holiday and period of fasting
Salaam	Respectful greeting — complimentary gesture
Shi'ite	A member of one of two sects of Muslim

ETHIOPIAN / SEMITIC

Falashas	A member of the Haematic Tribe living in Ethiopia and practising Judaism

FINNISH

Näkemiin, viehättävä Naine	Goodbye

FRENCH

Arrière-pensée	Ulterior motive
Au revoir	Goodbye
Carte blanche	Full discretionary power
Chéri	Dear or darling
Coq au vin	Chicken cooked in red wine
Cordon bleu	'Blue Ribbon' — French cooking style — meat stuffed with cheese, herbs, cream and wine
Coup d' état	Violent or illegal change in government
Coup de grâce	Finishing stroke
De trois, papillon	Threesome, butterfly
Encore, s'il te plaît	Again, please
Encore une fois	Once again or once more
En route	On the way
Escargots au beurre à l'ail	Snails in garlic butter
Faux pas	Mistake
Extraordinaire	Remarkable — outstanding
Fausse bonne femme	Lady who appears to be upstanding but isn't
Femme fatale	Lady who plays a fateful role in a story, situation, etc.
Force Majeure	See Commercial Terms
Gaie Paris	Gay Paris
Hors d'oeuvre	First dish or starter
Maître d'	Head waiter
Moules à la marinière	Mussels marinated
Nom de plume	Pen name
Nouveau riche	Newly acquired wealth

Forbidden Yesterday

Papillon	Butterfly
Petits fours	Small fancy cookies served usually with coffee
Pied-à-terre	Another home — some where to stay
Pret-à-Porter	Ready to wear (International Paris clothes show)
Salade niçoise	French salad with olives and anchovies
Sauve qui peut	Every man for himself
Son et Lumiére	Liighting and sound effects
Sirène	Provocative female
Touché	'You won that point'
Très joli	Very pretty or sarcastically 'how nice'

GERMAN

Ach, so	Exclamation
Auf Wiedersehen	Goodbye
Bierkeller	Pub
Bis morgen	Until morning
Bitte	Please or 'you're welcome'
Blitzkrieg	Lightning and overwhelming military attack
Blutwurst	Black pudding
Danke	Thank you
Danke, gut	Thank you, good
Deutscher	German
Die Ausweise, bitte	Identity papers, please
Ein grosses Löwenbräu	A large Löwenbräu (A large size premier beer)
Eine Minute bitte	One minute please
Fräulein	Miss or waitress
Freilager	Bonded warehouse
Frühstück	Breakfast
Geld	Money
Guten Abend	Good evening
Ich bin terrible	I feel terrible
Ich verstehe nicht	I don't understand
Ja	Yes
Kein Geld	No money
Knackwurst	Type of German sausage
Kraut	See Slang
Kugeln	Chocolates shaped like balls
Lederhosen	Leather breeches or short pants
Liebling	Darling
Messe	Fair or exhibition
Milch	Milk
Prima	Good
Noch einmal dasselbe bitte	The same again, please
Sachertorte	A type of chocolate cake originally made in Vienna
Sekt	Sparkling wine
Schinken mit Ei	Ham with egg(s)
Schöne	Beautiful
Schwarz	Black
Schwarz geliebte	One who likes 'things black'
Sitzbad	Hip bath
Sitzkrieg	Phoney war
Shyster	See Yiddish text
Stipp	From stippen — see Slang
Und Dir	And you
Und Sie?	And you?
Was ist los?	What's up?
Wie geht es Dir?	How are you?
Wunderschön	Wonderful
Zehn Uhr	Ten o'clock
Zwei	Two

Forbidden Yesterday

HEBREW — IVRIT / ASHKENAZI / YIDDISH

Alov Hasholom	Eternal peace (dear departed)
Bar Mitzvah	Ceremony of Jewish boy's coming of age
Blintzes	Pancakes filled with cream cheese or jam
Broygez	Annoyed
Capel	Skull Cap
Challah	Plaited bread loaf
Chuppa	Wedding canopy
Eretz Yisroel	The land of Israel
Frummers	Conservative Jewish religious sect
Gelt	Money (Geld=gold)
Glatt kosher	Strictly kosher
Gonif / Ganáv / Genevá	Crook – thief
Haimisher	Home made
Hatikvah	The Hope — Israel's National Anthem
Ivrit	Modern Hebrew — taken from the old Hebrew — God's given language
Katsas (singular & plural)	Mossad, overseas case officer — only some three dozen Katsas are ever active outside of Israel at any given time.
Knesset	Israel's Parliament
Kibbutz	Collective habitat and work-place
Koách	Strength
Kop – rosh	Head
Kosher / Kashér / Kóhsher	Conforming to Jewish dietary laws — legitimate — genuine
Kvitch	Squeal — let on
Landsman	Compatriot
Lechayim / Léchem / Le-cháyim	'To life / good health' (a toast)
Likud	An Israel political party
Lokshen	Noodles
Latke	Savory potato pancake fried in oil
Matzo / Matzá	Unleavened bread
Matzo balls	Crafted Matzos fried in chicken fat
Mavin	Expert / connoisseur
Mazel un Brocheh / Mazál un B'racha / Brokhe	'Go with good luck and prayer' — A binding Hebrew blessing and agreement when given with a handshake
Mazel tov / Mazál tov	Congratulations / good luck
Mezuzah / Mezuzáh / Mezúze	(Untranslatable?) A slime container (bearing the first few lines of the Shema) affixed to a doorpost / Hebrew home
Menorah / Menráh	Eight branch candelabrum
Meshugga / Meshugá / Meshuggeneh	Mad / crazy / silly
Meshugóim / Meshuggener / Mossad / Mosád	'The Institute for Intelligence and Special Operations'
Nebbech	Too bad —— hard-luck
Nebbish	Weak, insignificant and inept person
Noch	Yet
Ove sholem	Dear departed
Oy gevalt	Expression of dismay
Oy veh!	Oh dear! Oh dear!
Rosh Hashana / Rosh ha-Shaná / Shóne	Jewish New Year
Sabra / Tsabár	Native of Israel / born in Israel
Sayanim (Sayan — singular)	Overseas Jewish volunteers loyal to Israel — there are some 1500 active Sayanims in London and at least another 4000 on call.
Schmendrick	Fool
Schmuck	Stupid ass
Shabak	Israel's Counter-Espionage Service
Shabbos / Shabbes / Shábes	Jewish Sabbath — old Hebrew

Forbidden Yesterday

Shabbut	Jewish Sabbath — Ivrit
Shalom / Shalóm	Hello / goodbye — Peace / all is well
Shaygets / Shaykhes (singular & plural)	Non-Jewish man
Shikker / Shiker / Shikór	Drunk
Shlep / Shlepping / Shlepn	To carry or carrying around (a heavy parcel, bag etc)
Shema	Hebrew declaration
Shin Bet(h)	Former name for Shabak (see Shabak)
Simcha	Special occasion
Smoltz	Greasy charm
Shmoozing	Coaxing or chat up
Shtoomers	Adjective or sign — to keep quiet — mum's the word
Shysters	Professional unscrupulous persons
Tallis	Prayer shawl
Torah / Toráh / Tóre	Five books of Moses (the foundation of Judaism)
Trafy	Not Kosher
Tukkas / Toches / Túches	Posterior
Va'adat	(Va'adat Rashei Hasherutim) The top echelon of Israel's intelligence services. Function is to secretly coordinate all current field operations at home and abroad
Yiddisher	Jewish way
Yom Kipper	High Jewish Holiday day of atonement and fasting
Yugger	Male organ
Zhlub	Frumpy, slovenly person. Ill-mannered
Zugging	Nagging

ITALIAN

Alimento	Food
Antipasto (singular) Antipasti (plural)	First course (Hors d'oeuvres)
Arrivederci	Goodbye
Bella Donna	Beautiful Woman
Bellissimo (masc.) Bellissima (fem.)	Most beautiful
Buongiorno	Good morning
Cazzo	See : Me dia cazzo
Capriccioso	Freakish
Ciao	Hello / Hi! / Bye
Con amore	With devotion or zeal — love and tenderness
Con brio	With spirit
Grazie	Thank you
È'un piacere	Pleased to meet you
Fantastico	Fantastic
Favoloso	Fabulous
Farfalla	Butterfly
Fidanzata	Fiancé
Granmercé (rarely used these days)	Many thanks – Thanks for nothing (irony of)
Grazie — Grazie mille	Thank you — Thank you very much
Il contrasto	The contrast
Interessante	Interesting
La magia	Magic
La dolce vita	The good life
Laguna	Lagoon
Mafiosi	Mafia
Magnifico	Magnificent
Mama mia	Exclamation
Me dia cazzo	Give me your (penis) body
Maschile petto	Masculine chest
Meraviglioso	Marvellous

Forbidden Yesterday

Mia fantasia	My fantasy
Mi poui dare	Can you give me
Mi scusi	Excuse me
Molte grazie	Many thanks
Motoscafo	Stylish power boat
Osso buco	Knuckle of veal and rice, stewed and served with highly-flavoured sauce
Possibilmente	Possibly — maybe
Prego	Not at all — you're welcome
Presto	Hurry
Piú tardi	Later
Prima Signorina	First class — beautiful female / women
Rapido	Fast — with speed
Scicciolina (Ciccionlina)	Nickname of a female Italian Cabinet Minister — dubbed the Pornodiva and whore by the Italian media
Si, grazie	Yes, please
Signora	Mrs — or Italian lady over 28 years of age
Signore	Mr
Signorina	Miss
Solo	Alone, single
Sogno	Dream
Spaghetti al tartufi nero	Spaghetti with flaked black truffles
Tardi	Late
Tu credi troppo alla mia fantasia	You believe / see too much of my fantasy
Ultimo	Last — the most
Un attimo	A moment — instant
Um restorante specializzato im pasta	A pasta restaurant
Un fulmine	Lightning — thunder bolt
Vaporetto	Large motor boat used as / for public transport in Venice
Zabaglione	Italian pudding made from beaten egg yokes, sugar and Marsala wine

LATIN

Mons veneris	Rounded mass of flesh on woman's abdomen above vulva
Novus Ordo Seclorum	New World Order — as depicted on the back of an American one dollar bill
Speyria Aphrodite	Aphrodite Fritillary: bisque — khaki coloured butterfly

SPANISH

Adios	Goodbye

SLANG / AMERICANISMS

'A bren on'	A rag trade term — when trade is busy
Big white telephone	A toilet
Boys in blue	Police or the like
Butter boy	A novice cab driver
Choked	Unable to talk
Dagwood sandwich	At least a treble-decker sandwich, based on a U.S. cartoon character Dagwood Bumstead
Daisy chain	Large amount of expecting brokers
First base	To accomplish the first step
Flaky	Unreliable
Funky	Off-beat music / lively / earthy
Galloping Dominoes	Dice
Greek	Anal sex

Forbidden Yesterday

Karzy	Privy — Public W.C.
Kraut	Pejorative term for a German
Mark one's card	To closely inform
Sugar Daddy	A person willing to finance a deal
Rain check	Option — invite for later date
Quim	Vagina
'Ten Case Camel'	A camel that can transport ten cases of whisky across a desert
Slip-skin	Shake hands / intimate greeting
Stipp	To give — have sex
Twicer	A two-faced person — not sincere
Wet back	Illegal Mexican immigrant
Whitee	Caucasian

COMMERCIAL TERMS

D.A. terms	Draft Acceptable
Bonny Light	Nigerian produced crude oil
FOB	Free On Board
Force Majeure	Unforeseeable course of events from fulfilment of contract
Fringe Commodity Broker	Broker acting outside the Stock Exchange
Intrapreneur	A person within a large organization who uses his entrepreneurial skills to develop other business
RWA	Ready Willing and Able
Vertical Manufacturer	One factory or one company that processes from raw material to finished product

CURIOUS ENGLISH WORDS AND PHRASES

Batwittedly	A foolish act
Bissextile	Leap year
Bonobo	Intelligent, extrovert chimpanzee — habitat south of the Congo River
Gavaging	Feeding through a sucking tube (proboscis - snort) as a butterfly
Glozing	Talk — Explain away
Happenstance	A chance or accidental happening
Intrapreneur	See: Commerial Terms
Phizog	Image — expression — face
Promisedland	Hopeful
Pumpkin Time	When the good life stops
Mercury retrograde	When the planet and things in life go backwards
Negromania	A love/obsession for Negroes
Recce	Reconnaissance
Rimic	Rhyme — poem
Summerlove	Author's expression for a summer love affair
Wedge and Veering	Area of two high depression and changing
Wompstered	Bible punching
Zulu Time	The present time

GLOSSARY OF ACRONYMS

AEU	United Arab Repulic
AJEX	Association of Jewish ex-Servicemen
ARP	Air Raid Precautions
AWAC	Airborne warning and control system

Forbidden Yesterday

3 D	Three Dimensional
DA (haircut)	'Duck's Arse' chevron back parting haircut
D.A. terms	Draft Acceptable
DAKS	According to Simpson's, perhaps subconsciously derivnd from DAD and SLACKS!
D-Day	6th June 1944 — Allied invasion of Nazi Europe (On a day which any operation starts)
El Al	Israel Airlines
BOAR	British Army of the Rhine
FOB	Free On Board
EU	End User Certificate
GATT	General Agreement on Tariffs and Trade (UN Agency that attempts to regulate world trade)
GRID	Believed: Guy Relations Immune Disease
HMQ	Her Majesty the Queen (By appointment)
ICI	Imperial Chemical Industies
ID	Identification
KLM	Royal Dutch Airlines
LA	Los Angeles
LB(J)D	London Board of (Jewish) Deputies
L/C	Letter of Credit
LMS	London, Midland and Scottish (railway)
MOD	British Ministry of Defence
MT	Motor Transport
NAAFI	Navy, Army and Air Force Institutes (canteen for servicemen)
NNPC	Nigerian National Petroleum Company
OPEC	Organization of Petrol Exporting Countries
Pan-Am	Pan American Airways
PFLP	Popular Front for the Liberation of Palestine
P&O (POSH — Port Out Starboard Home)	Penisular and Orient (shipping line)
PLC	Public Limited Company
PLO	Palestine Liberation Organization
PTI	Physical Training Instructor
RASC	Royal Army Service Corp
RWA	Ready, Willing and Able
RM 20/20	Red Mercury
RSM	Regimental Sergeant Major
SA	South Africa
SABENA	Société Anonyme Belge d´ Exploitation de la Navigation Aérienne
SAS	Special Air Services
SAS	Sportsman's Aid Society
SS	Steam Ship
TWA	Trans World Airways
UN	United Nations
UAR	United Arab Republic
VE Day	Victory in Europe
VIP	Very Important Person
VJ Day	Victory over Japan
YMCA	Young Men's Christian Association.

SYMBOLS

Start of a flashback	* * *
End of a flashback	* * * * *
Flashback within flashback	* * * *

Forbidden Yesterday

Forbidden Yesterday

St. George's Hotel – London

Crest Hotel – Bournemouth

London Kensington Hilton

Royal Lancaster Hotel – London

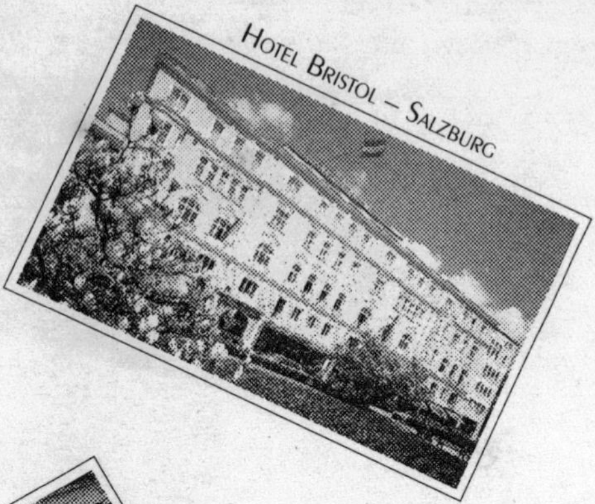

Hotel Bristol – Salzburg

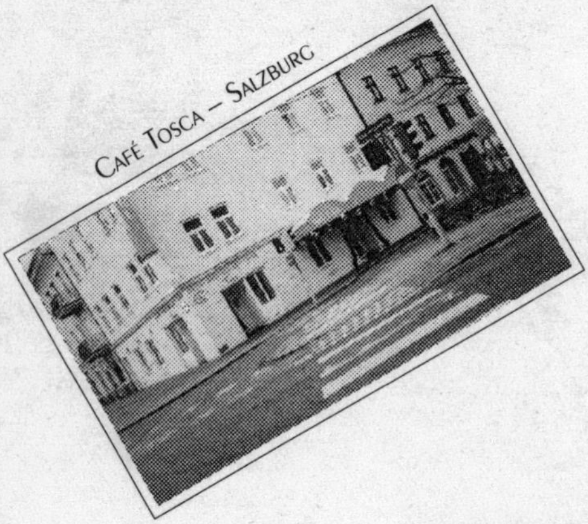

Café Tosca – Salzburg

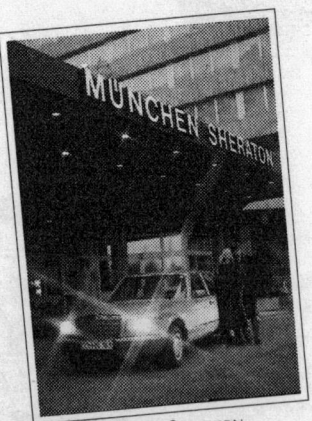

Munich Sheraton

Forbidden Yesterday

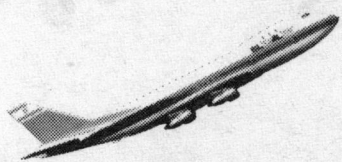

Forbidden Yesterday